All That Lives

All That Lives

Melissa Sanders-Self

WARNER BOOKS

An AOL Time Warner Company

Warner Books, Inc., 1271 Avenue of the Americas, New York, NY 10020

Visit our Web site at www.twbookmark.com

 An AOL Time Warner Company

Printed in the United States of America

First Printing: May 2002

10   9   8   7   6   5   4   3   2   1

Library of Congress Cataloging-in-Publication Data

Sanders-Self, Melissa.
    All that lives / Melissa Sanders-Self
      p. cm.
    ISBN 0-446-52691-6
    I. Title.

  PS3619.A266 A79 2002
  813'.6—dc21   2001017753

Book design by Charles Sutherland

This work is lovingly dedicated
to my grandmother
Mary Kathleen Self

acknowledgments

I want to thank the Spirit in all of its forms, and my husband Nigel, and my sons Dylan and Luke. Their love and faith in me is a great source of inspiration. Anne Edelstein has encouraged me endlessly and given me smart advice, and Jamie Raab at Warner Books read my manuscript with a rare kind of detailed attention. Without her perceptive editing *All That Lives* would be a different book.

My grandmother Mary Kathleen Self is responsible for telling me this story when I was little and for keeping it alive as I grew. My mother, Sharon Mayes, and David, Connie and Henry Katzenstein all helped turn my idea of this novel into a reality. In 1997 I had the good fortune to receive an artist's residency at the Djerassi Foundation, and I am extremely grateful to that program. I am also fortunate many of my best friends are willing readers: Barbara Joan Tiger Bass, Jim Bierman, Kit Birskovich, Karen Donovan, Ann Friedman, Lindsey Roscoe and Valerie Rich read my rough drafts, and I owe them. I am also grateful to Jenny McPhee for her early and insightful editing.

Harriette Simpson Arnow's work on pioneer life in the Cumberland was invaluable in my research, as were the writings of M. V. Ingram in his *Authenticated History of the Bell Witch,* published in 1894. I am also indebted to Charles Bailey Bell's publication *The Bell Witch: A Mysterious Spirit* and also the investigations of Hereward Carrington and Dr. Nandor Fodor into the psychosomatic possibilities that might explain the recorded phenomena. *The Foxfire Books,* edited by Eliot Wigginton, provided me with all I needed to know about hog slaughter, spinning, weaving, wild Tennessee plants and herbs and other affairs of plain living. All biblical references in this novel come from the King James reference edition.

Finally, I want to thank all the people of Adams and Robertson County, Tennessee, those with us and those no longer present, who kept the tale of the Bell Witch alive, passing it down over nearly two hundred years. All those people unknown to me made this book possible.

table of contents

All That Lives

how it began

In the autumn of 1815 when I was nine I walked into the woods past the cornfield near our stream, filling a flat garden basket with leaves the color of cherry skins, rooster necks and Chloe's boiled corn. My prizes dropped from the gracious limbs of oaks, poplars, maples and elms standing tall as God above me and I was grateful, for we were soon to have our first schoolhouse harvest pageant, and Professor Powell had requested all of us to gather fall leaves for decorations. The stream played a loud song, running high from recent rains, and I searched carefully with my bare toes for round stones I might step to. I felt very content, admiring my beautiful leaves, but I was struggling to keep hold of my pile, for it had grown so large, some flew out on the breeze of my movements and when I jumped to catch them, others sneaked over the edge.

All of a sudden, I stepped into a cold spot. The air was abruptly brisk and also very damp, the way it is when you progress to the back of a deep cave. The bare skin of my forearms began to tingle and a shiver straightened my spine. I looked about, dusk was falling quickly on the land, the way it does that time of year. I saw the tree trunks turning black with night. In the distance, across the cornfield and up the hill, I could see the back side of our house, faintly glowing with the lamps already lit behind the window glass of the kitchen. Our house was hewn from the finest double logs in Robertson County and though it was far away and partly obscured by the trees in the orchard, it was a sturdy and comforting sight.

I had the impulse to bolt away but at that moment I felt a pair of icy hands on my shoulders and I cried out in fear, for they were real, yet there was no one there. I started forward, slipping up the bank, and when I reached the field I tore across it and up the hill into the orchard, my precious leaves flying from my basket. I saw a few pretty blood-red maple ones caught in the folds of my skirt. I looked over my shoulder to where I had walked by the stream and there I saw a light flash. I stopped, thinking there must be someone there. I called my brothers' names, suspecting Drewry or John Jr. of playing a game with me, but I only heard the early hoot of an owl in response. The light did not appear again and I saw no movement in the darkening woods. I stood still by the side of the road, frozen, watching to see what was coming, but then the dark wind of evening brushed my cheek and rustled up under my skirts and I ran, lickety-split, away.

I was late for the evening meal and when I entered our hall I saw Mother, Father and my brothers waiting to be seated at the table in the dining room. Father frowned at me and I was so ashamed, I said nothing at all about what had happened in the woods. Our entire family was present, and my eldest brother, Jesse, took the chair to the right of Father, who sat across from Mother, and as though we were arranged in order of age, John Jr., Drewry, myself, Richard, and Joel took our seats. Father said the blessing and Mother said Amen, then Chloe began serving boiled hominy, cornbread and sweet potatoes roasted in the ashes. A tense silence reigned at our table, as no one made any effort at conversation, and the only sound was the clicking of our forks on Mother's treasured china supper plates and from the kitchen came the hissing of the fire.

"Let us retire to the parlor," Mother said, folding her napkin by the side of her plate. She stood, leaving the lamps for Chloe, to aid with the washing up out back. Some nights Mother and I cleared the plates but most often Chloe managed it alone. I was happy not to do it and I quickly rose and followed Mother across the dark hall.

Father pushed his chair back from the table and came after us, taking one of the two lamps. I watched him carry the light to his handsome writing desk that occupied the front corner by the parlor window. Reaching inside, he withdrew his silver whiskey flask, his book of accounts in which he documented the running of our farm, and his quill pen and ink. I watched as he took a long drink and prepared to write.

"Take this candle, Betsy, and bring me out the hairbrush." Mother passed the light to me before settling in her chair with the velveteen cushion by the fire. I obediently went into the dark bedroom she shared with Father off the back of the parlor. I found the wooden brush with the wild boar bristles on her bedside table and I gripped it tight, hurrying from the room, for the dark shadows in the corners reminded me of the coldness I had encountered in the woods. I wanted to tell Mother what had happened. I returned and knelt in front of her on the hooked parlor rug before the fire, tucking my legs under my skirt.

"Betsy." Mother bent forward and whispered in my ear while untying and loosening my plait. "Your father cherishes your yellow tresses and the rest of you, as if you were real gold. He adores you so, try to be worthy of his affection." Her hand rested on my spine, warm as the box iron. This was a gentle reprimand, but I drew my chin closer to my chest. I knew Father loved me in a special way and I did repent my lateness, but into the silent atmosphere I could not tell my story. Even Joel and Richard, who often had to be prevented from wrestling after supper, sat quietly on the wooden bench by the entrance to the parlor, swinging their cotton-stockinged feet from their dresses, loath to provoke Father. I focused my eyes on the carpet as Mother gently began to brush my hair. The rug had a bright border of red and blue flowers entwined and I found the pattern lovely to contemplate. Father put his flask, book and pen back inside his desk and closed the writing leaf with a bang. He stoked the fire with another log, then sat beside it in his hickory rocking chair, opposite my mother. He liked to read to us from the good book after supper.

"Darling daughter," he looked to me and I saw a certain brightness in his eye that told how he loved me like no other and would protect me always. Maybe I could tell him about the cold place in the woods. "Come and sit beside me, here." My hair was all undone and fluttered like the yellow flames of the fire when I stood. He bade me turn and kneel and he positioned his chair so the hem of my skirt was trapped under its wide legs.

"Tonight we shall hear no less than salvation history, for it shall instruct us on the right true path, eh, Betsy?" He placed his hand on my head and pulled my hair gently back so my neck twisted slightly and my chin tilted up. His eyes met mine.

"Yes, Father," I answered, feeling his genuine loving concern for my welfare and education. His fingers stroked the line of my jaw and came to rest on the nape of my neck. Perhaps I would not mention why I had been late. I wanted nothing more than to be worthy of his love.

"God," he cleared his throat and began to read, "at sundry times and in diverse manners spake in time past unto the fathers by the prophets . . ." He stroked my hair between the turning of the pages and his fingers grew heavy on my head. My movements were greatly restricted by the trapping of my skirt and soon my legs turned numb to pins and needles, but I did not protest, for it was Father's will that I should sit that way and I felt blessed to be his darling daughter. The words of the good book in my Father's deep voice acted like a lullaby on me and I began to feel myself drifting away. As I passed into sleep I wondered if perhaps I had imagined the cold place in the woods, for how could there be such a thing on God's good earth?

something unnatural

Our family was destined to be forever associated with the horrible evil that visited us, and yet it was not always that way, and it was not all we were. For years we lived as the other upright families in our district of Adams, Tennessee, sharing in the wealth and abundance of nature, in accordance with the laws of the Divine. Truly, our troubles simply unfolded, as if God spread a great black sheet across the bed of our lives. Our trials were not anticipated and the harmonious time before did not seem so very special, or precious, as it most certainly was. Four years of bountiful harvests followed that afternoon in the woods before our family experienced any further unusual disturbances.

It was a mild spring night, near my thirteenth birthday, and a soft breeze blew in my open window, bringing the smell of warmer days to come inside my room. I was lying in my bed curled into a ball with a cramp in my stomach preventing me from drifting into sleep, when I heard a sharp *tap* on my window glass. I wondered what it was but remained squirming in my position under my spring quilts.

Tap-tap.

It came again and I had the feeling it needed my attention, so I got up and went to the window. The moon was new and there was not much light, only the brightness of stars. I looked for a twig caught by the wind, or a squirrel confused, banging a nut against the glass, as that was how it sounded, but there was nothing there.

The pain in my stomach distracted me and I thought as long as I was standing I would take the opportunity to use my chamber pot. I felt something warm and sticky on my legs and smelled blood where I had never smelled it previously and I grew frightened. *Tap-tap* came again at the window and with my legs shaking and trying not to cry from fear, I hurried down the stairs through the dark parlor and off the back into Mother and Father's room.

"Mother, help me, for I am ill." I bent over her sleeping form and whispered urgently into her ear.

"Shhh, Betsy. Pray, what is the matter?" Mother woke easily and I gave her room to rise.

"There is a tapping at my window and blood between my legs!" She took me in her arms, and I could not prevent myself from crying. She smelled of sleep and held me close, tucking a stray lock of hair loosened from my braid back behind my ear.

"There, there, Betsy, hush. You are not ill, no, you are a young woman now." I had no idea what she meant, but I allowed her to lead me from her bedroom through the parlor, the hall and the dining room, back to the kitchen, so our conversation would not disturb Father's sleep. Her composure calmed me and I waited patiently in the chair by the woodstove while she stoked the embers and fed the kitchen fire to get it going. When the flames began, she disappeared into her pantry, returning with a jar of bark and a brick, which she placed inside the stove.

"Chew this willow for the pains." Mother handed me a chip of bitter bark and proceeded to explain to me the way it is for women. By the end of her speech I was not frightened, but proud to know I was no longer a little girl. I was a developing young woman who could someday carry a child in her own womb. I forgot about the tapping at the window completely until Mother left to fetch the thick red flannel petticoat and cotton cloths she had already stitched in anticipation of this certain occasion, and abruptly it came again, *tap-tap,* this time against the door. I went immediately and opened it, confident there would be someone there, though who at this hour would dare knock at our back door I did not try to guess. I need not have bothered, for there was no one.

"What are you about, Betsy? Close the door and come see how to fold these cloths." Mother carried the red flannel petticoat over her arm and a tower of white cotton squares were stacked in the crook of her elbow.

"There is something outside tapping! I heard it in my room and just now, at the door."

"Well never mind, it will be wind or rodent and no cause for alarm. Let me help you with your undergarments." There was blood on my nightdress and Mother helped me change it.

"You must launder your own cloths and soak them in cold water, to get the blood out."

"Could you explain the rest tomorrow, please?" I knew she had more to tell me, but I had begun to feel quite queasy. I clutched my hands across my stomach while she loosely tied the red petticoat around my waist.

"Of course, dear child." She gently held me to her and kissed my hair at the top of my head. "Miss Betsy, how fast you have grown." With her iron tongs she withdrew the brick from the woodstove and wrapped it up in another flannel, then led me back upstairs, fussing with my covers and the warm brick across my stomach until I was properly settled in my bed.

"Will you stay with me? The tapping at my window . . ." I was already drifting in my mind as it was very late, but I grasped at Mother's hand.

"Quiet, Betsy." Mother did stay. I shut my eyes on her loving face, glowing in the light of the single candle. I do not know if the tapping came again, for I fell solidly asleep.

In the morning my pains had gone and though I felt encumbered by the new cloth I wore between my legs, I decided to keep to the plan I had made the day before to accompany Father and my brothers John Jr. and Drewry on horseback down to the fields to inspect the progress of the newly planted tobacco seedlings. Drewry and I had to forsake a day of school to do it, which would have been no matter, except Father had recently paid Professor Powell for our lessons and Mother felt it was important for us to get our learning in. We understood her desires, but begged and pleaded desperately to be allowed to go. Father gave us his consent, overruling her concerns.

"Lucy, tobacco lessons are as valuable as book learning to our children." He winked at Drewry and me as he gave his final comments on the matter. "But before we depart, I will have a quick game of judge and jury with the little ones." Richard and Joel were disappointed they were not to be included on our outing and this was Father's attempt to cheer them up.

"I want to be judge!" Joel was fast with his request.

"Judge or juror, you must strive to be a rational man, a

consciously disinterested weigher of evidence." Father smiled, outlining the rules.

"I will be!" Joel's enthusiasm for the game caused Father to laugh outright, aware his youngest son knew not the meaning of rational.

"Your brother Richard will be judge today and you shall join Drewry and myself as jurors in the case." Father led them into the parlor, giving Richard his special chair. In a matter of minutes he had them decide the fate of a man accused of stealing land from his neighbor. "Remember, we need bold, brave judges who can see the truth," he advised when Richard wavered in his adjudication.

"The thief must build the fence anew, in its proper location, and perhaps pay the neighbor some monies for his trouble."

"Well done, Richard. Now, boys, as men of prominence, in the future you will undoubtedly be called on to act in public. You will cut fine figures with sound knowledge of justice and with skills for settling differences amongst your neighbors and friends." Father ran his hand through Joel's blond curls, well pleased.

"Can we play again?" Joel begged.

"Tell me, what law is the law above all others?" Father put his hand to his ear, encouraging their loud response.

"God's law!" Both the boys repeated in unison, practiced at the finale of the game.

"We will play again, but not now, for it is time for us to depart." Father stopped in the hallway where his guns, shot bags, powder horn and hat were hung on pegs by the door. He opened it wide and we followed him across the porch and down the steps. I took my time ambling down our hill, unused to the clumpy feeling of the cloth between my legs. Father insisted our home occupied an ideal location at the top of the knoll, for drainage was never a problem and the location afforded the most lovely views, but it did make for a strenuous approach and difficult descent. Drewry stopped for a drink at the well beyond our two immense pear trees, and then we carried on, past the horse tie, turning right, toward the stables. Zeke, our stableman, held the horses ready for us outside the door to the barn. I liked him tremendously, for he let me brush the horses' manes when Father was out on the lands.

"Morning, suhs, Miss 'Lizabeth." A smile wrinkled his dark skin.

"Betsy, you and Drewry may share the double saddle." Father patted the shining leather of it, inspecting the clever design that allowed two bottoms to ride comfortably on one horse's back. He was proud to have paid only ten dollars for it after trading tobacco with the saddler in Springfield.

"And a bright sorrel mare to take yous there," Zeke hummed under his breath, checking the shoes of the steady girl who wore the saddle. We called her Dipsy, for the long swoop of her back. I was disappointed not to have my own horse, but I did not argue with Father, as it was not a lengthy trip.

Drewry mounted first and busied himself arranging his gun across his back. Father helped me up and I wondered if Mother had informed him I was a young woman. I grew uncomfortable at the thought, circling Drewry's waist with my arms. I supposed I would not tell my brothers about it, but I did look forward to discussing it with my best girlfriend, Thenny, when next I saw her. It must not have happened yet to her, or surely she would have told me of it, for it was in her nature to talk of everything.

We set out, taking the southern path behind the stables so we might walk along the stream and approach the planting fields from behind. I heard the rushing spring water before I caught a glimpse of it, for its bubbling energy filled the woods. Rabbits and birds scattered into the stands of green budding elm, oak and maple, alerted by the farm hounds that raced ahead barking, their noses full of scent. We clopped single file slowly down the path and a family of deer leaped suddenly beside us, hopping over the grassy banks.

"Look, those deer are an easy mark!" Drewry shifted his rifle to his front and I saw the group stop to drink by a small stand of spring cress and silver bells at the river's edge. I was surprised they stood so close, usually the deer ran swiftly away, aware of the danger men on horseback posed.

"Drewry, we have other plans today," Father cautioned him against shooting, and though Drewry made a clucking sound of disappointment with his tongue, he said no more. I twisted as we passed the band, watching the deer step gently into the water. I wished we could ride after them and allow Dipsy to splash her knees in the shallows, but Drewry held the reins and guided us sure behind Father and John Jr., trotting up the bank toward the fields. I squeezed my arms tighter around my brother, pleased he had moved his gun. I liked breathing in the comforting smell of his wool jacket as we drew alongside Father's closest field, between the hog pen and the slave cabins. Red and muddy, it spread before us in the early stage of planting.

The Negro men had hoes and worked the dirt of half the field while the women squatted in the rows, working the other half with their hands, some with infants wrapped across their backs. The women had the job of removing each tiny green seedling from the germination crates, and planting it two hands apart in rows of red dirt made up by the men. Father's boss man, Dean, sat supervising on the split log fence bordering the field.

"Make certain the earth is tamped down well about the roots," Father called from his horse, abruptly cracking his whip in the air to signify his presence. The slaves did not look over, but Dipsy gave a start at the sound so Drewry had to speak to her.

"There, there . . ." he stroked her neck.

"Yes, masta!" Dean jumped down and cracked his own whip, but only lightly and to the side. He was not young but had the appearance of a straight sapling, tall and strong and determined to grow. Father said Dean was worth two men, especially in a clearing, so skilled was he with the ax, the maul and wedge. Dean possessed know-how as well as strength, for Father liked to craft our furniture, rockers, tables, bed frames and chairs and he enjoyed no one as his apprentice better than Dean. He had even bought a brass hatchet for Dean to chop splits for the woodstove, and it served as a great measure of his trust.

"We be done wit' this field by evening, suh." Dean bent to stroke the back of a hound that curled against his legs, but kept his head tilted to Father, respectful.

"'Tis good, for we have an early spring this year." Father bent way forward in the saddle, inclining his head to Dean. "We also have whiskey fresh from the doubler," he smiled. "Come down to the still at sunset and we shall sharpen our ideas a touch and you might take a jug back to the cabins."

"Yes suh, masta Bell." Dean looked well pleased at the thought of this reward at the end of the day.

"Make certain each plant is well watered," Father said as he straightened, giving him an obligatory caution before turning his horse and snapping his whip again, leading us trotting down the muddy path past the slave cabins toward the further fields.

Two ancient women, whose names I did not know, sat on their stoops at the cabins. Everyone else was out at work. The elderly two were engaged watching three toddling children, too big to be carried on their mothers' backs and too small or too ignorant to work, at play in the mud of the road. The old ones stood as we clopped past and bowed their heads to Father, while the little children stopped their game and watched us without moving. I stared back at the small brown faces wondering what imaginary lives they were creating in the muck, but then Father's horse let loose its bowels and my attention, along with the children's, shifted to the pile of steaming horse waste left oozing on the road. Drewry laughed and Dipsy delicately stepped over it as we rode on.

When we reached the planted fields I saw the young green tobacco there was already arranged in tight rows and all the slave children, dressed in white, squatted behind the plants, making a pattern greatly resembling Mother's woven checked tablecloth. Their hands worked quickly and, above the sound of water rushing at the southern boundary of the field, I heard the sound of stones, irregularly clapped together.

"We are here to look for worms," Father informed us of our purpose as he dismounted and tied up his horse under the budding elm on the edge of the field. "You know how." He dismissed John Jr., who had already tied his steed and turned his back. I watched him walking away, toward the far side.

"Come with me, Drewry, Elizabeth, I will learn you the method."

We dismounted and I allowed Drewry to go ahead of me, following Father. The mud was sticky beneath my feet and,

holding up my skirts, I walked unsteadily. The ride had jarred
my insides a little more than I'd expected and my stomach
was cramping again, but I tried to regain my poise. Father
stopped at the top of the first row, empty of children, and I listened attentively while he described the task at hand.

"The young tobacco plant is delicate and tasty to a fat
white worm, as you can see." He bent down and without a
long inspection pulled three slimy round white worms off a
wide green leaf. He dropped them from his gloved hand and
squished them against a stray stone in the row with the heel
of his boot. "They make our soil the richest in the district," he
said. Behind his shoulder I noticed the slave children casting
uneasy glances in his direction and I could tell they were
frightened of him, though I did not immediately guess why.

"'Tis of utmost importance every worm be plucked out of
hiding and killed with a stone, for if there is carelessness, the
worm will crawl back and eat and eat and eat, that is his purpose." He paused, gazing out across his field as though distracted. "Our purpose is to educate those ignorant of the
proper technique." Father glanced with squinted eyes in my
direction but before I could discover his meaning he turned
and walked quickly to the next row where there were children
picking worms. Drewry and I followed, finding it easy to keep
up with him as he stopped often, bending to peel apart the
new green leaves in search of the fat white worms. I looked
beyond his figure to the backs of all the children and I saw
that the clapping of the stones was the killing of the worms
and it seemed to me the tempo had increased since our arrival.

"See here," Father stood and held again in his gloved hand
a pile of the wriggling pests. He advanced to the closest child
picking, who happened to be Little Bright. She was our

housemaid, Chloe's, youngest daughter and we had played together for years until Little Bright was put to work in the fields and Father disallowed our friendship. I had been extremely fond of her, but I had not seen her for some time. I noticed her breasts had developed more than mine. Our eyes met and I saw she was afraid.

"We shall not tolerate worms on our green livelihood," Father said.

I watched with horror as he bent and stuffed the live worms from his hand into her mouth. "You must pick off every one," he warned and stepped back, waiting, making certain she chewed and swallowed. My hand flew to my mouth and I felt an uncomfortable knot rise in the back of my throat, for I could easily imagine the worms there. I shut my eyes so I might not witness her punishment further.

"Open now." On his command to her I was compelled to open my own eyes and watch, as he pulled her red tongue out with his gloved fingers and peered down her throat. Satisfied the dreaded grubs had disappeared, he patted her head and continued his walking inspection, but I could not follow. I wanted to sink to my knees in the mud and comfort Little Bright, if there could be any comfort. I wished to hold her or offer my clean apron so she might wipe her mouth out, but I was too frightened of what Father might do to me. Whenever I behaved not as he wished he took me out to the barn and whipped my bottom with his riding crop to impart the right true path into my mischievous heart. I feared to upset him. A sudden nausea I could not contain wrenched my insides and without looking at Little Bright I turned, tripping my way back down the muddy row toward the tree where the horses were tied. I leaned my forearm against the smooth bark of the elm and took deep breaths of the clean spring air to prevent myself from vomiting. I heard a rumbling whisper rising above the clapping of the stones.

"Pick-'em-all-off, Pick-'em-all-off, Pick-'em-all-off!" the slave children chanted fearfully.

I was afraid Father would be angry with me for abandoning the task, but when his inspection was complete he returned to where I waited near the horses and hugged me close.

"I know this teaching may be hard for you to understand. It may seem harsh and low-minded to you, dear Betsy." He pulled gently on my braid while patting my back, almost allowing me the time to release the tears gathered in my eyes and throat, but before I could, he carried on. "Yet, this is the most efficacious method and by it the new plants are thriving in the field." He lifted me up onto Dipsy, avoiding my eyes. He turned away and mounted his horse and I saw him nod with satisfaction at the quick moving hands of the slaves.

"His crop is the finest in all of Robertson County," I said softly into Drewry's back, resting my head against his jacket. I wished to look at the billowing white clouds of the sky and not at the little Negro children at play in the mud on our way back past the cabins.

That night I was awakened, shortly after retiring, to the same tapping I had heard the night before. I stayed in my bed listening, and I heard it in regular intervals, *tap-tap, tap-tap*. It struck the windowpane, then moved along the wall of my room. What was it? It was as if someone floated outside and knocked for entry, but I knew that could not be. It had to be the wind, a bird or rodent, as Mother had suggested. I pulled the quilt up to my ears and lay still, listening, immobilized, afraid as if I'd wakened from a horrible dream and found it to be real. TAP-TAP, the sound came louder and sharper and I tensed my body, for I thought my window glass had cracked.

"What is that noise?" John Jr. appeared in my doorway, a lit candle in his hand. He did not wait for my reply but crossed firmly to my window and opened it, looking out.

"How does it seem to you, dear brother?" I was much relieved to see him and his presence allowed my curiosity to prevail over my fear. I threw off my covers and went to stand beside him, finding the wood floor painfully cold under my bare toes.

"I see nothing, but I heard something, and it came from here." His thick eyebrows twisted downward, much perplexed. He shut the window and immediately it came again as we stood watching.

TAP-TAP! TAP-TAP!

For certain there was no visible explanation for the sound. The glass shivered in the candlelight when struck, but no twig or wind or animal did appear. We stepped quickly back away from the glass, afraid it might shatter as the noise came again, louder and more insistent.

TAP-TAP-TAP-TAP-TAP-TAP!

This time, it did not immediately cease.

"How can this be?" John Jr. looked at me and I could see the disbelief I felt mirrored in his eyes, flickering in the candlelight, disturbed by our quickened breathing. I shook my head.

"I know not, but I heard it last night as well." I shifted from one foot to the other, nervous and cold.

"Let us get your candle lit and fetch Father. He must witness this." My hands shook as I took the flame from John Jr.'s candle for my wick. I had a feeling the tap-tapping was something quite out of the ordinary and unpleasant and I did not relish waking Father to tell him of it. As it happened, I did not have to, as we heard his step on the stair and he entered my room.

"What is wrong here?" His voice was gruff with sleep, though he looked sharp enough.

"Hear it! Our sleeping is interrupted by rapping at the window, but we cannot see its cause."

TAP! TAP! TAP! TAP! TAP!

The knocking started up again like metal on the glass and Father was attentive. He cocked his head listening a moment before striding toward us and the window. His legs were long and bare beneath his nightshirt and he pushed up on his toes and leaned far out to ascertain the source of the noise, but as we had done before him, he saw nothing there.

"What could it be?" Father was genuinely puzzled and my concern deepened, as he usually had a quick solution to most problems.

Tap-tap.

"Perhaps a shingle has come undone. It is difficult to see." He turned away from the window and looked at me, accurately assessing my fear in one glance. "Betsy, sleep in Jesse's vacant bed, if you like." Jesse had married his girlfriend, Martha, months before and had moved to his own property further down the Adams–Cedar Hill high road, so his bed beside John Jr.'s stood empty. Having dispensed this advice Father shrugged his shoulders and left the room, communicating that whatever tapped on my window gave him no cause for great concern. John Jr. did not look at me, nor I at him, but I believe we both knew it was not a shingle in the wind, though we pretended it might be, as we silently retired together to his room.

We knew for certain it was *not* on the following day when a detailed inspection was made of our roof. Though we had planned a day at the schoolhouse, Mother allowed us all to participate in the examination of our home and the sun cooperated, shining strong on our backs, though it was still early in the spring. The tallest ladder was brought from the barn and Father and Dean and the boys climbed everywhere about the roof, but found no loose wood shingles, no stray branches, and no sign of rodent infestation.

"May I sleep in John Jr's. room again?" I requested this permission shortly before the hour to retire when Mother had finished braiding my hair and the Bible reading was accomplished. I'd found Jesse's bed plenty comfortable the night before.

"You may not." Father shook his head and frowned. Disappointed, I looked away. I had suspected Father would not allow it, for having found conditions satisfactory in the structure of our house, he did not intend to alter our regular routine.

"What shall I do if I hear it again?" I was most discomfited by the thought of what had knocked against my window.

"Be reassured," Father stroked my undone hair with his heavy fingers, "God made the darkness and called it night, but also He did make every moving creature, and called them good."

Despite his comforting words, I found it difficult settling into sleep and I twisted about in my bed. The moon was nothing but a sliver of God's thumbnail behind the glass of my window. My ears felt stretched with listening and there was mostly silence in the house. John Jr. snored lightly in his bed down the hall and from the younger boys' room I heard the regular breathing of Drewry and Richard, while Joel made a precious little sucking sound as if he were still a baby, nursing in his sleep. Without knowing it, I did fall asleep, but wakened suddenly with the sense someone had touched my shoulder. Rapidly I looked about but I saw no one in my room. The sliver of moon was gone and out in the pure dark I heard a sudden loud flapping, as though a great flock of birds beat their wings against my walls. I cried out and pulled the quilt above my head, squeezing my face between my elbows for I knew their beaks would break the glass and my room would shortly be invaded, whereupon I would be pecked to death.

Drewry and John Jr. came running and I heard their bare feet rushing to my window. They looked outside and declared in unison, "Betsy, there is nothing there!"

"There is! A flock of birds!" I refused to take the covers from my head and my speech was muffled through my quilts.

"It would sound so, but it is not!" John Jr. was upset.

"What is this grievous disturbance?" Father entered my room carrying a lit candle with Mother right behind. I felt her bottom sink against my hip as she sat down on my bed and gently removed the quilts from off my face. Gathering me into her arms, she spoke to Father over the thunderous flapping of wings.

"Perhaps they are confused of their direction, Jack."

"That would be so, dear Lucy, if only they were present! I cannot see what we can hear." Father opened my window and the sound grew so intensely loud I grabbed Mother's cotton nightdress in my fists and buried my face on her shoulder so as not to feel the talons and beaks I was certain would descend in the next moment.

"Impossible!" Mother pried me loose and bade John Jr. come and sit beside me, as she wished to see the source of the noise for herself. I clutched my brother's arm and peeked fearfully over his shoulder watching Mother squeeze in front of Father at my window. She bravely thrust her head outside and in a moment she drew back into my room and shut the window tight, diminishing the roar, but only slightly.

"This is most unusual." She stood frowning with concern and the light of Father's flickering candle accentuated a dark shadow on her forehead.

"Indeed." Father exchanged a glance with her, then looked away, into the empty raging night.

"Let us pray," Mother cleared her throat and spoke with her usual composure. "Let us entreat God, with all His wisdom, to allow us to discover the origin of these strange noises."

We joined hands around my bed and bowed our heads beneath the sound of beating wings. Mother led a prayer but I could not focus on her words for I felt my head would soon split from the pressure of the noise. The sound grew louder, then louder still, and Richard and Joel woke up and came in crying.

"It's all right, boys," Mother tried to reassure them. "Hold hands and join us in silent prayer." Joel squeezed my fingers tight as the thick log walls of my room began to tremble and the house began to shake. What was happening? What were we to do? We prayed. Only when we had burned three candles down and the gray light of dawn graced the edges of the sky, only then did the striking wings and rumbling cease.

Mid-morning we gathered at the breakfast table. School was not a question, as all of us were tired and distraught.

"The Reverend Johnston will visit us today and I shall make inquiries, but I forbid all of you to speak a word of these disturbances." Father looked first at me, then to my brothers, making certain we understood the serious nature of his directive. It was easily conveyed, for though we often saw him stern, he rarely was this somber. John Jr., Drewry, Richard, Joel and I avoided speaking to each other, since all we wished to speak of were the possible causes of the disturbance. Our house thundered an unusual quiet.

When the Reverend arrived, I made it my business to trail behind him and Father, as they took their walk out on our lands. The day was lovely and the air buzzed with the flitting wings of hummingbirds drawing nectar from the fruit tree blossoms. White butterflies flew out of the new grasses as the men took the back path through the orchard down the hill to the stream. I followed at a good distance, excited to see the young corn stalks uncrooking their new green necks when we crossed the flat field at the foot of the orchard.

" 'Tis a good and loving God who sends such a spring to Adams!" the Reverend called loudly to my father, apparently hoping conversation would slow his pace, for the Reverend was stout and wheezed slightly when he walked. His long silver hair lay over his collar, splayed out by his black top hat. I saw it glinting in the sun before I slipped behind a tree.

"We must give thanks at every step for our blessed fortune," Father answered and they carried on awhile in silence winding down the path through the woods until they reached the stream where the air grew full of rambunctious water song. They stopped at a small clearing of sandy beach, where a little waterfall the length of Father's boots rushed over gray stones into a shoal. I hid behind a large boulder on the bank above them and I was able to hear their every word.

"Pray, Reverend, what do you recall of the great earth

movements felt throughout this part of Tennessee in recent years?"

"I recall an angry God reminding us we are as nothing to the force of His will and nature." The Reverend bent and cast a stone into the stream with unusual playfulness for a man of his years. "I recall the tremors of the ground moved the souls of many, and attendance in the house of the Lord was greatly increased!" He laughed, watching the ripples he'd made in the water with his rock.

"Have you felt any such earth movements of late?" Father did not respond to his humor and appeared deeply preoccupied with unspoken concerns. He bent and cast his own stone, only it hit another rock and bounced to the other side of the stream.

"No," the Reverend turned to him, "have you, Jack?"

"I have felt something." Father nodded, and I wondered if the Reverend could see as I could, even from my distance, Father's reluctance to discuss the matter.

"Describe it." The Reverend waited.

"It was a rumbling, and shaking, and trembling of the house."

"A rolling of the ground, a tremor of sorts?"

"Something like that, yes."

I wondered why Father did not more accurately convey our experience.

"This was yesterday?"

"It was." Father bent at the knees and picked up another stone, casting it expertly to the center of the stream.

"Well." The Reverend moved his hands to his hips and flapped the tails of his jacket out sideways, appearing deep in thought. "I have just come from town where I paid a visit to Thorn's country store. There were several folks gathered there sharing pipes with Thorn and sampling the hyson skin and bohea tea he has recently carted in from Nashville. No one mentioned an earth movement and I do believe if anyone had felt such a thing I would be among the first to hear of it." He rolled his heels deeper in the sand, contemplating my father's face, but Father kept his eyes on the ripples his stone had made in the stream.

"Well, you are the first of whom I have inquired and I consider my original question now moot with your gracious reply." He stood again, showing his white teeth in a smile, appearing satisfied, but I was much dismayed, for the Reverend clearly could shed no light on what the disturbance in our home might be.

"Say, Jack, you have a sinkhole near the cold storehouse on your land, do you not?"

"We do," Father nodded.

"Well, might your rumbling be the ground settling around your sinkhole now that spring has thawed the frozen earth?"

"A good suggestion, Reverend. I will look there for an answer if we experience such rumbling again."

I thought of the place he mentioned where the ground curved down to make a grass lake of sorts by the entrance to our cold storehouse. How could a sinkhole be related to the flapping wings of invisible birds, or a tapping at the window glass? What could it have to do with the shaking of log walls? I laid my cheek against the smooth boulder that hid me well, and shut my eyes, tired and deeply concerned. I allowed the men to move away without me, continuing their stroll along the stream. They were clearly finished discussing the only subject I was interested in.

I was good for nothing the rest of the day, dreading the setting of the sun. I gathered warm eggs from the chicken coop for Mother, and attempted a spell of mending in the afternoon, but I feared each stitch brought me closer to the evening and the hours were not long enough, so soon was it time to gather for supper.

Our family joined hands around the table and bowed our heads to our wooden bowls. The steam off Chloe's early spring pea soup filled our noses as Father recited the usual prayer.

"O heavenly Father, dear Lord, we thank thee for thy gifts from Heaven and pray to serve with our souls, that they may be ever worthy of your blessings."

I prayed silently, Grant us an uneventful, quiet night of sleep, O Lord. I promise to be a better girl in every aspect, pleasing to my father and mother, compassionate to my brothers, and a dedicated listener in church, please God.

"Amen."

"Amen," we repeated, then sat in silence while Father sliced the biscuits in the basket.

"Children," Mother waited until all our eyes were turned onto her face. "The prayers we say at table have more depth of meaning than you may be aware."

Joel shook his golden curls, anxious to get at his food.

"May we begin?" Drewry lifted his spoon in inquiry.

"Listen to your mother." Father's tone was sharp as his cutting knife.

"You may," Mother answered, looking to Drewry, seeming somewhat distracted in her thoughts. She continued, "To be 'ever worthy' you must strive to put your faith in the Lord and know you will not be misguided. I wish each of you to remember this." I watched her competent fingers smoothing her napkin on her lap and I could tell she was concerned, and wished us to be brave. For her sake, I did want to try, but it was difficult. Already I felt unbearably anxious and as the last light of day disappeared from the windows, I found myself unable to lift my head and look at anyone. Chloe's normally light biscuits went down my throat like rocks, and I felt so tired I was barely able to raise my spoon to my mouth.

"Betsy dear, I believe you should retire." Mother excused me from the Bible reading after supper and, exhausted, I went directly to sleep in my own bed, only to be awakened in the middle of the night by Richard and Joel climbing on top of me, chattering.

"Sister, sister, there is a rat gnawing on our bedpost!"

"Quiet. Let me listen . . ." I cuddled them under my quilts and, stretching my ears into the darkness, I heard it too, faint but distinct, the sound of an animal, gnawing wood. Joel began to cry.

"What's the matter? Did it bite you?" I was relieved, thinking nothing of a rat at the bedpost compared to a flock of invisible birds beating down the walls. A rat could not produce a shaking of our house. The sound stopped and I heard Drewry's steps before I saw the light of his candle in the hall.

"There is nothing there again!" He entered my room shaking his head in disbelief. "I was quite near to it, sister, and plainly heard the gnashing of its teeth, but it took some time to catch a spark on my char cloth off the flint and steel in the dark. When I lit the wick I was standing right beside where I heard the rat but I saw nothing there. Nothing scuttered under the bed, nothing ran from the room. I saw no evidence of gnawing and the noise ceased with the light." Drewry pushed away the hair fallen on his forehead, struggling to make sense of his experience.

"But hear it now!" Richard cried and I realized the gnawing had started up again. The boys and I huddled close to-gether on my bed. With great courage, Drewry strode back to his room and when his footsteps ended, so the noise did stop. There was silence across the upstairs.

"Betsy, bring your candle and come quick," Drewry called and I did as he asked, repeating to myself, be brave, be strong and trust the Lord will protect you from harm. Joel and Richard each clutched one side of my nightdress in their solid fists and we made our way down the dark hall into their bed-room.

"Light it." Drewry took my arm and passed the flame to my wick and we held both our candles aloft. We searched every nook and corner, inspecting even the tiniest cracks in the plank floor, as if a rat could thin itself and slip between them, but we saw nothing. We stayed close together, uncer-tain of what we might find, investigating each shadow with great trepidation. Richard and Joel had a firm grip on our nightclothes and bumped against our backs as we moved along.

"Betsy, my neck's gone prickly," Drewry whispered in my ear.

"Shhh, the little ones are frightened enough," I answered. Neither of us knew what to do next.

"What is this about?" John Jr. entered and the way our lights cast shadows on his long jaw reminded me with com-fort how much he did resemble Father. We told him of the gnawing sound.

"Retire to my room," he insisted, but no sooner had we passed the landing and entered his dormer than the gnawing commenced again and this time it was accompanied by the ear-splitting sound of wood cracking apart.

"It sounds as though my bedroom furniture is on its way to kindling!"

"Run, Betsy!"

We raced across the hall to witness what could cause such destruction, but when our candles reached my door the noises ceased. Everything was as it always was. My rocking chair sat unmoving by the open window, my wardrobe stood in its place against the northern wall, my chamber pot was inconspicuous in the corner, and the china bowl of my washstand gleamed under our candle flames by the doorway. Only my quilts had fallen to the floor. All was silent.

"Fetch the lamps from the parlor, Drewry." John Jr. could even sound like Father when he gave commands and Drewry did respond, setting off downstairs. I picked up the quilts and wrapped up Joel and Richard on my bed, trying to keep from shaking with apprehension. I moved with caution, afraid the very bed stand might give way beneath us as we settled, for I had most certainly heard the sound of furniture breaking coming from my room.

"May we keep the lamps lit through the night?" I asked John Jr., hoping he would support such an effort. Father was not stingy with the lamp oil as many were, but he was not wasteful, and burning a lamp through the night without good cause would mean a certain trip to the barn.

"I know not." John Jr. looked confused regarding what to do. "Perhaps we should wake Father . . ." he suggested, but he did not start for the door.

"I am awake, my son." Father was on the stairs and spoke curtly. He entered with Drewry behind him carrying the lamps, unlit.

"Blow out your candles, I have brought the tinderbox should we need it." Father had a plan and we obeyed him, blowing out our flames, but I grew most anxious and concerned, for as Drewry had just described, I knew the flint and steel of the tinderbox could take an eternity to light. In the dark we listened and immediately there came again the sound of the rat gnawing the bedpost, only now it was in my room, right beside us, and the sound of wood splitting came from Drewry, Richard and Joel's room, accompanied by the discordant tinkle of metal screws falling to the floor.

"Don't let it bite me, Betsy!" Richard wailed, turning his face to my shoulder while Joel hiccuped a sob of fear. I pulled the two of them up to the head of the bed, moving as far away from the sound as possible. The gnawing grew louder, evolving into a hideous scratching on the floor, as though an animal as large as a dog or a deer was trapped beneath my bed. I held tight to the boys and was about to scream for Father to hurry and strike the flint and catch a spark when Mother appeared in the doorway with a lit lamp in her hand, revealing my bedpost, whole and uneaten, and nothing present except ourselves in the room.

"The good Lord gave us light and so be it. We will burn a lamp in each room this evening and consider this matter with the sun on our faces tomorrow." Mother was calm, as always, and made this pronouncement as though nothing was amiss that we could not address. "Richard dear, no rat will bite you, Father and I will guard your beds." She took Joel from me into her arms and there was no further discussion of the trauma. She managed to balance him on her hip so his curls mashed against her shoulder, while motioning with her other hand that held the lamp for Richard to follow her. He jumped quickly off the bed and rushed to her side, clutching her nightdress with tight fingers. I saw Joel gripped her waist with his legs and her neck with locked hands as though he planned never to let go.

"I want to sleep with Richard and Joel!" I cried, though I knew it was not brave. I was too scared to lie in my own bed.

"I will sleep with John Jr." Drewry volunteered to give his bed to me and I believe he needed his elder brother's comfort as much as I needed not to sleep alone. Father nodded his agreement, but his attention was not with our sleeping arrangements. He lit the two remaining lamps with Mother's flame and held them high above his head, illuminating as much of my room as possible.

"Give one to the boys, Jack." Mother saw him hand a lamp to John Jr. and then she left to tuck Joel and Richard in their beds. I wanted to jump from my bed and run after her, but her departure left a darkness at my doorway I feared to cross and I decided to wait until Father had finished his inspection so he might walk me down the hall.

"What is this, Betsy?" His voice was low and quiet and his inquiry so sincere I thought he had found something previously hidden. I stretched forward on my hands and knees, craning my neck to see off the edge of the bed what he was referring to.

"What is what, Father?" He did not reply to my question, but turned instead to face me, allowing the lamp to dangle from his hand so the room darkened and only a portion of the floor received the light.

"Darling daughter, shall I lie with you awhile?" He suggested this, but I could see he did not really want to lie with me. I could hear the tiredness in his tone.

"No, please, Father. Rather, I would go to sleep in Drewry's bed for I am frightened, and I wish to be near the little boys should they awake, for they will inspire me to be brave." I stood up quickly and Father took my hand in his and pulled me to him in the dark.

"Fear not, darling daughter, I will be close at hand." I was greatly relieved he did not wish to lie with me, for though his hand on my back was reassuring and his skin warm and comforting under his worn cotton nightshirt, I found the smell of the drink he had consumed after dinner sour and disgusting on his breath. He stepped out of our embrace but kept hold of my hand, raising his lamp to light our way down the hall.

Mother was tucking the quilts around Richard and Joel when we reached the bedroom. "Go to sleep now," she told the boys, managing to make it sound reasonable to try again.

"You too, Betsy." Father patted my behind as I hurried to be near Mother. Her lamp burned on the golden pine table under the window between Richard's and Joel's beds and there was plenty of light, enough to see that neither Richard nor Joel were crying, and they both looked fairly sleepy. I did not think I would sleep again, as my eyes felt stretched and widened by my furtive glances into the dark corners of the room, but Mother kindly agreed to stay awhile. We climbed together into Drew's bed along the wall and, pulling my body against hers, she snuggled her knees into my own.

"Do not be afraid, dear Betsy," Mother said, patting my leg with her hand under the quilts. "Your father will soon discover the cause of this disturbance." He had left the doorway and I heard his footsteps descending the stairs.

"I pray that will be so." I was calmed by her warmth and confidence and I allowed my lids to shut over my stinging eyes. Though we were troubled by no more noises that evening, I slept only fitfully in the well-lit room.

I woke early to the sound of furniture being moved about in the hall. I looked outside and saw the day was not a sunny spring one, but instead, the sky was overcast with a gray pallor that reminded me of the winter months. It looked not at all warm. I left Drew's bed and discovered Father, Dean, John Jr. and Drewry were in my bedroom, having moved my heavy wardrobe and my washstand out into the hall. They had upended my bed so it stood against one wall, and my whole floor was in plain view. Father held a crowbar in his hands and was set to pry up the boards.

"Some vermin could be hiding in between the ceiling and the floor," he explained, ripping the first board out. The creak it gave squawked like the wood splitting we had heard the night before. I shivered in my nightdress, unhappy to be reminded of it.

"What hides there, Father?" I wondered what he might find. On his hands and knees he leaned forward, peering into the empty space between the boards.

"I see no nests or evidence of animals, but I will look some more," he said. I realized he intended to rip apart the whole house if need be, to discover what visited such fear on us. A hopeless panic came over me that he would find no vermin. My stomach felt queasy and I put my hand across it as I wondered, if not vermin, what would he find? What could make the sound of birds and of gnawing and gnashing wood, and yet be invisible to the eye? My intuition screamed it was something unlike anything I had known before, something uncommon on this earth, and I wondered, why had it come to us?

I turned back into the hall, removing from my wardrobe cotton stockings and a plain cloth dress the color of the hickory nuts used to dye it. I walked to the boys' room to change and it felt odd to dress there, but odder still was the cause of it. I did it quickly, disliking the sound of ripping wood issuing from down the hall. I felt again the nausea in my stomach and I hurried down the stairs and into the kitchen where Mother was stirring a pot of beans and bacon at the stove. There were two brown vine baskets of laundry and ironing for Chloe and another of mending for me by the door and it made me tired to see them.

"Good morning, Betsy. How are you this day?"

"I am well, Mother." I know not why I lied to her, but I knew my true feelings would make her sad and I did not wish to add my fears to Mother's pile of burdens, like another basket at the door. Unfortunately, the smell of cooking beans was abruptly repugnant to me and I stood and ran out the back where I vomited into her blue flowering rosemary bush.

"Dear Betsy, I should say you are not well at all!" Mother followed me, and stroked my back. She scooped a bucket of cold water from the barrel where the rainwater was collected by the back door and washed my sick into the ground, before leading me back to the kitchen. "Sit, child." I sank into the chair by the woodstove and she brought me a wet muslin cloth smelling of comfrey. I closed my eyes while she gently wiped my face. "You have no fever . . ." She felt my forehead with the back of her hand, then stroked my cheek. "Sometimes with the bleeding, the stomach is upset." She ran her fingers over my eyelids, meaning I should open them, and when I did, she took up my chin, and tilted my face, so she could look me in the eye. "Are you frightened, dear girl?"

"Yes, Mother, truly I am!" I threw my arms around her waist and began to cry, while she combed my hair with her fingers. The touch of her hand pulled the truth from me. "I am afraid it is some evil thing that visits us and I know not what I might do to keep it from me!"

"Elizabeth! What nonsense. There is no evil in this house." Mother took a step away from me and frowned. "You know not the many possibilities of nature. We are greatly concerned with the noises we have heard, why else would your father at this moment devote his day to taking the house apart from the inside out?" I saw Mother was most distressed and upset herself, which frightened me the more. She turned to stir again the bubbling pot, lest it begin to burn, and I watched her shoulder blade rise up, spooning round the thickening beans. She sighed and turned to look at me. "Your father and I will solve this mystery, Betsy," she promised. "With the good Lord's help. And yours." She laid her wooden spoon across the top of the pot and placed her hands on my shoulders. I could see from the many lines about her eyes, she too was tired. She held my gaze with hers. "Of utmost importance is your health and constitution. Go lie in my bed and I will make you a peppermint tea."

"No, Mother, I will take the mending and sit in the parlor." I wanted to prove I too could be strong and brave in the face of our afflictions. I sewed all that day, finishing more than half the basket of mending, listening to Father move from room to room upstairs, prying up boards and replacing them, looking for he knew not what. I was not surprised when he found nothing at all, apart from dust and some old mouse droppings which were clearly unrelated to the noises we had heard. Supper was again solemn and silent, as a great heaviness weighted our necks when we bent them in prayer.

"Dear God, who art in Heaven, hallowed be thy name . . ." Father's voice held a somber intonation, ". . . for Thine is the Kingdom and the Power and the Glory. Amen."

"We will have a special Bible reading this evening, won't we, Father?" Mother's good cheer was out of place and though I did appreciate her effort, we remained a sullen group. Only Joel and Richard turned their heads, inclined to abandon their glumness.

"What story will you read, Father?"

"Whatever your mother likes." Father wiped his mouth with his napkin and smiled at Mother acknowledging her courage, but I noticed he was merely picking at his food.

"I should like to hear a story of God's love, perhaps John fourteen, on the coming of the Spirit, how He will be in you," Mother said, her eyes lit with good humor. She knew the connotations such a reading would bring. All around the table our mouths began to curl slightly upward, as each of us pictured Old Kate at the pulpit in her Sunday finery, imbued with the glory of the good Lord. Mrs. Kate Batts was called Old Kate by everyone, though she was about the same age as our mother. I was happy they shared few other traits, for Old Kate was quite unusual in her affect and appearance. Unpredictably outspoken, she weighed over two hundred pounds and dressed without regard to style or fashion. Our entire community took some delight in mocking her, and her strange ways were the focus of conversation as frequently as the topic of the weather. She did cut a distinct figure, traveling the district up and down the high road, peddling mostly stockings, woven from cast-off scraps of wool begged on previous visits from farm to farm, all to create an income. Her poverty was so severe, it was said she spun her cat hair into yarn. Mother both donated to her and bought from her. I'd heard Mother say that those who did not gave the excuse Old Kate worked her slave woman long into the night by the thin light of a single candle, but the more likely reason was they did not have charitable hearts. Old Kate's husband, Ignatius, was a crippled invalid, and we never saw him out-of-doors, not even in church. He sat hunched at the front window of their house, on the Adams–Cedar Hill high road, every day of his life. They owned a fair piece of property that bordered ours in places, but because of her husband's illness, Kate ran their farm, and it wasn't much to speak of.

Her best known eccentricity was her habit of filling with Spirit at our Sunday sermons. We recalled together how tolerant was the resignation on the Reverend Johnston's sturdy face when Old Kate shook the church, falling to her voluminous knees, wailing, "He is in me! Jesus, the Spirit of the Lord is in me!" Isolated titters of laughter from members of our congregation were usually hidden by the thunder of her declaration and by those who supported her religious impulses and called encouragement to her, "Praise the Lord, Kate! O praise the Lord!" The most humorous part came after the Spirit in her waned, and the sermon was accomplished and we were released outside. All across the church lawn groups of children gathered, laughing, pretending to be Kate Batts filling up with Spirit. Boys rolled on the ground and wailed and though their mothers called "Stop being silly!" from behind their gloves, no one was overly concerned, as it was all in fun. It was a happy memory Mother had conjured for us.

We adjourned to the parlor, and Father sat at his desk and drank from his flask for somewhat longer than usual, while John Jr. stoked the fire too much, his nervousness as apparent as the bright sparks shooting up the chimney. Richard and Joel sat either side of Drewry on the bench, and Mother had me sit before her on the rug, so my hair could be brushed and braided anew. Father settled himself in his chair and read slowly.

"If ye love me, keep my commandments. I be in my Father and ye in me, and I in you."

Richard and Joel giggled and made faces, as though they would fill with Spirit, and Mother smiled, indulging them, using her fingers to pick out a knot at the base of my neck.

"He that hath my commandments, and keepeth them, he it is that loveth me; and he that loveth me shall be loved of my Father." I listened, heartened by Father's reading.

"God loves me, doesn't he?" I asked Mother later, when she came to see me settled in my bed.

"God loves us all," she answered with certainty and waited at my bedside until I breathed regularly with sleep.

I awoke in the dark to the distinct sounds of lips, smacking near my ear, and from the foot of my bed came a gulping sound, as if some human being were gasping for air. I was terrified and paralyzed with fear, and abruptly my quilt was ripped off my body and my braid twisted from behind and pulled so hard my head was raised with a painful jerk off the bed. I feared it would be pulled off my shoulders, so violent was the force. I screamed, and heard both Richard and Joel in their bedroom screaming too. The gulping grew louder, a sound like someone taking too much liquid in their mouth, being forced to swallow. It sounded oddly familiar, and I knew I had heard it before but I knew not where or when. John Jr. came running, with his candle lit, and Drewry too came running, but only to light his candle and return to the little boys. With light, all our screaming ceased, for we saw nothing apart from our selves and our things in our rooms.

"Brother, it touched me! It hurt me!" I gasped, reaching out for John Jr's. hand. I pulled him to sit close beside me on the bed.

"What touched you? What was it? Why were you gulping like that?" John Jr. drew his eyebrows together in inquiry, inspecting my face.

"I was not!"

"I heard the same in our room." Drewry and the boys arrived, with Drew talking. "It was as if a person was swallowing too great an amount, and choking with the effort." His description agreed with mine. Behind him in the darkened hall the gulping came again. It was evil and it was at my door.

"Keep lit the candle! Get the lamps!" I cried, as Richard and Joel took my quilt up off the floor. I held my hand to the back of my head and felt where my hair had been pulled. The pain was gone, but I was certain it had happened. "It is something unnatural here with us." I spoke aloud my fear.

"How say you, darling daughter?" Father asked, arriving at my door with Mother behind him, both in their nightclothes, each carrying an unlit lamp in one hand and a candle in the other.

"It ripped the quilt from off my bed and pulled my hair so hard I screamed in pain, not only fear." I was upset.

Mother sat beside me, put her arm around my shoulders, and pulled me close. The gulping sound continued, accompanied by a raspy chorus of choking, and we all froze, listening to the grotesque smacking of lips, considering our situation.

"Jack, we must light every lamp and you must lead us all in prayer," Mother whispered, not frightened so much as greatly concerned.

"Let us move downstairs and see if we are still disturbed." Father turned and led the way. The gulping noise faded in and out in time to the flickering light of our candles in the hall. John Jr. displayed great courage walking toward it, with us as witnesses, and when his candle reached the boys' room, the noise did cease. We went quickly down the stairs, bumping against one another as we struggled to stay near.

The lamps were lit and set on the desk and on the side table in the parlor, then Father built the fire up into flames. We joined hands in a circle, standing on the parlor rug and Father began our prayer.

"Dear God, who art in Heaven . . ."

From upstairs came a frightening crash and thud, as though our wardrobes and chests were thrown to the floor. John Jr. dropped my hand, thinking he would investigate the noise.

"Stay here," Father ordered, and he continued to pray, "O Lord, deliver us from evil, for we are among the righteous." The sound of our beds being ripped apart was joined by the noise of a metal chain dragging what I thought might be a large stone or some other unfathomably heavy object across the floor above our heads. I was deeply afraid and I was not the only one. Drewry and John Jr. had their faces set in stoic imitation of our Father, but Richard and Joel had quivering chins, and even Mother bore an expression of dismay.

"Jack," she looked to him across the circle, "we must repent our sins."

"Who here has sinned?" Father glared at us and I felt unable to speak, so tight was my chest with fear, but Joel squeezed my hand.

"I have sinned," he cried through tears. "I stole a carrot from Mother's garden and fed it to the horse!"

"The Lord forgives you," thundered Father and I did wonder how he knew, but the sin was trivial enough, it could not warrant such persecution of us all.

"I have sinned." Mother did not raise her voice, and I

strained to hear her over the pounding destruction taking place above our heads. "I have sinned, for I have not trusted you and your wisdom in every moment, dear God. You must know what forces you have sent among us. I renew my covenant of trust in you, Father, though these horrid and unnatural events wreak havoc with my faith." We heard a clattering of stones cascading down our steps, so many and of such various sizes it was as if the Red River bottom accosted us.

"Look!" Drewry ran and grabbed a stone and brought it back to Father. "It is a rock, exactly as it sounded." Drewry's simple observation was accurate and terrifying, for if the rocks were actual and they obviously were, what would remain of our splintered upstairs?

"I have also sinned." Father took the rock into his hand and cast it down hard, in anger, against the floor. "Yea, I have sinned no more than most men! Why, God, do you inflict this trial on our good family?" To our surprise, the disturbance precipitously ceased. We sat a moment in silent shock, then I began to cry with relief, and I had to strain to listen while Mother continued her prayers.

"Father, forgive us and hear our promise unto you; we will forsake you not, and our faith shall be firm in adherence."

No one wished to return upstairs and Mother and Father did not request that we do so. They retired to their bed and squeezed Joel and Richard in with them, while Drewry, John Jr. and I made do with quilts on chairs before the hearth. The lamps burned without wavering, and the hissing of the fire was the only sound for the rest of the night.

The next day was a Sunday and at dawn, though the whole family was weak and fragile with no sleep, Father woke us.

"Get dressed, for we are going to church. I have been to your rooms and all is intact."

We made a path in the rocks piled on the stairs and went to dress. My room was not the heap of wreckage I expected, instead all was normal, except my bed was unmade and missing the quilts I'd left downstairs. From my window I saw the new day, and though the sun glinted under the clouds, there was the promise of it in the sky. I changed from my nightclothes into a cotton petticoat and my pokeberry-dyed church dress. The light of day made the dark experience of the night before more difficult to understand. How could it be that we should suffer so, and yet arise with our environment undisturbed and as it always had been?

I heard the sound of many steps in the downstairs hallway and I peeked out to see Father instructing Dean and Chloe in removing the rocks from the steps. A tight feeling of fear grew in my stomach, and I hoped Dean and Chloe could finish the task before we returned from church, as I could not stand the sight of those rocks. They were a too vivid reminder we were experiencing something very much out of the ordinary in our house. I hoped Father would tell the Reverend Johnston of our troubles, and I thought it would be a great relief for me to inform Thenny of my suffering, but at breakfast Father squashed that plan, reminding all of us we must keep a vow of silence regarding the dreadful disturbances.

"Tell no one," Father ordered, giving each of us his strictest gaze, insuring we would be circumspect.

We rode in our black buggy down the Adams–Cedar Hill high road, past Kate Batts's house to Jesse and Martha's homestead. We picked them up on Sundays, for Mother enjoyed the opportunity to converse with the newlyweds. Without permission to speak of the one thing on my mind, I found I could not speak of anything at all, and I paid no attention to the idle chitchat that passed between Martha and Mother, though I did notice Martha did most of the talking, describing in detail a problem she was having germinating peas.

At church, I found the sermon not particularly inspiring or relevant to our troubles. The Reverend read of Jacob and Esau, emphasizing how Jacob fooled his father, but not God. I prayed silently while he spoke, hoping in His own house I might have better success with my prayers and pleas for the Lord to pity us and put an end to our misfortune. When the sermon was over and we were released out-of-doors, Thenny tried to speak to me.

"What is the matter, Betsy Bell? Are you ill? Why was your family absent from lessons all this week?"

I only shrugged and I could not form a proper aspect to reply to her queries regarding my welfare, and the Reverend's talk of fooling people but not God made me feel guilty. I thought to tell her I was a young woman now, though the blood had nearly finished, but it was not the time.

"You *look* ill!" Thenny was irritated with me, I know, for she shot an injured expression sharp as a whittled arrow at me before running off without a backward glance to join our friend Becky Porter, who was talking with Ephraim Polk and Mary Batts beside the church steps. She said something to them about me, for they all looked in my direction, but then Father returned to our buggy and our silent family climbed inside.

Our Sunday supper began routinely. Father said the prayers and Mother said Amen, and Chloe served a hen, with ash-roasted potatoes. The smell of wild garlic followed her around the table as she bent to tend to our plates and I felt very hungry.

"Miz Lucy, I done most of the washing up and I done set the beans to soak for tomorrow, and I was wondering if I might leave a little early so I can get home to my girls. They like it when I'm there before the dark." Chloe spoke softly to my mother, but we all heard her request to be dispatched to her cabin.

"This chicken is so tender I believe you must've wrung its neck with kindness, Chloe. Certainly, you may depart." Mother waved her out the door and I chewed and swallowed my first delicious mouthful, thinking it was often lately Chloe did beg to be excused. Abruptly Father pushed his chair away from the table.

"I cannot eat." His voice was hoarse and he held his throat in his hand, assuming an expression of great discomfort.

"Jack, you look so pale. What is the matter?" Mother set her fork down and turned to him, concerned. Father shook his head, apparently unable to speak. He stood, one hand at his throat, using the table edge for support. Mother also rose and, putting his arm around her shoulder, she helped him to the parlor. John Jr. and I stopped eating and followed them, to see what was the matter.

"Something, a twig, is in my throat," he gasped.

"Good Lord, pray it is not a bone. Open your mouth wide, Jack." Mother held a lamp above him, peering down into his throat. "I see nothing there. Most likely you have swallowed a bit of salt bread the wrong way."

"Water," Father breathed, and John Jr. went to fetch it.

"Betsy, return to the table. Your father will be fine." Mother did not want me there and I did as she said, but it was difficult to believe Father would be fine, especially when I heard him choking out his words.

"Lucy, there is something . . . sideways in my throat. . . . I cannot swallow."

"Drink this, Jack. Here, John Jr., help me get him to the bed." At the table, Drewry, Richard and Joel looked at me, concern evident in their eyes.

"Is Father ill, sister?" Joel asked.

"So it would appear, but Mother says it's nothing, we must not worry. We must finish our supper without them." This was most unusual, as we always ate together, except during the harvest or market days when Father and John Jr. might be absent. We very rarely sat at supper without Mother. We chewed carefully, and did not talk. When we had finished, we had to clear away the plates and do our own washing up out back of the kitchen in the washing tub Chloe had thoughtfully filled with warm water. The light was fading slowly and the sky was a pure turquoise color, its shades of blue defined by the black silhouettes of the trees. I felt uncomfortable in the growing dark and I hurried through the task, running back inside with the boys. We slid the wooden bolt across the door.

Mother had dosed Father with valerian and slippery elm and he had fallen fast asleep. She and John Jr. had moved him to his bed and she had readied two lamps for the boys and me to carry upstairs.

"Will you tuck me in, Mother? Please?" I allowed my fear to be present in my plea, and she nodded and followed me up to my room.

"Is Father ill?" I asked as I climbed under my quilts, hoping she would stay with me until I was asleep.

"He is simply tired, Miss Betsy, and much in need of rest."

"What will happen in the night?" I feared he would be too

tired to awake and help us pray and defend against the coming unknown.

"Perhaps the Lord has heard our prayers and tonight our sleep will be undisturbed."

"Do you really think so?" It seemed unlikely to me, as I had grown quickly accustomed to expecting the worst.

"Would I say so, if I did not?" Mother bent and kissed my cheek and I could tell she planned to depart.

"I will say another prayer for Father before I go to sleep."

"Yes, Betsy, think of others always first, and the Lord will think of you." She paused briefly at my door to smile good night, before hurrying downstairs. It was difficult to sleep, as I expected any moment an obscene assault of noise and abuse, but remarkably I did soon doze, and did not awake until the day had come. I was amazed to discover the night had passed as Mother had predicted, unfettered with harassment.

the word is spread

At the breakfast table Father appeared completely recovered from what had ailed him the night before, as he was eating a hearty portion of porridge with molasses, and a plate of bacon, ham, red gravy and biscuits sat before him.

"Praise the Lord, children, for all His blessings." Mother nodded discreetly in Father's direction, but I was more impressed with our undisturbed evening of sleep than I was with his swift healing. "Your slates have been gathering dust." She smiled her pleasure over our quiet night behind the thin lip of her teacup as though she felt our trials were over. "Chloe has packed your dinners into your satchels and it's past time you set off for lessons."

"Yea, get your learning," Father said, ripping his meat into two pieces with his fingers. "But, Drewry Bell, I should like to feed my owl today, so you must do your duty there before you go running off." Father kept an owl as a pet in his tobacco barn, having found the creature when it was just an owlet while he was clearing a field in the autumn. Injured and left to die by its mother, Father had cared for it and easily nursed it back to health, as its problem was a simple sprain of the wing. The owl had grown into a magnificent tawny bird with a great ruffle of white around its neck, like the extravagant collars of French kings in our schoolbooks. Father had braided a long leather leash for it and kept his owl tethered to a post in the barn. On occasion he took him out to fly, but always trussed to the leash, so he could go no farther than halfway up the tall elms by the fields.

My brothers were required to catch sparrows and mice to feed the owl and they each had their own methods for doing so and they each said their method was the best, as boys do, but Drewry's seemed most sensible to me. He laid scratch and chicken feed in the dusty path as bait for his trap, then with a river rock he propped up a great wooden bowl, into the side of which he had driven a nail and affixed a length of twine. This string he carried in his hand while he hid behind the barn. When the sparrows came to peck the scratch, Drewry yanked the twine and brought the bowl down, trapping them inside. He used an old piece of tin to slide under the bowl, and when it was turned right side up the catch was handily delivered to Father, who liked to feed his owl privately. None of us ever asked to accompany him for we all knew when Father went to feed his owl it was his time alone.

"But, Father," Drewry answered his charge, "it will take some time for me to catch your sparrows, and Mother has just requested our lessons be attended to." Drewry poured innocence thicker than Chloe's molasses into his tone and I supposed he was not in a bird-catching mood.

"You then, John Jr., will you do my bidding?" Father exchanged a quick glance with Mother when Drewry bowed his head as though Drew had disappointed him, but John Jr. proved he was the son Father could rely on.

"I will gladly do the duty while my brother receives an education," John Jr. said, wiping his mouth tidily with his napkin. I wondered what method he would use. He was skilled with his rifle and had just the week before succeeded in barking up a squirrel. The poor animal had been secure at the top of an elm in the woods when the ball shot from John Jr.'s gun hit the trunk of the tree beneath its belly, driving off a piece of bark as large as my hand, and with it the squirrel, without a wound or a ruffled hair, killed by the long fall to the ground. I wondered if he could do the same to sparrows but I did not care enough to stay at home and see it. I was excited to go to the schoolhouse.

"The rest of you be off, then," Mother said, walking us to the door where she had arranged our satchels for distribution to our shoulders. "Remember, tell no one, Miss Betsy," she whispered in my ear, adjusting the leather strap of my bag.

"I know, Mother." I kissed her cheek, anxious to catch up with my brothers, for they were already running down the hill, past the well. I reached them where our path met the Adams–Cedar Hill high road and together we continued running and skipping, enjoying the glorious spring morning, smelling the delicious red earth, lush and steaming in the early sun. I wished to stop and stare at the brilliant stand of red sassafras and wild iris blooming by the roadside, but as a group we were anxious to reach the schoolhouse. We ran until we turned right off the road, onto our special trail through the hazel thicket, and there we were forced to walk single file through a tunnel of brambles. John Jr. had recently whacked through it with a machete, so no stray twigs caught at our clothing, but it did slow us down some. I was glad when we reached the place where the path let out and met the road at the wooden bridge where we could cross the Red River.

Steam rose off the planks as they warmed to the morning sun and, beyond the bridge, shining on its own green knoll, stood our pleasant white clapboard schoolhouse. Without warning, I was overcome with emotion and I had to stop a minute to collect myself. I felt as if I'd been released from a nightmare and was awakening to a routine I had previously taken entirely too much for granted.

"Hurry up, sister!" The boys and Drewry passed in front of me while I took a moment to fill my lungs with the spring air, adjusting the strap of my satchel across my breast. Perhaps I would have a chance to tell Thenny about becoming a woman. I looked down and saw a fish jump for its breakfast in the fast muddy water and I hurried after my brothers, marching up the hill in a triumphant parade.

"Good day, good day, pupils, lovely Miss Elizabeth." Professor Powell gave us a warm welcome, and I smiled and curtsied and took the closest seat, vowing I would appear more myself than I had the day before at church.

"Bet-_see_ had best-_be_ recovered!" Thenny cried, singsong, during our game of tag at the dinner recess. She caught my skirt and I gave chase to her all about the lawn, thankful for her good nature, as it felt wonderful to have a laugh and to play. It was not until I was amongst the other children that I fully realized how unsettling the sleepless evenings at our house had truly been. How to be myself without speaking of how I was altered? Who was I before I was scared out of my wits? I did not wish to think on my future at all. I marked my brothers' whereabouts from the corners of my eyes, but a tension I had not known I possessed began to slip off my body as my feet slipped over the slicker places in the new grass while playing tag.

"Watch out, Betsy Bell!" Joshua Gardner, who was several years older than me and known by all the pupils for his keen intellect, played the game with us and it gave me a sudden pleasure to hear my name on his tongue. Professor Powell rang the bell at the doorway far too soon, but during the geography lesson I stole glances at handsome Josh from under my bonnet ties, hoping he did not see me looking. He was Professor Powell's most exalted student and I had heard much was expected from his future. The Professor's sonorous reading allowed my mind to soak up new thoughts, about the woolly mammoths in China, grammar and geography. The hours of the afternoon passed swiftly by. At the end of the day Professor Powell loaded our satchels with new Dilworth primers, then dismissed us, and my brothers and I emerged from the schoolhouse into a pink spring sunset.

"So, Betsy, will you come again for lessons?" Thenny asked. She had to rush away, as her father expected her to lend a hand selling hard penny candy at the store after school. I looked and saw him smoking as usual on his porch. He waved his pipe, gesturing Thenny ought to hurry, as groups of the smaller children, freed from their lessons, were racing down the road. I regretted there had been no opportunity to talk privately with her.

"Tomorrow, Thenny." I waved goodbye and felt my throat grow tight as I knew I could not rely on tomorrow. I knew not what lay ahead of me in the dark evening. The days were lasting longer but already it was dusk. My brothers and I walked quickly over the bridge and through the hazel thicket, all absorbed in our own thoughts.

"Let's take the shortcut through the meadow," Drewry said, leaving the road and looking over his shoulder to be certain we followed him down along the riverbank. I let the little boys go in the middle between us, and we moved single file. All at once, I felt a cold spot like the one by the stream when I was nine, and I looked about, feeling a bristle in the air. There was a tingling bright as pins around me and I had to stop. I called ahead to Drewry.

"Look!"

Across the field near the woods I saw flickering lights skimming over the tops of the grasses, flowing toward the river.

"What's that?" Joel backed up instinctively and took my hand in his.

"Let's see!" Drewry set off running, but swift as he was, the lights had gone before he neared them. The boys and I ran after him.

"How fast those lights did shift!" Richard was intrigued.

"Where did they go?" I disliked the prickling tension in the air.

"There!" Richard spotted them again, drifting along the ground, moving in the distant direction of our house.

"Could they be lightning bugs, clustered for some unknown reason?" Drewry squinted, looking across the meadow, and I thought he had a most pragmatic soul. The brilliant glossy shimmer sparking from the ground and rolling up the hill was clearly no mass of insects. It was not a pleasant feeling to see it moving toward our house with the day growing darker by the minute.

"We must turn back and take the road," I suggested, afraid to go forward.

"No, Betsy, we must high our tails to home." Drewry took off across the meadow without further discussion, and Richard and Joel and I ran after him, not knowing what else to do. The tall grass whipped my hands and face so I felt it was tiny needles puncturing my skin and I clutched the strap of my satchel as it bumped against my hip. Please, God, keep us safe, I prayed, and with my eyes half closed I ran, trusting the Lord and Joel's hand pulling me, and soon we reached our own hill and I summoned the energy to bolt the final stretch behind my brothers. We clattered across the porch with the last light and threw open the great cedar door.

"Mother, Father, come quickly! There are lights in the fields and meadow!"

"Strange lights, with tingling!" We shouted our information, crowding around Mother, who came at once into the hall, frowning at the commotion we caused.

"What say you, children? Be calm!"

Frightened, we struggled to catch our breath, talking all at once.

"The lights were crawling to this house!" Joel tugged with two hands on Mother's skirt, his nose wrinkling, as if he were about to cry.

"'Twas heat lightning," Father said. He shut his desk with a bang and strode toward us raising his voice. "I have seen it myself." He maintained his tone of annoyance as the tears welled over Joel's lids, and Mother pulled him to her side, leading him into the parlor to sit on her lap in the hickory rocker placed beside the fire. The rest of us hung up our coats and put our satchels away in silence under Father's watchful gaze. Through the parlor window I glimpsed the lights flashing. They were not in the sky, but rather ran across the ground, sparking up in bursts, and they did not look like heat lightning or anything at all natural to me.

When we retired that evening, our troubles resumed. It began with the gulping sound beside my ear in bed, but before I could call out, the covers were ripped from my body and my hair was twisted at the nape of my neck and nearly pulled off my head. Father tested the affliction and experimented with not lighting the lamps until we could no longer stand it. Once the flame illuminated my room, all was revealed to be as it had been the evening before last, unaltered and silent as the dead night beating down around the house. We dozed unhappily in my well-lit chamber.

There was no question of school the next day, nor for the rest of the week, as each night the torment increased. In the day, we rested alone, or in silence together, and the feeling within our house was similar to illness, for discomfort accompanied our every breath. We attended only to the most necessary tasks, like visiting the outhouse and eating, to sustain our slight energies. We crept through the rooms as though the ground beneath us were a robin's shell and we were challenged not to crack it. Our souls focused on the too quick passing of the minutes as the sun moved overhead. We prayed and pretended to ourselves there were ways and means to stave off the dreaded setting and, thus, another night of torture. Meanwhile, Tuesday, Wednesday and Thursday passed each alike. The days were silent, and each night the torment increased.

Near the Friday supper hour, I was sitting in the chair before the front parlor window, for I had just finished mending a white cotton slip for Mother, when looking up, I noticed Reverend Johnston on his chestnut horse turning off the high road to our path.

"Reverend Johnston's come to call!" I shouted for Mother to come from the kitchen, for I had hoped some good person from our community would notice our days of silent absence from school and Thorn's store, and call, inquiring after us.

Mother did hurry, and looked only briefly outside to confirm I spoke the truth, before turning with some desperation to Father, who was at his desk, writing in his book of accounts.

"Jack, there is barely oil left for the lamps, and I do not believe we can stand many more nights like those of late. We must do something."

"Pray, Lucy, what is your suggestion?" Father turned his stoic face to hers.

"Understanding this phenomenon requires the help of God. Ask the Reverend to spend the evening here with us. Please." Mother placed her hand firmly on his shoulder and I held my breath for his response.

Father stood and pulled the heavy brocade curtain in the parlor farther aside so he could better see the Reverend engaged at our horse tie, delivering to Zeke instructions regarding the feeding of his horse down at our stables.

"He must mean to stay awhile without our invitation." Father's jaw was grave against the windowpane. "All right, Lucy. We will discuss it with him." His lips were tightly drawn and I could tell he wished it had not come to this, for he did not want to break his vow of silence regarding our family troubles. My feelings ran more toward throwing open the great door and racing down the hill to drag the Reverend in. I hoped he could do something to help us.

"Why, Miss Betsy, hello." When he reached our porch, huffing in his long black coat, and carrying his Bible in his right hand folded over his heart, I thought the Reverend was possibly the most comforting sight I had ever witnessed.

"Hello, Reverend Johnston!" I delivered an enthusiastic greeting to him, and he removed his hat, entering our hall.

"Reverend Johnston, we are delighted you have come to call. Never have we been more pleased to see a visitor."

Mother shared my enthusiasm and grasped the Reverend's hand in hers.

"I confess I came this way on purpose for there were rumors of illness here, and yet, I trust you are all well?" He looked about, seeming slightly bemused.

"We are well, and not so well." Father gave him a firm handshake and it was then I saw the Reverend raise his eyebrows, for Father was not known to be so inexact in his responses.

"How say you, Jack?"

"Please, join us here for supper and we will tell you all our news." Mother took the Reverend's arm and drew him to the table, enacting the regular social convention, yet clearly she was not her normal self either.

"I am happy for the invitation," the Reverend replied calmly, unaware of anything amiss. I took his coat to hang, and everyone got seated at the table while Chloe laid an extra place.

"We are experiencing unusual events in the evenings at our home," Father began, coming straight to the point.

"Is it related to the earth movements we recently discussed?" the Reverend inquired, settling his round bottom in his chair.

"Perhaps . . ." Father paused, as if he did not have adequate words to describe our trauma. "Yet, I wonder if these noises are earthly."

"How say you?" The Reverend smiled and balanced the heel of his hand on the table edge, awaiting Father's explanation of his claim, but it came from Mother, who touched the Reverend's arm and nodded in my direction.

"Our Betsy has had her quilts ripped from her bed and her hair pulled and twisted by invisible hands."

"Not only that, there is a terrible sound of lips smacking and gulping in the air, yet there is no person there!" Without requesting permission to speak I interjected, I so wished to relieve myself of the experience.

"And there are rodents gnashing their teeth on the bed-post!" Richard added. He was most frightened by the thought of being bitten in the dark.

"You could fill a riverbed with the stones dropped down our stairs," John Jr. said, for he had spent some part of every day carting wheelbarrows of rocks from the front of the house down to the stream.

"But if you keep the lamps burning it won't come in the room." Joel looked across the table at the Reverend with hopeful eyes, expecting a man of God would know what to do.

I could not ascertain what the Reverend was thinking, but he did not immediately volunteer an explanation for our complaints, though he did return his hands to his lap.

"I will happily pass an evening in your good company," he responded, "and if tonight is convenient, so be it. Mrs. Johnston is aware I planned to call on you, and she will assume I have accepted some kind invitation, and that I am not lost to bandits on the road, for Adams is blessed this year in having none about."

"To be certain I will send my man with a message to your home," Father reassured him. "We do not wish to worry your good wife."

"That would be kind of you indeed, Jack Bell." The Reverend folded his hands before his empty plate, with no expectation of trauma in his expression, despite what he had heard. I was surprised he asked no further questions and the conversation turned to how the crops were growing.

After the meal, Mother and I helped clear the table, and in the kitchen Chloe was bold, touching Mother's forearm.

"We done seen your house at night, Miz Lucy. Your double logs do shake and pulse as if it 'tis a livin' thing." Chloe's forehead wrinkled nearly into her kerchief with concern.

"We are gripped by a storm of violence inside, dear Chloe. Tell all the Negroes they must pray to God for our deliverance and never fear." Mother turned away to join the men already in the parlor. I wanted to ask Chloe if the slaves had seen the lights and heard the noise, and I wanted to discover what they did imagine it to be, but I did not dare, for I could tell it was contrary to Mother's wishes. I left Chloe alone in the kitchen without a backward glance, following Mother to the parlor.

The Reverend was seated in Father's usual chair by the fire with his good book in his hand so he might read to us. Father sat at his writing desk, drinking from his silver flask. I saw him upend it, shaking the last drop into his throat while I made myself comfortable at Mother's feet.

"I shall read to you from I Samuel," the Reverend announced, and Father moved to sit in the rocking chair, nodding his head, as though I Samuel was the text he himself would have chosen as appropriate for our situation.

The boys fidgeted on the bench, despite John Jr.'s presence beside them, but as the Reverend read how Samuel had heard a mysterious voice in the night and prayed to the Lord for deliverance and knowledge, they grew still and attentive.

"And the Lord said, Behold, I will do a thing at which both the ears of every one that heareth it shall tingle." I wondered how the Reverend knew about the tingling, but the fact he did greatly deepened my faith in his abilities. When the story was over, he asked us to rise while he recited a psalm. "We see not our signs. There be no more any prophet; neither be there amongst us any that knoweth how long. O God, how long shall the adversary reproach? Shall the enemy blaspheme thy name for ever?" I did not understand the Reverend's meaning in this, but to see him praying, with his eyes and hands raised to the ceiling, made me feel he sanctified our home, calling God into our presence. I grew excited, for surely God would protect us, God would grant us a respite.

"Betsy, will it now be over?" Joel turned his wide excited eyes to mine when we climbed the stairs up to our bedrooms. Mother walked behind me with a lamp and though I smiled, I deferred to her to comment.

"It will be what it will be, my little Joel," she answered, but her good humor added a great measure of trust and when I pulled the quilts around my nightclothes I was able to hope the night had arrived when our trials would cease.

"Blow out your candles, then, and let us sleep." The Reverend called good night from John Jr.'s bedroom, where he lay in Jesse's bed. I lay in my bed not even long enough to feel a feather poking through the mattress ticking, before I rose up and went to my door. I was surprised to see no candlelight wavering into the hall from the boys' rooms. I did not wish to blow my candle out and I decided I would not, but a sudden gust of wind accomplished the task for me and WHACK! I was slapped in the face in the dark by an icy hand. I screamed and heard the sound of chairs whipping to the floor all about the house, and then Mother and Father came running up the stairs. I saw behind the flame of their candles they hadn't yet undressed.

"Mother, it has struck me!" I held my hand to my cheek.

"How say you?" The Reverend entered and stood bow-legged before me in a long white nightshirt begged off my father. His candle dripped wax into its holder as he tilted it toward me.

"Look, there is a mark." Mother lit the lamp and held it up. The Reverend bent so near into the light above my face I could see the silver whiskers sprouting from his nose.

"It does look to be a handprint on her cheek," he said, verifying what I had felt. I watched him step back toward the doorway, appearing much preoccupied with the splintering sounds of breaking wood occurring throughout the rest of the house. Joel and Richard squeezed by him and climbed onto my bed. They were not crying, but very solemn, and they kept their eyes on the Reverend to see what he would do.

"What can this be?" he mumbled and held his candle high, looking to Father as if for sustenance, not at all the godly force I had expected.

"The light no longer has effect," Father dryly observed, for though the room was well lit with the lamp and candle, the gulping sound remained audible, as if all manner of animals were chewing cud inside our ears.

"I have never . . ." The Reverend concentrated, listening hard to the choking rasps that followed the smacking of lips.

"You must *do* something!" I was desperate, for what violent destruction would follow the gulping sound? What evil act? I despised the shaking of the house and I pleaded with the Reverend as my only hope, "Take action!"

"Yes, child," Reverend Johnston raised his fingers to his lips to silence me, "I will." He paused only a moment before determining he would speak to the entity as if it were possessed with human character. "In the name of the Lord," he pleaded, "what are you? What do you want? Why are you here?" Incredibly his queries brought a sudden silence to my room. Mother and Father exchanged a quick glance I could not interpret, then all of us spontaneously bowed our heads in silent meditation and prayer. I prayed and listened to each breath and shuffle of nightclothes with wide ears for the better part of an hour. Joel, even when frightened, had no tolerance for attentive waiting, and he had just fallen asleep when I felt a yank on my braid and the quilt wrapped about us was whisked to the floor.

"It's back!" I cried, receiving a sharp stab in my neck as though a straight pin jabbed me. The unseen hand slapped me broad across the face again and I shrieked in pain from the force of the blow.

"Oh Betsy," Mother whispered. Everyone else distinctly heard the slap. She sobbed and held her hands to her own cheeks, watching the red mark appear on mine.

"Dear Jesus!" the Reverend said. He placed his hands across my shoulders to steady me and better see my injuries but I was pushed from behind by invisible hands, wrenched from his grasp and thrown face down to the floor. The sound of choking filled the room as I lay prone on the wooden planks. I did not wish to move for I was afraid I would be struck down again. I closed my eyes and kept my cheek against the rough wood, while the smacking lips played in my ear.

"Get up!" Father commanded, lifting me by my waist. I was beside myself with fear and did not rise willingly. The Reverend Johnston took my arm to help him and I went limp as a slave to the whipping post, crying silently to my chest, leave me alone, evil, leave me alone.

"Miss Betsy, what has pulled you down?" The Reverend spoke sharply to me, squeezing my forearm with his pudgy fingers.

"I know not!" I cried, and then again, an icy slap struck

my face. I threw my hands up to protect myself from further blows, but it was no use, needles stung my cheeks and fingers. Father and the Reverend made a sudden grasp for my arms, to hold me, but I was pulled from them and thrown down by what I could not see, though I felt its strength, and it was greater than any man's. My forehead to the wood, I could not get my breath.

"In the name of God, I beseech you, cease your torture of this innocent! What are you and why are you here?" The Reverend threw his arms up to the ceiling, mustering great passion for his query. Again, the noise did stop.

My lungs opened and I dropped tears onto the floor. Mother kneeled beside me and stroked my back and the sudden silence felt as much a shock as the horror that had preceded it. No one knew what to do, but the Reverend began to pray.

"O God Almighty, our Father in Heaven, hallowed be thy name! This is a house of righteousness, inhabited by worthy servants of the faith! If there is sin, forgive us, forgive us Lord, for any abominable unclean thing, for we shun profane and vain babbling, knowing they will increase unto more ungodliness, and we are good, and strive to walk with you, O Lord." The Reverend's prayer was rambling and breathless, compared to his usual sound oratory. He too kneeled beside me and hissed into my ear.

"Miss Betsy, rise and tell me, what do you know of this disturbance?"

"I know only I am suffering with these torments you do witness." I raised my head and saw the Reverend studying my face as if he thought I might be the cause of the violence rather than its victim. "What do *you* know of them?" I responded, insolent, in tears. "Is this a punishment from God, Reverend? For what? What have I done?"

"Nothing!" Father was angry at the direction of the Reverend's inquiry. "Ask the Good Lord, not our Betsy, to explain to you the unexplainable, Reverend, so you may interpret unto us the right true path through this malignant force."

"It is unfathomable, Jack, until it is experienced. I know not how to act." The Reverend huffed and stood, nodding to my father, much subdued. He smoothed a hand down the round front of his nightshirt, stroking his belly in anxious contemplation.

"Your prayer has helped immensely, Reverend. Hear the quiet now," Mother said, attempting to console and encourage him.

"But will it come again?" Joel asked very softly, frightened.

"If it does," Mother comforted him, "I will hold you tight as before and we will pray to the Lord and trust He will keep us all safe, as He has so far. Look, are you hurt? Is your dear sister hurt?" Mother pulled Joel off the bed with one arm and pulled me at the waist with the other, so we were facing one another. His fearful eyes locked on to mine and he wrapped his arms about my neck. I found his curls the softest handkerchief for my tears.

"I am not hurt, little brother," I reassured him. I understood it was necessary to be brave, and I allowed Drewry and John Jr. to help me back to bed. I pulled them down to sit beside me, and once again we clustered together, a litter of siblings, guarded by Mother and Father and the Reverend too.

"Has your Betsy been singled out to suffer grievously at every visitation?" The Reverend turned to Father, pursuing aloud his thoughts.

"Yea, though she has not suffered on her own."

"Has no one else been physically abused?"

"These events have abused us all." Mother was absolute, and I realized seeing me suffer was as horrible for her as suffering herself.

"What connection do you postulate, Reverend?" Father seemed annoyed and impatient, and his voice flickered like the lamplight on the wall.

"I know not. I am grasping for an indication of a meaning here. Perhaps there is some connection, or perhaps there is none. I want not to offend you in any way, but we must strive to know all in our quest to expunge evil." Flustered, the Reverend turned his round face to me. "Betsy, do not be afraid, for the Lord is with you, but tell me, is there any cause or reason for the Devil and his demons to have business with you here? Is there a sin of yours of which we are not aware?"

"What say you, Reverend Johnston? Pray to God the answer to your query is within your soul this moment. Our Betsy is as innocent as the day she was born!" Mother stood, so upset I thought she might ask him to leave our home with his dubious speculations, but there came the metal tapping at the glass and a wind entered and blew out every candle, leaving only the one lamp, low on oil, burning darkly atop my washstand.

"Please, no!" I cried before I felt a thing, for I wished to attempt to communicate with my torturer as the Reverend had successfully done, assuming it had human character and could understand my pleas. It paid me no attention except blows to my cheeks and I screamed in pain. Slowly, the room began to shake with the thundering noise. The lamp rattled on the china basin and Father took it in his hand before it hit the floor. My brothers grasped my arms and I screamed again, "Please! No!" They tried to hold me to the bed, but I saw their hands stream past as I was wrestled from them to the floor. I struck it with enough force to know I would have bruises in the morning.

"Good God!" Mother threw her body over mine where I lay face down, struggling to catch my breath. I prayed silently, don't hurt me, don't hurt me.

"In the name of God, I beseech you, cease your torture of this innocent!" The Reverend resumed his tone of passion and intensity, his arms raised to the ceiling. "What are you and why are you here?" he yelled, and again the noise did cease. Flat silence and my quick breaths filled the room.

"Keep talking, Reverend." Father seemed annoyed. He lifted me in his arms as though I were a small child, and set me down on the bed where the boys embraced my battered body and I began to cry in despair, aware of how powerless I was in the grasp of unearthly torments. We endured this way until the early hours of the morning, when the attacks ceased and we were allowed a few hours of precious sleep before the dawn. No one left my room, we were all so exhausted. My parents, my brothers and the Reverend lay strewn about my floor like the quilts ripped from my bed.

"Jack, if I had not witnessed with my own eyes this phenomenon, I would not have believed such was possible." At breakfast Reverend Johnston and Father discussed our situation. "Clearly God must mean for us to find the righteous path amid evil in this instance."

"It is evil." Father stated this, but the tone of his voice conveyed a reluctance to believe that it was so.

"Evil is more often the province of man than God. Perhaps it is not evil, but of another nature?" The Reverend raised his eyebrows.

"What counsel have you?" Father was direct.

"Jack," the Reverend paused and set both his wrists on the table edge, leaning toward my father. "Jack, I believe you are experiencing what is called a supernatural affliction. In my opinion, all our community should be informed, so many minds can try all means of investigation and hopefully solve the mystery of why it plagues you." I held my breath and waited for Father to reject this idea but he did not immediately speak.

"Why, Reverend, would a supernatural force disturb my peace? I have no questionable dealings. The realms of both Heaven and Hell are beyond my days on this land." Father could not accept the injustice of it.

"Why, is not for us to ponder, but this, perhaps, we may discover. I suggest you read the Book of Job, and recall how the Lord can test our faith. I will return tonight with Mrs. Johnston, and we will pray together here again." The Reverend stood and Mother rose to walk him to the door, so he might speedily depart and recount to his good wife his strange experience at our home.

"Good Reverend," she said, "you are a true friend to our family and a wise man, clothed by the Lord. Look into your soul and ask the question you did voice aloud regarding our Betsy, and understand, Betsy is innocent, a mere child, suffering greater pains than you or I may know." Mother graciously opened the door for him.

"Dear Lucy, never in my imaginings have I envisioned such a scene as what I witnessed in your home last night. I was not myself, but overwhelmed by the presence of the power descended here. I confess I was thinking of the bygone days of Salem and the awful mistakes of that good congregation, all from the fainting fits of young girls."

"Reverend, you saw yourself, this is no fainting fit." Mother shook her head.

"I did see, Lucy, and you need not belabor it with me, I will hold to God in the highest what I witnessed here was not perpetrated by any person on these premises. I warrant the cause of this disturbance is unknown to all of us, and it will be my sole purpose to discover what it is and banish it from your home."

"Thank you, Reverend, we are much obliged. Whatever ails us, may your godliness be like water to its fire."

"Or perhaps my speech will be the fire of purification to its pestilence . . ." The Reverend stood lost in thought for a moment on our porch, a dreamy look shading his features, and I wondered if he entertained a grandiose vision of his own capabilities. How could he? I recalled his fear, his "I know not!" But I wished to be charitable in my assessment of him, for he seemed my best and only hope for salvation. He was a man of God while I was a mere girl, powerless and tortured.

"God bless you, Reverend." I bade him goodbye and came to stand under Mother's arm at the door. Together we watched him walk away down the path. He stopped at the well and turned to consider our house from a distance, then waved and went on. The pear trees were covered in white sweet-smelling blossoms and a light wind blew the petals down like a snow of flowers. The Reverend Johnston's black coat and top hat were dotted long before he reached the horse tie where Zeke waited with his horse, saddled and ready to ride.

"May I go for a walk, Mother?" I was overcome with a de-sire to be out-of-doors.

"You may, Miss Betsy," Mother answered, squeezing my shoulder. I could tell she thought it was a good idea. "It's near warm enough to sow beans today. Perhaps I'll do a row, when the pallets have aired." Mother, ever a gracious hostess, turned her mind to preparing the house for the callers we would have that evening. "Take your brothers with you, Betsy." She hugged me closer before she let me free. "And be mindful as you go."

I called to Drewry, Richard and Joel and they were happy to join me. We went out the back, skipping down the hill, running past the cornfield, where I noticed the grassy stalks were already ankle high. We turned onto the path by the stream and Joel and Richard raced to reach the pools forming under a small waterfall, hoping they might see some fishes. I had just come up behind them when Richard caught a crawdad and tried to scare me with it, in what I thought to be mean-spirited fun.

"EEEEE Betsy, I shall slap your face!" He held the ugly thing up, jiggling it, while its claws grasped the empty air and its legs and antennas squirmed helplessly.

"You are not amusing, Richard!" I pushed him so hard, he tripped over a rock and landed with his bottom in the mud, while the crawdad flew from his hand, hitting the ground with its legs running, scurrying to a safer hiding place.

"Look what you did!" Richard stood and bent over, turning the muddy behind of his trousers to my face.

"It was your own doing, not mine!" I shouted, annoyed that he had accused me. After suffering the Reverend's insinuations I could not bear to be held responsible for any wrongdoing, even something so trivial as mud on Richard's clothes.

"It was the combination of you both," Drewry declared. He pulled a handful of leaves off a budding elm and began wiping away the mud on Richard's backside. He said something into Richard's ear as he did so, but I could not hear it.

"Sister, I am sorry, truly." Richard stepped forward, and

looked me in the eye, and I saw his remorse was sincere. I did not wish to argue and I hugged him, feeling tears of weakness rising in my throat. Drewry and Joel moved to stand beside us and we formed a silent circle, as we had in the night, clustered on my bed. Richard's head was just the height of my shoulder, and his hair smelled of the fresh stream. I shut my eyes, inhaling it beside the bleached flax of Drew's shirt. Joel circled his arms around all our waists, as though he bound the corn, and the sun fell warm on my cheeks. I absorbed it greedily, hoping it was God-given strength.

That evening, the Reverend returned, and all the events of the night before were repeated for Mrs. Johnston's benefit, only with more intensity. The force abused me violently, with beatings to my face and body. Mother and Mrs. Johnston cried helpless tears, while my hair was pulled and my neck was stabbed with pins and needles, and though I did not bleed, the marks were evident. Again, we survived until dawn, Sunday morning, and though no one had slept and all tempers were short, we set out to fetch Jesse and Martha to go to church.

"Good morning, Father, Mother. God has blessed us with another lovely Sunday." Jesse seemed in a particularly good mood when he opened the door for Martha to climb into our black buggy. I thought it was a shame he would soon be burdened by the horror of our trials. Martha stepped up and settled in beside me, turning her head to admire my pokeberry dress as she did every Sunday and I saw her take in my bruised features under my bonnet.

"Why, Betsy, what happened? Are you ill?"

"What's this?" Jesse was about to shut the door, but stopped at the mention of illness.

"Ride in the buggy today, my son," Mother requested. Usually Jesse rode with Father and John Jr. up front on the driver's bench. He squeezed into the buggy, and Mother proceeded to tell the two of them what had been happening at our house. They listened silently, asking no questions, but glancing several times at my face while their expressions relayed concern.

"I felt it strike me, an invisible icy hand," I said, affirming the unbelievable, and the buggy rumbled over the bridge past the schoolhouse.

"'Tis true, 'tis true, 'tis true!" Joel clapped his hand against his leg, regressing in an outburst of emotion.

"Hush now, you must prepare to sit still and quiet through the Reverend's sermon," Mother reprimanded him, but only gently, and we rolled at a brisk pace past Thorn's store, shut up and deserted. We carried on down the next hill and then up again onto the ridge above the small valley where the river wound back on itself. Shortly we rode downhill and, crossing Johnston's bridge, entered the churchyard.

"Reverend Johnston means to inform the congregation of our trials." Mother spoke softly, but I felt an underlying warning in her tone.

"Why were we kept uninformed?" Jesse thought only of his own part in the matter, just like always. Annoyed, I turned my face fully to the small window.

"It was your father's wish." Mother was calmly unequivocal with him. I noticed the whitewash on the building gave our church the look of a bright beacon on its green knoll. I loved the tall windows and the pointed steeple above the belfry with the cross on top, standing white and pure against the cloudless blue sky. The great brass bell the Reverend had purchased with donations from the congregation rang peals of welcome. I recalled watching the fathers and the Reverend hang it high, the very day it was carted in from Nashville. We had all felt so proud our church was to be so distinguished.

Many carts were already tied up in the yard and I expected it would be a great relief to finally share my troubles with my friends, so I was very much surprised, when, after my family had filed carefully into our pew and been recognized with a nod of greeting by the Reverend, I became attacked by instability. I was suddenly weak and nervous, and I felt I might dissolve at any moment into tears. I bowed my head, glad of the wide cotton ties on my bonnet, and Joel beside me graciously slipped his small hand into mine.

"Good brethren and sisters of the Lord, today we will take our sermon from I Thessalonians *and* from events occurring among us, in our community." A murmur of whispering guesses breezed through the church and I thought some turned to look at us even before the Reverend told the story, but I could not be sure. I did see Thenny twisting in a pew to my right and I thought she flapped her arms behind her father's back for my attention, but I returned my eyes to my hands in my lap. I was extremely conscious of my tender skin and my arms ached where Joel and Richard pressed against my bruises. I listened to the Reverend read aloud.

"See that none render evil unto any man, but ever follow that which is good, both amongst yourselves and all men. Pray without ceasing, quench not the Spirit. In everything give thanks, for this be the will of God. Faithful is He that calleth you, who also will do it. Amen."

"Amen," answered the assembled.

"Now, were I to ask among you, name the man most formidable, steadfast and upright in following God's law, what name would you give? I believe the name John Bell would slip from many tongues."

Another breeze of whispers circulated through the church and Father shifted, uncomfortable, his movement shaking our entire pew. The congregation quieted, as any announcement in church regarding members of the community was almost always to do with an illness, a birth or death, so everyone's attention focused on what they did not know about our family.

"Our Brother John Bell has experienced strange and unearthly occurrences at his good home." The Reverend paused and in his silence I heard someone behind me whisper.

"'Tis true then, what the cook did say." I realized many in the church must have suspected some disturbance was occurring, for they must have heard the gossip of the slaves.

"I have stayed the past two nights along with John Bell and his fine family and witnessed for myself many horrific noises and some violent abuse of fair Betsy Bell. I ask all gathered here today, turn your prayers to the house of the Bell family, and apprise John Bell or myself with any knowledge you might possess to aid and remedy this dreadful circumstance."

"Ho, Reverend!" Kate Batts rose from her pew in the back, requesting attention.

"Yea, Mrs. Batts, speak freely."

"Ask John Bell to speak of what torments him!" Kate yelled her request as if we were across the bridge and needed to hear her many yards away. A chorus of other voices joined hers, shouting.

"Aye, speak! Speak to it, Jack." Nearly the whole of Adams was gathered in the church and most of Father's peers. I saw Mr. Thorn and Mr. Porter looking very much concerned. Everyone waited for Father's response, even the good Reverend at the pulpit. The murmurs quieted, while Father stiffly rose, clearing his throat.

"I know not what torments me."

"Might you know what form its actions take?" Old Kate had remained standing at the back, appearing very interested in the matter.

"I am no good at speaking," Father shrugged his shoulders, "especially on subjects I am not well versed in. The Reverend can relate the aspects of our suffering." Father sat down and looked at his hands. I knew he would say no more. The sunlight outdoors had reached the high window over the pulpit and it spread out in rays to the floor. I watched it reach the Reverend Johnston's back, producing a striking effect, as if God was sending his light down to us through the Reverend's arms.

"To speak and describe evil is not our business here. I shall say only never in my long experience have I witnessed such events as these, and blessed congregation of Adams, the Lord compels us to make our sole occupation as a community to rid John Bell's family of this visitation, whatever it may be! All who are well intentioned and strive to walk the right true path of the Lord shall gather at the Bell residence this very evening at six o'clock to this effect."

A rush of questions issued from the mouths of all present and the noise of everyone talking at once gave me a dizzy feeling. Mother and Father looked to each other and I wondered if they had known in advance the Reverend was planning such a gathering at our home.

"Let us sing our final hymn!" The Reverend had to shout loudly above the talking going on and when it did not immediately stop, he was forced to clap his hands, then bang them hard on the wooden pulpit before he had the assembly quiet enough to hear his instructions.

"Come now, Almighty King."

Throats were cleared and the congregation rose, buzzing with curious excitement over our troubles.

"Come now, Almighty King," our voices in unison sang with more enthusiasm than usual, as if all gathered believed we could summon the Lord.

> Help us your name to sing,
> Help us to praise Father all glorious,
> O'er all victorious,
> Come, and reign over us,
> Ancient of days.

At the close of the hymn I felt comforted, for faith in God and his power against any evil force was strong inside the church and in my heart. I was reluctant to leave but Father seemed anxious to set out, for he passed a whispered command down the line of his children.

"No talking in the yard. Get yourselves to the buggy for we will swiftly depart." I looked for Thenny and she waved to me. She was mouthing something, but Father and John Jr's. tall backs, as well as her father's wide front and too much distance across the church aisle, were in between us, and I could not make out her intentions. Father turned and frowned severely at me and I understood I was to hurry to the buggy in silence, absolutely. Whatever Thenny wished to say would have to wait.

I was quite disappointed that evening when the Thorns arrived, for they did not bring her with them. Neither did the

Porters bring their daughter Becky, and Kate Batts left her children also at home. Clara Lawson and the Randolphs stayed away, but the Reverend and Mrs. Johnston came. Drewry, Richard, Joel and I were alone as children amongst the many adults gathered at our house. Chloe had put away the Johnstons' pallets and every chair of ours was arranged in a wide circle around the parlor.

The community took their seats exchanging pleasantries, but were markedly intent with the purpose for which they had gathered. Only Kate Batts could not get properly settled. She made a show of laying her riding skirt over first one chair and then another as if none of our fine furniture suited her. She sighed loudly, then turned abruptly to Mother.

"Have you an extra hairpin, Lucy Bell?" She raised her hands to her massive head and shook her fingers in the nest of hair piled there. "I believe my hairdo is about to come undone."

"Of course, come with me." Mother led Kate back toward the bedroom, where her hairpins were kept.

"Witness how tolerant our community is in the face of the eccentric!" I heard Mrs. Thorn whispering to Mrs. Porter. "She's had a pin off me each time she's called."

"What does she do with them?" Mrs. Porter asked, at the same time raising her hand unconsciously to check if her own hair was held in place, secure.

"Most likely she plans to save them up and sell them back to us!" Mrs. Thorn and Mrs. Porter laughed together, though I did not understand why, since it seemed to me Old Kate could easily be guilty of inventing such a scheme.

Mr. Thorn had brought a jug of coal oil and extra lamps so though the evening darkened, our house glowed with golden light. The Reverend took Father's chair and put it before the hearth, for we had no fire. The night was gentle, with pleasantly cool breezes floating through the open front window.

"I am pleased to see you here this evening, but I must warn you, the phenomenon experienced on previous evenings, should it descend tonight, will most certainly be unlike anything you have witnessed before," the Reverend said. "Pray, keep your faith in the Lord at all moments. I will read from the text of John, how Jesus prays for his followers." He opened his Bible at its mark.

"That would be us, then, Reverend, Jesus prays for us!" Old Kate called out loudly as she and Mother returned to the room and crossed it to sit on the bench by the doorway. I noticed Old Kate took up most of it, leaving just enough room for Mother's delicate form on the end.

"Yes, he does, Kate, now hear the text." Mother spoke softly, giving Kate's fleshy arm a warm but prohibitive squeeze, for she wished to hear the Reverend read and I believe she was worried Kate might fill with Spirit and thus prevent the recitation. The golden air in the room was tense with expectations.

"I know the text, Lucy," Kate responded, not lowering her voice. "I came to see the torments. My girl says it is demons you have here." Mother dropped her arm and turned away and I saw a troubled frown pull on her usual calm countenance. How could Old Kate say that? Mrs. Thorn, on the other side of Mother, responded instantly.

"What do you know you about it, Mrs. Batts? My slaves say what ails the Bells is some old hag practicing witchcraft in these parts."

"Helen!" Mother looked upset with both of them and pulled her woven shawl close, folding her arms across her chest, her face terribly sad.

"And who might this old hag be? What say you?" Old Kate

raised her voice to Mrs. Thorn and the Reverend turned to her, clapping his Bible mightily to his chest, a gesture which brought the focus of the room to him.

"Have you some knowledge you wish to share with us, Mrs. Batts?"

"Ask Helen Thorn for knowledge, Reverend, as she claims to have some, but first, let us hear how Jesus prays for us." There was silence for a moment and Mrs. Thorn looked away, out the parlor window. The Reverend decided not to pursue the matter and instead cleared his throat, commencing his reading.

"Whatsoever ye shall ask the Father in my name, he will give it you. In the world ye shall have tribulation: but be of good cheer; I have overcome the world." I wondered, what did it mean exactly to overcome the world? Did it mean to die and go to Heaven? All my friends and family were on earth, and I did not wish to leave them to overcome my tribulations, however horrible they might be.

"Ask, and it shall be given you; seek, and ye shall find; knock and it shall be opened unto you." There was a sharp drop in the temperature of the room and a windy whistling sound descended on us. The Reverend continued quickly. "For everyone that asketh, receiveth; and he that seeketh, findeth; and to him that knocketh, it shall be opened."

Our great front door swung open at the close of the Reverend's sentence and gasps of shock came from the lips of the startled crowd.

"Is it an apparition?" Mrs. Porter spoke in a frightened whisper and the rush of wind walked through the hall, billowing Old Kate's skirts, chilling the boys and me on the floor.

"It is only the wind." Father crossed the room to shut and bar the wooden door but abruptly we heard smacking thuds against the wall of the parlor, as though someone threw cobblestones against our house with force. I drew my arms around my knees and Joel and Richard did the same. The adults rose and went to the windows. They opened the door Father had just closed.

"There's nothing there!" Mr. Porter shouted with surprise.

"But we hear it and can feel the strike!" Mrs. Porter was not brave enough to look, but she seemed to believe there must be someone outside, throwing the rocks.

"The stones do not always appear." John Jr. held a lamp aloft for Mr. Thorn, who squinted out the window. We heard the sound of wind rushing through the leaves in the forest, as if the forest stood inside the very room.

"What is this noise?" Mr. Thorn inquired.

"Look, there is no wind up in the trees, and yet, I hear it blow." Mr. Porter was puzzled and stood beside my father at the door.

"Pray, good people, grasp hands together now!" We stood and made a circle in the parlor, holding hands, while the blowing winds continued, so fierce I expected any moment the walls would dissolve and we would stand in a clearing under a rage of wind in the woods. I held tight to Joel and Richard's fingers.

"In the name of God, reveal yourself." The Reverend raised his hands and so did every pair about the circle. There came a sudden silence of the wind and stones, but the next moment the bristling coldness returned to the air, and I knew it meant to hurt me.

"No! Please!" I cried out, just before a stinging slap was laid into my cheek. I heard the noise of furniture flying apart upstairs and general cries of fear as all our eardrums were set to vibrating. I was pulled from my place and something grabbed my hair in fistfuls while I stumbled to the center of the parlor rug.

"The girl's possessed of demons! God forbid!" I heard Old Kate shout above the noise.

"I'll not have such blasphemy inside my house!" Father shouted back. "To speak of evil is to be of it!"

"Nay, to be of evil is to *not speak plainly of it* when it raises its ugly head inside your home. How long has this demon been in attendance here?" Kate demanded.

"What do you see? I see nothing but invisible tortures to my girl!" Father came to where I'd fallen to my knees and Mother was already there, stroking my back.

"Bear up, Betsy, trust the Lord will keep you safe," she tried to soothe me.

"Be quiet!" The Reverend silenced everyone in his loudest voice. "In the name of the good Lord, tell us, who are you? Why are you present here?"

An unnatural silence filled the house and everyone waited, surprised to feel they might hear an unearthly answer to the Reverend's query. I though it promising that when he spoke directly to it, the violence did cease. I sat up and did not cry, for I was strengthened by the numbers of people populating the room. I felt a cold shiver at the base of my spine, traveling up my neck, causing me to shake slightly. A high-pitched whistle was heard, faint as a sharp wind at first, but as we listened the sound grew so loud, all present were forced to cover their ears with their hands.

"If you can whistle, can you communicate with us?" the Reverend bellowed, and the whistling ceased. And as if in direct response, we heard a loud thud against the door. "Good!" The Reverend was obviously pleased, but Father looked grim and angry. "Jack, I believe we must try to communicate with whatever it is," the Reverend began to explain his enthusiasm, but Father cut him short.

"Reverend, I believe it is your responsibility to expedite its return to whence it came." Abruptly I was slapped again without a warning, so I reeled backward and the blow was loud enough for everyone present to hear.

"Look, it leaves a mark!" cried Mr. Thorn with concern.

"Don't let it hurt our sister!" Richard began to sob and Mrs. Johnston hurried to comfort him and Joel too. She drew them close to her ample chest.

"Good people, pray unto the Lord! Hallowed be thy name, thy kingdom come . . ."

I screamed in pain from a new slap to my cheek and fell forward pressing my forehead against the rug, suffering more blows descending on my arms and back. Mother and Father and the Reverend tried to shield me, but it was impossible. They were pushed aside, while the invisible blows fell fast and furious along my spine.

"Good Lord, is this the Devil's arm?" Old Kate did sound more curious than frightened.

"You would be the only individual to recognize it," Father snapped at her over his shoulder, as all two hundred and fifty pounds of Kate moved closer to see me flinching, beaten to the carpet.

"Darkness covers a multitude of sins." Old Kate looked down at me as if I were a squirming creature of the dirt.

"Be quiet, Kate, or leave this house." The Reverend spoke with severe authority, and I believe the larger audience was helping him adjust to the ways and means of the mysterious force. "The Lord will stand by us, and by this innocent, the Lord shall deliver us from every evil work." The blows increased against me while the Reverend prayed, and he was quick to return to speaking directly to the phenomenon, as if it could hear and understand.

"Cease this torment of Betsy Bell! Tell us who you are and why you are present here." At this, the blows stopped again. I lay prone, my knees to my chest, grateful for the woolen cushion of the carpet under my cheek. I saw the trousered legs and skirts and petticoats of our visitors and I heard them rustling in the sudden silence. The guests spoke softly, seeming very far away.

"What can it be?" I heard my brother Jesse ask.

"What should be done?" Martha posed the more relevant question.

"Pray, goodly assembled, let us combine our prayers. Deliver us from evil, O Lord . . ." The wind started up again and I heard a general gasping for air amongst the startled persons. There was the noise of a slap and a cry of pain, but it did not issue from me. Instead, the Reverend found himself abused.

"O Heavenly Father, deprive us not of our dear emissary." Mother closed her eyes and raised her arms to the ceiling in a posture of devotion.

"No, not my John!" Mrs. Johnston rushed to his side and put her hand to his cheek to soothe him but she too was slapped, whereupon she burst into tears. The Reverend bore his attack with great stoicism, barely flinching, and in this he was a fine example. I placed my arms above my head, expecting blows across my back, bad as a whipping, but instead the blows were laid unto my dear community, across the backs of my brothers and the adults gathered, so I was mercifully spared the full energy of the force. Amid the rushing wind and the furious whistling I heard the guests call out.

"Something has pinched my ear!"

"There's a pin stabbed in my hand!"

"I have been slapped!"

I felt a disgusting sense of relief that persons other than me were suffering the physical abuse, but as soon as that thought crossed my mind I felt hands jerking back my head.

"I will out from this cursed place!" I saw Kate Batts turn toward the hallway to fetch her coat.

"Kate, you cannot, the night is black." Mother stood and followed her with kind concern for her welfare, ignoring the storm of noise and blows about the room.

"I have a lantern, Lucy, and more would I trust the night animals of the forest with my fate than would I remain where evil is at work."

"Let her go if she is not inclined to help," Father shouted after Mother with disregard for Kate's welfare.

"I am inclined to return home and see what I can do to mix you up a remedy!" Old Kate shouted back across the room.

"Wait, you must not go alone," Mr. Porter called out, rising, with Mrs. Porter clinging to his arm, suddenly anxious to accompany Old Kate.

"Good people . . ." The Reverend rubbed his stricken cheek with his hand and looked after them with some dismay.

"When will this visitation take its leave of us?" Mr. Thorn looked to my father, and I saw his brow was deeply furrowed with fearful concern.

"Be there any amongst us that knoweth how long," the Reverend said, quoting what was apparently his favorite psalm on the subject, as an answer to Mr. Thorn. "O God, how long shall the adversary reproach? Shall the enemy blaspheme thy name for ever?" He offered it up as a prayer with his hands raised to the ceiling.

Mother bolted the door after Old Kate and the Porters departed and the rest of us endured the night alternating between our prayers to God, our direct entreaties to the thing itself, and our suffering of maddeningly cruel abuse. All suffered save Mother, who remained untouched. She ministered compresses and cups of tea and fervent prayers to everyone in torment, and eventually, in the early hours of the morning, she was able to hand out pallets and quilts and we were again allowed a few hours of rest before the dawn.

the constant passing of all things

Mr. and Mrs. Thorn departed as soon as it grew light and the Reverend and Mrs. Johnston followed, leaving even before Chloe had readied our breakfast. Jesse and Martha decided to remain another day and I could hear them upstairs talking with Drewry, Richard and Joel. The scratch of Father's pen across the paper in his book of accounts caused me to squirm on my chair at the dining table.

"May I *please* go?" I turned, most earnest, to Mother. I expected she would oppose my request and I sat up straighter, trying to appear as sturdy and robust as possible, hoping I could influence her decision.

"No, I would have you by my side today, Miss Betsy. And your brothers also." Mother had her mind made up, I could see, but I very much wanted to speak to Thenny and I did not think it right I should have to stay at home, as everyone would surely talk of our family at recess.

"I want to go. I want to hear my lessons!" I unfolded my hands and banged my palm lightly on the table for emphasis to my speech. Mother tilted her head at me and smiled slightly, implying I ought to know better than to tell such a bold lie.

"Betsy, to the spring for water go. Gossip is an evil thing." She frowned at the word *evil*, which held new connotations for us both. "That reminds me, you need to bathe and cleanse your body and soul. I will have Chloe build the fire and heat the water."

"But I *am* the spring here, Mother. I am the source to drink from regarding what ails our family." I did not like the picture in my mind of Thenny telling stories gathered from eavesdropping on her parents' conversations. And what of the Batts children, what would they have heard?

"Elizabeth! How say you? 'Tis false pride on your face! How does false pride seem to our Lord?"

"They will say what ails us is demons and my fault!" I don't know how I knew it would be so, but I was certain. Mother softened her features and a heavy sigh escaped her lips.

"A true friend of moral character will come to you for the facts of the matter. All in good time, dear child." Mother was possessed of a patience and certitude I did not have within me and she was absolute in her decision I would remain at home. She left me sitting on my own at the table while she went to heat the water for my bath. I laid my head down on my arms and breathed my own heavy breath, impatient with my inability to change her mind, but by the time the boiling water had pushed the lid off the pot, I knew there was nothing I could do but make the best of it. In the winter, bathing was accomplished in the kitchen in the large washtub and Chloe always built the fire up high, but in the spring, summer and fall, we took our baths outdoors.

"Fetch a pail of cold from where the stream runs fast,"

Mother handed me the light tin pail and sent me off while she and Chloe lifted the pots and carried the boiling water out. I ran down the stone path to our necessary house where Father had built a platform with a cedar hip bath on the southern side. I passed it and went to the stream where I could easily fill my pail, for the water ran close there, and Father had made a small dam of stones and laid a hollow hickory pipe to serve as a waterspout. I hurried back to dump my full pail in the bath and repeat the process, for I liked my water deep. When I returned from my fourth trip, Mother and Chloe were on the platform mixing my stream water with the hot water they had carried from the house. Mother had pulled the sleeve of her dress above her elbow and she was testing the mix with her hand. I shed my outer garments, climbed up the wooden foot stool, and stepped into the bath. The water was warmer than the breezy day and I sank luxuriously deep.

"Bring more hot, Chloe!" I called out as she started back to the house, but I had a feeling she was moving on to other chores.

"Use this to cleanse your head, Miss Betsy." Mother handed me a rosemary soap bar and I let it float between my hands, looking down at the water. Chloe and Mother knew how to mix the lye, the ash and lard to make a perfect soap. My cotton petticoat billowed up and I saw white fluffy clouds advancing across the sky reflected in the water behind my face. The sun was hot, but the feel of my wet petticoat against my skin gave me cause to shudder and I was reminded of cold prickly airs and pins.

"Will you help me, Mother?" I dipped my hair back to wet it.

"Oh yes, I will help you, Miss Betsy!" She crossed quickly behind me, smiling, and I could tell by the mischief in her voice she was set to play. She dropped the long wooden ladle by my knees and pulled it high, pouring streams of hot water over my forehead. I plunged lower in the bath and shook my hair, like a fish wriggling on the line.

"I've got a live one!" Mother teased me, imitating Father at the fishing hole. "Whoa, it's a big one." I held my breath and she dunked me under, but I sprang back toward her laughter, so welcome was the sound. She stood smiling down at me, then caught the bar of soap and set to rubbing the top of my head and the nape of my neck, her fingers massaging peace and spicy lather into my hair.

"Betsy, you are a beautiful girl . . ." Her fingers paused and I could tell she was finished playing and engaged in serious thought over her next words. I tilted my head farther back on the edge of the cedar tub to keep the soap from my eyes. I squinted against the sun, but I could not see the features of her face. "All your troubles, no matter how large, shall pass away like the days. You may rely on the constant passing of all things." Mother sighed as if distracted and I had the sense she was keeping something back. She had meant to tell me more, I was certain of it. She pushed my forehead down and separated the locks of my hair with her fingers, keeping my ears underwater, so they filled with heavy silence. The constant passing of all things did not seem a very inspiring or even comforting thought to me, but I knew that was how she meant it.

When I had finished washing, Mother wrapped me in a cotton sheet and I returned to the kitchen to dress before the cook fire. Martha had brought a pretty broomstraw yellow cotton dress she had stitched just for me and even though it was a little large through the waist and hung too low over my petticoat, Mother allowed me to wear it, I wanted a change so badly.

"Just for today," she told me, "I will tailor it tomorrow," but I doubted she would get to the tailoring anytime soon with so many guests and I planned to ask Martha if she might do it with me later. Mother had to set the house in order. The pallets had to be aired, the wood floors needed sweeping, and all the dishes had to be stacked in the cupboards, while Chloe prepared the food. I was afraid Mother would ask for my help with these tasks, but she did not. Instead she encouraged me to go out of doors.

"Go take in the sun, Miss Betsy, and dry your head, or you may well catch cold. I hope to join you soon, for I must sort the beans for seed."

I wandered out the front door and down the porch steps to our wooden swing, which hung on the lowest branch of the giant blossoming pear tree. I sat down on the board, worn smooth by all our bottoms, and held tight to the ropes, pushing my legs up to the sky, lifting my dress. I noticed the dye of the cloth was a perfect match for my hair. It smelled better than the blossoms and made a long yellow cape behind my back when I swung out far, my feet dangling over the grassy hill. I leaned back, then swept forward again, and the movement of the swing shook the branch, sending flurries of white petals down. I watched them sail lightly to the ground and thought how good God was to give us flowers in the pear trees. Perhaps knowledge of the passing of all things *had* comforted me, for I did feel quite content. Looking out, down the road, I was surprised to see Old Kate Batts appearing like a dark nut amongst the flowery blossoms.

She was by herself, with her mare in tow, her copperas riding skirt under her arm, and she was turning off the road onto our path. I dragged my foot to stop the swing and watched her tie up her horse, then maneuver her massive body into a fast waddle. I sat still, hoping she might not notice I was there, but when she drew level with me on the path she stopped and removed from inside her dress a bulky round bag about the size of my palm fastened and tied with a leather thong around her neck.

"'Tis you, Betsy Bell," Old Kate was out of breath and puffed her words, "the picture of a pretty girl today, I see." I thought she did not like me and I was not able to respond as I would have liked, so I just sat silent, attempting a closer inspection of the dark thing hanging over her bosom.

"'Tis an amulet to ward away your evil Spirit!" Kate followed my eyes and held the thing aloft so I could see it was a black scrap of velvet she had stitched with undyed wool into a bag. Bits of herbs fell out between her sorry stitches when she squeezed it. "I can now approach your home and discuss this matter with your good mother for I am protected. Run, tell her I have come to call." I did not like taking orders from Old Kate but it would have been disrespectful to ignore her completely. I jumped down without speaking and began walking slowly up toward the house and there I saw Mother sitting in her chair above the porch steps, sorting the seeds into folded pieces of paper. She could see Kate Batts clearly from her position and me as well. She waved.

"Good day, Mrs. Batts. I trust you had a safe journey to your home last night?"

"I did, and it was well I went." Kate climbed the last of the hill grunting, as she tried to speak and walk. "My girl had accidentally dosed Ignatius, the poor crippled and suffering soul, with his *morning* mixture before bed, so he was wide awake and much in need of company when I arrived."

"I trust he is settled and content today." Mother sighed kindly, empathetic with Kate and her trials.

"He is, thank God, but I have not come to discuss his interminably bad health. I bear a remedy to dose your young'un with." Kate nodded pointedly at me as I slid past her to stand behind Mother. I gripped the top of her chair and fixed Kate with a most impolite stare. Old Kate leaned against the railing of our porch and after fumbling inside the leather pouch she wore about her waist, she withdrew a small green bottle.

"This is a potion against black magic, to rid a person of bad demons, made from herbs off the African continent. I acquired it in a trade with that old slave, Nona. She lived near Clarksville, claimed she was a witch doctor." I was not surprised to hear Old Kate traded with the slaves. "I sold the poor woman a goat for some cash and a boxful of African herbs, and the hag swore the contents of the box were good to cure all manner of ailments brought on by the Devil or his demons. I have been thinking it was the worser deal for me, for even though my goat was old, she still ate the weeds and made the cheese, but never have I had the use for driving out the demons!" Kate paused and returned to me my assessing stare. "Until now." Her eyes were small and black and when she turned them on me I desired to climb onto my mother's lap, though I was much too big for that.

"Driving out the demons . . ." Mother repeated the phrase, as if she did not understand.

"Lucy, you know the whole continent of black people is packed with demons, so they know of what they speak. I expect this will do the job on your young'un and try it you must, for God knows where this possession of your girl shall lead." Kate looked down at the ground and cleared her throat of noxious phlegm and I thought she planned to spit like a man, but she did not. Mother took the proffered bottle silently and turned it about in her hands, as if she were examining the glass and cork, but I suppose she was wording her response so as not to hurt Kate's feelings.

"What have you made it of?"

"Ah, if there were anyone to whom I would reveal my secrets, it would be you, dear Lucy." Inappropriate laughter welled up in my throat and I put my hands over my mouth and nose to conceal my response to Old Kate's ridiculous arrogance. Mother could mix potions of greater healing properties than anyone in the district. "Simply trust it will quell the poison spirits in the young girl's heart," Kate continued. "Dose her with it, here and now!" Kate's insistence made me nervous and I found the situation suddenly no longer humorous. "Pardon me!" She did spit into the grass, then rested her hands on her enormous hips, awaiting Mother's response. I hoped Mother would not follow Kate's advice, as I did not like the look of the dark liquid.

"We know not the source of our ailment, Kate," Mother said. She set the seeds still to be sorted off to one side and got up from her chair, the bottle in her hand. "Come in and let us share a pot of Chloe's mint tea. It is already brewed." I was greatly relieved Mother did not plan to dose me with her remedy and I smiled, thankful one of Mother's many talents was the ability to turn a conversation well away from conflicting opinions.

"It won't hurt her, Lucy, and the source of the ailment need not be known before a cure is attempted." Old Kate was disappointed and frowned stubbornly, pretending to know the right course of action. "Regardless, a cup of tea would go down well with me, for I am inclined to spread my skirt. It is a long walk here. Might you have a new donation for my scrap collection?" Her usual self-interested manner returned and I wished heartily she had not bothered to make the journey.

My head was heavy with mean thoughts and I ran back to renew my position on the swing while Mother led Old Kate inside. Only moments before, I'd been happy, appreciating God's good nature, but even as I pushed my legs forward and back again, I could not regain my previous mood. My mind was darkened by Old Kate's demon ideas. I heard a single set of boots clopping down the porch steps and I knew before turning it was Father. He approached me from behind and stroked my still damp hair as though it were fine silk from China.

"Darling daughter, that Mrs. Batts has come to speak her blasphemy about our house again, and your dear mother has invited her inside." It was rare for Father to complain to me, and I took a risk confiding to him.

"She has brought some potion made of African herbs traded off a slave to rid me of my *demons*. Please, Father, don't let Mother dose me with Old Kate's mixtures!" I looked up, imploring him to take my side and I saw his eyes were bright and attentive, holding my own.

"You will not drink of it!" he responded, frowning.

"I am pleased to hear you say so, Father, for I do not *wish* to drink of it."

"With the likes of Mrs. Batts, the Reverend was correct in his advice; Job must be our teacher. The congregation of hypocrites shall be desolate, they conceive mischief and bring forth vanity. Their belly prepareth deceit." Father had been diligent in his reading of the text. I noticed the skin of his cheek was taut and drawn and the curly dark hairs of his eyebrows were not brushed into place but stood out wildly. He caressed my cheek with the back of his hand and delicately held my chin, smiling how very much he loved me. He bent at the waist and whispered in my ear, "Would you like a push, Miss Betsy?" From over my shoulder I saw the boys and Martha and Jesse clattering down the porch steps.

"Oh, yes please!" I answered, happy again, strengthened by my private moment with him. I wrapped my fingers tight around the rope. When Father pushed, he generally spared no effort, pushing high as the swing would go. I delighted in the rush of falling backward, for when I was not being thrown to the floor, it was a wonderful sensation. When John Jr. or Jesse pushed, they never gave their all, afraid of the trouble they would catch if I were hurt, but Father had no fear of anyone and he pushed with all his might.

"Higher, Father! Higher!" I cried, thinking of the many carefree times he had pushed me this way, tickling my waist, sending me out over the hill. Would there be many more? I wished I could return to those happier days, and not face whatever tortures lay before me, but I was old enough to know wishing could not make it so.

"My turn! My turn! I want a turn, sister!" Joel jumped up and down, impatient, on the large roots of the pear tree, and Father grasped my waist and slowed me down, so I could give it over.

"Come, Betsy," Martha reached for my hand. "Mother says we can tailor that dress for you now, if you like. We will spend the night again here and I brought none of my own sewing, so you must allow me to busy my needle." Martha was smiling and kind and I felt as if she were my own elder sister.

We hurried up to my bedroom and I stood near the window with my arms straight out at my sides while Martha began folding and pinning my hem.

"Did you know, Martha, near the time our troubles began, I became a young woman," I shyly told her my news.

"Well, Miss Betsy! Now you will fall in love, for now the fig tree putteth forth her green figs, and the vines with the tender grape give a good smell!" She laughed sweetly, quoting the Scripture.

"Oh no, I know no one," I objected, but immediately I thought of Josh Gardner's profile, bent over his lessons, and I felt my cheeks grow hot.

"Oh yes you do, Betsy Bell! I can see you already have a love in mind."

"No, honestly," I protested.

Martha moved around to pin the back side of the dress and I was glad she could no longer see my face. "Oh Betsy, the joys of womanhood are immensely pleasurable." She went on to describe aspects of becoming a woman I had never imagined. My thoughts stayed on Josh Gardner as I recalled the sound of my name on his tongue and I was well distracted from my darker concerns.

At dusk when the Reverend arrived, we discovered he had left Mrs. Johnston at home, but had brought with him the new Methodist preacher, Calvin Justice, from the growing settlement at Cedar Hill.

"Hello, Betsy Bell." Calvin Justice smiled and removed his hat to me as I descended the stairs. He had a healthy shock of chestnut-colored hair without a line of gray and his beard was solid and dark. He seemed much too young to be a man of God, but then, the Reverend Johnston was my only comparison.

"I've heard much about you and your sad troubles." He

reached for my hand and I was embarrassed. I wondered if all Methodists were so very forward.

"Preacher Justice has come to stand with us this evening to help us pray, for in the eyes of the Lord we must be as one," Reverend Johnston said, following Calvin Justice into our parlor.

"Attendance in all houses of the Lord has greatly risen as news of your troubles has traveled the district, Mr. Bell." Calvin Justice made a friendly joke, and I saw Reverend Johnston look to Father for his response, but Father was not forthcoming. He had taken a ride on the land while Kate Batts visited and on returning he'd complained again of something twiglike stuck in his throat that prevented him from swallowing. He had not joined us at the table during dinner, but stayed in his chair at his desk reading the good book, then writing in his book of accounts under the light of the lamp. He was there still, his face grim and his jaw tight. He gave an unenthusiastic nod of welcome to the new preacher.

"I believe tonight our troubles will be less," Mother told the Reverend, and I wondered if she was thinking back to the quiet night we'd had the last time Father felt unwell. She was very much concerned with Father's illness and she stayed near to him, looking often to see if he had drunk the tea she'd placed by his side. "Certainly with two such dignified men of God in our home," she encouraged Calvin Justice to settle in her own chair, "the Lord will favor us."

"There is much of Heaven and earth too advanced for our simple minds to comprehend. We must pray together," Calvin Justice said with great assurance and I felt immediately he was a man born to his calling. "Each chapter and verse in the good book is one I dearly love to read, so I am honored to take your request, Mrs. Bell."

"Jack and I had discussed a section of Hebrews eleven, on great heroes of the faith, for here we must emulate such men." Mother smoothed her skirt as she spoke. Calvin Justice found the page of her suggestion quickly and began to read in a clear church voice, commanding everyone's attention. I was sitting on a pillow of my skirts, on the rug, with the boys and Drewry beside me, while Martha and Jesse occupied the bench behind us. I leaned back against Martha's knees cushioned by her skirts and I closed my eyes as the list of the great heroes went on and on. I must have dozed a short time, for abruptly Martha was gripping my shoulders with tight fingers.

"Do you hear that, Betsy?" she whispered in my ear.

I listened and heard a soft rattling that turned our parlor into a field of thistles fraught with a winter wind, but there was a cadence to it like speech, as if inside the wind someone was talking in complicated tongues.

"What is it?" Everyone held their breath to hear it better and it evolved into the whistling we had heard the night before.

"If you can whistle, can you communicate with us?" The Reverend withdrew a piece of parchment from his pocket and we heard all at once a great knocking on the walls and doors.

"Sit down, Jack." I saw Father attempting to rise and speak but Mother held restraining arms on his shoulders, and tried to deliver his message herself.

"What say you, Reverend Johnston, what is your intention here?" She gestured to the piece of parchment unfolding from his Bible.

"Lucy, I believe this force may be intelligent and I have brought some questions, written down to keep my mind on my purpose. I have given the matter a great deal of thought and I believe we must try to communicate with this phenomenon if we are ever to be rid of it."

Mother was silent, considering.

"There are many mysteries in God's plan for each of us, Mrs. Bell. Our work is to bear up under what hardships He imposes," Calvin Justice said, supporting the Reverend. His lithe form was taut with attention and I felt he must have had a hand in crafting this approach. The whistling intensified so there was no sound but it, piercing and shrill. I covered my ears and prayed my head would not burst, for the noise was truly painful. I shut my eyes and huddled against Martha's knees, expecting the worst.

"We wish to know your meaning here, for we believe you can communicate!"

As if in answer, a violent shuddering split the air, ending with a thud, then silence. We took our hands away from our heads and looked about, seeing only ourselves, frightened. The Reverend held his parchment to the lamp and persisted. "If you can hear us, give us a sign." I saw Father squirm in his chair. He made a sound as if he meant to speak but could not, the speech died in his throat and then the clear bell of a *tap-tap,* like metal on glass, sounded against the parlor window.

"Good, good!"

"With all respect, this appears not so very good, Reverend," John Jr. voiced what I was certain Father was thinking.

"How many people are here in this room?" The Reverend ignored my brother and gripped his parchment more tightly, for his shaking hand made the light flicker on the wall.

Tap, tap, tap, tap, tap, tap, tap, tap, tap, tap, came steadily with clear pauses in between, a rap for each person present. It was plain the phenomenon had answered. Martha bent and gripped my hand in hers.

"It understands!" she whispered into the shocked silence.

"How is it possible . . ." Jesse shook his head in disbelief and looked across the room to Father, listening intently.

"If you can understand us, tell us, who are you? Why are you here?" The Reverend was excited with his success and he stepped to the center of the room, waving his arms, gesturing to the "here" of which he spoke.

"Wait, John . . ." Calvin Justice rose and meant to speak, but before he could, the sound of the whistling wind commenced again, voracious in our ears, and above it we heard the sound of numerous slaps and blows. The Reverend Johnston flinched with pain as he was struck. I dropped Martha's hand attempting to cover my head. Fingers cold and hard as winter icicles stabbed at my hair and tore it from my braid. I shielded my face with my elbows and drew my knees up to my chin, protecting myself as best I could.

"BE GONE from this good home, you evil being!" Calvin Justice crossed the room and laid his strong hands on the Reverend's thrashing shoulders, attempting to steady him and perhaps wrestle his invisible foe. His countenance was pure passion for righteousness and through a crack in my shield of elbows I saw Father attentive to his ways and means.

We heard the _clap_ of a hand and the roomful of persons groaned in unison as Calvin Justice did recoil. The red mark of fingers slowly appeared where his face had been struck and we were all saddened, for Calvin Justice had seemed, however briefly, a possible worthy opponent for our evil affliction. He did not cry out, but put his hands to his face in disbelief. He reached into the air as though groping in total darkness and I watched the white cuffs of his shirtsleeves grasping nothing.

"Where are you that would strike me down? Return that I might feel your hand and shake it in peace before the Lord." I felt a jerk on my hair and I was thrown to the floor at the preacher's feet.

"Torture this innocent no longer. Forgive us and return from whence you came!" Mother left Father's side immediately and came to me, crying her prayer in earnest. The whistling ceased but the sound of the wind, rattling thistle heads, returned. We froze to listen and within it heard a dangling metal noise, like the bell of the church being carelessly cleaned, *scrape, screek, scrape, screek*. It was not completely unmusical and I listened carefully, thinking I heard a conversation buried in it. It died away and the wind went with it slowly, until there was only the Reverend's hard breathing and our own general sighs of relief and amazement. For certain whatever it was had gone from us, at least for the moment.

"Good Reverend, Preacher Justice," Mother said, her voice composed but strained, "if I may be so bold to ask, pray, tell us what ways and means you plan to employ to rid us of our suffering?"

"The Lord may mean your suffering to be lived and not relieved." Calvin Justice softened his opinion with a kind tone and appeared to contemplate his words while stroking his dark beard. The Reverend looked to him and scratched at his own sparse stubble.

"I believe *you mean to say* this suffering must be *understood* for it to be relieved." The Reverend spoke nervously, looking to my father, who sat silent in the corner. Calvin Justice was about to say something else but Mother interrupted.

"Let us focus our humble powers of intelligence on that one purpose. Let us work together to solve this mystery. I request you read of Paul at Corinth."

"Of course! The perfect text!" The Reverend Johnston pulled his Bible close and nodded to my Mother with respect, impressed by her gracious manner. "Please, you begin," he looked to Calvin Justice.

"God that made the world and all things therein . . ." Calvin Justice raised his hands to the ceiling while the rest of us bowed our heads. This was a popular section of Scripture and when I recognized it, tears, absent all the evening, arrived in my eyes. "Neither be He worshipped with men's hands, as though he needed anything, seeing he giveth to all life and breath and all things . . ." I listened and cried silently until Mother's voice joined the Reverend's and Preacher Justice's, reciting the last line, ". . . For in Him we live, and move, and have our Being. Amen." I felt a momentary warmth shoot through me, as if a genuine healing was occurring in my soul, brought on by the words of the Lord. Yet, even as I encouraged the good feeling of filling with Spirit, I tried to grasp it too deeply, and in that moment the feeling slipped away.

the mysterious spirit speaks

The next day was my thirteenth birthday and again I pleaded with Mother to allow me a day at school. Against her better judgment, she relented but made me promise to be most cautious. Jesse and Martha departed our home as my brothers and I left for the schoolhouse. I hugged Martha tight and told her I hoped they would return soon to stay with us again. The weather was gray, for a spring rain had fallen at dawn and a wet green mist hung about the path. Drewry, Richard, Joel and I breathed deeply of it, relieved to be walking away from our house.

"Sister, how will you tell it at school?" Richard walked beside me, his leather satchel bouncing on his back.

"I will speak the truth of the matter," I said, shrugging my shoulders, rebalancing my bag.

"What is the truth of the matter?" Drewry kicked a stone and Joel ran ahead, chasing it.

"What do you believe?" I wished to hear his thoughts, for he was frowning, his expression limp as the bent grass.

"I know not, but likely the truth will be discovered."

We reached the hazel thicket and were forced into a single line. At once, from every side, a thick barrage of thin twigs, wet with the rain, fell down on us. I held my satchel before my face and ran, tripping over the hem of my new yellow dress. It caught on a branch and tore about the bottom as I fell. Scrambling to get up again I ground my knees into the wet red mud under the grass and dark stains spread across my skirt. The sticks pummeled my cheeks and hands.

"Hurry, sister, away!" Drewry grasped my arm and we ran together to the bridge Richard and Joel had already reached. Out of the thicket the torture ceased and I stopped with Drewry beside me. We turned to look back at the path littered with sticks.

"Of this I shall say we were attacked by flying wood!" My heart was beating much too quickly, and I recalled Mother's warnings and concern for my safety. "How would you describe it, brother?" I was out of breath and more upset over the soiled state of my dress than the scratches I had received from the twigs, but I tried to make light of it.

"Perhaps it was a birthday greeting for you, Betsy," Drewry joked. He removed a twig from the top of my braid and we managed two short laughs, but they flowed uneasily from our throats.

"Perhaps it was just the wind," Joel called, running back to fetch us, anxious to get to school. "Carry on, carry on!" He played as though he were the overseer in the field and Drewry and I both gave real laughs to see him so resilient. Across the bridge we saw a recess was in progress in the schoolyard.

"Look, there they are!" Thenny spotted our little group and everyone immediately stopped their games and came running to greet us. I looked for Josh Gardner, but he was not present.

"How are you, Betsy Bell?"

"I am well and pleased to see you all, and today I am thirteen." I curtsied my greeting.

"What has happened at your home?" everyone asked at once.

"Tell us! Yes, please, tell!"

"There have been many rumors," Becky said, looking at Vernon Batts as she spoke.

"And perhaps some rumors are the truth." Vernon was quick with a retort to her unspoken accusation. "How often do we see Miss Betsy Bell arriving late in the day in a mud-streaked dress? No doubt her demons now accost her in the woods!" Clearly Old Kate had spoken of us in her home.

"I stumbled in the thicket!" I cried, feeling a sudden reluctance to tell the truth, regretting having shared that it was my special day. "At our home, it is as the Reverend said on Sunday, better not to speak of it, but pray it would soon be gone, so we might join our goodly peers in studies and games." I saw Professor Powell about to ring the bell outside the door and I waved to him, noticing he clanged the iron triangle with exuberance. All turned, mumbling, thinking later I would tell them more, but I thought, later, I would not.

We entered the schoolhouse and took our seats on the benches and I withdrew my slate from my satchel. Professor Powell stood behind his large oak desk waiting for our attention.

"Before our mathematics lesson I should like to announce the prize for best composition." He shuffled some papers in his hands. Thenny had the seat beside me and she sat up straighter, expecting it would be awarded to her.

"The best composition was penned by Miss Mary Batts for her essay, 'From Sheep to Cloak.'" There was an audible gasp from Thenny, and Mary Batts was the picture of surprise as she rose to receive the blue satin ribbon.

"Thank you, Mary, for your excellent work," the professor smiled. "If any of you girls have questions regarding warps and cards, just ask Miss Mary."

"I expect she has to win with her family so pitiful," Thenny whispered in my ear and I knew why she was so mean-spirited about it, for I had seen Ephraim Polk give Mary an enthusiastic smile. Thenny had no great liking for Mary Batts because *she* liked Ephraim, who was known to visit the Batts house on the pretense of talking with Vernon, whom nobody really liked, but clearly, he went to catch a glimpse of Mary. It was no wonder Thenny narrowed her eyes and fell into a sulk. I realized she coveted honors more than I did, but I tried not to think any worse of her for it. I had much else on my mind.

Professor Powell began to read out numbers for the mathematics lesson and I exchanged a glance with Drewry, who sat to my left and up a row. I knew he would not talk about our trials if I did not. I had not planned to be so restrained but once I had begun that way, I could not see how to tell the truth of the matter. I began to feel quite sorry for myself, as it *was* my birthday and I had chosen to come to school and I was not enjoying it. I wished Josh Gardner was present. I could not concentrate on the lesson and I was grateful Professor Powell did not address me with any questions for I was truly elsewhere in my mind. I drew a vine down the side of my slate and decorated it with leaves when I was meant to be doing sums. At the close of the day we were dismissed from our lessons and a small group gathered again around me and my brothers in the schoolyard.

"Will you come back, Miss Betsy, or be too tormented by

your demons to suffer instruction?" Vernon Batts stood with his legs wide apart and I thought perhaps I should tell him he ought to have his mother stitch him a new pair of trousers, for the ones he wore were much too tight and short.

"What do you know about it, Vernon?" Drewry asked, challenging his insolence toward me.

"I've heard it said demons dance on the roof of your Betsy's room."

"Have you also heard of the man in the moon? No demons have been seen by anyone at our home so keep yourself quiet regarding what you know not." Drewry stepped forward and took my arm. He was taller and stronger than Vernon and if it came to blows, I was certain Drew would be victorious. Though his mouth was large, Vernon was a coward at heart.

"So tell us, what is the matter of which the Reverend speaks?" he asked, persistent.

"Go on, tell, Betsy." Thenny popped up beside me, encouraging me to answer these inquiries.

"We must not speak of it . . ." I shrugged my shoulders, implying I was obedient to a wish not my own.

"Recognize *this* is the truth." Drewry took another menacing step toward Vernon. "Our father has commanded our silence, but on the day when we may speak freely of our disturbance, you best hold your ears onto your head for whatever you imagine, it is much more than that." Drewry reminded me of Calvin Justice for a moment, so inflamed was his tongue.

"May that day be soon," Vernon spoke this last to our backs, as we departed.

"Sister," Joel tugged at my hand demanding I keep him amused as we crossed the bridge and prepared to enter the hazel thicket. "Mother will set a special table for your special day. What treats are you predicting?"

"The first strawberries and Chloe's sugar cream." I could already taste them on my tongue. I took a deep breath of woody thicket and I was not surprised when abruptly the sticks began to rain on us again, only much fewer in number, and this time they did not strike us with much force, but landed mostly just ahead in the path.

"Stop, sister, we must investigate." Drewry pulled at the hedge with his fingers, looking as if he wished he had brought his gun to school.

"Drewry, it is obvious no person, animal or wind is the culprit here." I wished to make haste to our supper and I strode ahead. Richard plucked a stick from the ground and, removing his knife from his pocket, he notched the wood, making a game of the harassment.

"Take this, demon!" He threw it back into the hedge growth and I thought it a sign of our real progress we were able to laugh, a few paces farther on, when the same stick was returned to him, striking him lightly on his behind.

"So how was your day at school, dear children?" Mother poured tea from the china pot at our celebration, inquiring after us.

"Uneventful, apart from many new lessons." Drewry and I exchanged a glance, having agreed we should not worry Mother with the curiosities of our peers, or the sticks in the hedge.

"Sister, I have a birthday treat for you." John Jr. stood up from his place at the table and left the room, returning shortly with his wooden flute. He played a lively tune and I did feel grateful for his effort and tried to tap my feet. The notes fluttered in my ears and I was overcome with emotion. Bitter disappointment regarding my day at school, combined with my birthday, and my overall exhaustion, gave rise to an uncomfortable sorrow in my soul. I tried to listen to the lilting tune but nothing seemed purely good to me. Even John Jr.'s sweet song was fleeting and momentary, while the tortures of the night loomed ahead, certain and frightening. What good was it to be a growing young woman when torture and suffering was my future? Tears spilled from the sides of my eyes.

"There, there, Miss Betsy." Mother came to me and held my head against her breast so the rough linen of her smock tickled my ear. "'Tis a day to give thanks to the Lord for your incarnation. You are growing up a lovely girl."

"'Tis true." Father came around the table and patted my back and I did feel warmed by the two of them standing either side of me. John Jr. allowed the last note of his song to roll off his tongue, and as he took the instrument from his lips we heard a knock on the door. I expected the Reverend, arriving to sit vigil with us, but instead it was the Thorns, with Thenny.

"Good evening to you, we hope we are not imposing."

"Come in, come in, you must share our tea," Mother said, inviting them to join us.

"No, please, we have come with an invitation to extend, for your Betsy to spend the evening at our home, and if it is your pleasure, we will collect her now." Mr. Thorn removed his hat but held it in his hands.

"How kind of you." Mother looked uncertainly to Father, then to me, assessing how she should respond. Mr. Thorn cleared his throat as if he was unsure he wished to speak.

"We thought perhaps your dreaded affliction might not follow her elsewhere," he said, admitting his reasoning. Mrs.

Thorn nodded her head, nervous with concern and agreement.

"'Tis a thought we have not tested." Father squeezed my shoulder giving a pragmatic response.

"Please, Betsy, please, say you will." Thenny was excited and hopped from one foot to the other, awaiting my reply. To see her did make me smile.

"May I, Mother?" Was it possible the evil might stay away from our home if I was not in residence?

"Well, all right, if you desire it so. How say you, Jack?" Mother tucked a stray piece of hair from my braid behind my ear with affection.

"John Jr. shall fetch her in the morning," Father replied and I was pleased to hear him give his permission. I raced upstairs with Thenny to pack my nightdress and fresh stockings.

No sooner were the covers pulled about us and Mrs. Thorn withdrawn from Thenny's room than Thenny did start in with all her questions.

"Tell me everything. You must." She sat up on her elbow and her dark brown eyes glistened with the light of the single candle by our bed.

"It is difficult to speak of . . ." I lay on my back looking sideways at her eager face. It felt odd to be in a home other than my own.

"But you must, I will tell no one, and swear to it." Thenny waited, putting her hand on her heart, knowing her exuberant will could pull bats from a cave in the daytime. I sighed, giving in with some relief.

"Tell no one, as 'tis Father's wish we should be circumspect, despite the Reverend's exhortations." I propped the pillow further up behind my head and turned to her, relating much of my tortures and experiences with many details. I kept my feelings and conversations with my family members to myself, but the violent actions were enough to absorb Thenny. She listened with attention, stopping my monologue only to express sympathy and anger toward all I had suffered, though I sensed she was greatly enjoying the plotted nature of my recent days. I was exhausted at the close of telling it, but Thenny was infused with energy.

"Betsy, a witch must be the source of your bad troubles."

"The Reverend believes it is a supernatural force."

"Think, did you but once give Old Kate Batts a brass pin of your own? I hear say she can curse the one whose pin she has." I felt irritated, for if Thenny could hear my story and believe it came down to a pin in Kate Batts's hand, obviously she had not understood the extent of my torment.

"I wear my braid only down my back, not on my head." I could not remember Kate Batts ever begging a pin from me.

"But you have pins, for special do's. Perhaps you did lend her one. Or perhaps your mother lent her one, without your knowledge." Thenny seemed to feel sleep had eluded me for so many nights I could not be trusted to know what I had or had not done. "Old Kate Batts might be a witch and you and I not know it," she surmised.

" 'Tis worse than a witch's conjuring at our house." Though I felt no liking for Old Kate, I doubted she possessed the know-how to create such violence as was ours.

"We know not the ways of the witch." Thenny's eyes grew unfocused and I saw she was picturing all manner of possibilities.

"I know no reason for Kate Batts to suffer our family any trials. My mother is her friend and neighbor." I discouraged Thenny, growing further annoyed that I had not conveyed the immensity of our malignant manifestation, for if I had, she would not insist Old Kate could be responsible. I looked at her, suddenly recalling her sour expression when Mary Batts won the prize in composition, and it occurred to me perhaps she was making her suspicions up for her own ends.

"This is why I say so . . ." Thenny tapped my arm with impatience in a hurry to explain her reasoning, and I was anxious to hear it, for I did not wish to think she would accuse Old Kate of witchcraft simply because the boy she liked favored Old Kate's daughter.

"Two months previous, I went with my mother to the store. There was still muddy snow on the ground and I waited in the carriage while Mother went inside. I heard voices and around the side of the porch I saw your father and Old Kate, involved in an exchange of words. She was talking of *her boundaries* and your father answered something about *his land,* but I could not make out any more. It ended when he tipped his hat and turned his back on her. She shouted after him, *'I'll remember this, Jack Bell, and you will be the worse for it.'*" Thenny shook her finger, imitating Old Kate brilliantly. "I heard her say so plain, Betsy!" She gripped my arm, as if she could squeeze a proper response from me, but I did not know what to say. I'd heard Father complain Old Kate was a jealous landowner, but I was unaware of any specific incident between them. I recalled her standing arms akimbo at our porch, suggesting I be dosed with her demon potion, and I felt sick to my stomach. I knew if I told Thenny of it she would call for Old Kate's lynching. I thought of Mother and decided I should wait and see regarding Mrs. Batts.

"Thenny, I have yet to tell you of another thing entirely!" The subject of my becoming a woman was enough to distract her for a few moments. It had not happened yet to her and she wished to know all about it. We heard Mrs. Thorn's footsteps in the hall, and she entered the room.

"Say your prayers, dear girls, for it is time to rest."

"Oh no, Mother, we must have light all night or the witch that tortures Betsy will descend!" I knew Thenny was not afraid of what she called the witch and she did not expect it to bother her in bed. She was simply wide awake and filled to the brim with new information for her busy mind, and so did not wish to extinguish the candle.

"Thenny Thorn, you are an embarrassment to me." Mrs. Thorn frowned at her daughter, but smiled warmly at me. "Pay no heed to her silliness, Miss Betsy, for I am certain whatever has visited your home will not bother you at ours. Commence your prayers." She sat on the edge of the bed and picked at a stray thread from Thenny's red patch quilt. Bowing her head she began reciting the Lord's Prayer along with us. "Our Father, who art in Heaven . . ." I heard her nervously snap the thread off, right when we said Amen.

"Now, quiet." Mrs. Thorn blew out the candle and left us alone. I looked around after her departure, noticing Thenny's room was much smaller than my own. There were no windows and so it felt like a cozy burrow. I breathed deeply, relaxing into Thenny's luxurious feather bed, hoping evil and violence could be left behind by way of a simple carriage ride. But as I snuggled beside my friend, I heard the harsh descent of whistling wind enter the room.

"Betsy!" Thenny screamed and grasped me with both hands. "My hair, something pulls my hair!"

The violence attacked us both with as much force as it had ever unleashed. It ripped the covers from the bed and simultaneously pulled our braids, slapping us with strong ice fingers. I tried to protect myself, curling with my head between my knees on Thenny's bed. I hoped she would follow my example but she was hysterical, screaming and crying even when the invisible let up actively assaulting her. Mrs. Thorn appeared in the doorway and behaved as though the visitation had not been expected in any way. I peeked from under my elbow and saw she held her candle high.

"Stop it now! This can't be! I won't have this in my house!"

Thenny's screams were louder than the whistling wind, but I detected the smack of lips near my ear, and as I listened it evolved into gulping swallows. I felt senseless having imagined it could have been otherwise.

The next morning, when my brothers came to fetch me, they reported in my absence the disturbances were no less at our home, so we came to know the presence could occupy two places at one time. Over the next few evenings our trials continued and Mother would not allow me back to school. "I would have you near to me, Miss Betsy," was all the reasoning I could pull from her. The boys and Drewry were allowed to make the journey and I depended on them to tell me all. Unfortunately, Drewry reported that despite her assurances she would not, Thenny had spread the tale that an evil witch attacked our family.

"Did she speak to the source of the witchery?" I felt a coldness in my chest at the thought of what Thenny's tongue could do, but Drewry frowned and shook his head.

"I did confront her, Betsy, on the inaccuracy of her speech, but Thenny Thorn defended herself to me, relating how the class has buzzed with malignant suppositions concerning what ails us, including the idea that all is the product of your overimaginative mind! *'I know your Betsy would never concoct such trouble even were she able!'*" Drewry managed a cloying imitation of Thenny to make me smile, aware how deeply I felt the pain of these false accusations. "Thenny declared herself to me your true friend and confidante, but at recess she did mesmerize the schoolyard with stories of the evening you spent in her bed accosted by the thing."

"'Twas nothing to the many evenings you and I spend here!" I was frustrated hearing this gossip. How could Thenny be so unkind as to speak of it without me present? And who was saying I had brought it on myself? Though during the day I might suffer the emotional pains of false accusations and fear, come evening I knew I would suffer the real affliction itself, a fact that penetrated my every moment. "Why would I bring such trauma to our home?"

"Never mind, I put a stop to her outrageous talk and hopefully did squash the rumors like so many worms on rocks." Drewry kept his eyes on mine and his lips twisted in a sly smile.

"Thank you," I looked away, disinclined to hear what harsh words he had used. I knew it hardly mattered, as there was no stopping malicious gossip once it had begun.

By the next Sunday morning at church, the lack of sleep and physical abuse suffered by all of us was apparent on our faces. The night before, Reverend Johnston had expressed grave disappointment at his inability to communicate with what he believed was an intelligent supernatural force. The whistling wind had developed a voicelike quality and more than before the Reverend expected an answer to his favorite query, "If you can understand, please speak to us, tell us, who are you? Why are you here?" But only indistinct utterances inside the cloud of noise responded. Weak and faltering, what it might answer had been impossible to decipher. He stood slump-backed, leaning heavily against his pulpit while reading his sermon on God's law, ignoring the murmurs of concern rippling through our congregation.

"Brothers and sisters," he took a deep breath, "I must speak again this week on the tribulations of the Bells and those who care for them. How great is the darkness! We must pray ever more for the Lord to lift us to the light."

"Pray, Reverend, is Jack Bell inclined this Sunday to speak to his torment, for all to hear and better know its aspect for their prayers?" Old Kate spoke freely from the back of the church and stood to emphasize her broadcast. "I have seen it myself and would have all know its nature, so they may guard against it."

"Yea, Kate, I would speak against corrupt minds who talk of what they know not." Father did not stand but spoke sharply over his shoulder, twisting his jaw like a dog biting its fleas.

"Speak to it, Jack, go on!" A round of spontaneous encouragement for Kate's suggestion went about the church and Kate sat down, vindicated.

"I will ask you all to do as I have done on the good Reverend's advice." Father stood reluctantly, nodding to the Reverend. "Read the Book of Job and ask yourselves as I ask now, Shall vain words have an end?" He quoted the verse and though his voice was solid, it was deep with emotion. A silence fell over the congregation and he remained standing, as upright and sturdy as ever I saw him. I felt full of pride, witnessing his demand for the respect he deserved from our community. Several members shifted uncomfortably on their benches, and I looked to Thenny and saw her head was bowed.

"Please, continue, for verily this sermon teaches." The

Reverend opened both his arms out wide, with serious fatigue in his gesture, inviting all to listen to Father.

"I also could speak as ye do," Father quoted the text in his firmest tone. "I could heap up words against you and shake my head at you." I saw Kate turn to her neighbor and make some remark, and a few others began to mumble, but how could they take offense, when we were the ones who suffered? I could see Father interpreted their talk as more of the same treatment we'd already received behind our backs and decided to end his speech without requesting prayers to help us. "People, I know not why, but God has delivered me to the ungodly, and turned me over to the hands of the wicked." He sat down and I saw his eyes were angry and his back too straight.

"Yea, surely God will not do wickedly," the Reverend said, looking surprised at the direction Father's speech had taken. He tempered the effect on the congregation by speaking calmly, with pure confidence. "Neither will the Almighty pervert Judgment."

"O Lord, O Lord, O Lord!" A disturbance and gasping began at the back and I turned to see Kate Batts on her feet, wobbling from her bench down the aisle to the pulpit. "I am filled with the Glory of God!"

"Blessed be, she is filled with the Spirit of the Lord!" Mrs. Randolph called out her condition and everyone sat up taller to see Old Kate falling to her knees, her straggly long hair loosened from its pins, flying in every direction. Her head jerked rapidly back and forth and she laughed uncontrollably, waving her arms to the sky before the Reverend as if she were drowning and reaching out to be saved.

"Bless this woman for she walks with the Lord." The Reverend gave the blessing somewhat perfunctorily I thought, and Father looked away from the scene, an expression of disgust on his drawn features. I understood his feeling, as I was also suspicious of Kate's motives, but I noticed no one tittered as they usually did, though no one called out "Praise the Lord," either. For the first time our congregation as a whole was uncertain how to act, so no one spoke. We sat in silent witness to her filling with Spirit and it was not long before she collected herself and walked back to her place, wiping her nose with a bit of tattered white lace.

The Reverend ended the service with a short prayer and by the time our family had reached the doorway I saw Old Kate had her wooden cart down at the bottom of the road. She had quickly recovered from the Jesus in her and was attempting to hawk amulet bags of herbs like the scrap she wore around her neck.

"Guaranteed to ward against witchery and demons!" she called out to the crowd.

"How dare she mock us?" Father wished to speak with her and I wondered what harsh words he would say, but Mother insisted we must depart immediately.

"It would be unwise in our situation to issue unkind words to anyone, even someone engaged in profit at our expense," she said. I thought Father would ignore her advice but instead he listened. He kept his lips tight and drove our buggy swiftly home.

After the Sunday supper I retired to my room, hoping to rest a few moments before the Reverend and Preacher Justice arrived and the evening trials began. I lay down on my bed but I could not get comfortable. On my back all I could think of was the harsh jerking which nearly pulled the hair from my head, and when I rolled over, the beautiful star pattern on the quilt Mother had made for me gave thoughts of the covers flying off. I was sad to realize my bed was no longer a place of rest. I rose and sat in front of my window in the rocking chair Father and John Jr. had crafted. In the distant woods beneath the orchard, beyond the cornfield and past the stream, I saw a light steadily moving through the trees, as if someone walked there, carrying a candle or a lantern, but I knew it was no person. For the first time, I experienced something that was not entirely fear in connection with the presence. I *knew* that night the thing would speak, as though it whispered its intention in my ear. I had the feeling once it spoke I might discover why it had chosen to torment me and the knowledge gave me strange comfort, though I did not yearn to hear what it might say. I felt soon the violence against me might lessen and I would be protected by the very same force that now abused me. This did not seem possible, but I felt it was. My room was darkening and I heard many footsteps coming up the path, then greetings at the back door. I looked to the light in the woods and saw it flash brightly, sparking from the ground. It was time for me to go downstairs. I held my skirts as I descended and prayed to God most earnestly, please, please, let our torment come to an end.

In the parlor three men I did not know occupied chairs beside Calvin Justice and I assumed correctly they were members of his church in Cedar Hill. Mother shared the bench by the doorway with the little boys, and Mrs. Johnston, Jesse, Martha, Drewry and John Jr. occupied all the remaining chairs, which were placed about in a circle. Father took a quick drink from his flask before sitting in his chair. Everyone faced the hearth where the Reverend stood, clearly anxious to begin his reading from the good book. Mother moved to make room for me but only the edge of my bottom fit on the bench.

"In keeping with the text of this morning's sermon, I will read from the Psalms in praise of God's law." The Reverend took his time turning the pages of his worn Bible and I shifted, uncomfortable in my spot. "Open mine eyes, that I may behold wondrous things out of thy law. It is good for me that I have been afflicted; that I might learn thy statutes."

I bowed my head, listening for whatever noise would announce the arrival of evil, but there was only silence.

"My soul is continually in my hand: yet I do not forget thy law," the Reverend read on. Mother took my hand in hers and I in turn took up Joel's and very near us, from the direction of the front staircase, came the windy whistling. The air in the room bristled with feeling as those visitors not accustomed to being in the presence of the phenomenon confronted their fears. I attempted prayerful meditation. I closed my eyes and tried to breathe deep to the limits of the laces of my dress, praying, God help me to endure all pain and suffering, for I knew it would soon be administered to me.

"I am small and despised: Yet I do not forget thy precepts." The Reverend spoke with confidence and faith. I felt the warmth and strength of my mother's hand in mine and I tried to pass the same current through my other hand to Joel, *think of others always first.* On my cheeks I felt a sudden burning flush, but the room grew noticeably colder. The wind rushed around the room yet not one person cried in fear. All were riveted to the Reverend Johnston's upturned face or attentive to me. Abruptly the heavy cedar door flew open and slammed shut again so forcefully I thought it would bust off its hinges. Father and John Jr. jumped up and pressed themselves against the door to hold it shut, but it blew open again, hurling them to the stairs before crashing back with a tremendous bang, like a gunshot.

"Reveal yourself," cried Reverend Johnston. "What or who are you? What do you want? Why are you here?" The lamps were suddenly extinguished. We heard one long tone develop from the myriad of sound inside the wind and the lamps spontaneously lit again. Instead of the indistinct utterances and weak whispering, we heard word for word, in a faltering but clearing distinguishable voice, the sermon Reverend Johnston had read on his very first evening at our house.

We see not our signs. There be no more any prophet; neither be there amongst us any that knoweth how long.

I listened, squeezing Mother's hand, strongly reminded of my feelings in my room when I had known the Presence would be verbally forthcoming. I wondered if I should tell the company assembled, when all of a sudden I felt as if I was falling from a great height into a dark place. My body was roughly torn from beside Mother and Joel and flung onto the floor where I twitched with unnatural movements, locked in violent convulsions.

"It is a seizure!" One of the visitors from Cedar Hill had been schooled in elementary medicine and pronounced it so.

"I fear she is in the grasp of what speaks to us." The Reverend looked about the well-lit room with trepidation.

"Jack, she does not breathe!" Mother came to my side and listened at my heart, near hysteria. I wished to comfort her but found I could not speak.

"Release this innocent, evil fiend!" Father used his great strength to lift me onto his shoulder and, clapping my back hard, he forced air into my lungs until I coughed. As suddenly as it began, the seizure ended, but I fell into a state of semi-consciousness where I could not speak and breathed as though I slept. They laid me out on the bench.

"I shall fetch Dr. Hopson," Calvin Justice said, greatly concerned. His visitors rose to leave with him.

"John Jr., you and Jesse go along, accompany the doctor to our home. Tell him it is most urgent, and Godspeed," Father commanded them to action. The Reverend, Mrs. Johnston, Mother and Father stayed in prayerful vigil around my sleeping form, but nothing more occurred until several hours later when the doctor knocked at our door and I abruptly awoke.

"How does your Betsy fare?" He entered our parlor, removing his hat. Dr. Hopson was of my father's age, but his hair and beard were pure white and well trimmed. He wore round spectacles with immensely valuable gold frames. They glinted in the lamplight as he approached me and I was reminded of the sparks in the forest.

"She was cast down unconscious," the Reverend began explaining.

"And her poor body twitched like a fish out of water," Mrs. Johnston continued.

"Jack had to pound her back to force her breathing," Mother said as she took Dr. Hopson's arm and pulled forward a chair where he could set his large black leather bag.

"Hello, Miss Betsy. Open wide." The doctor began his examination by looking down my throat and his glasses reflected away the light so I could not see his eyes. He attended our church, despite its distance from his home, so I knew he had heard of our family troubles, but he said nothing regarding them.

"She appears the picture of good health." He gave his assessment with a puzzled frown. "She was most likely the victim of fainting. Did you eat your supper, Miss Betsy?"

"I did, sir," I replied, confused as to why exactly he was there.

"Take these smelling salts." He rummaged in his bag, placed a packet in my Mother's hand, then lowered his spectacles before giving over his advice. "I would prescribe less excitement for the girl." He looked up at the Reverend and my parents as though he wished to scold them for rousing him from his bed late at night and forcing him to ride through the dark for no discernible cause.

"Excitement was not the cause of this," Father disagreed.

"Pray, know you the cause, John Bell?" The doctor stood tall before him and Father was forced to sigh and bow his head.

"I know not the cause. I know only she did suffer."

"Yet, I have examined her and found her fine, of robust constitution even, and surely, this must be some excitement for the girl, the sheer numbers gathered at your home this evening." He looked briefly about the parlor. "'Tis late for a young girl, or an old man." He nodded to the Reverend and frowned at the assembly without saying more. Father and the Reverend exchanged a glance, but neither spoke.

"Have a cup of tea before departing, Dr. Hopson. What news have you of Mrs. Hopson? I trust she is keeping well?" Satisfied I was indeed no longer in danger, Mother took Dr. Hopson's arm and led him to the dining table. Father and the Reverend did not move. They stared down at me as if my body held some hidden clues to what they wished to know, but did not know, and Father shook his head, dismayed.

"I must take our Betsy to bed." He scooped me off the floor, curling my body to his chest with great strength.

"But, Jack . . ." The Reverend looked as if he wished he had not spoken, but could not help himself. "Are you certain you are able?" I thought he was concerned Father had consumed too much whiskey to carry me.

"I am able as always, Reverend." Father lifted me up, grunting, and I closed my eyes against the Reverend's worried concern, limply allowing Father to carry me upstairs without speaking. I heard Reverend Johnston's footsteps, and then his voice as he joined Dr. Hopson, my mother and brothers in conversation in the dining room, far away. Father lay me down on top of my quilts and shut my door, so I knew he intended to spend some special time with me.

"Darling daughter . . ." His breath stank of sour whiskey as he bent over me, and I turned away, so his whiskers scratched against my cheek. "Let me help you with your nightclothes." He rolled me onto my side so I faced the wall and he made room for himself on my bed. He untied my smock while I held my breath, as anxious as I had been on many dark nights previous, while I waited for the jerking of my braid and the slaps across my face. Father's callused fingers walked across my ribs, undoing all my stays. "I find our trials are most disturbing to my soul." He cupped his hand gently around my breast. "And you are a young woman now," he sighed and pushed his hips against my bottom. "Give me refuge in your loving ways, Betsy, though it must not be as it was, still, darling daughter, you are a great comfort to me." He placed his heavy hand on my hipbone and pulled me flat. Father's breath was hard to face and I did not feel capable of satisfying his desire for comfort, but I feared the absence of his love much more than I feared his unwanted touch. I wished I could leave my body as I did when the Spirit spoke, but that power was no more under my control than the Being itself.

In the morning, I awoke feeling weak and quite worn out, but Mother had decided to set up the spinning wheel in the parlor and make it her day's business to occupy my hands and mind with instruction in manipulating the cards, the wool and spindle.

"Betsy dear, not like that, try this." Mother was patient and soft-spoken with her teaching, but I knew myself to be more adept with a needle and thread, and my heart was not in the lesson. My breaking cards would not separate the fibers, and my fine cards made lumps instead of rolls. Mother had already filled a corn shuck spindle on the wheel. I sighed as she passed it to me for inspection. I felt I could not do it. I wished Martha and Jesse had decided to stay on at our house so I might have an excuse to sew instead of learn, but they were occupied at their own home. I imagined Martha out-of-doors, planting her kitchen garden. I wondered what Mother would say if I suggested we put the spinning wheel aside and plant some beans. Averting my eyes from the spindle to the parlor window, I was rewarded to see a visitor walking up our path.

"Isn't that Josh Gardner, frail Elsa's son?" Mother set the unspun wool in her hands on her lap, following my gaze. We had been at it for several hours with little progress, and I believe she too was grateful for the interruption.

"It is," I said, fumbling with the balls in my lap, ashamed to be wearing my plainest cloth work dress. Mother tilted her head to the side, inquiring.

"I wonder why he's calling?" She left to greet him at the door and I busied myself wrapping the spindle, attempting to appear as though I was well experienced with it. Josh Gardner had been in the back of my mind since that day long ago when we played tag at school, shortly after the Spirit's arrival. There was something about the curl of his lip when he said my name that caused me to catch my breath and grow warm inside. I thought of what Martha had said, how I would soon find my love, and although I did not look my best I hoped to impress Josh in some way. Mother ushered him directly to the parlor.

"Miss Betsy Bell, we have a caller, young Joshua Gardner." Josh was already the height he would stand as a full-grown man, which was almost as tall as our front door. His dark hair coiled around his cheekbones like the twists of rope he'd used tying up his horse. I met his eyes only briefly, but I saw they were gray as a dark summer sky when it's hot and holding back rain. I stood to curtsey and forgot the full spindle on my lap. It struck the floor and came unwound, rolling a white line of new-spun wool from me to him. I felt my cheeks grow red hot with embarrassment.

"Hello, Betsy," he smiled, most warm.

"Will you have some cake and tea with us?" Mother distracted him from watching as I rolled the yarn.

"I'd be honored, Mrs. Bell, but take no trouble on my account. I call to ascertain your daughter's welfare and I bear a book from Professor Powell for her long days at home." He withdrew a thin green book from the satchel over his shoulder.

"How kind of you. I'll fetch refreshments for us all." Mother excused herself and I directed Josh to take a seat, surprised when he chose Father's. I settled across from him in Mother's chair beside the unlit hearth and it felt odd indeed to sit that way with him.

"How do you fare, Betsy?" He leaned toward me with great concern, setting the Professor's book on the floor with disregard so I knew it was not his real reason for calling. "I hear say you were cast down in a fit last night by your evil menace." His straightforward nature pleased me greatly.

"And yet, I have no memory of it," I answered.

"At school they say it is a witch or demon that attacks you.

Would it were a dragon, and I, its princely slayer!" Josh spoke with passion but wore a wide smile on his face, and the image of him armed and dueling with a mythic beast did make me giggle.

"Would it were so!" I encouraged him, smiling, but quickly sobered. "I can tell you of what led to my unconsciousness . . ." I looked at my hands, still holding the roll of wool, and I remembered the words of God uttered by the faltering voice of the phenomenon. *We see not our signs.* It was enough to remove the smile from my lips, but Josh was such a sensitive soul he put his hand up to stop my speech, and leaned forward.

"Betsy, do not torture yourself further by speaking of it," he begged me. "Might we take a stroll by your stream?"

Mother entered the parlor and I saw by her frown she had heard his request.

"Please, Mother, we will be so careful and when I return I will have new energy for the spinning." Mother studied my face and for certain she was thinking of the cake already cut in the kitchen, as well as how improper it was to allow me unchaperoned with a young man out-of-doors.

"You may go," she agreed, recognizing I suffered experiences which circumvented all etiquette, "but ask Richard and Joel to join you. Walk where you will, but tarry not over long for you must return to the house for your cake."

"We will not fail in that, Mrs. Bell." Josh smiled with polite enthusiasm and his fine manners impressed me.

"Most likely it will do Betsy's constitution a world of good." Mother spoke aloud her thoughts, opening wide the door for us. Richard and Joel were engaged in a game of ball under the pear trees, but they were fast in running to join us. We set out walking to the stream in conversation.

"Which of you can skip a stone the farthest distance?" Josh was an only child and knew not the joys of a large family, but he was ever so friendly with my little brothers.

"I can!"

"No, me! You'll see!" They raced ahead of us, eager to find the best flat rocks to show Josh their abilities. The elms were in full leaf and the wild iris and sassafras bloomed on the banks, filling the lush midday air with their fresh scent. There was no wind reminding me of evil and I was enjoying myself, picking out a path through the grass, listening to Josh tell of his adventures out rabbit hunting with Alex Gooch. I felt we were in our own private world, secluded in the forest, and it was so much the better world. Josh was describing the rabbits jumping in the field like popping corn when I slipped on some slick moss and he caught my arm, preventing me from falling to the ground.

"Careful as you go, Miss Betsy." He steadied me and the kind concern in his touch filled my heart with excitement. I was sad when he politely dropped my elbow as we reached the stream. Suddenly, I wanted to tell him about the way I'd felt alone in my bedroom, before the Spirit spoke. I wanted to tell him how I had known beforehand what would occur. I sensed he would try to understand, but I couldn't find the words. He carried on with his stories, lighthearted and cheerful, and I gave myself up to listening, allowing laughter to flow from my soul like the water flowing beside us, careless and calm, held fast by the red mud of its banks.

the spirit disturbed

Josh's visit was a great comfort to me and I thought of it often during the following weeks of isolation I endured. I attended the Easter sermon with my family but other than that grand outing, Mother continued to keep me at home, where I spent long days engaged in chores and tasks she insisted be performed, though they seemed meaningless to me. The days passed quite slowly, and the only surprise in them was how I had begun to look forward to their closing, for as the Spirit used its energies to develop its speaking ability, the violence against us was growing less.

The Being had continued its established pattern of arriving after the supper hour, when the evening lamps were lit, with a rush of cold air and various noises, including knocks on the walls, splitting bed frames and gulping swallows of air. Yet, it wasted no time in blows but cast me down unconscious straight away, beginning its vociferous imitations, repeating phrases of Scripture previously recited by the Reverend and Preacher Justice in our home. The fainting was nowhere near as painful to me as the nightly slaps and jabs and pulling of my hair had been, for I quickly learned to prepare myself for the loss of breath by closing my eyes, and relaxing all the muscles in my body so I might not be further injured if it chose to thrash my limbs about the floor. No one suggested calling Dr. Hopson again. In this matter the Reverend and Calvin Justice had joined forces. They had instructed Mother and Father to trust in the Lord, for He would make certain that I would survive the fits.

The Reverend's and the Preacher's amazement at the visitation's ability to speak at all was quickly giving way to overwhelming curiosity regarding what the force did mean by speaking. It could mimic the Reverend Johnston's cadence so accurately, it was difficult to believe it was not himself. One evening, he insisted Father cup a hand over his mouth and search for evidence of ventriloquism, but Father found no such thing. Not that he expected to. On the next evening, the voice adopted Calvin Justice's passionate tenor, as if to prove its versatility, and it read with eloquent force. When the Being finished its talks, it left and I awoke, whereupon I was told of its antics.

A new interest in the force was growing inside of me, for I enjoyed puzzling out the meaning in its recitations as much as anyone, especially since I was not privy to them. I was amazed to hear how the amorphous and intangible violence now parlayed the words of God while I slept unconscious, and I hoped Mother was correct when she said the Being was clearly altering itself into a new personality with a range of aspects beyond evil. Nevertheless, I remained uneasy as I scooped fish guts from the bucket to fertilize the garden and sewed through my afternoons, for despite its new regularity of action, I knew from experience what troubled us was entirely unpredictable.

One lovely spring night, the Reverend Johnston and Calvin Justice and my family were gathered in the parlor in our customary places discussing our supernatural visitation.

"Its tone reminds me of the marvelous talking bird we witnessed at the fair of Knoxville years ago. Do you recall it, children?" I closed my eyes and breathed the fresh night-blooming stock and the scent of Mother's roses, heavy in the cooling air, drifting in the open windows. I had a picture in my mind of being small and craning my neck up to look at a large black carriage. There was a man standing tall before it with a wildly colorful bird on his shoulder, but I could not remember hearing the creature speak. I looked to Drewry and John Jr. to see what they recalled, but they had their eyes closed, and I could not tell what they pictured in their minds.

"If a bird can learn to speak, what of other lower forms?" The Reverend Johnston pursed his lips in open inquiry and I suspect he wished to discover if the Being could do more than repeat Scripture to him. Could it speak for itself? As his enthusiasm for the entity had grown, so had his Bible. I saw the leather binding of it strained to hold the many parchment notes he had stuffed within it.

"This form is low indeed, Reverend," Father said. He did not look well. His brow was twisted down with ever growing concern. "Plead with the Lord, Reverend, on our behalf, plead that this demon would trouble us no more." Father let no opportunity pass him by to remind the Reverend of what he hoped was his true purpose in the matter.

There was a general rustling of clothing as everyone sat up, in a position of alert meditation. I bowed my head, beginning to concentrate on my own breath, filling my lungs with the scent of flowers and my mind with peace. This was not as difficult as it had been previously, for I was not frightened of feeling nothing. I listened for the Reverend's reading but before he could begin, cold air filled the room and I experienced a swirling of images, including the hearth where there was no fire filled with sparks, before I fell into unconscious darkness. When I awoke, I was lying with my belly and cheek pressed against the parlor rug and my toes touched the smooth wood of the floor.

"Who are you and why are you here?" the Reverend Johnston demanded, irritating me, for I felt I was just waking up from a too short nap, when into the cold silence I heard the voice distinctly reply.

I am a Spirit; I was once very happy, but I have been disturbed.

"Look, Jack, her eyes are open." Mother kneeled beside me, her face concerned. I wished to tell her, do not be afraid, for I am well, but I found I could not force myself to speak. I struggled to move my tongue but it was as if my mouth was frozen still. I closed my eyes. For a moment I felt it was speaking only to me, expressing my own true feelings: I once was happy, but I had been disturbed.

"Mark its words!" The Reverend was excited.

"They are the first not taken from the Scripture," Calvin Justice whispered.

"What do you mean?" the Reverend Johnston asked the air.

I am a Spirit; I was once very happy, but I have been disturbed.

It repeated the phrase once more, and I heard it, but pretended to be sleeping, as I could not speak of what it called to mind, an ugly incident our family had hoped would remain forever forgotten. With my body frozen stiff as my voice, I recalled it fully, measuring the import of the Spirit's words.

Years ago, Father and the slaves had cleared a plot of thistles and brush up on the plateau at the northern boundary of our land above the river and in carrying out the work, they came upon a small mound of what appeared to be graves. Father surmised the site was an Indian burial ground and gave orders to work around it. A few days later, Vernon Batts came calling to our home, as at that time he was trying to make a friend of Drewry. Together the two boys went out to hunt down the spot of the graves, hoping to find some relics the Indians were thought to bury with their dead. When they reached the mound, Drew had suggested they leave well enough alone, as the graves did not seem fanciful up close, but Vernon maintained they would have to look inside them to be certain. Drewry had foolishly agreed and they had proceeded to scatter the rocks and dig up the earth, and in the process, they disinterred the bones. There was nothing of value in the grave but Vernon did not wish to leave empty-handed. He had removed the jawbone from a skull and carried it back to our house, devising an elaborate plan to scare Richard and Joel and myself. I was sewing in the parlor when they ran in, wildly excited. I had seen Vernon slip on Mother's clean and polished wood, whereupon the jawbone flew from his hand and struck the wall with such force a tooth was knocked loose, and it disappeared from sight through a crack in our floorboard.

Unfortunately for Drewry, Father had been passing through the house at that very moment and hearing the scuffle he had entered the hallway and demanded a full account of their doings. Once informed, he had reprimanded both boys severely. Vernon was sent home and Drewry was taken to the barn for a whipping. Father sent Dean to take the jawbone back to the grave and he was instructed to replace the bones that were disinterred and told to make certain the rocks were piled high to protect the graves from future marauders. The following year, Father had allowed the thistles to reclaim the area.

"She is waking now," Mother said. I had opened my eyes but remained still. As I focused on Mother's cotton dress I realized she had moved my head onto her lap. She stroked the hair off my forehead and I felt as though it was true, I was waking from a long and restful sleep though I was unaware of having slept at all.

"It has departed." The Reverend shook his head with some consternation and his silver hair fell in front of his ears. I felt sorry for him, none the wiser on his mission.

In the morning, once the Reverend and Preacher Justice had departed, our family sat all together at the table, discussing the Spirit's meaning in using the word *disturbed*. The same recollection of the lost tooth had visited all of us. Drewry, brave soul that he was, suggested perhaps our family troubles had been brought about by his own thoughtless and horrible mischief from that day long ago.

"I have thought it over and I must speak of how it seems not right." Drewry set his elbows firmly on the table and raised his eyes to Father. "I cannot understand," Drewry said nervously, "*why,* if the Spirit belongs to the bones I did disturb, *why* has it come to settle at our home rather than Vernon's, since Vernon was the one who plundered the bone from its grave?"

"It would come here, Drewry, searching for the tooth it lost!" Richard was on my left and as he spoke I turned to him with great concern. Did he not realize our father was unaware of this significant detail?

"What say you, Richard? What tooth?" Father set his spoon beside his bowl.

"It was wrong in every aspect—" Drewry began his explanation but once it was revealed how the Indians' tooth had fallen under our house Father became enraged. Slamming his fist down on the table, he ordered Drewry out to the barn. I squeezed Drew's arm as he stood, for I saw beneath his mask of stoicism he was crumbling inside.

"Father, I would have you know I do repent that incident more than any other from my short lifetime and if I could but live that day again, never would it be the same."

Mother looked as if she might cry, as it was sad for her to hear her son's repentance, but she said nothing aloud. It was useless to dissuade Father from implementing punishment once he had decided on it. We all knew it was better not to speak. As Drewry left the room, Father rose and went not directly to the barn as I expected, but instead into the hallway. Removing his short knife from his belt he stuck its sharp end into a crack between two floorboards, meaning to pry it up right then, with his bare hands. He exerted all his effort and though I expected it was an impossible task he had set himself since our floor was well laid, I did not say a word.

"This floor is solid as they come," Father grunted with frustration, unable to loosen it. John Jr. rose and stood behind him, waiting for the instructions he correctly sensed would be forthcoming. Mother, Richard, Joel and I sat at the table holding our breath, unable to touch the grits and fresh milk in our bowls. When he had exhausted the possibility of removing the board with his knife and hands, Father sat back on his heels. "Fetch Dean up to the house, John Jr., and the crowbar and the claw hammer," he ordered.

Father spent the rest of the morning disassembling that section of our floor. Our hallway was demolished, board by board, and the creak and split of the wood coming up induced terrible fear in my heart, as I associated the sound with the previous violence of the Spirit. I remained seated at the table, but Richard and Joel moved to sit above the action on the stairs. I expect they wished to jump down and play under the house, but they were too frightened of Father's anger to ask if they might. Father himself climbed down through the open floor when it was large enough to do so and stood firmly on the cold earth exposed below. Dean had brought the fine rake and Father combed the dirt carefully, but he found nothing.

"Lucy, get the sifter," he commanded, and I saw Mother frown.

"Goodness, Jack!" She shook her head all the way to the kitchen as if she thought his was a foolish pursuit, but she brought the sifter to him with no further remark. I followed her example and kept a silent vigil, but moved to the parlor so I might engage my hands at mending and have an excuse to look away from the consternation on Father's features as he sifted the dirt beneath our house, cup by cup. He kept at it all the day, but he did not find the missing tooth.

"If ever a tooth did fall here, the earth has claimed it for its own." He climbed from the hole defeated, and after John Jr. and Dean had helped him replace the boards, it was near time for supper.

"Betsy, fetch your brother," he looked to me, wiping dirt from his cheek with a white muslin cloth Mother gave to him. He apparently had no energy left for whipping Drewry, who had waited all day in the barn.

"Tell him make haste to return to the house and to his room, where he might pray to God for forgiveness for his sins." I hurried to the stables, relieved to be outside, for I had not known the day was so lovely. The sun was soon to pass behind the trees and the land glowed with the pink goodbye kiss of day. The grass seemed greener and the air more still and I heard the whippoorwills starting their evening song. Despite my relief at being out-of-doors, I felt a tingling fear, walking alone down the path, and I ran the final yards to the stable barn, throwing open the door when I reached it. A group of flies, warmed to buzzing, spun about my head, and I saw Drewry pacing through the dusty straw littering the rough barn floor, his eyes downcast and his face pale from fear.

"Father has not the heart for whipping, Drewry. All the day he has searched for the tooth and found it not. He instructs you to your room to pray for forgiveness for your sins." When Drewry stopped his movements and turned to face me, his features were without the joy and relief I expected.

"Dear sister, do you know why we are so cursed?" His face seemed to crumble and he stepped forward clutching me to him in a hard embrace. In the troubled lines around his eyes I saw my own inner feelings and I struggled not to give in to tears.

"At least Father's crop will not be laid across your backside," I said meekly, squeezing my arms around his waist in an effort to console him.

"If all my sins and yours, sweet sister, and all the sins of every one of us within our family were combined and offered up to God, along with all our resolutions *never to sin again,* what would be the outcome? More of the torture we have received as good, God-fearing Christians?" Drewry had clearly thought about it in the day. "Tell me, Betsy, what horrific crime has any one of us indulged, that we should be singled out for such punishment?" Drewry's hands gripped my back and reminded me of Father undoing my stays. "I do believe what haunts us here has naught to do with God," Drew continued, "and God's forgiveness of our sins has naught to do with our continued torment." I could not answer him and though it was blasphemous to do so, I well understood the feelings he did voice, for the injustice of our suffering weighed heavily on us all.

"We will be transfigured by our affliction," I said, repeating a phrase I'd heard the Reverend say to Father. I tried to utter it with hope for a positive transformation in our future, but I too was filled with dark foreboding thoughts. We remained standing together as the last rays of sunlight filtered like the long fingers of God through the cracks in the barn siding. The last pure beams of light fell well short of our two figures, and as we gazed, it disappeared entirely.

Several nearly identical nights of Scripture recitations followed, then passed away, so many I lost count, for the only inconstants were each evening our home held a different configuration of callers from around the district, as the word spread regarding the Spirit's abilities. The Thorns and the Porters came, and the Polks, whom we did not know well, came from the east and brought old Mr. Harris and Mr. Gooch. They witnessed deeply engaging religious talks in place of the violence of before, but all that was discovered was only that no one could compete with the Spirit's pious knowledge. No one could successfully argue with it. The Being could give correct interpretations of the Bible passages, and it could recite more than one translation, as well as patiently inform the community which verse was most authentic and original.

"This is a most unusual parlor game," old Mr. Harris concluded when he left our house and I thought it was an accurate description for those evenings spent indulging the Spirit's intellectual development, amid the rush and whir of turning pages.

Before long it had impressed everyone with its mastery of Scripture, and then abruptly the Being grew bored with theology and turned to mischief. It began to gossip, tattling fervently on all members of our community. It told how Mr. Thorn had fallen asleep in church during Reverend Johnston's Sunday sermon, and it accused Sarah Ellison of regularly cheating Thorn's country store by filling her sack with five pounds of flour while only paying for three. Calvin Justice recalled how the Spirit had spoken of truth, *whatsoever he shall hear, that shall he speak,* and he suggested the purification of our souls through upright moral behavior was perhaps the visitation's true intent and meaning, but I did not believe it was so. Even with our daily sins and trespasses, I felt our souls were infinitely more pure than the Spirit's intent.

Toward the end of April the days had lengthened so it was not necessary to light the lamps until well after supper. We had the windows open all through the house and I was in the kitchen helping Mother and Chloe prepare two trays of tea for our guests. The Randolphs were our callers and they had brought their cousin Clara Lawson with them. Though she was many years younger than Mother, Clara's husband, George, had recently passed away and made her a widow.

"Smell the roses and the charlock, Betsy," Mother said as she shook the tea cloth out the back door of the kitchen.

"We are privy to one sweet spring," Chloe said, and she held her nose high, looking out at Mother's garden.

"Let us add fresh flowers to the tray." Mother took my hand and pulled me down the path past the blooming orange calendula to her bed of roses. We had no basket and she bade me hold my skirt up so she might gently place the thorny roses there as she cut them from the bush.

"Observe perfection in these blossoms, Betsy." Mother smiled at me and touched my hand. "Striving not, they are an example of beauteous nature unto the Lord."

"They are flowers, Mother." I sighed, wishing to accomplish the task and return to have a slice of Chloe's custard pie, but Mother frowned at me and I realized I had given the wrong response. She felt compelled to correct me.

"Elizabeth, think on it. The Lord has given us perfection in His nature, that we might strive to emulate such beauty. Pray, you shall one day blossom to such perfection as this rose." She clipped a stem and tossed it so the thorn pierced the plain cloth fabric of my skirt. I looked at the growing pile of blossoms, noticing the petals curled like lips, the edges darker than their centers, like real mouths. If they could speak, what would they reveal of beauty and perfection? The last light of day touched the garden and I sensed someone near, watching. The bright tinkle of Clara's laugh fluttered from the house sounding like a spoon dropped accidentally in its saucer and beyond it the crickets and katydids screamed, night has come, night has come.

"That's plenty," Mother said and stopped her clipping. She looked around, listening carefully, as if she too felt the Presence in the air.

"Mother, do you feel the Spirit?" I was frightened, but Mother turned me toward the house and spoke calmly.

"Yes, Betsy, I feel the Spirit. The Spirit of the Lord and the Spirit of the roses, and the Spirit of the katydids too, for all living things are Spirit."

The kitchen was warm and reassuring and we carried the trays into the parlor to serve our guests their tea. The Rev-

erend cleared his throat and was about to start his reading
when a clatter of stones fell down the stairs and the room became cold as a cave in winter.

I would speak to you of an ugly thing.

"Speak not, but return from whence you came." Father
was ever vigilant with his requests.

_I would speak of adultery, and charge within this room there
are some partaking of it._

A general gasp of shock, expressed by a sharp inhalation
of breath, swirled about the parlor, as this was a most serious
accusation.

"Charge thee before God?" Reverend Johnston narrowed
his eyes and looked keenly at the Randolphs and Clara Lawson. "For He is all knowing and all seeing in such matters."

"How does a demon charge before God, good Reverend?"
Thomas Randolph looked to Father for support.

_Speak not, Old Sugar Mouth! In this purpose, I am the tri-
bunal._

A strange and most disturbing silence followed.

"Old Sugar Mouth, what does it mean?" the Reverend
Johnston mused, hugging his Bible to his belly, frowning. I
saw Father look away and smile slightly and I remembered I
had heard him say to Mother our Reverend did indulge the
sweeter words of the Lord, as he did the fat corn cakes.
Thomas Randolph shifted his feet as if he was uncomfortable
in his position and I saw Clara look to him, but sideways
without turning her face. Abruptly, I knew what the Being said
was true, plain as if it spoke into my ear alone. Clara Lawson
was engaged in a romantic tryst with her cousin Alice's dear
husband!

"How can you berate so good a man?" Mother rebuked the
voice.

The wicked boasteth of his heart's desire, the covetous blesseth himself and abhorreth the Lord.

"Dear Lucy, I feel most suddenly unwell." Clara stood, nervously smoothing the folds from her skirt.

"It is common to feel unwell in the presence of our visitation." Father turned to her with reassurance.

"You shall spend the night with us, Clara." Alice Randolph stood and took her arm and Mr. Randolph also rose.

The wicked are snared in the work of their own hands.

"'Tis not wise to ride when you are not sound." Mother was concerned. "We have pallets and plenty of beds." She followed Clara, who hurried from our parlor attempting to fetch her cloak. "What ails you, Clara? I will make you a special tea."

I turned in time to see Clara trip and stumble on the pile of rocks at the foot of our stairs. Her lithe form fell heavily onto the hallway floor.

"Clara! Are you hurt?" Mr. Randolph was quicker to her side than Mother or Alice, and I saw Clara raise fearful eyes to focus on his face.

Let thy sentence come forth from my presence, behold the ways of the wicked.

At this Clara fainted into unconsciousness and Mother and Alice Randolph kneeled beside her.

"She must not be moved," Mother said as she lifted Clara's hand to feel her pulse.

"Indeed she must! It is the evil of this house that makes her ill!" Mr. Randolph was quite upset.

"I have smelling salts . . ." Mother rose to fetch them from the kitchen but Mr. Randolph ignored her.

"Open the door, Alice!" he commanded his wife, and we

watched him cradle Clara's limp form to his chest. He carried her out onto the porch.

"I believe we will depart," Alice said hastily, grabbing her cloak and Clara's from the pegs. The Spirit slammed the door after them, letting loose a malicious laugh.

The wages of sin is death.

"Judge not, lest you be judged . . ." The Reverend's eyes were downcast and he was disturbed and Mother stood helplessly gazing at the shut door.

Be quiet, Old Sugar Mouth, for you know nothing of it.

Mother had placed the cut roses in a blown glass vase on the table beside the tea tray and their perfume sweetness filled the air. I breathed deep their luxurious scent, pitying poor Clara, for though she had a friendly disposition, the Spirit clearly felt unkindly toward her, and the natural outcome of the Being's dislike would undoubtedly be great tribulation for her. I did not suspect it could be greater than my own. I realized I had witnessed the entire exchange without being made to suffer pain or unconsciousness, and I wondered as I fell asleep that night, Was there any meaning to the Being's actions?

I do not know who first repeated the Spirit's accusation, I know *I* did not, but perhaps it was destined to be known, for only a few days later Alice Randolph came calling alone, intent on speaking with Mother.

"Hello, Mrs. Randolph!" I heard Richard greet her from the bottom of the hill where he was playing. It was wash day and I was hanging the bed linens on the line that ran beside the garden. "Mother's clipping lavender," Richard informed her, skipping along, accompanying Mrs. Randolph up the hill to Mother's garden. She seemed unaware of him, walking quickly, but Richard carried on talking. "My father has said I might be allowed to bring the corn to your mill, come fall."

"Has he? Are you already so big?" Mrs. Randolph answered, but from her preoccupied tone I could tell she was not at all interested in whether my little brother was of age to be trusted going to the mill. "I shall not forget to look for you," she politely reassured him anyway. They arrived at the edge of the garden and I saw that Richard's face was lit with happy thoughts of a fall paddle in the mill pond, but Mrs. Randolph wore a serious expression.

"Mrs. Randolph, why hello! Might I offer you some lavender to scent your wardrobe?" Mother stopped her work, her sharp iron clippers suspended in midair.

"No, thank you, Mrs. Bell. I call with a delicate matter on my mind." Mrs. Randolph wore a dark woolen cloak dyed from walnut hulls and I saw her fingers were busy with the somber material about her throat. Mother set her tool down and placed the long lavender blooms into a basket at her feet.

"Shall we repair inside and hold our discussion over tea?" she asked her guest.

" 'Tis not necessary, as the matter is brief." I peeked from behind the wet sheet I was pinning and saw Mrs. Randolph appeared to be struggling with the task she had set herself. She was a skilled miller's wife, adept and practical, but clearly she was more comfortable grinding corn than discussing the unpleasant aspects of life. Mother quietly and politely waited for Mrs. Randolph to reveal her trouble.

"Malicious rumors regarding my good husband, Thomas, and my cousin Clara issue from your home." Mrs. Randolph sighed, confessing her concerns. "I come to beg you, please, you must affect this evil gossip, for tarnish grows on our good name!"

"Were it possible to affect this visitation, do you believe that I would not?" Mother touched Mrs. Randolph's arm. "This Spirit is not influenced by me nor by any other."

"There are many who say it speaks the truth!" Mrs. Randolph was close to tears, and allowed Mother to comfort her in an embrace.

"It speaks both lies and truth in equal measure." Mother's countenance was thoughtful as she stroked Mrs. Randolph's back. "No one of good upbringing gives credence to its tales." She moved back a step but kept a reassuring hold on Mrs. Randolph's arms, searching her face, encouraging her to be stalwart. "You are unconsoled," Mother sighed, as if she knew not what to say.

"There are many in these parts with upbringings leaving much to be desired!" Mrs. Randolph pulled her arms free, with some impatience. "This talk is hard for Thomas, and how will it affect our livelihood if folks refuse to use our mill?" She used a corner of her cloak to dab her nose. "And what of our dear Clara? She is of a delicate constitution, as you know. When she was small, often she did spend the winter months in bed, with fevers and the like. Her mother went to an early grave caring for her, and now Clara is widowed so young. I believe she can weather no more suffering." Mrs. Randolph shook her head and I could see she was more deeply concerned for her cousin's welfare than she was for her good name. "If my Thomas consoles her with his company, what is the sin in that?"

"Rest assured, I will do all I can for your benefit and Clara's." I knew Mother's word was good, but what could she do? "Shall we have that cup of tea?" Mother left her basket at the bush and took Mrs. Randolph's arm in hers. They walked together down the path into the house, where I could no longer hear their conversation.

The Spirit did not speak of Clara or the Randolphs again during the week that followed, but Mr. Thorn came with a cartload of supplies, and while he smoked his pipe and shared a drink with Father, Thenny and I were allowed a brief visit.

"Betsy, have you heard of the affair?" Thenny's eyes shimmered with the excitement of her knowledge.

"Of course, for I was present at the accusation." I felt proud of this fact though I knew it was wrong to be boastful.

"The store is buzzing with it! Mother says Alice Randolph ought to tie that Clara flat down on her husband's stone and grind her up like corn to grist." I said nothing in response to this, recalling Mrs. Randolph's worry for her delicate cousin. I had a strong sense of discomfort and foreboding as she went on, describing the gossip at her father's store, and it grew so intense, I changed the topic, asking what she knew of Joshua Gardner.

"Josh Gardner no longer comes to lessons regularly and I suspect the reason is *your* long absence!" This news was a great distraction from Clara and the Randolphs' troubles and we worried over it until Mr. Thorn was slapping the reins of his mares and ordering Thenny to climb in the cart before he left her behind.

It was only one week later when we received the devastating news that Clara Lawson had hanged herself inside her barn. Mr. Randolph had found her swinging from the rafters when he called to give his customary help about her lands. No one was privy to the scene when he cut her down and most certainly considered his own role in her sin, but we were all at church that Sunday when he rose and spoke.

"The evil curse hosted by the Bells attacked our poor Clara, God rest her soul, with gossip and fear, and they put no stop to its vile lies!" Thomas Randolph was a tall man and wiry, and his voice rang strong with angry conviction.

"How say you? What relationship do the afflicted have with what has cursed them?" the Reverend spoke in our defense. "I hesitate to remind you, Mr. Randolph, your cousin Clara sinned against the Lord in taking her own life." Thomas Randolph sat and I saw Alice put her arm around him for comfort, but he shook her off.

"Please, do not further pile our sorrows," Mother begged, standing to face him. "The loss of Clara Lawson is a heavy blow to all gathered here." She meant this most sincerely, but I could see from the hard set of their faces that the Randolphs would forever hold us responsible, despite Mother's woeful insistence we were not to blame.

"Get on with the sermon, Reverend," Old Kate called from the back, for once representative of most of the congregation, who felt the Spirit had simply hastened the affair to its natural conclusion. Most were satisfied to hear of it no more.

We did not attend Clara's funeral, held the next day, but the Reverend Johnston said her eulogy, despite her sin, for he was a kind and forgiving soul. When he arrived at our home that night, he told us it had been a nasty business, for a hard rain had fallen all afternoon.

"'Twas mud they buried the poor girl in." The Reverend shook his head with some sympathy, removing his wet hat and coat in our hallway.

"Perhaps they might have waited . . ." Mother lingered at the door and held her lamp aloft. She stared unseeing at the great drops of water falling on our porch. "God's tears fall hard for poor Clara." The whole incident had greatly disturbed Mother and we were well aware of it, for at suppertime over Chloe's fried chicken and fresh peas, she'd prayed for Clara to enter the Kingdom of Heaven, despite her sins.

"Better it is over and her body in the ground." The Reverend spoke not unkindly, but with resignation. He turned away and entered the parlor, greeting my father, my brothers and myself with a sigh. No one else was present, and though I knew it was only the rain and a symbolic gesture of community respect for the Randolphs that kept the curious away, I felt an overwhelming loneliness at the thought of Clara Lawson's frail bones buried in the ground. I recalled her sewing at a quilting session, her long black eyelashes vivid on the pale skin of her cheek, focused on her work. The Reverend waited for Mother to come away from the door and join us.

"I shall read tonight, as I did at the grave, from Genesis, of Eve's original sin." Mother frowned, but I realized the Reverend needed to atone for having given poor Clara any eulogy.

"God hath said, ye shall not eat of it, neither shall ye touch it, lest ye die."

The Spirit entered the parlor like a small leak of rain speaking softly.

Luce . . .

It whispered Mother's name and brought the scent of wet roses and lavender with it.

Luce, it was her fate and his to be thus severed. The wages of sin is death.

It said nothing to show mercy for Clara's pale skin and long black eyelashes, forever closed and buried under mud. No mercy, and no remorse, entirely culpable as it was.

witch creatures

It rained constantly for one long week and the stream below the house rose to dangerous levels, as did the Red River. Mother kept me sequestered inside, along with Richard and Joel, for she feared one of us might carelessly fall in the water and be drowned, or perhaps she had even greater fears. She did not reveal them, but forced us to do her bidding. The sound of the harsh rain pelting against the roof and window-panes was an incessant drone accompanying the many monotonous chores she set for us. Every morning she had me on my hands and knees beside Chloe, scrubbing the mud tracked in by Father, John Jr. and Drewry off her smooth wood floors. Father and my brothers spent all day along with the hands, working in the wet, digging berms around the fields to protect the young tobacco plants from flooding. I thought the rain would never end and God's tears would fall forever for poor Clara, but finally the clouds extinguished their supply and the night came when the rain did cease.

The next day I went for a walk beyond the stable and the hog pens toward the fields to see the puddles for myself. It was near the dinner hour and as I came around the corner I saw Dean, Father's boss man, standing under the whipping tree, holding forth to the rest of the slaves. They sat on tree stumps and upended germination crates, eating corn cakes, and they looked completely absorbed by his talk. No one noticed me slip off the path and sneak behind the honeysuckle bushes where I could hear what he was saying.

"You all know I was among the folk most pleased when this recent rain did stop, for it had been a week since I could make the journey to visit my Aggie." Dean's wife was called Aggie and she belonged to the Thorns. Her cabin was full of Dean's children, and he usually spent some nights there. "Now, Aggie, superstitious like she is, she thinks it is black magic here happening to the Bells and to protect me she done made a witchball."

"A what?" someone interrupted.

"A witchball. Out a hair from both our heads. She done made it up in a tangle a fur culled off the back of a red fox."

"Lord, whose idea was that?" The woman who spoke smiled and slapped her knee, amused.

"She got the idea for it from Corrine, Old Kate's woman. Aggie made me promise I would carry it and she said it was sure to work to protect me good. So last night, when I saw the rain had done, I set out down the road. I had the witchball in my pocket and my ax in my hand. The moon was waxing so I had some light and I was just at the hill near the poplars when I heard something in the brush and a large black dog come out of the trees."

"Were it Caesar? That farm hound, he always running off," a man with a floppy hat sitting on an upended crate asked curiously, without looking up from the stick he was whittling while Dean told his story.

"No, it were not Caesar, but at first, I was thinking it was, just a wild dog, or a lost dog, so I spoke to it, nice and easy, low and sure. *Hey there, doggie, go on wit' you.*" Dean imitated himself, talking to the dog, but then he changed his tone and imitated the voice of the Spirit. "*Where are you going?* came from the mouth of the dog! I saw it was a witch creature and I done prepared myself for a fight."

"No strong arm can keep away what tortures the masta's family." One of the women brushed crumbs of corn cake off her smock onto the ground. "But here you be, so what did happen?"

"It asked me, *What's that you have in your pocket?* I felt it could see right through my trousers. I said nothing, I got nothing, and it growled and called me out, *That's a lie! You got foxfire wrapped in your wife's hair rolled into a ball just to pester me!* It pawed the ground and I fell to my knees in the mud. I put my hands together and I prayed, Lord Almighty, I been bad, but redeem me now." Dean held his hands aloft in a posture of prayer, but remained standing. The crowd had stopped fiddling and chewing and waited, barely breathing, for Dean to continue. "*Foxfire to pester me!* it kept saying and I talked to it straight. What you want with me? *Give me that ball of yours or I'll turn you into an ass and ride you into the river.*"

At this several of the men laughed nervously, and Dean paused to share a smile with them.

"Lord knows I'd do most anything not to be magicked into an ass and ridden by a demon into the river, so I reached in my pocket and got the witchball, but the damn thing was hot as a coal from the fire! I threw it at the dog and in the air it done swelled to the size of a watermelon and when it struck the road, it burst into flames. The dog moved off then, but I saw it was ready to rip me to pieces."

"Pray to Jesus!"

"How did you survive?"

"The Lord He work in unexpected ways. I was standing there thinking I might meet my maker when all at once I had the memory of the day masta Bell and I chopped the giant oak we used for the cold storehouse door. Whooping like an Injun warrior I charged the creature. I could see pretty good with the light of the blaze and I brought my ax down hard. I hit that dog square in the middle of the head and it split wide open. Blood poured out, then I done seen that dog body leap up and roll over three times before it fell forward right into the flaming ball of fire, and shot up from the ground like a star across the sky. Lord, I never seen such like that! I ran fast as I could all the way to Aggie's door."

"I would stay at home now." The woman who had spoken before shook her head giving this piece of advice.

"But I do love to visit Aggie, and she will form a bad impression if I do not go."

"Rather a bad impression than no you at all!" I recognized Little Bright's sweet voice, filled with concern for Dean, and my eyes watered with unexpected tears. How many lives were to be altered by what tortured us? I ran home and found Mother on the front steps with Chloe shelling peas and before them I repeated all I had heard.

"He said it was a black dog the size of a foal, that could talk and make fire in the road. He said it was a witch creature." I was out of breath from excitement and running, but Mother and Chloe remained calm. Chloe gave me a look as I told the story that made me think she had heard it already from Dean. She expertly split the pods with the sure edge of her nail, and as I caught my breath, resting in my thoughts, a memory of strange winged animals Drewry and I had spied in the meadow years ago came back to me. Had they been witch creatures?

It was around the time when I was only nine and collecting leaves in the woods for the harvest pageant. Drewry and I had gone for a walk beside the meadow and I had been behind him on the path when suddenly he had stopped and pointed into the tall grass, where there were a cluster of unusual creatures. They had appeared to have wings as well as fur and they half hopped, half flew away from us into the woods. Neither of us recognized the animals as any we had seen before, but Drewry had surmised they were probably creatures particular to Father's land. One had spread its wings and turned its furry head to look at us, aware of our presence. Larger than a turkey buzzard, its fur had been white as a snowy jack rabbit's and its tail had swished above the tall meadow grass like a horse tail swishing flies. We had taken off running, low and sneaky, through the tall meadow grass to get closer and then we had heard the flap of wings. When we reached the wooded place where the animals had been, we saw nothing. The grass was not trampled down as it should have been and though we searched the ground, there was no scat, nor fur, nor feather. The wind that day had brought a rain of blood red maple leaves swirling down around us. I remembered playing a game where we tried to catch the leaves, making wishes. We had looked a little longer for the animals, then we had given up and returned home. I had forgotten all about them. Were they witch creatures? Drewry and I had never spoken of them since. I supposed I should find him and ask his opinion before I brought it up, considering how it had gone regarding the tooth. I took a pod from the basket between Mother and Chloe and burst the shell in my palm too quickly so the fat peas inside went bouncing over my skirt and down the steps.

"Careful, dear," Mother said, dropping a handful of her own into the pot. "'Tis Dean's only weakness, his love of a good story," she commented, seeming disinclined to believe the witch creature tale, but later, during supper, I heard her mention it to Father.

"For certain he has made the matter worse with vivid details." Father sighed, leaning his elbows on the dining table. "We'll have no slaves out in the nighttime now." He correctly perceived the effect the attack on Dean would have. The May Day holidays were approaching and it was sometimes necessary with so much work and so many gatherings for the slaves in the district to run messages for their masters after dark. However, after the attack on Dean, none of them would leave their cabins once the sun had set, and all feared the witch creatures in the night.

"We must protect them and ourselves from further harm," Mother insisted, and she asked Father to speak with the Reverend and Preacher Justice about it. He raised the subject that Sunday as soon as the two men settled into their chairs in our parlor.

"You have heard the tales of my man Dean, as trustworthy a slave as ever there could be?" Father said.

"Oh yes, we heard the tales." Calvin Justice pulled his riding gloves off with a snap, and I wondered why he was so dismissive. He had the chair farthest from the window and I saw the last daylight caused his chestnut hair to gleam dark red.

"Witch creatures in the night! Are they varied in their aspect?" The Reverend raised his eyebrows to my Father, expressing his great interest. "What do you think?"

"I think we must ask Dean." Mother set her teacup on the

side table with determination in her attitude. "John Jr., fetch Dean and bid him make haste here to our home." I could tell Mother and Father had already agreed on this course of action, and I was amazed how the conventions governing our lives were falling away. What had seemed unthinkable was now easily practiced. John Jr. rose and left without a word.

"'Tis well we should discuss the matter with your man." The Reverend seemed to look forward to the accounting and leaned back in his chair, opening his Bible to choose the passage he would read.

You would do well to speak to me of Dean's exiguous troubles.

The Being's voice caused all of us to sit up straight as ladder-backed chairs, for it had arrived without warning, bringing with it no noise, or sudden faint, but only a small cold bristle to the air. I shivered, for I was dressed in a spring cotton and I wrapped my arms about my front as much for warmth as for protection from the unknown. Our lamps spontaneously lit.

"Why, thank you for the light, but could you kindly cease to visit us each evening?" Mother spoke the plea softly, with respect and deference. Father twisted in his chair and looked upset with her.

"Be gone, evil demon from Hell! Return to this world no more!"

"Jack, Jack, I would know what it has to say." The Reverend put a restraining hand on my Father's shoulder, and I felt suddenly immensely tired of their petty arguments.

"Tell us, what constitutes a witch creature?" The Reverend directed his voice to the unseen.

You will know when you see one.

"I do not wish to see one!" The Reverend shook his head, smiling as though he shared a cup of whiskey at the still with the Being. "Are there many such creatures in this district, or is it yourself, inhabiting other forms?" He bent forward, inclining his ear around the room, listening for the location of the voice, his perpetual curiosity displayed as vivid as his Bible held against his chest.

They are many and all are me.

"What do you mean?" The Reverend looked at Calvin Justice and my Father, puzzled by the Spirit's bold assertion.

Old Sugar Mouth, you are a potbellied ninny!

Mother gasped at the affront to the Reverend but I wondered how she could expect good behavior from a force so evil in its ways and means.

"Cease your insults in my good home!" Father stood, casting his arms wide as though he might catch the Being and throw it out.

O long-suffering Jack, so it is with you.

"The Lord knows my character." The Reverend stood beside my Father, about to give a patient listing of his own best qualities, accompanied by a statement of his intent to learn the true nature of the visitation, but the Spirit cut him off.

I saw three unclean spirits like frogs come out of the mouth of the dragon, and out of the mouth of the beast, and out of the mouth of the false prophet!

"'Tis Revelation . . ." Calvin Justice remained seated and I observed the line of his mouth was pure concentration. Behind me the door opened and John Jr. arrived with Dean.

I smell a slave in this room!

Dean entered the parlor with his chin set down but his shoulders straight, as if John Jr. walked him to a whipping, a stance uncommon for Dean, as Father certainly had not had the occasion to whip him so often as he found it necessary to praise his skills. He did have an unwashed smell though, for his plain cloth shirt reeked of a hard day's labor.

"Have you appeared as a dog tormenting this Negro who goes by the name of Dean?" The Reverend put on his church voice, interrogating the Being.

I am many things in many places. I am everywhere at once. Know you not the truth of this, Old Sugar Mouth?

"Speak, man, for you are among the good and righteous. In the name of God, tell us, what meets you on the road at night?" Father ignored the Spirit, addressing Dean, encouraging him to tell his tale.

"I met with a black dog what has the witch in it, masta." Dean spoke with his eyes on the parlor floor and I thought how much smaller he looked indoors than when I saw him in the fields.

"What sin stains your footsteps? Why does this creature of the night acquaint itself with you?" asked Calvin Justice. There was a harsh, unnatural tone to his query and Mother looked sharp in his direction.

"I practice religion, suh, there ain't no black magic on me!"

Nay, there is no longer magic on you for I have cast it out! Foxfire to pester me! Get out! Get to the road and dare to raise your ax and strike again!

"O Good Lord God Almighty help me Jesus!" Dean fell to his knees and clasped his hands up toward the sky in an exact imitation of what he'd done on the road in his story. His eyes were shut so hard the wrinkles ran like streams along his upturned face.

"What say you, Spirit?" Calvin Justice maintained an edge in his voice.

Get rid of the slave, for I cannot abide his smell and I will tell you all you need to know of witch creatures in the night.

"Go, Dean, but do not leave this property." Father helped him to stand and Dean began to walk to the door.

"Look! There are marks on his trousers!" Joel pointed to Dean's leg and I saw a patch of cloth was missing. Dean stopped walking and Father raised his eyebrows, waiting for his explanation.

"Suh, last night the dog done come again to me on the road and now he got two heads and both of them full a snapping teeth. I ran fast but he did nip the cloth. But only cloth suh, he got no skin of mine against his teeth." For a moment I saw Dean as I knew him, strong and unafraid.

"Stay home tonight, Dean," Father said again.

"Masta, I can brave the black dog now, for I done seen the worst of it!" Dean trusted my Father and confided in him.

"Perhaps 'tis true, but it is not worth the risk. Stay home and tomorrow we shall send a message to your wife regarding your confinement." Father opened the door, but Dean hesitated and I could see he was thinking of Aggie. Father saw it too, and sighed.

"You can carry the message yourself in the daylight, if you like."

"Thank you, suh, I am most obliged." Dean left and Father bolted the door. He returned to the parlor and the Reverend Johnston was the first to speak, directing his words to the empty air, to the Spirit.

"Tell us more about the witch creatures aforementioned."

I shall.

The loquacious Being changed its tone completely and the cold bristle was replaced by a heavy summer air, so thick I could hardly breathe. It spoke in a soft girl's voice I could not identify as that of any particular youngster.

Amanda Ellison and Gertrude Harris of families to the east of this homestead will soon meet a heron on Kate Batts's pond that is no regular bird.

The girls the Spirit named were known to me. Both attended school and though they were of Richard's age, I could easily see them in my mind. Amanda had a long blond braid, much like my own, while Gertrude's hair waved and curled, and frequently broke loose from its plaits, becoming ringlets around her face.

These girls are playing games together while their fathers speak of business, and tarry at the forge. They wander, a short way, down Piney Woods, then on they go, along the eastern boundary of Old Kate's farm. Their eyes are to the ground, searching for the special cones strewn about the forest floor.

I thought of the many times I had wandered with Joel and Richard in the Piney Woods, the smell of Mr. Ellison's charcoal fire pungent in the air. He shod our horses and had crafted our andiron and grate. I looked to the hearth and listened.

Amanda feels someone watching her, and looking up, she sees the witch creature, a heron, standing in the path ahead. "Hurry, Gerty, hurry. There is a beautiful grand bird," she calls out to her friend.

The Spirit duplicated Amanda's young lilt accurately, and Joel slipped his hand in mine, moving closer to me on our bench.

They chase the lovely heron and its white wings shine in the woods like God's light, beckoning them farther and father on. Many times they think the graceful fowl is settling its feathers, ready for a rest, and their hopes ignite, for they want to be near it, but just as they come upon it, the heron vanishes, reappearing farther on, until the light of the day draws to a close.

They come suddenly to their senses and realize they are deeply lost within the woods. Darkness falls around them and they hear gunshots in the distance, and understand their fathers are firing their rifles, hoping they will hear and make their way toward the sound. They try, but they cannot return. Their progress through the trees is halted by the reaching arms of branches, grasping at their clothes and hair.

The Spirit added the frightening sound of branches scraping together to its recitation.

These girls find a tree large enough to support both their backs. Bravely they lie down together, side by side, to await the morning light. The heron now appears and spreads its great white wings like an angel, covering and sheltering them. The girls sleep peaceful as new babies in a cradle, but just before sunrise, the heron speaks, insisting Amanda must come down to the lake to greet the day, while Gertrude must wait by the tree, as her father will shortly arrive. The girls are reluctant to separate, but the heron waves its wing and Amanda follows. This parting will be their last in this world. By mid-morning Gertrude will be found by the fathers beside the tree, but Amanda will be drowned in Old Kate's pond. They will find her body with her arms spread wide, like the wings of the witch creature heron.

The soft girl voice the Spirit used to tell this story ceased at its end and the more regular tone of the Being returned, taunting Reverend Johnston.

Are you educated on witch creatures now, Old Sugar Mouth? Do you want to know more?

"We have heard enough from you, forevermore! Be gone, you evil teller of tales," Father said, clearly disturbed by the tragic prediction.

You are idiots, and recognize no truth, even when it is before you.

The sound of water lapping at the edge of a lake filled the room, then died away, and I felt the Spirit had left us.

"'Tis likely nothing more than a twisted fairy story," Mother softly reassured Joel and Richard and I noticed both of them had tears in their eyes. I hoped they would not go blabbing it to Amanda Ellison or Gertrude at school, for I immediately thought it best not to give strength to the Being's prophecy by repeating it.

"Should we tell those girls what we have heard tonight? Perhaps they should not be allowed any trips to the Piney Woods." The Reverend clearly felt the opposite approach would be wisest, but Father agreed with me.

"The thing speaks lies, Reverend. Why scare the girls for no reason?" There was a startling knock at the door and we looked about, confused, for it was late for a caller and, since Clara Lawson's suicide, only the Reverend and Preacher Justice had visited us. Mother answered it, admitting Mrs. Batts.

"Hello, Lucy Bell, know ye no creatures accosted me on the road this evening, and I am here to tell you of it." Kate entered the parlor talking, with utter disregard for the assembly gathered.

"Greetings, Mrs. Batts, we are engaged here with serious concerns." The Reverend Johnston frowned at her, looking as though he wished she had not interrupted.

"As I am, Reverend, engaged in the very same serious concerns. I should have been here earlier, but I had to attend to bedding Ignatius, so my girl could easily care for him in my absence. Speak ye of serious concerns . . ."

"Sit, Kate, and tell us your cause to call." The Reverend sighed and we all watched Old Kate settle her massive form onto the edge of a sturdy wooden chair John Jr. brought in from the dining table. She leaned back, straining to reach the pouch she wore about her waist, for it was buried under her folds of fat encased in her plain cloth smock.

"Here," she breathed, yanking something from it. "'Tis the foot of a witch rabbit I shot and killed in your southernmost field, John Bell, this very day. Look, it bears the telltale sign." Kate extended her fleshy palm and we all rose and gathered around to see what it contained. She held a lean hind leg butchered off a white rabbit, marked with an unusual spot of black fur in its center under the pink pads of its toes. Father looked at her grimly.

"How did it happen you were hunting in my field, Mrs. Batts?"

"'Twas less than one hundred yards into your boundaries, Jack Bell, and I had chased it a good mile!"

"You rattle like a bell clapper up a goose's ass." Father was annoyed.

"Jack!" Mother frowned.

"Let me have it, Kate," said the Reverend Johnston. He pushed forward and was about to take it from her hand when she closed her plump fingers over the fur and returned it to her person.

"Nay, good Reverend! This is the foot of a witch creature! It must be buried before morning on the north side of a mossy log."

"You better get on with it then, as the hour grows late." Father turned away from the circle and sat heavily in his chair by his desk, no tolerance of Kate's eccentric ideas in the straight of his back.

"'Twas my intent to share with your good family a charm to ward away what ails you, Jack Bell." Old Kate looked after him, narrowing her eyes.

"Jack, we must not allow our kind neighbors to wander in the woods alone at night," Mother said, crossing the room to stand beside him. She stroked his shoulders, as though she would impart new manners into him.

"'Tis no matter, Lucy, I am adept at my way in the woods." Old Kate leaned back again in the chair, replacing the foot into the pouch about her waist. I saw the Reverend and Calvin Justice exchange a solemn glance, and I understood the mood was such no one there was inclined to laugh at her strange ways. Instead, our experiences were so out of the ordinary that Calvin Justice and the Reverend were prepared to go along with Kate's bizarre ideas.

"We shall accompany you, Mrs. Batts, and facilitate the burial." Calvin Justice politely offered his hand, and Old Kate rose, smiling.

"Let us pray all future witch creatures will be deterred!" Kate called over her shoulder as she and the Reverend and Preacher Justice departed to find a mossy log in the woods.

Father waited until the door was closed behind them, before removing his silver flask from his desk.

"What must we bury to deter Old Kate?" he asked, but clearly he did not expect an answer from us.

The following day, I was sitting in the parlor near the dinner hour, engaged in sewing, pondering Kate's witch creature rabbit. I wished there were someone who might know if Kate's methods and means of protection could have any measurable effect. Looking out the window, I saw the only man who possibly might, dismounting at our horse tie. His arrival was so unlikely, I hesitated and rubbed my eyes. Father was writing in his book of accounts at his desk and I glanced over to him, then jumped up to pull back the heavy brocade curtain so he might see Frank too.

"Father, I believe Frank Miles is calling!"

It was a great coincidence, for Frank Miles the trapper was one of Father's favorite friends, but we saw him rarely, as he lived a nomad, most often encamped in the Great Smoky Mountains trapping coons, badgers, bears and the large river beavers abundant in those parts.

"What luck! It has been some time," Father said and I ran to throw open our door, surprised when Frank reached it how completely his wide girth did fill the space. He set his gun down inside the door, near Father's, and held out his arms for me.

"Hello, Miss Betsy, why, you've grown a foot." Frank hoisted me into the air so easily, I might have been a feather in his hands. He wore a deerskin coat unlike anything I had ever seen, and I reached out to touch the collar of rabbit fur circling under his bushy black beard. He laughed and drew me closer, tickling my face with it. "Aye, and you weigh near as much as a doe!"

"Oh, Frank Miles!" Mother hurried in from the kitchen, wiping her hands on her apron, smiling. "'Tis a joy to hear your voice!"

"Greetings, Miz Lucy, greetings, Jack." Frank shook Father's hand with both of his and Father pulled him forward into an embrace, revealing how much he had missed his friend during our period of torment. Mother readily wrapped her arms about his waist, smiling, then pulled back to admire his coat.

"Where on earth did you get this?"

"'Tis doeskin, and winter rabbit fur. I had an Injun stitch it up for me in trade for a sack of grist this winter." Frank held his sleeve out for us to marvel at both the delicate work of it and at his bravery for trading with the red men. "Yea, Jack, I come to call, though I am still stinking of my winter ways, for yesterday when I arrived in Clarksville I heard serious gossip against your good family name." The mood of merriment and celebration induced by our lively greetings plummeted, and Mother and Father exchanged a look of dismay. "I was standing in the store the unwilling recipient of grievous insults, as men claimed you are haunted by some demon at your farm."

"Say what you heard, good friend, for I would know it," said Father.

"A man, who said he knew you not, but knew a preacher man who knew you, said the Devil has staked a claim on your fair Betsy, so she was thrown about the room despite the strong arms of steadfast men." Frank put his hands on his hips, incredulous, and I was surprised how far behind our experience the gossip in Clarksville was.

" 'Tis true, in part, what you heard said." Father reluctantly shook his head, pained anew by our situation before his friend. "Come share a meal with us and we will tire you with our tales of woe."

"Tell me only how we might put an end to this deplorable affair, for nevermore do I wish to hear a slur against this house!" Frank removed his coat and handed it to Mother and I marveled at the wide leather belt he wore, equipped with three knives of varying sizes, a wound length of silver chain, and a bead-and-feather-embroidered pouch.

"Ah, Frank, would it were possible." Father shook his head, resigned.

" 'Tis possible! How say you? Look about you, man! Yours is the home which comes to mind during my coldest winter nights, for yours is overflowing with righteous living." He smiled warmly at my Mother. "We shall rid your house of evil, and oust it permanently, like vermin to the night." Frank's confidence in his own ability to remedy our situation was a welcome attitude, and we moved to the parlor to discuss various plans and strategies heretofore not mentioned by the Reverend or Preacher Justice. "We shall catch it and roll it in a blanket and put it in the fire so it might burn in Hell where it belongs." Frank's white smile stood out, splitting his black beard like the white stripe on a skunk.

Mother cast an uneasy look to me when Frank began to scheme, wishing to ascertain the resonance such violent thoughts might have on my countenance, but I felt nothing more than pure and delicious excitement at the thought of Frank Miles willing to do battle with the Being.

"Have you ever seen a witch creature, Mr. Miles?" I asked and he nodded his head, quite slowly, in assent.

"Have you seen a *rabbit* witch creature with a black spot on its white left hind foot? And did you kill it and cut off its foot and bury it in a field on the north side of a mossy log?"

Frank threw his head back and laughed as though I'd told the greatest joke he'd ever heard.

"God granted you imagination in abundance, did he not, Miss Betsy!"

"'Twas not my tale, but that of Old Kate Batts!"

"'Tis true, Old Kate did say as much." Mother put her arm around my shoulder and we both laughed with some relief, as Frank clearly felt Old Kate's theory was absurd.

"Has that eccentric woman called often at your home?" Frank grew serious, inquiring.

"Not so often as some," Mother said, shrugging her shoulders. She looked sad thinking back on the many callers we'd experienced. Some had not fared well.

"The Reverend Johnston and the new Methodist preacher, from Cedar Hill, Calvin Justice, they come each evening," Father explained.

"I heard 'twas so. Perhaps the demon is attracted to their spiritual ways . . ." He laughed and I could tell Frank's thoughts in this regard appealed to Father, for he laughed also and called over his shoulder for Chloe to come from the kitchen.

"Go to the field and have Dean deliver this instruction to the Reverend and Preacher Justice. 'Respectfully, we do request you stay at home this evening, for Mr. Frank Miles is at our house and will hold his own with our visitation.'"

"Yes suh." Chloe bowed her head, memorizing the message.

"Tell Dean also, he might surprise his wife this evening, as he likes." Father related Dean's experience with the black dog and Frank laughed until he rumbled like a snoring bear.

"Tonight we shall see what your demon is made of!" He nudged Father's elbow with his own, not at all frightened by the prospect. "I have a brew that will fortify our souls in preparation, Jack." Frank turned to Father. "How say you? Have you strength enough for a hearty draught?"

"Come, Betsy, let us help Chloe with the supper preparations," Mother said, taking my hand as she led me to the kitchen where I did not wish to be. It took near an hour to prepare the succotash of corn and green beans seasoned with bacon and after that Mother found more chores for me. I heard Father and Frank laughing together from the front porch where they had taken out two chairs but I did not see them again until it was time for the meal. I noticed Mother served Frank and Father strong cups of fresh ground coffee with their supper, and when the meal was finished she made certain they each carried another cup of the dark brown steaming liquid with them to their places by the fire.

"Tonight I shall read," Father declared, placing his feet

square on the floor. He leafed through his Bible as he sat down, well satisfied at the prospect of returning to his own routine.

"Darling daughter, come sit beside me . . ." He crooked his finger, inviting me to move.

You shall not!

A rush of air whisked his Bible off his lap and the Spirit arrived before I could rise from my place. His good book struck the rug with a thud, and the incongruent nature of Father tossing the word of God to the ground caused Frank Miles to burst out laughing. Richard and Joel laughed also, relieved to see Frank make light of the Being's antics, but I thought their boyish giggles sounded more nervous than hearty.

"Shhh," Mother scolded them, not amused. She sat down on the bench between them. "The good book is the sacred word of God and we honor it holy as such."

Mr. Miles, you cannot catch me like a common coon!

"You knowest not the mind of a trapper," Frank responded, placid as if the Being were no more than a new acquaintance he wished not to pursue. I was greatly impressed by his calmness. Ignoring its claim, he spoke to Father as though it were not present.

"How fares your crop this year, Jack?"

"The tobacco grows well in all my fields." Father followed Frank's lead and kept his temper, ignoring the Spirit.

The worms grow fat in all his fields!

Frank stood up suddenly, affronted.

"Who are you, demon? Why are you here?"

To wrap you in a blanket and throw you in the fire!

The Being repeated Frank's own scheme in a teasing singsong, revealing it knew of his plot.

"Ho, you should try it, for I doubt you would succeed!"

Frank Miles rolled his large shoulders back, ready for any attack against his person.

"Be careful, Mr. Miles," Drewry spoke, rising from his chair. "We have seen this force flatten the strongest among us." No doubt he was thinking of Dean and the witch dog, and the many nights of violence we had endured before the Spirit started to speak.

"We _have_ no fire this evening, Frank." Mother stood and coaxed him back into his chair, also worried violence would be the natural result of his bravado. "The evening is quite warm enough without it." Frank understood her unspoken meaning and returned his manner to exemplary politeness.

"I should like to shake the hand of a demon, Lucy, for I desire to add the tale of it to my repertoire." I marveled how he used the French with ease.

Why should I wish to touch a man as filthy and odorous as you, Frank Miles? The Being spoke in a soft flirtatious tone to Frank and I wondered what it intended.

"For the same reason I should like to touch your hand. You might tell the tale, how you did stroke the open palm of Frank Miles, Tennessee Trapper Extraordinaire." Beguiling it to respond, he held his hands out, palms open to the ceiling. "Shake my hand, demon, or are you frightened?"

I fear no man.

The Spirit slipped what Frank attested was a delicate and ladylike hand into his own, and as he felt the unbelievable touch of the invisible, his mouth fell open, amazed to find it was more luxurious to him than the softest fur across his fingers.

"You are a velvet lady . . ." Shocked by his experience, Frank grasped at the silk feeling, but the Spirit would not allow him to hold on.

I am all things.

"Be gone, you evil demon, be gone from here this night!" Father rose to stand beside his friend, reminding him it was their purpose to expel the Spirit from our home. Frank lunged forward, flailing his arms wildly through the air, hoping to grasp a piece of the Being, and Father's Bible rose off the floor and struck Frank a hard blow on the back of his head.

Know your traps are full and your Injun friends collect the skins before you.

"Creature, recant your lies for they are foul." Frank rubbed his head and hissed at the Spirit.

Get to your camp if you do not believe it so.

The Being struck him again, this time across his face with Father's Bible, and to see Frank punching and flailing at the good book, his wild black hair flying about his face as his cheeks grew bright red, caused me to laugh out loud.

"Elizabeth!" Mother was annoyed, and looked to Richard and Joel, who were forced to cover their mouths with cupped hands to keep from giggling. It was uncannily amusing to witness Frank wrestling the holy word of God.

"Enough!" Father managed to wrench the Bible from the force that held it to Frank's face and with great effort he pulled it to his chair and sat on it. His jaw was clenched in anger and the wheezy laughter of the Being filled the room, abruptly ceasing at its highest pitch. We were silent, realizing it had gone from us. I recovered myself quickly, no longer inclined to laugh.

" 'Tis a foe to be reckoned with." Frank wiped his brow with the back of his hand and remained standing. I glanced at Drewry and John Jr. near the door and saw disappointment on their faces. Drewry cleared his throat before he spoke.

"It has told the truth of the future in the past, Mr. Miles."

"Eh? How say you, young man?" Frank raised a bushy eyebrow at my outspoken brother and tilted his head. John Jr. and Father looked annoyed with Drew, but I sympathized with his desire to share his knowledge.

"The Being does sometimes speak the truth." Drewry sighed and I thought of Clara Lawson, and I expect everyone present, except Frank, did likewise.

"I would concur with our good son on this subject," Mother added.

"The Injuns know not where my traps are laid." Frank Miles looked to my father, but Father turned from him and crossed the room to his desk without speaking on the matter.

"The Injuns fear the wrath of Frank Miles as much as any white man," Frank declared as he straightened his back and squared his shoulders, cutting a formidable pose.

"Share this flask, my friend." Father withdrew it from his desk.

"Do they know you are off the mountain?" Mother was concerned and stared bleakly at the untouched cup of coffee Father had placed on the side table.

"Oh yea, they know when I am gone." Frank scowled and took the whiskey.

"Perhaps you should return and discover if it speaks the truth." Joel tilted back his golden curls and spoke aloud the obvious suggestion with childish innocence. His feet dangled above the floor and we watched them swing, waiting for Frank's answer.

"And will you come along, little man?" Frank smiled and rustled Joel's hair with the same hand that had felt the Spirit's touch. I could see he had not planned to make his journey back so soon.

"Will you be departing?" I knew I should not ask forthright, but I could not climb the stairs without knowing, I so enjoyed Frank's presence in our home. Even though he was dejected, merriment seemed never far from his grasp.

"'Tis likely that I shall, Miss Betsy, but sooner than a weasel down a hole, I will return to prove your demon is a liar."

Verily you shall return, Frank Miles, but not on the day of your imagining.

The lamps flickered and the candles sputtered out and the boys and I froze in our movements toward bed, surprised by the Being's return.

"Look, it's lightning!" Frank squinted at the window confused by the flashing of the ground.

I am no liar, though I have tales to make the best of your small stories fit only for the children's ears.

Mother pulled Joel closer, covering his ears with her hands in case the Being might begin to tell the tales of which it bragged.

"Please, I beg you, torment the children not one day longer. Say farewell to us this very night." Mother spoke to the Spirit but looked to Frank Miles with some desperation, as if she hoped he could take the Being with him on his travels.

No, Luce, I will stay awhile. And you, Frank Miles, you shall return here at my whim, for I do like you.

"I do not like you, demon!" Frank responded with honest disgust. "Your hand is smooth, alas, your curse is hard on John Bell and his fine family."

You know naught of it, and you bore me when you dabble with convention. It hangs like an ill-stretched skin on you. Yet, you inspire me to share a song.

We were silent as the Being sang a hymn with such sweet timbre an angel from Heaven could not have equaled its tone.

Come my heart, and let us try,
For a little season,
Every burden to lay by,
Come and let us reason.

What is this that casts you down?
Who are those that grieve you?
Speak and let the worst be known.
Speaking may relieve you.

We were astonished to hear it possessed so lovely a voice, certainly unlike any I had ever heard before. It flowed over us as if we were stones in the river, caressed by waters of smooth serenity. I felt I would sleep well and soundly in my bed, lulled into sweet dreams by the music.

"How beautiful!" Mother expressed sincere praise unto the Being, for failing to make it depart, she wished to encourage its best nature.

I shall sing for you another.

The Spirit responded like a child made bold, strengthened by adult attention.

"I shall listen no longer." Father was irritated and stumbled clumsily across the parlor. "I refuse!" His gait was unsteady and slurred with whiskey and Mother rose, to take his arm and help him, but he jerked away from her, bumping his hip against the side table by the door of his room. "Curse the evil thing!" He spit on the floor crossing the threshold, then Mother blocked my view. She lingered at the doorway of their room, watching to be certain he fell into the soft feather down of their bed and not onto the floor, for clearly he was drunk and not mindful. She left him fully clothed and already sleeping, then turned back to us, as we prepared to be audience for the Being's concert.

Frank Miles moved the chairs and laid out his pallet before the empty hearth. I sat cross-legged on the rug by his feet. He gave his quilt to the boys, who rolled themselves into a cocoon shape, resting their heads on his broad side. We listened to the Spirit sing for several hours and it was a most remarkable experience, for as the voice rose high and low, so too did the lights outside the window and in the lamps. Even Frank with all his knowledge of the world declared he'd known nothing like it, ever.

I enjoyed the warmth of cuddling on the rug and the beauty of the lights did move me, but I found myself looking often to the doorway, missing Father immensely, and looking also inside myself, at what I truly felt. I settled my head beside Joel's, against Frank's unusual deerskin trousers, reminding me of wilderness unknown. Could there be places wilder than my home? I recalled the hateful laughter and cruel torments the Spirit was capable of and I felt the beautiful voice it used for singing was false. I was quiet and though I nodded agreement when Mother praised the Being for bestowing on us such a harmonious recital, my thoughts were entirely otherwise. I preferred the lovely singing to its other voices of evil, mischief and Scripture, but I perceived the Spirit's true nature was simply pain and torment when it came to me, and even its sweetest notes fell flat into my ears.

the spirit's treasure

I remained dejected for days after Frank Miles left our home, and I was not the only one. Mother and Father and my brothers were similarly depressed. The Spirit's ability to control the lives of everyone it came in contact with was terribly oppressive. Though I had grown accustomed to my own life being directed by the Presence, I could not adjust to it holding sway over the grown men I admired.

In one way only were we fortunate; Frank departed near our May day celebrations, and they were a great distraction for us. We prepared as usual, the only difference being as we stitched new bonnets and polished boots, we were serenaded by the unearthly voice, for after Frank had gone, the Being was able to speak in the day as well as the night.

"What experiment that godless trapper performed in your good home, Jack Bell, apparently had the opposite effect from your desire." When the Reverend Johnston called, he was smug regarding the failure of Frank's strategy, but I believe he regretted his insensitivity a moment later when Father replied.

"It hardly matters when the demon chooses to speak, Reverend, for every moment of its existence, silent or not, is a shrill and constant noise inside my soul."

Constant was the garrulous Spirit during the days leading up to the holiday. It sang hymns a plenty, including some we had not previously heard. Mother fretted, for she was afraid the Spirit planned to attend the church services on May Day, and who could judge what the response of the entire congregation would be if the Spirit sang like a trouvère through the holy hour?

"We are privileged indeed, privy to your entertainments here," she spoke softly to the Being while she sewed in the afternoons. "But, please, stay silent for Reverend Johnston's sermon." She rocked and sewed as she pleaded, finishing fine lace for the collar of my new white May Day dress. The Being did not directly reply to her, but chose instead to sing an enigmatic "Song of the Bee."

> *Buzz, buzz! buzz!*
> *This is the song of the bee.*
> *His legs are of yellow;*
> *A jolly good fellow,*
> *And yet a great worker is he.*
>
> *In days that are sunny,*
> *He's getting his honey;*
> *In days that are cloudy,*
> *He's making his wax:*
>
> *On pinks and on lilies,*
> *And gay daffodillies,*
> *And columbine blossoms*
> *He levies a tax!*

Buzz! buzz! buzz!
From morning's first light
Till the coming of night,
He's singing and toiling the summer day through.

Oh! we may get weary,
And think work is dreary;
'Tis harder by far
To have nothing to do!

I took this song to mean the Spirit intimated it would be bored, if it was capable of such emotions, without attending the Reverend Johnston's sermon, but contrary to our expectations, when our bright May Day dawned, the Being was remarkably silent and our family was allowed a lovely sunny afternoon, strolling in our finest clothes in the company of our entire community, along the gently sloping grassy banks where the river ran slow near the church.

What an excellent time I'd had, visiting with Thenny, and viewing Josh Gardner across the river. Thenny had winked at me and cast her eyes slyly under her new bonnet in Josh Gardner's direction, while complimenting me on my fine dress, but our parents' ears had loomed above our conversation. If my brothers and Mother and Father had not been present, what would she have said? I exchanged only a brief glance with Josh, for he and his family had walked the path on the church side of the river. His mother had appeared very frail, needing the support of her husband on one side and her manly young son on the other, but when Josh saw me, he did wave. I had returned his gesture, wondering if from that distance he could appreciate Mother's fine lace stitched about my sleeve.

The thought of him was still a consolation to me, but it was not so vibrant as before Clara's death and Frank's departure. A heavy sadness born of my continuing isolation and out-of-the-ordinary experience pressed down on me. I wished Mother would allow me to return to school, for I had not been since my birthday, but she was disinclined to do so, preferring to keep me close by the house. I was lonely, for Joel and Richard and Drewry went to take their lessons with Professor Powell, and John Jr. went with Father, on horseback, to the fields. Jesse and Martha were still involved setting their small homestead in good order for the growing season and I was all alone, my only company Mother, Chloe and the invisible voice. Maybe Father would allow me to go with him when next he rode to Thorn's store. Or perhaps he could bring Thenny back with him? I planned to ask him about it at dinner, but in the evening the opportunity did not arise and right as we were finishing our meal, the Reverend and Preacher Justice arrived.

As we settled into our places in the parlor Mother related to us all how the Being had upended the milk jugs in the dairy during the day.

I did, I did!

The Spirit acknowledged the mischief in a childish tone and the Reverend Johnston decided to interrogate the Being regarding its afternoon prank.

"Pray, tell us the significance of milk spilled on the floor?" His brow was puzzled and concerned, for he took his inquiry quite seriously.

Old Sugar Mouth, not every act has meaning.

The voice spoke from inside our empty fireplace and the Reverend Johnston turned toward it, clutching his Bible to his chest, addressing the invisible.

"And yet God's Will inhabits every action. How is it with you, Spirit? Who are you and why are you here?" The Reverend's continual inquiry was made fresh with his eternal optimism, for he clearly believed one day the Being would reply. I sighed and pulled Joel closer to me on the bench where we had settled, wishing the Reverend would find a new line of questioning, for I did not anticipate an answer.

I am the Spirit of an early immigrant.

"Listen, Betsy, it has a foreign voice!" Joel's observation was accurate, and I sat up straighter, interested.

When I came to this country I was rich beyond measure, having inherited a vast amount from my father's estate in the Old Country. I had a fine home, but it burned to the ground before your time, and nothing remains of its earlier splendor.

I had never heard a voice with syllables so keen and articulate and I felt transported to the pages of a book where castles stood on rocky bluffs surrounded by the sea.

I was an unfortunate man, for I was burdened with many poorer relations who wished to benefit from my wealth without any cost to themselves. I was informed they were to visit me and thinking myself clever as the fox, I hid my gold coins and most valued treasures in a place not far from here. A place I will reveal to you.

"Sister, when has it told such an excellent story . . ." Joel snuggled against me, whispering his remark with great excitement, but I told him to hush so I might better hear the fine and elegant voice continue.

When my relations arrived, they found not the excess they imagined, and a dreadful quarrel ensued, the result being, I lay dead, by my own cousin's hand. My riches lay hidden in the earth, and my house was burned to the ground.

I felt a sudden leap under my breast, as if my heart

jumped up, for I knew the intention of the immigrant before the Being spoke it to all present.

I am the Spirit of the immigrant, and I have harassed you this many days only to divulge the secret hiding place, so Betsy Bell may have the treasures, to live blessed and prosperous all of her days.

I nearly jumped out of my chair, overcome with the possibility that I might finally be the recipient of some good fortune rather than suffering and misery at the hands of our visitation.

"This cannot be! You demonic spinner of tales. Who has heard of such a man in these parts?" Father objected to the rapt engagement and wonder seeping into the persons gathered in the parlor.

"There were many men before us, Jack. We know not every history . . ." The Reverend looked to Calvin Justice, hoping he would concur, and say something wise to calm my father.

I want you to be the guardian of these riches, Old Sugar Mouth. You must go when it is unearthed, to witness the counting and take it into safekeeping until Betsy comes of age for it.

"How preposterous! The demon mocks you, Reverend! Do you not see?" Father turned away in disgust, and Mother took up his hand, speaking quietly.

"Suffer no indignities to a man of God, Jack."

"Tell us where your treasure is hidden, and we shall most speedily move to investigate the veracity of your claim." Calvin Justice spoke his practical suggestion to the empty fireplace in his most commanding tone.

I will tell you, only when all involved promise to adhere to my conditions. Swear it will be so, and I shall reveal the place.

"I shall agree to no conditions put before me by a demon from Hell!" Father shook his head.

"Look, Jack, God's Will is not meant to be understood at every juncture. Perhaps this is the Being's final revelation to us." The Reverend Johnston was obviously excited, and anxious lest Father refuse to swear. "Mark the accuracy of the immigrant's accent and tone in the Being's speech! It could be what has plagued you and our community speaks to us now in its true form. Recall, it has previously claimed to be a Spirit disturbed. The early immigrant of whom it speaks could have met his violent end too soon to be remembered in these parts." The Reverend paused, and I had a sudden image in my mind of a man in foreign dress standing alone on the plateau where the thistles grew. Was it possible the Being spoke the truth?

"Mr. Bell, if it is so, we must allow this soul redemption. Pray, give your consent to its conditions." Calvin Justice urged my Father to agree.

"I doubt the veracity of this story in its every aspect, and if Frank Miles were in this room I expect he would laugh at you and all." Father held his mouth in a sour frown as if he wished to spit.

"But, Father, Frank has gone to check his traps and could not stay." Joel's innocence was precious as the imagined hidden jewels and he did articulate the facts of the matter.

Frank Miles will find them sprung and empty.

Everyone ignored the Being's comment, for the Reverend was intent on proceeding to discover the whereabouts of the buried treasure.

"We have heard accurate predictions here already, Jack, and in this your own dear daughter may profit from our action. How say you?" The Reverend impatiently snuggled his Bible under his arm, insisting on an answer. Father looked not about the room at our anxious faces, but hard, at the empty fireplace.

None shall dig except Jack Bell, his son Drewry and his man Dean. The Reverend and Betsy shall go, but must promise not to participate in the excavation. No one else may be present.

"In good faith we agree to adhere to those conditions, in the hope that doing so will allow you to return peacefully to your own world." The Reverend voiced the promise and prodded Father, "Eh, Jack? Agreed?"

"So be it." Father was most solemn, but everyone else seemed to have been holding their breath, as a general exhalation of relief floated around the room.

Whither I return is not your concern, Old Sugar Mouth.

"Where are they to search?" Calvin Justice was disappointed not to be included in the party but he maintained a keen interest in the organization of the affair.

On the hill of the most southwestern corner of this property, there is a large flat rock above the mouth of a small stream. This marks the place and beneath it lies the treasure.

The Being went on giving directions to the spring through the surrounding area on the high bank of the Red River, describing the paths so minutely there could be no mistaking the way. I closed my eyes and the powers of description the Spirit possessed transported me through a stand of blooming dogwood beside the rushing river. It was a curious feeling, for though I certainly remained sitting on the wooden bench in the parlor, rays of sun touched my arms and the gentle breeze swayed the many beautiful green leaves about my eyes.

"Listen, sister!" Joel clutched my dress in his fists and we both heard the bubble and trickle of the stream at the base of the flat rock where the Spirit said the treasure lay.

"I want to go . . ."

"No, Joel, we know not what will be found on this expedition." Mother turned to him but still gripped Father's hand.

"What, if anything," Father snapped, withdrawing from her grasp, standing abruptly. "I believe I know the place and I should like to make an early start, so I will now retire. Gentlemen, I bid you a good night."

"Are you certain you have heard enough?" The Reverend's round face had a dreamy expression and I believe he was greatly enjoying the Spirit's recitation of our upcoming journey through the woods, but Father gave him only a cursory nod.

"I am certain I have heard more than enough, Reverend."

I followed his example and hurried upstairs, and Drew ran after me, catching my hand on the landing.

"An adventure . . ." He smiled at me before we separated to our rooms, and I could tell he shared the general feeling of excitement born of faith in the Spirit's tale.

I did not undress, for I knew I would be up early. I crawled under the quilts of my bed and lay there listening to the sound of the Reverend and Calvin Justice arranging their pallets in the parlor. I did not think I could sleep and I wished morning would quickly come. What if the secret of the treasure was revealed in town and someone beat us to the spring? That was impossible, I knew, for all who had heard of it, apart from the creature itself, were sleeping here at our house. The Spirit could broadcast the news, only why would it, if it truly meant for me to have it? I lay worrying about many silly things like that, until I reached the most legitimate fear of all. What if the evil Being was lying and meant only to torment me with impossible hopes? Unable to accept that was the most likely outcome, I fell asleep.

At the break of day we set out from the stables in a line, Father and the Reverend Johnston in front, followed by myself and Drewry in the double saddle, and Dean in the rear, leading the mule laden with tools and the luncheon Mother and Chloe had packed for us. The farm dogs ran ahead, down the path, wagging their tails and yapping at the birds, as if to tell the world we were off hunting treasure. It was more than an hour's ride through the woods above the river to the head of the southwest trail, but once there, no one wished to take a break, as the ride was exhilarating and we desired to proceed directly to the spring. The sun shone favorably on us, and the skin of my arms grew warm with it, as they had the night before in the parlor during the Spirit's recitation. I leaned lazily against Drewry, rocked by the rhythm of our trotting horse.

Soon we turned into the hill and as we progressed deeper into the woods, the green leaves formed a thick canopy above our heads and the light became the color of moss. The trees were suddenly taller and thicker and rose on all sides so we were cramped, even in single file.

"'Tis an excellent location for hiding," the Reverend observed, twisting about in front of us and I looked to him, for his voice was nervous. By straining my head I could see Father, up ahead. He had brought his machete, had unsheathed it, and was hacking at the vines and saplings clogging the path before us. Some snapped back and others flew out in every direction, and the Reverend's horse backed up, skittish, with good cause. Drewry expertly guided our mare back, shouting, "Back, Dean," over his shoulder to successfully avoid a disturbance from the animals.

"I'll wait with the children," the Reverend called to Father, who had disappeared from our sight into a wall of green bramble and vine.

"Ride assured, we are nearly there," Father called back and the Reverend reluctantly kicked his mare forward, instructing us to keep our heads down, for it was narrow. Leaves and vines raked at my hair as we clopped through what seemed to be a never-ending tunnel of bramble.

At the end of it we found ourselves at the top of a hill in a most wondrous location, for the wooded area was actually the back side of a high rock outcropping. We had a marvelous view of the twisting Red River far below us on our right, and spreading to our left was a small meadow of young trees. A great flat stone marked the mouth of a spring that bubbled up near us, flowing down over the rock outcropping toward the river. I dismounted the moment I realized it was indeed the place of the treasure. Without pause, I ran and jumped up on the stone and spread myself flat across it. With my arms stretched out and my toes pointed, it was just the size of me, some five feet in diameter. The stone was hot, warmed by a morning in the sun, and I realized, absorbing the delicious heat through my stomach, it was impossible that anyone other than the hand of God could move such a rock. The treasure could not be dug from under it. All this way, for nothing. I sat up and saw Father and the Reverend and my brother, still mounted on their horses, staring at me, clearly thinking the same thing.

"This will not be an easy task," Drew spoke, breaking the circle of silence. The men dismounted, led the horses to drink at the spring, then tied them to trees in the woods, but spoke not another word. I sat on the stone watching the pretty lacy patterns made by the sun filtering through the trees. The Reverend shifted his feet and sighed a few times, contemplating the project. I imagine he was turning over in his mind the right words to speak, such as, "be not defeated before you begin," or "strong as Samson are the righteous." He cleared his throat, but said nothing. There was a terribly solemn tension in the air and no one seemed able or willing to break it. I expect the thought was in their minds, as it was in mine, that apart from the strength of the Spirit itself, nothing was going to move that rock. After a few minutes, Father sighed and kicked the boulder with the heel of his boot.

"Break out the tools," he instructed. They'd brought three spades, a mattock and the maul, and Drewry exchanged a woeful glance with me while rolling up his sleeves. With noticeable fortitude, Father set to thrusting his spade in the dirt and the Reverend cried encouragement.

"The first thrust is the most difficult." He had unpacked his Bible from his saddlebag and clasped it tightly to his chest for comfort, watching Father begin the digging. According to the Being's instructions he did not attempt to help with the hard labor. He merely watched with sympathy, as Father, Dean, and Drewry grunted with the effort of shoveling wet earth.

For hours they dug around the perimeter while the Reverend and I watched, following the growing pile of dirt in a circle around the great stone, listening whenever Father, Drewry and Dean attempted to analyze from which position they might most easily lift the stone from the ground. They had discovered it was most firmly embedded as they had expected. The spring bubbled up beside the rock, ensuring the red earth was wet and heavy, and the process slow and arduous. Dean was sent into the forest with his trusted ax to fell two pole trees to use as levers.

"We ought to fix a prize for the first man to lift the stone from the ground," the Reverend suggested, pacing helplessly by the edge of the growing ditch. Standing to his knees in mud, Drewry set his shovel in and leaned on it.

"Endowing my dear sister with wealth for the rest of her days and providing solace for the Spirit of the immigrant is prize enough for me!" He was trying to improve the atmosphere and I laughed with him, finding the thought of riches for the rest of my days and the return of the disturbed Spirit back to where it had come from delightful.

"I would use such funds, unlike the poor soul who lost them, for the betterment of my relations," I announced, skipping around the circle to stand with sincerity before him.

"Dig, Drewry," Father commanded, frowning at our attempts to lighten the task. I watched for a while longer, then around midday I busied myself laying out the luncheon of cold meat and cornbread. The men took a break and the Reverend blessed the food and our mission, and after they had finished eating I packed what was left away again in the saddlebags. I returned to the edge of the stone to watch, but quickly grew restless with the monotonous heaving and piling up of earth, so I wandered to the edge of the outcropping, following the spring in its path to the river.

I climbed down the hill a ways, and there I saw the stream progressed over a steep embankment, cascading in a long series of waterfalls to meet the larger river. It was a dizzy and exciting view. I looked over my shoulder to wave to the Reverend but I was too far down to see the men and the rock anymore. I made my way to the edge, pulling up my skirts so as not to wet them. There was a comfortable rock just above the first fall, and carefully I made a place for myself there. The noise of the bubbling water was peaceful and I was enjoying myself, feeling the strong sun on the top of my head. Leaning way out, I braced my elbow on a dry stone and was able to take a long drink from the spring where the water ran fast and clear. There is nothing so lovely as fresh spring water. When I'd drunk my fill, I turned to the carefree pleasure of slipping make-believe boats into the rushing stream. Each twig I dropped was propelled over the edge and carried off down to the river with great swiftness. It had been a long time since I sailed leaf and twig boats, and I began to daydream about the treasure.

What I wanted most was the Spirit's swift return from whence it came, but if it should leave treasure in its wake, that could be some compensation for the trials we had endured. I wished for a satin ribbon for my hair, and a pair of white silk stockings to put away until the day I married. I thought I would purchase pounds of hard candy from Mr. Thorn for Richard and Joel, and I would give a new velvet bonnet to Mother. Drewry should have an adventure storybook and John Jr. a beautiful new gun, and for Father, I knew not what to purchase. I was not sure what he most would like. I gazed at two green maple leaves I had dropped in the falls. They were caught in an eddy in a small pool beneath me, swirling in a perfect circle, chasing each other madly before being swept down to the river. It came to me that Father might like a new riding crop, as I'd noticed the leather on his current one had begun to fray.

I heard a rise of voices and excitement from the spring above and I jumped to my feet, practically tripping over myself in my hurry to see what they had found. Through the combined efforts of Father, Dean and Drewry, and with the direction of Reverend Johnston, I saw the men had managed to prize and tilt and raise the stone from its bedding, and it lay overturned beside the mouth of the stream. Where it had been was a large circle of dark earth.

I reached the edge, and felt the air suddenly cold and dank, giving rise to tingles in the flesh along the back of my neck and arms. I recognized the presence of the Spirit, but reasoned it was just the cold wind let out from under the rock.

"Look, there is nothing." Father thrust his shovel into the damp red earth. Drewry dropped to his hands and knees, and began digging with his fingers, mindful of any glittering or hard substance he might discover.

"The immigrant said it was beneath the rock, buried *beneath* it." The Reverend stood close to the edge, leaning over the hole. "That's it, Drewry boy. If you are tired, Jack, have Dean continue the digging. It cannot be much deeper." He had not given up. Father looked at him and then at Drewry, whose hands and forearms were caked with red mud.

"Use the tools," he said, thrusting the shovel into the earth close beside my brother. I felt a sinking in my chest as though the great stone removed had fallen down inside me. If the treasure was under this rock which took three strong men near all day to lift, how had the immigrant sunk it there? I watched the men dig deeper and deeper, and I watched the Reverend's face for some sign that God's hand had worked alongside the immigrant, allowing the tale to be true, so I might buy my family presents and be released from future torment, but soon the hole stood six feet wide and near as deep, and no treasure had been found. The water which fed the stream had opened rivulets in the walls, and Father, Drewry and Dean were wet and exhausted from their labor, full of mud and hungry, as it was near the end of the day.

"You have dug deeply here." The Reverend shook his head in dismay, reluctant to be disappointed.

"There is nothing." Father did not say he had known it would be so, but it was apparent he had finished with the task.

"It tricked us, evil thing, to satisfy its own malicious nature." Drewry made a ball of mud and threw it down in anger.

Fools!

We had not heard a word from the Spirit all day, but I was not surprised when its wicked laughter rose from the pit the men had dug.

What else will you do for the promise of riches?

No one responded. Instead, we made haste to load the tools and mount the horses, all of us despondent and much chagrined.

What fun we will have this evening!

The Spirit shouted, filling the forest with its nasty laughter before growing quiet.

We rode home in silence wishing the whispering leaves and the chattering of birds preparing for the night could stifle our ugly thoughts.

"Why is it so mean?" Drewry slapped the reins gently on the horse's back, speaking softly. I could not answer him, and only shook my head before laying my cheek against his dirty sweat-filled shirt. I berated myself for having been foolish enough to believe the Spirit, and I closed my eyes when we passed the stand of dogwood, for it glowed silver and recalled to me the many coins lost to us. Even the farm hounds that ran ahead kept their noses to the ground and gave no bark.

Twilight was well settled when we rode into the yard, but a bright half-moon hung above the stables and we were surprised to see no fewer than ten carts and buggies parked there.

"What's this?" I heard Father grumble at the discovery.

Zeke was waiting by the stable and he quickly took Father's reins in his big hands.

"While you was riding on the lands, suh, these folks done pulled up and pitched their tents, assured you were hospitable. Miz Lucy had me see to all their horses."

"From where have they come? I do not recognize the carts." Father dismounted and assessed the numbers, gravely calculating the extra feed and water he must dispense.

"They hail from far away, from the mountains of Kentucky, and the folk who own that wooden cart over near the hog pen say they are Shakers, from the north."

"Good gracious, Shakers!" The Reverend also dismounted and conferred quickly with my father. "No doubt now that the weather is sublime you will be inundated with visitors who are curious regarding the phenomenon." The Reverend took a deep breath, causing his chest to barrel up, as if he must prepare to give a sermon. He brushed the dust of riding from his coat in anticipation of addressing a crowd.

"What am I to do? Host the entire state of Tennessee and beyond, on my small farm?" Father stood annoyed and muddy, in his working clothes, in no mood to be hospitable to strangers.

"You appear to have little choice in the matter, Jack." The Reverend sighed and turned to his horse, unpacking his Bible from the saddlebag. "Take the boy and clean up, and when you enter the house, strike as fine a form as only a man like you, John Bell, can cut. I will entertain them for you until then."

"Listen," I interrupted. Drifting from the open windows of our home we heard many voices raised in song, led by the strong timbre we recognized as the Spirit's voice.

"Clearly," Father's tired eyes looked directly into my own

before he spoke to the Reverend, "they are already entertained." He and Drewry went to the bath to wash, and I was sent to fetch new clothes for them. The Reverend took the path up to the front door, but I strode up the hill from the stables and cut across the orchard so I might enter through the garden into the kitchen. I did not wish to report the failure of our mission to anyone until Father and Drewry were by my side. In the kitchen, two lamps burned and Chloe raced from the pantry to the stove, sweat pouring from the edges of her kerchief. A steaming iron pot shook with heat on the woodstove, and Chloe took no notice of me, busy as she was. I kept my head down, surprised as I entered the dining room, for it seemed a hundred people occupied our house, and I recognized not one of them.

In truth, the number of persons present was less than half that, but still, I had to force my way through the crowd parting for me without knowing who I was. I slipped behind a line of visitors perched along the banister, all the way up the stairs, and glancing back I saw every chair in the parlor was taken, though I could not spot Joel or Richard, John Jr. or my mother. The crowd occupying our house was involved in singing a song, led by the Spirit.

> We walk by faith
> And not by sight
> And when our faith is done,
> In realms of clearer light . . .

I managed to fetch the clothes and slip back down the stairs, holding close to the wall, bearing a new suit for Drewry from his wardrobe, and an old suit of John Jr.'s for Father, since I did not wish to cross through the crowd in the parlor to get one of Father's own. I kept my eyes down but I felt no one looking at me, and as I walked through the dining room unnoticed, I had the sense every stranger there was hypnotized and under a spell, so completely were they oblivious to me.

"It must be an angel, for it knows what only myself and my dead mother are aware of!" A small man with dark hair shouted this revelation to the crowd as I stole out through the kitchen into the warm night. I glanced at Chloe but she turned her back, withdrawing into the pantry.

I glided down the dark path to the necessary house, stepping lightly, stone to stone. Father had lit a candle by the hip bath and I could see him and Drewry waiting. They had cleaned their bodies and faces in piggins, and stood in their underwear on the flat platform. Father hastily reached for the linen trousers, cotton shirt and woven coat I'd brought, while I explained there were too many people in the parlor for me to fetch his own.

" 'Tis no matter. Who is present?"

"I saw no one known to me," I told him, and stared up at the moon and stars, for they looked suddenly closer than normal, and I felt dizzy, as if I were falling into the sky.

"What of your mother?" Father caught my arm and roughly drew his opposite arm into John Jr.'s jacket. "I did not expect to see the day when an invisible demon would host a party of strangers in our home."

"They are singing hymns, Father. 'We Walk by Faith.' "

The three of us looked up the hill across the garden to the house, pulsing with light and the noise of many voices. We heard talking and laughing, and a song of unintelligible syllables drifting down to us, and without speaking Drewry and Father each took up one of my hands in their own.

"Undoubtedly, it means to mock us with an audience."

Drewry shook his hair and lingering drops of water from his wash were thrown onto my cheeks.

"S'cuse me, folks, is this the outhouse?" A stranger had wandered down the hill, searching for a place to relieve himself, and Father sighed.

"It is, good sir, and you may light the candle on the left, inside the door, with this one." I realized Father planned to take the Reverend's advice and cut his finest figure of strength, authority and hospitality for the evening.

"Come, children, we must go." He ushered Drew and me up the path through the garden and into the back of the house. I did not want to participate in the parlor gathering and Father seemed to know my thoughts, or they were the same as his. He had us take up stools around the flaming woodstove.

"Dish us up some dinner, Chloe, for it has been a trying day."

"There's only white beans and corn pone, masta Bell, the meat's done gone." Father frowned, but Chloe made three plates instantly, and Father sent her to find Mother amongst the crowd to tell her we were home, and merely wished to eat our supper before joining the gathering.

We ate slowly, trying to stretch out the chewing of bread and beans, for our hearts were loath to join the party. We heard Reverend Johnston's familiar voice rising above the strange ones, while the Spirit led the group in a test of their Bible knowledge. There was a round of applause, then we heard a man cry out, "Having witnessed several hours of this magic I do proclaim it greater than the rumors! Mark this occasion, fellow travelers, we witness here the haunting of the century!"

"Jack! Children! Please, join us!" Mother burst into the

kitchen, her cheeks pink with fetching cups of tea for the many unexpected guests. I could see she greatly desired our presence.

"The time has come," Father said, rising and setting his plate on top of the sideboard. I noticed he had barely eaten a morsel. Drewry took my hand and I kept my head down, pushing forward, but still it was difficult following Mother through the crowd to the parlor.

"Look, there is the father! And the girl too!" A ruddy-faced and pudgy man I had never seen before stood by the door and made this announcement, and the revelry died down. Whereas before I felt invisible, I now felt like a pussing pimple on otherwise clear skin.

"Sister, sister." Joel and Richard popped up from a place on the rug where they had been hidden by unknown boots and skirts. "Did you find the treasure? What happened in the woods?"

The room was abruptly still of all but breathing and Joel snuggled his face against my skirts looking up, expectant of good news.

"We found nothing . . ." I bent down and whispered in his ear.

Nothing but the good earth of the grave.

The Spirit's tone abruptly altered from merry to malicious, and I felt a tremor of nervous anxiety electrifying the persons assembled.

Old Sugar Mouth stood about prayerfully, and Drewry's hands worked the dirt better than a spade. As if he were made for it.

The Spirit described everything exactly as it had occurred.

Dean staved the mattock in up to the eye, every pop, pop, pop! And sweat ran off the slave like water.

Having a raucous good time, it laughed with glee between

observations, and I kept my head down not wishing to see what I knew were the stricken faces of my family, humiliated before a crowd of strangers.

Old Jack dug and dug, better than the man employed in the trade of gravedigger in Clarksville. Old Jack the gravedigger! He has the knack.

I could not bear to look at Father.

Miss Betsy planned her purchases, so certain was she. She would have candy! and a gun! a book! a velvet bonnet! and satin hair ribbons too!

I covered Joel's ears, whispering through my fingers, "The candy was to be for you." I resented the caricatures it made of us, presenting Father as inept, and myself as a spoiled and vain young girl, but someone in the room laughed, and then there was another giggle. Though meanly done, the Spirit continued describing our party in such a humorous tone, so accurately depicting those unflattering aspects of each of us that there were many in attendance who could not help but laugh. Perhaps they could not hold it back, as it broke the highly uncomfortable tension created when our intimate thoughts were revealed. I know not the reason, but all of a sudden, in the center of the crowd of strangers, I felt again the invisible hand, twisting my hair around my throat, and I could not breathe amid the laughter. I was frightened and my heart threatened to burst inside my chest, then all went black.

I was propelled onto the floor in a violent convulsing fit, and it appeared to all gathered I was smothering under some invisible force. I panted as if for my very life, and one of the strangers in the crowd in possession of a pocketwatch and the mind to use it declared my breath was lost for up to a full minute between great gasps. This struggle went on in my body despite Father's and Mother's attempts to force air into my lungs. I could not breathe and I appeared to be unconscious but I was aware of everything as it happened. Mother and Father pleaded with the Spirit to relent but the Being did not respond.

"Jack, we must send for Dr. Hopson." Mother felt she could stand it no longer, and Father asked John Jr. to ride and fetch him. "What if this time she does not recover?"

"Release this innocent!" proclaimed the Reverend. "You sinners who did laugh at the Being's rendition of our misspent day, beg for forgiveness from our Lord." The Reverend commanded the strangers, even the Shakers, to follow his instructions, but their well-meaning prayers were futile. The fit carried on without abating for two hours and the Spirit was silent throughout, answering no entreaties, and giving rise to general speculation that its energy was thoroughly used keeping me captive.

"You demon of Hell, in the name of God, be cast from my home, be brought to your Judgment Day for the torture and torment of this innocent child! Go from here and appear before the Lord, our God, who is all powerful and stands to conquer you!" Father attempted to distract the Being, and save my life, by shouting above my writhing body, and his forceful nature seemed to have some effect on what grasped me, for the Spirit released my lungs to breathe, and Father lifted me from the floor to the chair, where Mother bent over me.

"Thank God, the fit has ceased!"

"Make way! Make way! What is the nature of this gathering?" Dr. Hopson pushed through the crowd in our parlor.

"Good people," the Reverend Johnston spoke in his church voice. "You have abused John Bell's hospitality enough this evening. Let us all retire and allow the doctor his examination in more private circumstances." The Reverend enlisted John Jr.'s and Drewry's help to clear the house.

My head was sore at the back where I had struck the floorboards and I looked about with my eyes half open, not caring when I saw departing looks of fear and sympathy cast in my direction. Why did they look at me that way?

"You fainted again, Elizabeth Bell?" The doctor adjusted his gold glasses on his nose, having removed his coat and hat.

"Good Dr. Hopson, we feared entirely for her life, so virulent was what seized her!" Mother said, stroking the hair loosened from my braid off my forehead. I felt as if I might cry. Dr. Hopson sighed, and opening his leather bag, he withdrew new smelling salts.

"I am much recovered now," I breathed, straightening in the chair. I was uncomfortably embarrassed by the doctor's deep assessing stare.

"Indeed, you appear to the eye most sound and fit." Dr. Hopson did not remove his gaze from my person.

"Doctor, you cannot imagine the horror we endured!" Mother took Dr. Hopson's arm with pleading fingers.

"Verily, I cannot." The doctor placed his hand briefly over hers, inquiring, "What home remedy has she imbibed?"

"None, sir! For her ailment is not constant and I have no remedy in my pantry for ailments such as these."

"Lucy, let us have a cup of tea. Elizabeth, I will give you a dose of laudanum to be certain you sleep, for I believe you are in great need of rest." Dr. Hopson removed a brown glass bottle from his bag. Without pause he dropped a full spoon of liquid down my throat.

"Children, to your beds." Father spoke forcefully and we all readily obeyed. I was pleased I would not be subjected to further prodding and poking of my body, as I felt sore and achy, from the long horse ride as much as the fit. The medicine dispensed by Dr. Hopson left a sweet taste on my tongue.

My brothers helped me upstairs, but left me alone to rest. I did not undress immediately, but stood at the window in my room, looking out. The laudanum had made me woozy and I steadied myself with my hand on the wall. I saw lanterns moving in between the tents pitched at the foot of the orchard where the ground was flat, and I realized the strangers were many, camping on our land. From downstairs I heard the sound of voices raised in argument, and I listened to Dr. Hopson exchanging words with my father and the Reverend.

"It is my considered opinion that these meetings at your home, John Bell, are of an anti-religious nature and I am greatly surprised, as they are attended by some of the finest, outstanding members of our community. Including yourself, Reverend, our spiritual leader!"

"You know not what ails her, but we have seen it, and we know." The Reverend Johnston spoke most passionately in his own defense.

"Tell me why the phenomenon you so readily ascribe to is not in residence when I am called? And how has it happened, Reverend Johnston, that this religious festival grows outside John Bell's door? Who are these Shakers from the north? Who are these strangers descending on our district, and for what cause?"

I felt certain Father wished to know the answer to those queries much more than the good doctor and I wondered how he would respond.

"I know without experience of the visitation present in this home, it is difficult to fathom—" The Reverend Johnston spoke most patiently, but the doctor interrupted.

"I find it most difficult to fathom why you do not put a stop to these gatherings!"

"We are powerless before it." Mother and Father spoke in unison and I could hear the pain of their situation so evident in their tone, it must have been powerfully strong on their features.

"The fainting girl is merely an expression of the general hysteria dominating your assemblies." The doctor was frustrated and expressed his own opinion freely, with anger.

"Without a doubt, some supernatural phenomenon afflicts this family," the Reverend insisted, begging Dr. Hopson to accept his word, but I knew the Spirit must speak with the doctor in the house before he ever would believe in its existence. "If you could use your medicinal arts to decipher some possible cure, as I have used my divinity schooling on the entity, perhaps—"

"My medical skills are of no use in the treatment of willful mass delusions." Dr. Hopson did not allow the Reverend to complete his thought. "I removed myself from my domicile at urgent request and rode near two hours in the dark on a road most dangerously rutted these days, to find I am not needed, but merely a guest at your strange carnival."

"Please, Dr. Hopson, let us drink some tea . . ." I heard Mother's calm voice, raised with authority. "Let us argue no longer, for vials of the wrath of God have poured over us already here." Her sorrow effectively silenced the men. "Let us sit at the table and take a moment to thank the Lord our Betsy has been delivered from her fit, and thank Him also for gracing us with such ill trials that we might strive to righteous behavior."

"Amen," the Reverend declared.

"Let us encompass minds of wisdom, and discuss what

remedies you might suggest, Dr. Hopson." Mother's voice grew faint and I supposed she led him to the dining table for the tea.

Outside, the lanterns flickered in the tents, and my eyes were tired and heavy. My dress was done up down the back and I knew Mother was not on her way to help me with it. I lay down, uncomfortably aware of the bone buttons lining my spine, yet how far away seemed the days when sleeping in my clothes was undesirable. I closed my eyes, and fell asleep at once.

the strangers on our land,
head lice and the summer storm

In the morning, bright sunlight poured from the window onto my bed, so I awoke hot and sticky with the feeling I had slept over long. My first thought was to change my clothes and I threw off the quilts with as much violence as the Spirit itself. I decided I would find Mother and request her help to bathe and dress anew, but as I passed the window, movement below in the strangers' encampment caught my eye and I stopped.

"Look! There's the girl!" the same red-faced pudgy man from the night before pointed up at me from where he stood, hanging a wet washing cloth on a tree branch in our orchard.

"That must be her room, where the thing began . . ." A bony woman I did not recognize came to his side and waved at me.

"Hello, Miss Betsy Bell! We are your neighbors from Kentucky! How do you fare?"

I did not answer, horrified to face a crowd of inquiring

strangers first thing in the morning. I stepped back from the window, slid along the wall to my doorway and out onto the landing in the hall where I ran into Mother.

"Betsy, I would like you and the boys to accompany me to Thorn's store in the wagon, for we are in need of certain provisions for this company."

"Will they be staying long?"

"They have not made their intentions known to us, but as long as they are present we must be considerate and care for them."

"I must change my dress, Mother." I held out my skirt displaying the many wrinkles of the night.

"Bring your books. You may partake of a lesson at the schoolhouse with the esteemed Professor Powell, before we return." Mother smiled at me, knowing I would be pleased she had granted me this opportunity to visit with my friends. "I believe summer has arrived," she breathed deeply, "for it appears to be a hot day in the making."

I hurried to get ready, relieved Mother had not requested I remain at home to entertain the gawkers. As I changed I heard Mother and Father downstairs discussing J. Bratton, the cobbler, who had recently announced in church that he was making shoes designed for left and right feet, rather than the standard two of one kind.

"We must have him round to size us, Jack," Mother insisted, "and also the slaves, all of them, men, women and children, should be shod before the cold weather."

"Their feet are tough as cowhide, Lucy, and they have the shoes we issued last year." Father quickly objected to having the cobbler down at the cabins. "We can give them extra tallow to rub the leather up, and they can turn their stockings over the tops come winter."

"Chloe tells me plain all their shoes are worn too thin for extra tallow to do the job." Mother was exasperated and I wondered if the company was simply too much for her, as she did not generally involve herself with Father's methods in the running of the farm. "Jack, you must have seen it yourself!" She did sound annoyed.

"They will last another year." Father held firm, as was his custom, to his decision, and I knew Mother would not have her way. Beyond their arguing voices I became aware of a high-pitched screaming outdoors. I paused, and soon recognized the wailing as the squealing of a hog. I wondered if Father planned to slaughter a pig for the strangers. I finished dressing and ran downstairs, finding Father in the hall, about to leave the house.

"I must make haste to the barn," he said, the scream of the hog punctuating his speech.

"Is that the pig we'll eat for supper, Father?" I asked.

"It is," he nodded without looking at me, engaged in pulling on his leather work gloves.

"Why do they cry like that?" I had always wondered, but never asked.

"Every marked hog will squeal until it hangs from a short rope." Father allowed the heavy door to bang shut behind him as he hurried out.

"How is the hog marked, Mother? How does it know?" I turned to her, watching as she tied her bonnet, preparing for our trip to Thorn's store.

"Your father and the hands decide in conversation, Betsy, and it is a mystery how the hogs do know, but know they do." She must have read the puzzlement on my features, for I was thinking, a mystery? How is it possible? "All God's creatures are imbued with certain knowledge and the hogs do know when it is time to call their angels down." Mother seemed to think this was perfectly understandable, but I wondered if a *person* were marked to die, would they know it? Would they sing songs like the Spirit's sweet hymns to bring their angels down? Or would they scream and wail like hogs? These were curious thoughts and only momentary, for Mother wished to leave and I was sent back upstairs to bring the boys down. While searching for Joel's slate, I heard her talking with Chloe.

"Miz Lucy, on your way, will you tell masta Bell, Dean done stacked a pile of green hickory in the smokehouse and tell him to make a memory of how we need the hog guts to fall in the big kettle for the soap making."

"Last time Jack sold the lard off, didn't he? We nearly had to buy it back." Mother laughed at Father's unusual error. "All we had from that pig was the hocks, the crackling bread and sausage."

"If he do catch the blood, I'll make us up a pudding." Chloe banged her bread pans on the porch to clear the crumbs and I licked my lips recalling her blood pudding as most delicious. I hoped Father would not waste the innards.

"I'll deliver the message now, before the blood is spent into the ground. Hurry, Betsy! Boys!" Mother walked out the door as we ran down the stairs.

Lessons were in progress when we reached the school-house and I found it difficult to open the large painted door. I looked over my shoulder at Mother riding on to Thorn's store. Her back was straight and her bonnet tied tight and from behind she appeared relaxed, as Zeke slapped the reins on the horse's back, forcing them down the hill. I took a breath and stepped back so Joel and Richard would enter first.

"Why, class, it is Elizabeth Bell and her brothers, come to join us! Greetings." Professor Powell smiled warmly across the heads swiveling in our direction, and I curtsied, noticing most everyone's feet were the color of summer dirt. The room was not full and Joel and Richard promptly took their customary bench, but I did not know where to sit.

"Good day, Professor Powell." I kept my head bowed, feeling Vernon Batts's black eyes narrow on me. Josh Gardner was not present, nor Becky Porter. Where was Thenny?

"Here's a place, Miss Betsy!" I looked up and saw Thenny was forcing Amanda Ellison to move and make room for me. When I saw Amanda, I froze and felt I could not walk the seven paces to the bench where I was meant to take a seat. Her long blond braid swung out behind her head as she settled into her new spot, and I imagined her long hair undone, floating like translucent angel wings, face down in the lake.

"Please, be seated." Professor Powell smiled, but gestured I should make haste to the bench, as he was waiting to continue the lesson.

"Forgive me the disruption," I managed to speak and found my limbs capable of crossing space, but I could not look at Amanda. I kept my eyes most purposely averted from her, for the feeling in my soul was overwhelming and oddly embarrassing. I wondered if Father had been right deciding we should keep the Spirit's morbid prediction quiet. What if we did not warn her and it came to pass? I felt uncertain but I believed it best to keep quiet about my thoughts.

"Miss Mary, please continue with dictation."

"Honesty," Mary spoke the first word and everyone labored to write it out in cursive on their slates.

"Miss Betsy, I would have you be my assistant examining the quality of our dictation today, but I wish not to ask too much of a pupil so seldom seen." Professor Powell stood and examined my slate. "Your absence has in no way affected your abilities, I see. Class, behold a perfect 'honesty.'" He held my slate up for the class to see and I blushed with the extra attention, but it felt wonderful to be in an environment where the old routines still functioned. I said a silent prayer to the Spirit, please leave me be, allow me this, speak not.

Mary dictated "obedient," "sought," then "cherished," and Professor Powell stood over me all the while.

"Very good, class. Now, Miss Thenny, display for us your quick tongue in reciting our June poem." Thenny stood, and curtsied, and flashed her teeth in a smile to me before she began.

> "Cheerfulness"
>
> There is a little Maiden—
> Who is she? Do you know?
> Who always has a welcome
> Wherever she may go.
> Her face is like the May time,
> Her voice is like a bird's;
> The sweetest of all music
> Is in her lightsome words . . .

Thenny faltered and Professor Powell frowned.

"Take a seat, I would have Miss Betsy read the rest, from the primer, as she was absent during the memorization."

I rose and Professor Powell placed the book, open to the

page, in my hands. He guided me through the simple verse with his index finger.

> By old folks and by children
> By lofty and by low:
> Who is this little maiden?
> Does anybody know?
> You surely must have met her.
> You certainly can guess;
> What! I must introduce her?
> Her name is cheerfulness.

Professor Powell smiled at me above the primer and I was touched by his efforts, though I felt no affinity with the maiden of the poem. He clearly had no idea how far from cheerfulness my emotions dwelled.

"An appropriate muse for such a lovely day, eh, class? We shall have a recess, and enjoy the sunshine out-of-doors."

I ran down the steps grateful to be released so I might talk to Thenny, who led me eagerly to the mulberry tree where we could talk alone.

"I heard a crowd of strangers have settled on your land." She grabbed my arm, excited.

"Yes, but how did you know?" I felt slightly annoyed I had not had the pleasure of telling this news myself.

"I was at the store early in the morning helping Father load the bins with fresh sugar from Clarksville and a stranger entered, professing to be amongst the crowd of traveling folk gathered at Jack Bell's farm."

" 'Tis true, there are many strangers camped on our land and the mood is of a carnival and all." I decided to make it sound as exotic as I could.

"Will it be fun as a lynching fest?" Thenny rubbed her hands together.

"'Tis better, for the Good Lord wills no one must die!"

"He wills mostly mystery surrounding you, Miss Betsy." Thenny embraced me, tickling my hips with her fingers. "I will beg my Father to call on you this evening, for I would like to see the strangers. Are they poor whites, drunk on rotgut whiskey who will eat your dirt?"

"Gracious, Thenny, what outrageous gossip! Do you honestly believe my father would tolerate such visitors?"

"He has tolerated much." Thenny grew subdued to solicit more information and I complied.

"These strangers hail from Kentucky and they are traveling with slaves who are encamped beside our own, in the cabins. But there is also a pair of slaveless Shakers from the north."

"Blasphemy! Shakers on your land!"

"The Reverend knows all about it," I assured her, momentarily anxious she might not wish to join us.

"I also heard the Witch cast you down again and Dr. Hopson was brought out to your home." Thenny looked at the ground as she spoke and I saw her neck tense, knowing her inquiries were sinfully curious.

"It did, but I cannot recall it rightly." I waited until she looked into my eyes, "For Dr. Hopson dosed me with some laudanum after it was done."

"Laudanum! Goodness, Betsy." She grasped my arm, her voice full of fear. "They gave it to my cousin Edwin before he was consumed!"

"I am not near passing, dear Thenny." The pleasure of impressing Thenny with my woes was one of the few pleasures left to me. I smiled and placed my hand over hers on my forearm. "I experienced no ill effects apart from a sublime drowsiness from my dose."

"Look! Your mother arrives to fetch you off already . . ." I turned and saw Zeke and my mother walking up the hill beside the cart, full of hoop barrels and burlap sacks. Thenny embraced me again and held me tight, speaking falsetto into my ear, "I will high to your home tonight or I am not Thenny Thorn!" I laughed at her playful ways and kissed her cheek, running to meet Mother on the road.

True to her word, Thenny did appear early that evening at our home, along with her parents, Calvin Justice, the Reverend and Mrs. Johnston, Jesse, Martha and many others from the community of Adams who had not come calling for several months, since Clara Lawson's death. The news of strangers on our land had caused everyone to put aside their reservations so they might see the tents and hear the Spirit sing. They dressed up in their party clothes with excitement and curiosity, brimming with apparent goodwill toward us, and they arrived bearing corn cakes and pies, so we hosted a spontaneous party.

"For you, Jack, I have brought this large bottle of fine whiskey, fresh from the doubler, with the express intent of keeping yourself and your visitors in superior moods all evening long." Calvin Justice handed Father the bottle, then sought the Shakers, so he might engage them in religious debate. I helped Mother and Chloe set out tables between the strangers' tents and the stables, for our feast included no less than ten fried chickens and twenty pots of boiled hominy and rosen'yers, the early corn roasted in the ashes. The boys ran races on our front lawn and spit water from their mouths at the well, and thanks were given all around for the warm setting sun, for it had so far bestowed on us all a prosperous growing season. The Spirit did not speak until supper was finished.

I have attended the sultans' banquets and the Romans' feasts.

Jesse, John Jr. and Drewry lit the lanterns and torches to keep the mosquitoes off.

Extravaganzas your pitifully small imaginations cannot fathom.

"Please, cast no aspersions this evening." Mother stood at her place and raised her arms to the sky, addressing the crowd and the Being. "See here, the beauty of the fading light, the rising moon. Hear the song of the katydids." She paused, allowing the company a moment of silent listening, and during it the doves in the stable obediently cooed goodnight. "Hear the melodies of affection between family and friends, gathered at this table." Mother sat down smiling and cups were raised to toast her sentiment.

For you, Luce, we must celebrate.

The Spirit spoke as if it smiled on Mother and she did look angelic in her summer dress, her face shining in the lantern light, moist with the heat.

"I would celebrate your departure from our home." Father's words were slurred but I thought it was impossible for him to have already consumed too much of Calvin Justice's whiskey. I saw Mother take up his hand with some passion, turning patient eyes of long-standing love onto his face. I wondered if she too had whiskey in her pewter mug, rather than her usual tea.

I enjoy nothing so much as a good party!

The invisible Spirit's incantations danced around the table, raising everyone's expectations.

"A party!" cried a stranger, "how shall we celebrate this witchery?"

"The Lord has blessed us, and we must celebrate not witchery, but in His name." Calvin Justice raised his glass off the table. I knew he had not convinced the Shakers of his opinion during his debate with them, and I believe he preferred a party to continuing that discussion.

"I fear the sap does rise tonight!" The Reverend Johnston made a joke, and everyone laughed, and the light summer heat reverberated with ease and comfort. I saw the Reverend take Mrs. Johnston's hand into his own under the table, following Mother's example. John Jr. sat beside him, looking quite jovial. He raised his mug to me.

"In Betsy the sap does rise bewitchingly!" he teased and a chorus of knowing laughter circled the table.

What a clever boy you are, John Jr.

" 'Tis true, eh, Betsy?" Father ignored the Spirit and, turning his back to Mother, he looked into my eyes as though none were present with us. "Darling daughter, do you feel the sap surging in your breast this evening?" I was shocked he had addressed me so before a crowd of strangers. Did he mean to come to my room later? I could not think how I should answer, but Mother made light of his comment.

"Jack, all the young girls here are as lovely as the breeze at night. Let us have a dance and celebrate the summer season now upon us!"

The crowd pulsed happy agreement with her words and whatever oddities they expected to experience, they seemed satisfied to dance instead. I looked down at my hands so I might meet no curious stares, for I noticed my breast was rising with excitement and I supposed it _could_ be sap.

"Get your fiddle, William," called one of the strangers to

another, removing a bright pennywhistle from his shirt pocket. John Jr. ran up to the house to fetch his wooden flute, and in an instant a large square was made for dancing beside the tables in the flat part of the path. The men built up a bonfire, and laughter and music paired off in the night as everyone chose a partner and took their places in twos, like the lightning bugs mating in the deepening dark about us.

Play "My Lady Fair"!

The Spirit called the dance in perfect time to the musician's notes. Thenny was my partner and we passed between Jesse and Martha on our left and Joel and Richard on our right. I watched Mother coax Father off the bench by sitting on his lap, covering his legs with her wide flouncy skirt. She held his face in her hands, then stood and pulled him up. I watched him smile reluctantly, lengthening his body. He stiffly turned her on his arm, and they joined the top of the square, dancing beside Jesse and Martha.

"The Virginia Star"! Take the lady on your left . . .

I was amazed the Being knew every reel and step, and could change its voice most unctuously, so I was uncertain if it were a stranger calling out the dance, or the Presence I knew so intimately. It hardly mattered, for we were a mixed-up mass of spinning folk. I noticed Mother's hair fell down, hanging in brown curls around her face and in a long thick rolling wave all down her back, causing her to look like the young girl she must once have been. Her dress too was loosened, and when she leaned her head back, laughing, I saw the delicate white skin of her neck exposed to the top of her bosom. I looked away, feeling as I had earlier when I had seen Amanda Ellison, oddly embarrassed, as if I knew something I should not. Why had Josh Gardner not been present at the schoolhouse? Thenny and I took our turn casting off and I skipped down the line, my feet in perfect time with hers. We formed a bridge with our hands held high for our line to pass under and we laughed breathlessly, squeezing our fingers tight as the couples ducked through. I wondered if I would ever be so lucky as to share a dance with Josh. Thenny swung me round onto Jesse's elbow and I flung my head back like Mother, looking up at the bright stars, the few remaining lightning bugs hovering at the line of trees. From the cabins I heard the mellow beat of a pigskin drum and deep Negro voices engaged in song, Zeke's rising above the rest. The warmth of the firelight on Thenny's flushed cheeks and her delighted giggles filled me with tremendous happiness as we spun through our moves. I felt no fear, for I was certain no violence would be enacted on me, and none was. I was allowed to swing and roll my body in time to the music, at one with the sap coursing through the veins of the trees and through my breast.

Before long, all except the youngest children had exhausted themselves with dancing, and the musicians were forced to quit, complaining of sore fingers, and being in need of refreshment. All returned to the tables to share whiskey and cold water carried fresh from the well.

"Drewry, take the young'uns to the house . . ." John Jr. slurred his words dreadfully, and sat with only one leg around the wooden bench between Jesse and Father, who laughed, realizing he had imbibed more strong drink than his young body was accustomed to.

"How say *you* to retiring, young'un?" Together they helped him to his feet and I followed, with Mother, Thenny and the boys, all of us laughing so hard tears leaked from the corners of our eyes and made the torches blur.

I will tell the rest of you a story, if you like . . .

I heard the Spirit cajoling the folk who remained with the

promise of a long evening, and I felt extremely grateful to the strangers as I held my skirt up climbing the hill. Though they might be unaware of it, they occupied the Being, involved as it was with their entertainment, and we were allowed a peaceful night of rest.

A month of long hot days passed by while we endured the company of the strangers. They seemed intent on remaining on our farm until their supplies and ours were completely diminished. They urged the Spirit constantly to sing new songs, or to entertain their small minds with long tales, and I thought though they were fine to dance with, these outsiders had revealed themselves to be ignorant indeed. They did not understand even the simplest of concepts, and continually expressed great fascination regarding the Spirit's ability to be in two places at one time, or to exist in both the past and the future. Their interest seemed to feed the Being tremendously, and it was most always present, night and day.

I was sitting on the porch steps with Mother, engaged in stripping the leaves and twigs off dried slippery elm and the Spirit was with us, singing a sweet tune it had introduced as a French gardener's song.

> *When the day is warm and fine,*
> *I unfold these flowers of mine;*
> *Ah but you must look for rain*
> *When I shut them up again!*

Mother quietly hummed along, happily employed by her work, but I frowned, wishing she would in no way encourage the Being. I was also thinking they did not call it slippery elm for no reason. Each time I grasped hold of a twig, the branch twisted in my hand and poked my belly or caused another twig to break off and peck me on the cheek and I was having a difficult time. The Spirit's song was like the drone of a menacing bee to my ears.

"Ouch!" I sucked my pricked finger against my teeth, annoyed that I must learn such a laborious task in which I had no interest. The Spirit broke its song and laughed at me, but Mother was too patient with my frustration.

"Look, Betsy dear, it's simple, like this." She took the branch from my hand and snapped each twig off, efficient as the saw blade at Polk's mill. She held the final stick imprisoned between her knees and expertly sliced downward with her paring knife, separating the bark away. "'Tis for Father's throat and we need much of it." She laid the thin bark into a tightly woven vine basket by her side. I had suspected Father's throat was troubling him, for he had been mostly silent for days. Though amongst the chaos engendered by the strangers on our land, his pain was barely noticeable.

I was reaching for a new branch from the pile between Mother's feet on the porch steps to make another attempt at my labor, when I felt a sudden vicious itching on my scalp.

"Mother, there is something biting at my head." I bent over for her inspection and I was not pleased to hear her moan.

"I believe it is head lice." She yanked a hair out and held it up to look more closely.

The wooden cart of the Shakers rode up to the horse tie and I was surprised, for since they had camped on our land, the strangers had not often ventured out in their carts. The tall man in the black coat shouted up to us.

"There is a plague of lice so severe amongst us, we are motivated to leave your farm." He scratched his hat across his head. I was not sorry to hear they were going but I found a plague of head lice to be a disturbing thought. Mother and I laid our task aside and walked down to see them off. Behind the Shakers came the couples from Kentucky, who had already packed their carts and gathered their slaves from our cabins leaving flattened grass at the foot of our hill.

"Farewell, Mrs. Bell, Betsy Bell. We will keep you in our prayers." The woman who had waved to me that first morning waved again now from her seat in the wagon, then returned her hand to itching her neck. Her husband, the red-faced pudgy man, thanked Mother for her hospitality but then remarked, "I hope to cleanse my skin of every pest, invisible or not, when I away from here!" I understood a new attitude had risen amongst them. They had witnessed enough of our torture.

Get gone, Shakers!

The Being spoke from the blooming honeysuckle vines lining the road and the horses were shocked, bolting dangerously for a short spell, then stopping, as if they'd run smack into an invisible wall and could go no farther. The Spirit laughed when the Shakers' wide brim hats blew off and it sicced the farm dogs on them.

Caesar, Harry, Domino!

The Being called the dogs by name up from the barn and we saw them run, barking at the Shakers' cart as if it were a cornered rabbit they had hunted down, urged by the Spirit screaming.

Go, hounds!

The horses bolted, then halted, bolted, then halted, so it took nearly three hours for them to travel less than five hundred feet down our road. I watched the whole scene squirming as the red dry dust of the path disturbed by the horses rose and settled on my skin, contributing to the irritating itching of my head.

🌿

We soon discovered everyone on our farm, including the slaves, had the nasty lice. It was easy for the Negroes; they lined up like sheep in spring and Zeke shaved all their heads, but our family, having suffered profoundly so many afflictions of the Spirit, felt our pride in this instance and wished to show it through the keeping of our hair, infested or not. The boys' locks fell only to their shoulders, and once trimmed, it took less than an hour to pick over their heads, but my braid was well past my bottom and it took over four hours from the day to oil, wash, comb and pick the nits off the million fine blond tresses down my back. I cried in pain as Mother pulled them out, hair by hair.

Two weeks into the scourge she told me she could no longer devote so many hours to my grooming. The cucumber and okra pickling was behind schedule, not to mention the cheese making. She bade me braid my hair and tie a silk ribbon on the end, and she cut near a foot of it off. I tied up the other end and she put it away in her keepsake box, a small consolation to me.

Every moment of our day not absorbed in picking nits, or oiling and combing our hair, we spent boiling pots of water for washing and disinfecting our living quarters, for they swarmed with the tiny live bugs, especially where the visitors' pallets lay. Mother and I scrubbed on our hands and knees alongside Chloe with brushes and rags, until the wood shone with the vinegar and tea tree oil meant to repel the pests, but the following morning there they would be again, wagging their pincers at us, as we sopped them into the pails. Like infinitesimal scorpions, they dug into our scalps laying prodigious quantities of eggs, secured with a glue of life most certainly unequaled in all of nature.

Mother frequently burst into tears, frustrated when her greatest efforts could not produce a cure. The final insult came the morning she discovered her leather kitchen book infested.

"Chloe, look!" I heard her cry. "These parasites have feasted on the pages where my most prized recipes are recorded!"

"Ah, Miz Lucy, the good Lord put the knowledge in your head and there it is still." Chloe tried to comfort her as best she could, but it was awful to see Mother's face, forced to burn what was left of her precious recipes, as the lice had eaten them to shreds. The Being did not speak, or give an explanation for the plague it visited on us, preferring to sing songs, quote passages of Scripture, and make meaningless disparaging remarks, through the long summer. I thought most of its energy must be used conjuring fresh bugs each day.

It was endless. Pots and cauldrons steamed through the oppressive summer heat, as we boiled the clothes, mixed the oils, scrubbed and nit picked, day after day, week after week, until nearly the whole summer season had passed. We were prevented from going to school, or church or even to the store. Messages were carried and provisions dropped at our horse tie, and I began to wonder if we were the only people left alive on earth, could it feel any different?

Twice I did the washing clad only in my petticoats, I was so certain no one would be about. I stood over the boiling iron cauldron of hissing cloth and the bare skin of my arms and legs tingled in the hot sun. I could feel the sun burning my skin to a darker color, but I did not care. I stirred the pot with the long wooden wash paddle and felt my near nakedness in our yard was in some way truly liberating after so many weeks under the critically watchful eyes of strangers. I found myself thinking of Josh as the linens boiled. It had been too long since I had seen his handsome face. Without a doubt he had heard of our lice and had been prevented from calling. As I stirred, my breasts lifted and fell and it seemed to me they had recently grown a bit larger. Sinful as it was, I amused my-self imagining Josh Gardner hiding in the bushes watching me work, admiring my bare skin and round, lifted bosom.

One afternoon, late in August when I had finished the washing and scouring, Mother took me out on the porch to oil and braid my hair. It hurt when she plucked the nits and then she pulled it extra tight behind my ears, making a worried clucking sound with her tongue.

"Listen to the shoals, Betsy. I fear a thunderstorm is brew-ing." I sniffed the air for rain, but all I could smell was tea tree and thyme oil in the soggy humidity, and underneath it the musty smell of blooming tobacco floating over from the fields.

"Hunt down your brothers and fetch them from their fish-ing hole, for I would have them home." She patted the tight braid lying down my back.

"Yes, Mother." I ducked away from her hand, pleased to be sent on an errand and released from further cleaning.

The day was gray, but hot as the inside of the kettle when it would blow the lid off. I set out slowly, for it was difficult to move in the thick heat. No one, not even Zeke, was around, not by the stable or the dairy house, and every animal had re-treated to what shade it could find and lay in it, unmoving. All the hogs slept in the shadow of their trough, or in the mud hole under their tree. The cows were asleep in the pasture, and in the stables even the flies were quiet. The only creature I witnessed with any energy was a young golden kitten batting at a cobweb on the corner of Father's tobacco barn.

"Here, kitty, kitty," I called to her and she came quickly to my hand, allowing me to stroke her soft hot fur. She pulsed her head against my fingers a moment and her fine whiskers tickled my palm before she darted off, leaving tiny paw prints in the dust. I turned behind the barn and crossed the field to meet the path down to the stream. Passing under the green canopy of leaves, I drew a deep breath, and for the first time, I smelled the coming storm. Looking up, I saw the sky had turned a blackish blue, and I knew I ought to hurry.

I jumped from stone to stone enjoying the cool smoothness of rock hidden in the shade all day. I listened for the boys in the woods, but heard nothing more than the rush of the water. I knew my brothers would most likely be on the beach where the stream met the larger river under the cavern. There the water fell over the rocks to make a near thirty-foot pool, perfect for fishing. It was some distance and I felt as I pushed through the green tangle of leaves the Spirit was with me, helping the branches to lift and part, but the air gave no bristle, and the Being did not speak. Time seemed melted by the heat of the day, and though I felt my limbs moving, my destination remained distant. The air did not circulate freely as it usually did above the rushing river. It hung heavy, viscous and menacing. I trudged on, and on, and then, just as I crested the hill where I might see the fishing hole spread out beneath, a breathless fear gripped at my throat and a great wind descended so harsh, the wide green leaves were whipped from the branches and flapped across my eyes. There was a rumble of thunder and the ground moved beneath my feet as if it were God's plan to raise me up. I looked above, to the mouth of the cave, set some seventy-five feet deep into the rock outcropping. Where were my brothers? The rock rose in a sheer cliff near two hundred feet above the bottom of the riverbed and I felt suddenly dizzy.

"Drewry!" I called out when I saw him, down by the water's edge, near the giant elm shading the fishing hole under the cavern.

"Betsy!" He turned, but only briefly, and I saw he was struggling with something in the water.

"Sister!" Joel jumped up and down behind Drew and I could not make out what excited him. Thunder cracked the air and I ran down the path, fighting a gale force that sent branches twirling from the trees.

"Help me! He's stuck and sinking!" Drewry held Richard's arms, at the elbows, and the rest of him was disappeared in the red mud.

Fools! There is not time for this!

The Spirit arrived, along with drops of rain pelting from the sky.

"Help us!" I cried, and Joel joined me begging, "You must help us! Please!"

We had all heard tales of slaves and Indians sucked into whirlpools of quicksand by the Red River, but I had not believed them until now.

"I'm losing him!" Drewry lost his slippery grip on our brother and Richard's arms flailed wildly before he was sucked completely under the mud. I screamed and threw my body down, thrusting my arms into the mud to try and fish him out, as it seemed impossible he might die before our eyes. Drewry fell beside me, and Joel shrieked in hysterics on the bank.

"Hold to me! See if you can grasp him!" Drew anchored himself to the elm tree on the bank and fastened his fingers to my dress. I plunged my arms into the mud, but felt no reassuring limbs.

Tell your brother next time, keep his toes from muddy whirlpools.

Again I heard the roar of thunder and lightning flashed about us. To our profound amazement Richard's body shot out of the quicksand like a lead ball from a gun. It was clear the Invisible had pulled him out, for there was no other explanation. He landed roughly at the foot of the elm tree, sputtering and choking with mud in his mouth.

Quick, children, get away!

"Richard, Richard, are you sound?" I scooped lumps of muddy sand from his eyes so he might open them, and his solemn face reminded me of when he was small. He nodded, clearly too exhausted to speak.

Quick, go now!

The Spirit slapped us with sharp fingers, and pricked our skin with pins, and the rain fell so hard I could not tell if it was needles or drops of water striking my cheeks.

Move at once!

"We must fetch him home to Mother." Joel ran to the path and Drewry took up one of Richard's arms, while I grasped the other. We carried him between us, stumbling through the hot rain and wind toward the path above the fishing hole.

All at once, there was a CRACK, much louder than any thunder, and we turned to see a flash of white light and the giant elm struck by a bolt of lightning. It split the tree in two and a plume of black smoke rose into the rain as the trunk smashed down across the river, solidly covering the quicksand whirlpool forevermore.

"Sister! The Being has saved our lives for certain." Drewry's posture froze, looking back at the scene of misadventure. I adjusted the thin body of Richard against my hip.

"Thank you!" I could not have been more grateful, for Richard's life spared and all of ours. My heart raced with confusion, for all had happened more quickly than I could conceive it. Beneath the fast beating in my chest, I felt the real power of the Spirit, as it demonstrated sway in matters of life and death. I wondered, why did it curse us one day and spare us from natural disaster on the next? The dark part of my heart supposed we were perpetuated as play toys for the Being. If we were gone, who would it torture?

"You are not so evil today, mysterious Spirit!" Drewry called into the air, and seeing his face full of relief gave me cause to think more positively on the subject. Drewry smiled at Richard, muddy, but in one piece, alive. That the Being was capable of great acts of kindness was a thought I struggled to apprehend. The lightning bolt that caused the tree to fall had left a putrid sizzle and stink in the air and the smoke filled my eyes, choking my throat, as we struggled through the wind and hot rain toward home.

That night at dinner we told the story of our rescue to Father and John Jr., while Mother heard it for the second time.

"We'll have to fetch Polk's giant tree saw," was Father's only remark on the subject.

I suppose you would prefer I let the little darlings die?

The Spirit joined us with this caustic insult to my Father, who threw his spoon down on the table, and stopped eating, though Chloe had served his favorite mint and summer squash soup.

Why do you not praise me, Jack Bell? It is you who are evil, ignoring me, day after day.

The Spirit took a coy feminine tone with Father and he did not much like it. Without speaking, he withdrew from the table and I heard him pass through the parlor, removing his flask from his desk, retiring early into his bedroom.

"Pray, we will be eternally grateful for the good deed you have done for us today." Mother soothed the Spirit and we heard it sigh, contented.

"Drewry, did you pass your brother Jesse on the road this morning?" Mother's query was an abrupt change of subject. I knew Jesse had traveled to Springfield to ascertain the price Father's tobacco would bring in the coming harvest, but I did not know Mother was worrying over his welfare, as the journey was not a difficult one and Jesse often made it.

What, Luce? Are you concerned for Jesse?

"Yes, for he has never liked a storm," Mother answered affirmatively, smoothing her dress on her lap. I saw she still fretted over her firstborn, though he was a man on his own.

Wait just a moment and I will see where he is at.

There was silence in the room except for Joel slurping the last of his soup from his bowl.

Your Jess is safe at home. He sits at his pinewood table discussing with his good wife, Martha, the positive results of his journey.

"I must thank you again, gentle Being, for you have set my mind at rest on the subject." Mother rose, smiling, turning to my brother. "Come, Richard, let us sit a spell on the porch together. There is still light and the rain has ceased."

I went to the parlor to pick up the mending I was working on before joining them outside. Joel had busted the seams of his linen summer trousers and I was adding a new strip of cloth in the crotch. Mother had Richard on her lap when I came out, and they were rocking in her hickory chair.

"Were you very frightened, love?" She spoke softly into his wavy brown locks, shining from the oil treatments.

"Yes, Mother. I never shall play near a whirlpool, never, ever." Richard's bare toes, cleansed of the red mud by the bath Mother had given him before dinner, reached the floor, yet he rested his head on Mother's shoulder, and rubbed his cheek against her. It made my heart crack like the split-open elm, to see him, such a big boy, and so solemn.

The air had cooled slightly, and showery drops of water fell from the round pears weighting nearly every branch of the tall trees in front of the house. The smell of the rain was delicious, sweet, green and delicate, and the wind had turned to refreshing breezes. A blue jay preened his feathers at the well and gave a shrill cry that startled me. I accidentally pricked my finger with my sewing needle and, though it bled, I did not cry out.

my brothers depart

The next morning Jesse came round to see us and after divulging his good news of high markets in Springfield, at which we all rejoiced, he set his hat ceremoniously on the table and gave this report.

"Yesterday, shortly upon my return, I was set at the table talking with Martha, when the wind blew open our door." Jesse paused to be certain all of us gathered at the breakfast table were listening. "This was after the storm had passed. All of a sudden, the wood beneath my hands began to shake so violently I suspected an earthquake, or I knew not what. I was quick to my feet, and taking Martha by the arm, we ran outside, only to find nothing moving, not even a wind in the leaves. In truth, it was unnaturally still in our yard, and at once I recognized it was that evil menace that haunts this family, come nattering at us. I know it to be so, for finding the natural world in order, we returned into the house, *very much disturbed,* and on the table lay a pile of stones which certainly were not there moments previous." Jesse did not need to convince us of the Being's capabilities, but no one interrupted him to say so, for clearly he was not finished. He took a sharp breath in.

"The time has come when we must be rid of this affliction. Martha and I will make our way to South Carolina, as others before us have done." Mother locked her knuckles tight together on the tabletop and was about to speak, but Jesse nervously continued. "Think on my life here! When I travel to our church or store, I must along the road pass Old Kate's stall—*Get your Bell Witch amulets!* She uses our good name! Mine and my father's good name, in the hope strangers passing through our district will pay to fend off the demon that accosts us." Jesse looked to Father, who did not meet his gaze but clearly understood. I felt the pinch of a louse biting at my scalp and I too clearly understood my brother's emotions.

"Dear Jesse, I hesitate to confess *I* was the cause of yesterday's discomfort, for I did wonder aloud regarding your welfare after the storm." Mother reached across the table to take Jesse's hands in hers, to quell his thought of leaving.

"No, Mother, you are not the cause of my misery." Jesse pulled his hands from under hers and banged his fist down, raising his voice. "I seek only a life unmarred by stones across the tabletop!" A silence fell on all of us, contemplating his declaration. I wanted suddenly to tell him how the Spirit had saved Richard's life, but he spoke again. "I shall escape this torment. I wish to journey where the weather is warmer and where the Indian corn increases with no effort, so little pains will subsist a large family. I wish to go where the grounds are low and a great variety of mast is said to thrive." It was clear Jesse had thought carefully, creating his plan, all the while saying nothing to us. He tried to soften the blow it was for Mother to hear the news. "I cannot stay here, Mother," he took up her hand regretfully, "for my heart is weak as a rocky ridge, so wretchedly poor it could not grow potatoes."

"Jesse, you need not grow potatoes with your heart." Mother patted his hand in hers and frowned. "You have land a plenty here and Father has offered to help you in tobacco, and what of Martha?" She turned to her daughter-in-law. "Martha, what say you of this plan?" Mother expected Martha to object wherein Mother promised with her eyes to support her, but Martha sighed and looked to Jesse.

"It will be as Jesse wills, for I have put my faith in him," she said, sliding her hand under her husband's. "But surely, I will miss you all!" Martha's acceptance was the clearest indicator my eldest brother was quite serious regarding his imminent departure from the district. Mother let her head drop into her own arms on the table, and began to cry.

"Jesse, Jesse, how can you leave us? How do you know the Spirit will not follow you wherever you may go?"

I will not.

The Spirit broke gently into the discussion, and I realized it must have been present all the while.

"Damn you, evil menace!" Jesse cursed it loudly, looking up.

"Please, speak unto this boy, promise you will trouble him no more!" Mother pleaded with the Being, beside herself with frustration.

Luce, Luce, how I hate to see you unhappy, but in this, your desire will not be fulfilled. Your Jesse will do well in black-eyed peas. His wife will rise out of bed early, while he lies and snores until the sun has risen one third of its course, and dispersed all the unwholesome damps, and even with this tendency to laziness, his crops will prosper and the fruit of his loins will multiply.

The mention of her future grandchildren stopped Mother's

tears. It was as if their ghosts danced happily around the table on some future summer day, and we all absorbed the Spirit's prediction of my brother's life, seeming a likely and accurate one, for Jesse had always liked to lie in bed in the morning.

"Will you return, to visit?" Mother reached again across the tabletop, covering Jesse's hands with hers.

"We are not leaving this moment, Mother. It will take some time to set our affairs in order," Jesse reassured her. He was a grown man. He did not need their permission, he had only intended to inform them. Slowly he withdrew his hand and patted Mother's, a half smile on his lips.

"What say you, Father?" He turned to Father, who had been silent all the while.

"I have the names of kinsmen for you, Jesse." Father nodded, but I saw Jesse's decision irritated him. I wondered if he was jealous his eldest son might actually escape the torment Father himself must continue to endure. The good news of the markets was heavily shadowed by the sadness that fell over us all, as we contemplated the prospect of no more Jesse and Martha chattering on our Sunday ride to church. No more girlish talk over sewing. I wished heartily the Spirit would go away rather than my brother, but I knew it mattered not what I wished.

The September morning after Jesse and Martha departed, our lice infestation ceased. From one day to the next, we were freed from the pestilence. Our first Sunday back amongst the congregation, the Reverend Johnston and Calvin Justice came to our home after the service for the Sunday meal, and the Reverend wasted no time inside the door before complimenting Mother for her gracious invitation.

"We have suffered, lacking your good company through so much of the summer season."

"And we have missed you also, dear Reverend. We are at last redeemed from our scourge here on this farm, and yet, another worldly inconvenience now assails us." Mother took Calvin Justice's topcoat from him.

"Pray, what can it be?" the Reverend inquired, hanging his own coat on the hallway peg. I watched him from where I sat in the parlor, sewing the new gray linsey-woolsey trousers Mother and I were making for John Jr.

"We have had some news." Mother bade the men to take their seats. I nodded to them but did not rise, for I was on the crucial final knot of a trouser leg. I held the needle up as my excuse, and the golden evening sun from the parlor window flashed over it, sending a spark of light into the room.

"Miss Betsy," the Reverend nodded to me and settled in Mother's chair, while Calvin Justice sat on the other side of the hearth. "What news?"

"We have had a message regarding a share in an estate I hold in North Carolina." Father cleared his hoarse throat and entered the parlor with John Jr., each of them carrying a straight-back chair from the dining table. Father did not go to his desk for his flask, but set himself beside Calvin Justice to further explain.

"Affairs in this estate are coming to a close and I must send a representative." The Reverend and Calvin Justice listened intently, and I believe they wondered if Father was seeking volunteers, for they both looked troubled. "John Jr. will depart in the morning and we seek your wise advice and counsel for him, on this, his farewell evening."

"Goodness, Jack." The Reverend's round face was surprised, but I thought I saw a shade of relief in his frown.

"Must he travel over the Great Smoky Mountains, with the winter on its way?"

"'Tis hardly winter yet, Reverend, but yes, he must cross the mountains. We are planning his route across Newfound Gap, and from there he may rest at beautiful Lake Lure." Father clapped a hand down on John Jr.'s knee, to reassure him, speaking of the journey ahead.

"I hear bandits line the road along the French Brood River. He ought to stay his horse from there." Calvin Justice leaned forward and clasped his hands together, squeezing his knuckles, sparing the details. "However, there is a wayfarer's house of excellent report just this side of Cullowhee."

"Were it not Cullowhee where the Injuns retreated?" The Reverend Johnston turned to him with surprise.

"It was, but there are none left living there, and a pleasant station exists in that place today. You have my word on it, for I rested there myself on my journey from the Methodist seminary."

"In that desolate mountain territory, thieves and other anti-religious men are known to prowl." The Reverend shook his head with worry, but Mother adopted a positive attitude.

"Be not overly concerned, dear Reverend, not every non-believer is a dangerous man." I thought of Frank Miles and his good soul, as the man who proved her statement absolutely. I knew Mother was unhappy, as I was, that Father was sending John Jr. off to North Carolina, but she was making the best of it. I tied the final knots in the thread most reluctantly. Since Jesse and Martha had departed, I found I missed them much more than I'd expected and losing John Jr. felt unbearable. Who would be next?

Your John should stay at home where he will be useful. This journey will prove futile, as the estate is not yet settled and cannot be settled for some time to come.

The Spirit offered its own view of the situation.

"Go from here!" Father shouted, standing, his face noticeably red with anger. "Return to Hell, where you belong!" The fury of his voice caused everyone to tense and sit up straighter. No one wished to provoke the Being into violent tortures on the night before John Jr.'s departure. We were all surprised to hear the Spirit laughing its retort.

You know nothing, old Jack. If John Jr. leaves this house tomorrow he will have a hard trip without reward. The sky will throw fire and storm after storm will deluge the roadways until his finest horse sinks to its knees in mud. He will grow ill from lack of nourishment and cry bitter tears. All for nothing, for when he reaches his destination, he will discover several months must pass until the money will be available to him. Good son that he is to you, he will trouble himself greatly with the persons there, and stay long in torturous expectation of an outcome other than this truth I here predict, yet when he returns, John Jr. will be empty-handed and so much the worse for wear.

This picture was bleak indeed and I shuddered as the images so accurately described filled my mind. I was nearly overcome by the urge to cry out and throw myself across John Jr.'s feet to beg him, please, listen to this vision of the future, but the Spirit spoke before I could, in a greatly softened tone.

Soon to this farm will come a young lady from Virginia, wealthy and in possession of charms more plentiful and sweet than the blooms on Luce's roses. Her slaves are numerous and her family is outstanding, of old money. She will please you, John Jr., unlike any other in this lifetime, and if you stay at home, you will certainly win her heart.

I believe John Jr. was affected, as I saw him glance at Father, suddenly uncertain. For my own part, I thought I saw the beautiful girl appear in the wavering flame of the candle Mother was lighting. The sun had gone from the parlor window, and the yellow flame flared up the wick, revealing a young woman with a soft expression of love on her face.

"Seek not to deceive, you Devil, for it shall be your undoing." Father's voice was determined. "John Jr. shall not adhere to fantasies from a manifestation evil as you are. Leave my house. Leave the decisions of God-fearing men apart from your concerns." His timbre was full of effort yet restrained, and I wondered if he was suffering the pains of his throat.

The Spirit laughed again, sounding like the creak of a wagon wheel stuck in the mud.

They that hate the righteous shall be desolate.

"How could a Being such as yourself be considered righteous?" Father was outraged and sat heavily in his chair, looking toward his desk. I believe he wished he had his silver flask in hand.

I am righteous. And everlasting.

The Spirit departed suddenly, as if offended, and we sat uncomfortable in the silence it left behind.

"*Is* this journey truly necessary?" The Reverend Johnston raised a hand to Father. "Perhaps it would be better for all if the estate could be settled without your representative, Jack?"

"Speak not, good Reverend, of altering our plans to align ourselves with demonic predictions. What must be, will be." Father sighed and clapped John Jr. on the leg again. "Son, if you would have an early start, you must retire." Father seemed to relish this exercise of his will over the Spirit's talk and I felt annoyed with him.

"We will not pass the night here. Jack, Lucy." The Reverend Johnston and Calvin Justice stood to take their leave.

"John Jr., God bless your endeavors and your travels. Numerous temptations you will meet along the road, but we will pray for you and know the Lord walks with those who walk the right true path."

"I will recall your counsel often, I am certain, Reverend." John Jr. smiled and hung his head a little.

Upstairs, as I undressed, I hoped some sense would lodge inside John Jr.'s head instead of dreams and he would rise in the morning and tell our Father he simply could not go, for the Spirit had said it was unwise. Besides, the opportunity to meet a girl who *would please like no other* could not be missed, for everyone knew such matches in life were not easily come by. I thought of Josh Gardner's gray eyes and of his arm steadying my own months ago when we had walked on the path to the stream. I felt he pleased me like no other, but I did not see enough of him, and soon I would be missing two of my brothers instead of just one. I crawled into my bed and pulled the summer cotton quilt up high, though it was warm. I wished to wrap up my thoughts in the blanket, for I knew whatever passion lay inside John Jr.'s adventurous heart, he took after Father in most ways, and I expected he would rise before the dawn to leave.

I woke to the sound of voices, and I ran outside, clad only in my thinnest nightdress, afraid I had missed my brother's departure. I saw Drewry, Richard and Joel already gathered at the horse tie. Father was slipping a rolled-up map through the leather straps of John Jr.'s. saddlebag and Zeke was busy with last-minute instructions regarding the care of the horses to his boy Isiah, who was to accompany John Jr. The horses stamped at the ground, impatient to be off.

"Farewell, and God bless you, my son." Mother embraced him, wrapping her arms around his waist, pressing her cheek into his shoulder. He was slightly taller than Father and looked every inch a man. Joel ran and hugged his legs and I believe Richard and Drewry may have wanted to, but they hung back, waiting. John Jr. lifted Joel onto his hip, then swung him down to the ground, tickling his sides.

"Be a good boy, Joel, and learn your tasks, and one day you and I may ride together."

"I want to now!" Joel bounced up and down with desire, but John Jr. laughed.

"You want to, but you cannot!" He spanked Joel friendly pats on the bottom until he ran away to climb and swing on the horse tie and John Jr. turned to me.

"Betsy, I will bring you home fine silk or lace, which do you desire?"

"I desire only you would not leave," I answered truthfully. The first rays of sun cut through the wet half-light, illuminating the stubborn set of his jaw along with the certain knowledge in my heart that his journey would be as the Spirit foretold, full of pain and suffering for no great end and the sweet match he left behind would never appear for him again.

"Don't cry, dear sister." He kissed my cheek and embraced me, misunderstanding the quivering in my chin as concern for myself with him gone away. "I will return to you." I saw Mother was busy, discussing some aspect of John Jr.'s route with Father, and because they could not hear me, I pressed him.

"Brother, did you not hear the Being's warning? Will you not listen?"

"Betsy." He frowned and held me squarely by the shoulders. "Be a good girl and helpful to our mother and father. Speak not of our evils but endeavor to lead a good life, and pray to God." He turned away, much preoccupied, and I saw in the set of his shoulders the same stance he took patrolling the fields alongside Father looking for worms in the tobacco. He was going to do it whether he wanted to or not. I put my index finger in between my teeth and bit down to keep from crying, for I suspected John Jr. knew, as I did, his journey would be arduous and most likely all for nothing, yet he was obligated to complete it. I thought the Spirit's words must have dampened his enthusiasm for the ride ahead, particularly if he thought of the beautiful young lady in the candle flame, but John Jr. gave no clue as to whether these thoughts truly occupied his mind. Instead, he mounted the horse Father had chosen, and waited for Isiah to do the same.

"Ya!" He flicked the reins and they set off walking deliberately down the path to the road, where he turned and waved, before kicking his horse into the brisk and steady pace he would set for his journey.

"Will he come back, Betsy?" I felt Joel lean against my side, wrapping his fingers into mine.

"Of course he will, of course," I reassured him, certain it was true, John Jr. would return. Only I had the strongest sense, watching the back of his sturdy horse swaying from our farm, when we did see him again, some vast change as yet unpredicted in our lives would have altered the faces we turned to one another. I wished I could know for certain what trauma lay ahead.

the accusation of kate

I thought of John Jr. often, and said prayers at night for his safety, but the harvest time was on us and I was constantly at work. The skies were cloudless and blue, day after day, and the air was crisp and dry, allowing near perfect conditions for tobacco curing. In August each tobacco plant had been cut off close to the ground, impaled on slender iron sticks with sharp points capable of pushing through their tough stalks, and then each plant had been hung in the barn to cure. Now they were being culled and carefully bunched into flat fan-shaped hands so they could be stacked into burdens and loaded into the hogshead drums Father would take to market in spring. The boys and the hands did most of that work, and I spent my days beside Mother and Chloe, sorting the beans for drying and seed, canning tomatoes and squash.

One afternoon, early in October, I told Mother I must go for a walk out-of-doors before I could pay careful attention to the afternoon's task of stripping slippery elm again. She gave her permission and I walked out through the orchard. The air was warm but no longer heavy as it had been most of the summer. I could hear the thud-thud of ripe fruit dropping to the ground with the breeze and I picked up a golden apple to eat as I walked. I looked down the hill toward the stream where the flat cornfield was dotted with pumpkins, bright orange and ready for harvest. Chloe would soon be making pumpkin soup, a treat of unsurpassed goodness, and I looked forward to sampling this year's crop.

Father had already harvested the corn and only the stalks were left in the field, tied into bunches and laid in stacks. They would soon be dissected into kindling and powder. Chloe had shown me when I was Joel's age how to make a doll from a corn husk and there was nothing I had liked better, when I was little, than spending an afternoon in the cornfield indulging this pastime under the blue autumn sky. It seemed long ago when I played, mindlessly happy. I made a pillow of my skirts in a flat place between the bundles and managed for a few moments to focus purely on my own enjoyment. I chose the best husk from the pile at my feet. Sufficiently dry, yet supple. Carefully I smoothed it to shape a face and tidy bonnet. What fun it was, caressing the silk skin in my hands. I twisted and tied, and soon had a lovely little figure. She was sweet, but lonely, so I made another, then another, and before long I had a party of dolls. I got to my feet and used a stick to make roads in the red earth, pretending the dolls had come to live in pumpkin houses surrounded by prickly green leaf lakes and cornstalk mountains. I did not think of the mountains John Jr. was toiling through, I thought only of my game. I contemplated what lives my dolls might have, and I was about to give them names and invent the stories of their town when I was startled from my play by the shwoosh of a bird wing near my ear. I looked up. It was so peaceful and quiet in the field, a swallow traveling from tree to barn made a great sound. I looked to the woods beside the stream and saw dust rising from the bank and in the next moment I saw a horse and rider. I held the edge of my cotton bonnet to better shade my eyes, pleased to recognize Josh Gardner riding toward me. I waved and walked to greet him, leaving my dolls where the wind might take them.

"Hello, Betsy," he called out happily. "Might you be allowed a short ride with me? I have my father's saddle and it's plenty wide enough for both of us." He smiled and I felt he was even better looking than I recalled, for his face was tanned to the color of his dark saddle and his gray eyes stood out like the fox grapes ripening on the vines. I looked hastily over my shoulder pleased to realize from where we were in the flat space between the field and the stream, my house could not be seen.

"We needn't be gone long and I would have come before, but every minute of every day I have been in service to my father on our farm." Josh offered his arm to pull me up, his smile sincere. When I did not immediately take it he placed his hand on his hip, impatient. "I have but a short time now, Betsy Bell, and I did use it to make haste to your lands in the hope we might share a short ride along your lovely stream." The way he said my name caused my stomach to tighten. I wished to go, but I knew Father would not allow it.

"I am uncertain . . ." I stalled, assessing if it would be worth the possible consequences.

"We won't be long . . ." Josh spoke of it as though it was no great matter. He let the reins of his mare droop and she nuzzled my face, inviting me herself, so I felt I must consent.

"Why, yes, I'll come, but let us ride preferably away from my abode."

"Of course." Josh laughed and leaned down, extending his

arm to me again. I blushed, but grasped his elbow and nimbly climbed up the side of his horse.

"Betsy, you are graceful as the beautiful heron recently residing on Old Kate Batts's pond." He watched me twist my skirts to fit in sideways behind him on the saddle.

"I have heard of no heron in this vicinity," I lied, not wanting to reveal what I knew of the witch creature predicted by the Being.

"Have you ever seen one?"

"Never."

"Then we must go there," he declared, snapping the reins. It seemed quite a sensible choice of direction, for we were nearest the trail to our southern boundary and to take that path we need not pass my house.

"Hold tight about my waist and we will get there all the sooner." Josh was friendly even when commanding. I did as he requested, discovering the white cotton shirting of his back had a fresh smell much different from the lye of our laundry. We galloped at a good pace on the trail without speaking, while I pretended to admire the lovely yellow and red colors of the many trees, but really my eyes absorbed nothing more than Josh Gardner's jaunty angling of his reins, and the sure movement of his buttocks in the saddle.

We reached the log bridge Father had built over the river near the boundary of our land and Kate Batts's and we slowed considerably to cross it. The golden light of the sun filtering through the autumn leaves in the woods made the air around us glow with warmth. I felt secure and happy with my arms around Josh Gardner, and I wished our ride could last for days. All at once, a sudden shower of sticks and stones from the hedge growth by the bank caused Josh's mare to whinny and neigh and rear up sharply and I found myself fallen to the ground, his horse's hooves stamping dangerously close beside my head. With expert skill, Josh rode forward through the barrage and across the bridge, where he dismounted, left his horse to recover on its own, and hurried back to me.

"Betsy, are you hurt?" I saw him running but as he moved closer the falling sticks intensified, such that I could not answer or even uncover my head, for fear my eyes would be put out by the twigs attacking. I was surprised, as the Spirit had not been violent with me for some time. Nonetheless, it felt as I remembered, appalling and hideous. Josh fought his way through the storm of branches and tried to shield my body with his own, but it was no use.

"Get up!" he urged, pulling hard on both my arms, managing to drag me upright. I kept my hands over my eyes and I do not know what Josh did so he might see, but somehow he led me stumbling after him over the bridge and there the pelting ceased.

"How do you fare?" I could tell Josh was shaken, for his face had grown pale beneath his tan, but he focused all his attention on my welfare.

"I have seen much worse than that!" I tried to laugh.

"Dear girl!"

"The twigs did not strike strong enough to injure . . ." I did not want the Spirit to ruin my ride with him, though I knew it already had.

"But your cheek is scratched and your hands are bleeding." Josh took my fingers in his gloves and I saw he was correct, fine scratches lined the backs of my hands, and they lightly put forth blood. Josh dropped them suddenly and running back across the bridge he shouted loudly in the place of our attack.

"Come out, you Spirit of the Devil, and let me have a

round with you!" He picked up a large branch from the side of the path, preparing himself for a fight with the Invisible. I ran back after him.

"Stop, stop, dear Joshua. Please, take me home, it is useless to provoke this Being further." My hands began to tremble uncontrollably and my knees were weak with the weight of me, as if I carried the large boulder of our fruitless search for treasure in my belly again.

Betsy Bell, do not have Josh Gardner.

The Spirit spoke from every golden leaf in the surrounding canopy.

"Leave me alone . . ." I managed to whisper.

"Show yourself, that I may beat you to unconsciousness!" Josh raised his stick high above his head, and all around us the wheezy laughter of the Spirit issued from the shrub and woods like wind. Josh whipped his head from left to right, expecting blows, but none did fall.

"Otherworldly demon, fight or go! Trouble the innocent no longer!" Josh reminded me of Father for a moment, his jaw set, defiantly stern.

How do you know Miss Betsy is so innocent?

The sound of the Spirit's laughter made my heartbeat quicken, and I worried I might faint. I did not want Josh to engage the Being in conversation, as there was no telling what it would say or do.

"Josh, please." I stepped toward him and placed my arm on his. "I feel most suddenly unwell. Let us depart." He turned to me.

"If you wish it to be so, I will take you," he said, placing his stick down on the ground. He grasped my bare and bleeding hand gently in his gloved one and walked me back across the bridge.

"I am heavy . . ." I began, for when we reached the horse, he turned, and circling my waist with both his hands, he lifted me up so I nearly flew into the saddle. I hoped perhaps Josh *could* be a formidable opponent for the Being, but as my Father, the Reverend, Calvin Justice and Frank Miles all had failed, it did not seem likely any man, even so fine as Josh, could ever prevail against it. He mounted behind me, circling my arms with his arms and the reins, his left leg pressing against my skirt, holding me up. I felt protected and found the warmth of his body most comforting, but as we crossed the bridge and trotted through the space of air where the Being had unleashed its tortures, I grew cold and weak inside, and I shivered, distressed by the event.

"Do not be afraid, Miss Betsy," Josh spoke with confidence, and kicked his horse into a trot. I did not reply, for what could I answer? I did not wish to bore him with my fears.

"Shall I deliver you to your front door, or to the spot of our rendezvous?" Sensitive soul that he was, he recognized I was unhappy, but might wish to keep it to myself. The thought of meeting Father or even Mother while riding with Josh Gardner with my hands cut and bleeding and having to explain did not appeal to me. Josh read me rightly.

"To the spot of our rendezvous," I answered, repeating the sophisticated French, able to smile at the lightness of his choice of words. I liked him immensely.

We reached the field and Josh dismounted, holding his arms out for me to slide down. I was careful not to fall into him, but to remain arm's length away. He gripped my elbows and made me look into his eyes. Earnest was his gaze and something passed between us that made the moment lengthen and be still. Our stance together felt just right.

"You must promise you will make your way to where you

will be safe." He dictated a course of action for me with utmost seriousness.

"I am safe right now," I answered boldly, staring back at him, forgetting for a moment about the Being, thinking I would be frightened only if Father were to happen by and see me alone with Josh. He sensed my thoughts and looked up to the orchard, allowing his hands to gently slip over my forearms and clasp my fingers.

"No doubt you have not been missed, Miss Betsy, for that was a short ride indeed."

"I am sorry it came to such an end." I bowed my head and looked at his gloved hands holding mine. Truly, I had enjoyed it, despite the violence.

"On my word, we will meet again, and we will not be maligned. This incomprehensible horror can not long torment you." Josh lifted my chin with one gloved finger, forcing me to look again into the gray pools of his eyes, reminding me of Kate Batts's pond and the heron we had not seen. "Betsy, I know it is forward of me to say this, but with your circumstances as they are, I feel the regular conventions for relating do not apply." Josh took a breath and I could see he was slightly nervous in his speech. "It's just that I would have you know I think of you most constantly. You are so beautiful, Betsy Bell. Do not despair. Go, and care for yourself, for you are most precious and deserving." He smiled and I blushed at his strong words to me, pulled my hand from his, and turned away, setting off as if the Spirit chased me.

Betsy Bell, do not have Josh Gardner.

The phrase echoed in my ears, stronger than the feeling of his finger on my chin. Why would the Being say such a thing? Why was it so committed to my unhappiness? Why had I allowed myself even for a moment to think I might have happiness? I knew the Spirit had its ways and means and did not want me content, but why had it chosen to torment me so grievously? I slowed to walk through the cornfield, the prickly pumpkin leaves catching at my skirts. How wasted was my happy playtime. All the dolls of my game and joyful moments had disappeared, blown by the wind into the river, scattered amongst the rocks, I knew not where. Such was my fate, blown and bloodied by forces I could as much control as the wind. I felt Josh's eyes on my back, but I did not look over my shoulder until I reached the hill and began the climb up through the orchard. There I stopped and saw he had mounted his horse and was waiting to leave until he could see me no more. I waved, suddenly aware he had revealed a deep liking for me and I had shared nothing with him. I turned away, miserable that I had not told him how very often he was in my mind. I ran up the incline, arriving breathless at the gate of the garden. There was Mother standing at the kitchen doorway, shielding her eyes against the sun with her hand. I hoped she was inspecting the plants in between us, but I had the feeling she was about to shout my name.

"Elizabeth! I wondered where you'd gone." I felt if she saw my face she would see everything that had happened and I did not wish to sadden or anger her with my experience. I walked as slowly as I could, keeping my eyes to the ground, but it was difficult to keep secrets from Mother.

"Betsy dear, are you unwell?" She came to me when I stopped at the barrel by the side of the house where the rainwater was collected. She stroked my braid as I rinsed the dried lines of blood off the back of my hands. "Your hair is in a massive tangle, child, come inside, we'll give it a good brushing." Mother led me through the house into her bedroom, where she sat me down on the bed, facing the small high window above her bedside table that let in a cheerful bright blue square of sky. She took the wooden brush from the top of her chest and gently unplaited my braid, without speaking. I appreciated her silence, but found without her questioning me, I could do nothing but feel my sadness, and the tears welled up in my eyes and spilled onto my cheeks. I let them drop onto my dusty dress, and Mother ceased stroking the wooden brush across my hair, forced to pull out the twigs and brambles with her fingers. I cried a little harder, relieved to feel Mother's concern.

"There, there, little one." These simple words made me feel the way I used to, when I was nothing but a tiny girl and Mother could hold all of me in her lap when I was hurt.

"This is the matter . . ." I told her all, concentrating on the punishment I had received at the bridge.

"I was attacked in an evil way, with more violence than I have witnessed from the Being for some time. Look at my hands, scratched to pieces, for I used them to shield my eyes. It meant to scratch my eyes out, Mother, laughing all the while!"

Betsy Bell, do not have Josh Gardner.

"See?" I turned quickly for the Spirit spoke from beside my mother. "I hate you, demon! I hate you!" I yelled into her face, though my words were meant only for the Being.

"Betsy!" Mother threw her hands up, and for a moment I was frightened she might smack me with the back side of her brush, but she was only startled by my turning or by the Spirit's interruption, and her hands quickly dropped.

So what if you hate me? So what?

"Leave her be," Mother spoke seriously to it, but without over much concern. She reprimanded the Being as if it were Richard, caught teasing Joel, and I soon heard why. "Elizabeth, it was indeed wrong of you to go riding with Joshua Gardner unchaperoned and without permission."

She believes she will make her own rules.

"She knows the right true path," Mother said. She turned her head to answer, for the voice now emanated from the blue square of light. "And she will walk it, I am certain. Take no pleasure assaulting and abusing her, for then what will she learn?" Mother picked up the brush to return to the task at hand, reasoning with the Being.

Your Betsy would go "preferably away from my abode."

The Spirit taunted me with a perfect imitation of my voice and I saw Mother frown to hear the words I'd spoken, but good that she was, she had me turn my head so she might continue brushing, rather than chastise me. She put her attention to distracting the Being by sending it on an errand.

"Be useful, and let us hear news of John Jr.'s travels."

I will bring you this, dear Luce, though I can not guarantee it will please you.

Mother's artifice was effective and the room grew silent except for the swooshing of the brush.

"Mother, I believe it would be best not to trouble Father with this tale of my misadventure." I spoke quietly though I was still upset.

"Betsy, I shall not tell your father, solely because he has far greater concerns, and it will serve no one to disturb him further, but what our mysterious Spirit will say of it, I would not try to guess." She sighed and dropped my hair, ready to plait it up again. I did not see how she could remain so calm and my chin began to shake with tears again. "Betsy," Mother pulled my hair back, "you are a young woman now and must constantly endure more than most. Be certain the Lord does have a special purpose for you. He loves you more than you can know, and He has assigned you suffering. Though it is hard to reconcile, pray constantly, and someday, perhaps, we all shall know God's meaning in our special trials. You must trust it will be so." Mother's knuckles moved from the nape of my neck to the top of my spine, braiding swiftly.

"In truth," I sobbed, covering my eyes with my scratched hands, "I do not feel my special purpose or that love of which you speak! I see only God's punishments, for He does not protect me." Mother paused only a moment in her plaiting, thinking on my desperate words, before resuming at the same rate as before.

"That's blasphemy, Betsy, and you cannot mean it." She pulled my hair tight. "You must have faith and that is the end of it, for the ways of God are as mysterious as our affliction. I tell you, trust the good Lord will provide and care for you as you trust your father and me to provide and care for you." She tightened the knots quickly and I felt her tying the leather thong around the end of my braid before I could respond. What if she was wrong? What if there was no God in Heaven watching over me, directing my sad trials for some higher purpose?

"Let the tightness of this braid remind you of this wisdom I impart, for somehow you must keep it in your head, Elizabeth." Mother patted my leg with the back of the brush, with more lightheartedness than she held in the tone of her voice. "Come now, we must turn our attention to the slippery elm, for your father's throat is a great nuisance to him." I threw my arms around her before she could rise, grateful my braid was fresh and tight, grateful, even though I could not grasp it, that Mother believed I had a special purpose to my trials.

We sat on the front steps for near the rest of that afternoon in silence, amused only by the golden yellow leaves falling from the pear trees. I had finally mastered the art of twisting and paring the slippery elm bark. My knife cuts were exact and deep enough to cause the bark to peel its own self off the twig. When it recoiled back, I grasped it easily, pulling free one long sturdy strip for Mother to store in the jars she'd lined up on the rail of the porch. The scratches on my hands were making the task more difficult, but working slowly I was accomplishing it. Near time to get ready for supper, I heard the racket of wagon wheels, and looking out, I saw a fine black carriage traveling down the Adams–Cedar Hill high road, and in its dust, a wooden cart full of Negroes dressed in white, laughing together.

It is the young lady from Virginia, come to visit.

I was not surprised to hear the Spirit make this pronouncement. I had been waiting for this visit since the night before John Jr.'s departure. The wheels of the fine coach rolled steadily toward us, and I saw the window open and the head of a young woman pop out. I recognized her face, for I had seen her in the candle flame. The carriage turned off the road onto our path.

"Tie up the bundles and stash them at the end of the porch." Mother stood and wiped her hands on her apron before reaching back to untie it. "Will they be staying long?" she asked the Spirit as though she trusted it to know, but it did not respond nicely.

Long enough for you to see what folly John Jr. has committed.

I dropped my pile of deadwood in the corner, wishing I could switch the Being's backside with it. I returned to tie up Mother's bundle and saw she was already hurrying down the path toward the horse tie to greet the visitors. The young woman from Virginia was delicately stepping from her carriage, assisted by the hand of an elderly gentleman with a long gray beard. My tight braid reminded me, trust in God, but it also made my head ache. I sat down to collect myself in Mother's rocker on the porch, for I did not look forward to the coming evening. I ran my fingers over the scratches on my hands and thought of Josh's worn leather gloves, the heat in his eyes by the bridge.

Betsy Bell, do not have Josh Gardner.

"I will have in my thoughts what I please." I spoke aloud, though I was alone, for I was uncertain if the Spirit had actually spoken to me or if I simply heard its words strongly in my mind. The Spirit laughed, unquestionably speaking out loud, for I could feel the vibrations that were its breath around my ear.

You will witness what it means to lose a love, Miss Betsy.

"Why must I witness my brother's spurned opportunity?" I stamped my foot on the wooden porch, covering my ears with my hands. "You need not cause me further pain, and I will have my own opportunity to make the match I please!"

Do you think so, Betsy Bell?

The Spirit teased me.

"You are not my maker, and know not what will be!" I was angry with the Being, and insisted it no longer dictate my actions, but abruptly I felt a hand grab my braid and yank my head back, as if its intent was to divide my scalp from my soul. I cried out.

I am all things, and your future is known to me. You would do well to remember it.

The Spirit laughed and caused Mother's bunch of slippery elm to bust its jute and gather into a massive round ball of sticks. Before I could stand and grasp it, the giant sphere of twisted wood bounced down the porch steps, rolling with great accuracy toward the horse tie at the foot of the hill. I jumped from my chair and flew after it, calling to Mother.

"Look out!"

The Spirit's haphazard sculpture was near the size of me and moving with such speed whoever was at the end of its path would certainly be hurt.

"Aiii, 'tis a whirligig!" The young woman from Virginia heard my cry and with great presence of mind she grabbed her escort by the hand and flew so quickly up the lowered steps of her carriage, the plume of her fancy hat went fast as a real bird through the sky. She shut the door with a bang and when the ball of sticks passed the horse tie, it miraculously lost its invisible glue, dissolving into a pile of wood.

"Praise the Lord!" cried the old black man who drove the cart, "this must be the place."

"If you have come to see the Bell Witch you will be greatly disappointed, for what haunts us is unseen, except by mischief such as this." Mother looked forlornly at the batch of slippery elm, so dusty and cracked I doubted it was usable.

"Mrs. Bell, I presume? This is my uncle, Sir Thomas Barton, and I am Miss Sallie Barton." The young woman popped out of the carriage again and descended the steps, withdrawing a gold case from the brocade purse swinging on her arm. I had never seen anything like it and I watched mesmerized as she took from it a card, placing it urgently in Mother's hand. There was an elegant quality to the swish of her light blue skirt and I saw the fabric was fine.

"We hesitate to impose on your good graces, Mrs. Bell, but we are traveling to Nashville and at the inn in Springfield we heard remarkable tales of stimulating activities about your farm, and we thought it worth the short journey to come calling." Sallie Barton looked sideways at her uncle for confirmation and he nodded, clearly accustomed to allowing his pretty niece to speak for both of them. "Already we have experienced excitements beyond most days!" She smiled, so her face lit up with charm, expressing her clear beauty. "Please, Mrs. Bell, if we are any inconvenience, we will turn our horses straight, but if not, might we tarry just a short while?" Sallie Barton spoke so politely I was not surprised to hear Mother invite her to supper and to stay the night, adding that her slaves were welcome to join ours in the cabins.

Before we could lead the young lady and her uncle up the hill and into the house, two new sets of travelers, strangers who had met Miss Sallie Barton at the inn in Springfield, turned off the road and onto our path. Mother greeted them, and also Calvin Justice, who rode in behind the company.

"I heard the Negroes singing, Mrs. Bell," Calvin Justice said. "I thought perhaps someone had passed away without my knowledge."

"Why Calvin Justice! There is no such calamity." Mother stopped and put her hands on her hips, sounding annoyed the preacher would jump to such a morbid conclusion. "Merely visitors from the state of Virginia. Meet Sir Thomas Barton and Miss Sallie Barton."

Calvin Justice dismounted and removed his hat and I wondered if he realized whom he met. I expect he did, but what could be done about it? He was invited to share our supper of mince and pumpkin pies, along with the unknown travelers. I looked at no one, trudging back up the hill. I concentrated on the tip of my nose and the base of my neck, still tingling from the tight braid and the jerk of the Spirit.

"I feel an autumn chill," Mother remarked, after our supper was finished. She led our guests into the parlor. The front window was open, but no one moved to close it, for it let in the pleasant undulating and unfamiliar songs of Sallie Barton's slaves, rising up from the cabins, through the crisp fall evening air.

"Drewry, build us a small fire," Father said as he crossed the room and stood at his desk, removing his silver flask from within. I had watched him casting studious glances at Miss Sallie Barton throughout our meal as she spoke of her plantation in Virginia and her travel on a ship to England and back. I wondered if he was thinking of John Jr.

"'Tis warmer than Virginia in this season." Sallie had a heavy fancy shawl intricately woven in a cup and saucer pattern, wrapped loosely on her shoulders.

"Sister, she's so pretty . . ." Joel tugged my arm, whispering his observation.

And a perfect match for your absent brother.

The strangers gasped as the voice of the Spirit entered the room on the crack and spark of the flames Drewry built up in the fireplace.

"Oh goodness, you must be the Bell Witch!" Sallie Barton smiled, as if pleased to be introduced.

I am many things. No longer will I lie to you. I am none other than a witch of Kate Batts's making, here to torment Jack Bell out of his life!

There was a general intake of breath amongst the gathering, for though none present, excepting Calvin Justice and my family, knew Old Kate, all knew the name of the master of the house they visited, and they turned their eyes to Father, who had taken a seat in the hickory rocker next to me. His chair commenced rocking so unnaturally fast, Father had to grip the arms to keep from being flung from it. Before us his limbs grew stiff and he was seized with sudden contortions of his face. His flesh twitched and danced as if invisible hands attempted to rearrange his features. It was horrible to see, and it was made worse knowing there was nothing we could do to help him. The Being laughed, and magnified the crunch of the wooden rocker striking the floorboards, apparently enjoying its torment of Father tremendously. One of the strangers jumped to his feet.

"Who is this Kate Batts? In what direction lies her home? Let us bring her to justice tonight for the torture of this good man!" There were murmurs of enthusiasm for the suggestion rising from the strangers and I was abruptly unable to take a breath. I felt my body grow cold, for as much as I disliked Old Kate, I was as certain as ever the evil menace was not of her making, despite the Spirit's claim.

Calvin Justice stood, and raised his hands high, so all would look to hear him above the noise of the rocking.

"Good people, if the Devil speaks to you, believe him not! For he will lead you down the path of no return."

"Yea, but Preacher Justice, look, it is as the Witch proclaims!" The speaker gestured to Father, rocking madly in his chair, bits of white frothlike spittle appearing in the corners of his mouth. He did not look well.

"Friend, indeed we all are witnesses to the sufferings of John Bell, and his family, on this occasion and on many others, but to believe such as the pain they have endured could be magicked by a woman in our district whose only sin is in her strange eccentricities, is to give credence where none belongs." Calvin Justice spoke with passionate authority and managed to quiet the impulse building to hunt down Kate and drag her from her bed. The grip on my lungs was loosened and I gasped for air.

I shall torment Jack Bell out of his life!

"I beg you, cease at once this torture." Mother spoke in a quiet but desperate tone. "Let us join hands together and pray the eyes of God will look down on us here and take pity on our troubled souls."

"Repent, Jack Bell, if you have sinned, is my advice," urged the stranger who had previously denigrated Kate, but Miss Sallie Barton gave him such a look he should have put his tail between his legs, were he a hound. She took up Mother's hand and with an earnest glance at Father's seizing form, began the prayer.

"Our Father, who art in Heaven . . ."

Your prayers mean nothing. I am a witch of Old Kate's making, here to torment Jack Bell out of his life!

"Hallowed be thy name. Thy kingdom come, thy will be done . . ." All our voices in unison continued the prayer, watching, hopeful of a change in Father's fearsome twitching, but the attack carried on until I felt again the heavy stone fall in my chest, as though my heart had turned to lead and dropped down along my spine, exactly as I had felt with Josh. No one seemed to notice, but I found I could not speak, my throat was closed, strangled with a weighty darkness. I knew, as I had known with certainty the night the Being first spoke, the Spirit would accomplish the evil deed of which it spoke. The light of the flames in the fire filled my eyes, and I had just a glimpse of Father released from his shaking, before I saw darkness and found I could no longer breathe. I fainted onto the floor but remained oddly present, though I could not speak or open my eyes. I felt Miss Sallie Barton kneel beside me, crying as though I were a sister to her.

"I beg you, whatever you may be, cease the torture of this pretty innocent!"

Who ever perished, being innocent?

"Do not quote Job to us, for gathered here, we are the faithful," said Calvin Justice, kneeling beside Miss Sallie Barton. I felt a twinge in my chest as though the Being stabbed a needle at my heart.

"O my God, I trust in thee: Let me not be ashamed, let not mine enemies triumph over me." Calvin Justice spoke the Psalm of David. The Spirit opened our great cedar door and slammed it, sending a cold blast of air into the parlor.

Miss Sallie Barton squealed in fear and jumped to her feet, and her uncle spoke to her firmly.

"Sallie, this excitement is more than I find necessary for any day."

I stayed frozen on the floor, unable to move. The Being slammed the door a second time, shaking the house.

"Prayer is the only recourse," Mother spoke into the silent room, realizing the Spirit had gone.

"Are you fit, Jack?"

"I am, but I do seek _some_ recourse." Father's voice was strange and tight.

"Jack Bell, you appear to have triumphed in your struggle with the Being," Calvin Justice exclaimed. "I am glad of it, but I feel you ought to take some rest, and I will take my leave."

"Mr. Justice, would you be so kind as to carry our Betsy up to bed before departing?" Mother spoke of me as though I were merely resting on the floor, not choked and stiffened by unnatural forces.

"Of course," Calvin Justice said, taking a step toward me, but Father interrupted his movement.

"No, Mr. Justice, I will carry my darling daughter myself."

Father's tone was deeper than before and I felt his strong hands cup my bottom and my back.

"Jack . . ." Mother was concerned he could not manage it. "Are you certain?"

"Of course," Father answered, and with great effort he lifted me and held me to his chest, staggering only slightly.

"Is sleep possible under such circumstances?" Miss Sallie Barton spoke nervously.

"If you are weary, as we are," Mother tried to reassure her, giving over the brand-new pallets we'd made, with fresh sheets and a stack of quilts. Father carried me through the hall and up the stairs. He paused when he reached the landing, breathing hard, and I heard Mother escorting Calvin Justice to the door.

"It would be my wish to keep quiet the recitation uttered here tonight, and I thank you for your voice of reason."

"My pleasure, and of course, I will not speak of it."

I nuzzled my forehead into Father's neck and felt it slippery with sweat. The underside of his beard prickled my nose.

"Betsy," he grunted, crossing the threshold of my room. He shut the door with my foot and I shivered, for the air upstairs was as cold as the outdoors. He lay me down on my bed and collapsed beside me, exhausted. "Darling daughter, all will come out right," he whispered, but seemed too spent to say more. His skin beneath his shirt was soaked with perspiration and some of the frothy spittle that had issued from his mouth was drying on his neck.

"Dear Father," I whispered. I curled into his arms and found him hot and comforting, though his breath stank of whiskey and he held me in a slightly painful posture, with my hands trapped between his legs.

if god is with you

Over the next month, the Spirit went about the community broadcasting that its origin was in Kate Batts's kettle and there were many who were ready to believe this was the truth. The Randolphs, the Porters and Mrs. Hopson all closed their doors to her, and Mr. Thorn would no longer eye her wares for possible sale inside his store. At church no one would sit near to her, but contrary to what I did expect, Old Kate did not speak out against the treatment she received. Instead, she continued to be the first and only member of the congregation to fill with the Glory of the Lord every Sunday without fail, and no one present could equal the loud voice she used to proclaim her pure faith. While she wriggled her fat under the pulpit, the congregation whispered—Even if she had not *created* the evil presence, she clearly practiced magical arts of some sort, for what other explanation could there be for her unusual attitudes and ways, as well as her overly zealous nature, both undoubtedly a ruse for her secret dark beliefs? Despite the talk, Old Kate continued to drive into the churchyard her cart of amulets and elixirs to ward away the demons.

As our good name seemed as though it would be forever linked with the entity that tortured us, so it seemed Kate Batts's name would be linked to what caused our suffering. This did not trouble me, as I did not believe it was true, and I did not care about Old Kate particularly. I was much more disturbed by the Being's other proclamation and I wondered often, did it truly intend to torment the life from Father? It said no more about it for some time, spending its energy in gossip, songs and Scripture recitations.

By November, the weather had solidly turned to winter, and one night the temperature took a truly sharp drop. I woke in the morning to a thin film of frost on my windowpane. I put on the sturdy leather lace-ups with the thick soles Mother had just recently gifted to me, and I went outside before breakfast. Lovely white crystals of frost were sprinkled like raw sugar over the red and purple leaves shed by the plum and cherry trees. I admired the colors in the orchard, but I had taken only a light woolen wrap, and I was cold. I decided to visit the tobacco barn, where the heat of the year was extended and stored, released in the good smell of bittersweet leaves, culled and stacked high.

I ran past the stables, the dairy and the hog pen, and entered the barn just as Father was engaged in supplying his owl with its breakfast. The light was dim, slipping only through a few small cracks in the roof and walls, but I saw Father had let the sparrows loose on the plank floor and he stood beside the perch, unwrapping the strands of his owl's tether. He had his back to me and I do not believe he saw or heard me come in the door.

The sparrows were two little brown birds, with white- and black-tipped wings. I wondered why they did not fly to the beams of the ceiling and attempt an escape. It was odd how still they stayed, allowing the owl an easy mark. He swooped down, caught the first bird in his talons, and cracked its neck with one thrust, before pecking it to pieces in the most gruesome but expedient form. His eyes were black as pebbles in the stream, and even as I watched him repeat the horrible predation on the second sparrow, I could not deny Father's owl was a tremendous bird.

I felt abruptly the smothering weight again as if a heavy stone pushed against my breast, and I sat, right where I was, onto a hogshead drum full of tobacco. I heard the voice of the Spirit in my mind, *torment John Bell out of his life,* and I knew it was only in my mind, because it was so much fainter than when it spoke out loud. The satisfied cry of victory released by Father's owl devouring its prey filled the barn. I could not breathe and I felt I would soon expire, but I did not, though the oppressive grievousness in my chest would not lift through the effort of my will alone. Father suddenly turned and noticed me, and I saw his trousers were unbuttoned and his shirt hung loose, and I wondered if he had a special reason I had not previously imagined for feeding his owl alone.

"This is not the place for you, Betsy Bell." He strode across the room, irritated by my presence, or perhaps he assumed I was upset, having come upon the killing. I could not move or respond, because of the weight in my gut, and I wondered if it was fear that kept the sparrows still. I expected he would lay me out on the drum and lift my skirts, but Father ignored me, and I realized it was early and he had yet to take a drink. When the truss was completely stretched out, he turned his back on me and began winding the leash back to the tether. I watched his tall form turning the leather in his hands, and the stern angles of his shoulders rolled under his wool coat. He was oblivious to what I felt and heard, and I was suddenly glad of it, for my thoughts frightened me, and it was better he did not know them. As soon as I was able to take a breath, I jumped up and pushed open the great barn door, never so relieved to feel the crisp air in my lungs.

Near one month later, in the first week of December, Father was sent a message from the magistrate, Abraham Byrns, who lived thirty miles from our home past the growing settlement at Cedar Hill. Mr. Byrns requested that Father, as one of the most intelligent, prosperous and distinguished men of our community, appear at his home to serve on a jury to settle a law dispute.

"I wish you would decline, dear Jack," Mother said, attempting to discourage him from going.

"Nay, 'tis my duty, Lucy. I must attend."

On the morning of his departure I woke up late, and I could tell from the light in my room the first snow had fallen. I rose and stood at the window admiring the white fields. All the land was covered, like Chloe's applesauce cake under a generous cream frosting. I missed John Jr. quite heartily, as he could be relied on to support my brothers and me in hitching up the sleigh at the slightest dusting, to go riding over the hills.

Downstairs Mother and Chloe were beginning to prepare the Christmas fruitcakes, and I had to make do with cold biscuits. I spooned heaps of blackberry jam inside them while Mother sat across from me, absorbed in writing the recipe on fresh paper since she no longer had her kitchen book. I knew Mother's fruitcakes would take near an entire day of her devotion, and it occurred to me I had the perfect opportunity to command a horse from Zeke and take a ride by myself.

"Would you like to chop the nuts, Miss Betsy?" Mother did not look up from writing with her request.

"No, Mother. If you do not mind, I should like to play outdoors in the new snow. I dislike the process of making those fruitcakes, for there is too much stirring and thickening involved!"

"As you wish, Miss Betsy." I was correct in assuming the cakes obsessed her, and she was unconcerned with me. I finished my breakfast, meager as it was, and returned to my room announcing my true intentions to no one. I pulled wool stockings over my cotton ones, then my thickest undergarments, followed by my winter wool dress. I laced my boots too quickly, but I took my time pulling on the lovely soft gloves and hat Mother had just finished knitting for me from last season's lamb's wool. I hoped Father had left a pair of his leather riding gloves in the stable, as he often did. I felt a certain wild abandon realizing he was absent and I hurried downstairs, leaving quietly out the front door.

Drewry, Richard and Joel were having a game in front of the house, practicing their aim throwing snowballs through the bare limbs of the pear trees. I wanted to avoid them as I wished to be alone, so I turned sharply to my right and slipped around the side of the house, following the washing line. The snow crunched beneath my feet, a delicious feeling I enjoyed, but as the hill grew steeper I had to run to keep from slipping down. I burst into the barn and there was Zeke about to take the saddle off of Moses, one of Father's favorite horses. I thought Father must have asked Zeke to saddle an extra horse, in case the need arose.

"Father intended Moses to be exercised by me," I said quickly, telling Zeke a bold-faced lie.

"Mighty long stirrups he intended for you, Miss 'Lizabeth."

Zeke gave me an indulgent smile and laughed at his own joke. He helped me shorten the leather straps of the stirrups and placed the climbing stool beside Moses' flank, so I might mount like a lady, important as Miss Sallie Barton.

"Be mindful, Miss 'Lizabeth," he cautioned. "Lord knows the beasts get excited by the first snow. Our God wouldn't want no red blood shed across it." He gave Moses a pat on the rump and waved me out of the stable.

The feeling of riding Moses and leaving the barn so high above the world was unlike any other happiness. I set out sedately walking, keeping the reins short to impress Zeke with my control, but once out of sight, I encouraged Moses to canter, then trot, and we bounced across the snowy fallow cornfield down toward the stream. I wished to observe where it had frozen fast and where it managed to rage in falls over the icicle-covered rocks. The morning was both gray and bright at once and Moses' breath combined with my own painted white frosty curls in the air around my face. The branches looked blacker than they really were in contrast with the new snow balanced on their edges. I had to brush aside the laden elm to pass and I turned in the saddle to watch the random pattern created when the snow fell to the ground. The stream was quiet, much of it beneath ice and snow, and the only sound was the clopping of Moses' feet as he overturned stones hidden in the path.

I had gone quite a ways and was nearing the bend where the stream widened to meet the full river below the cavern where the elm had been struck by lightning during the storm in the summer, when I was surprised to see Josh Gardner standing in the clearing, his horse drinking where the water ran fast beneath his feet.

"Betsy . . ." He smiled and turned to me as if he had been

waiting a long while. " 'Twas you I had in my thoughts this minute and here you are!"

"I would be on your thoughts, dear Josh, as you are on my land." The sheer unlikelihood that we should see one another alone in the woods emboldened my tongue. I had desired it so, but I had not allowed my heart to conjure such a fortunate possibility.

"I must confess many times I have stood alone on your land, Betsy, hoping you would venture out. At last my efforts are rewarded." I felt my cheeks grow hot in the frosty air. Josh reached up to take the reins and help me dismount, which I did with enthusiasm, too much perhaps, as my foot slipped and I fell into him in such a way his arms had to come about me to steady us both. I looked to his face, laughing my apologies, and ever so quickly he drew me yet closer and kissed my mouth with his. Moses jerked the reins, held too tight by Josh's arm around my back.

"Whoa, there," Josh quieted him, and removed his arm from me. I stood solid, my lips tingling from the cold or the kiss I could not tell. It had happened naturally and been so brief I was not certain it had happened at all.

"I'm sorry, Betsy. I should not be so forward. I did not plan to kiss you. It's just . . . you are so pretty, in the snow." Josh shrugged, embarrassed, and I did not immediately soothe him.

"I am a girl of good repute!" I decided to tease him a little, holding my nose up and turning my face away, hoping he would know I was not serious. Almost instantly I longed for him to kiss me again.

"Shall we walk the path a ways?" Josh suggested, changing the subject, loosely tying the horses to a tree. "I saw the mouth of the cave has icicles of glory."

"Did you see them last year? They grew almost to the length of the opening!" I was excited we were to walk together.

He reached for my hand and I gave it to him, happy when he squeezed my fingers inside the lamb's wool gloves, acknowledging the heat that passed between us in the bitter cold. The ground was frozen hard beneath the snow and it was slippery going as we climbed the bank. Down below, the river grew wider, cutting an ever deeper swath through the rock. I had not come this way since the summer storm. The path was steep and we labored in our ascent, until we reached the top and achieved the best view of the cavern and the clearing below. Winded, I gasped at the winter glory before us. The ten-foot-square mouth of the cavern held icicles the size of horses' heads hanging across the top.

"Which one is the longest?" Josh asked and I pointed to the center one. It occurred to me if I were standing with my brothers instead of Josh, they would be hurling snowballs across the river, hoping to strike an icicle and send it tumbling below. I felt decidedly pleased they were not present and I squeezed Josh's gloved hand in mine.

"Did you know . . ." I thought to tell him a family secret, only it wasn't really a secret, just something private. "Did you know, that cave leads all the way to our cold storehouse near the sinkhole? We have a rocky knoll in the hillside way behind the orchard and across the stream where the entrance lies. You must see it, Josh, for inside the storehouse far in the back, there is a passageway underground leading after some time to the mouth of that cavern." I raised my arm to point and noticed Josh was slow to follow my gaze, preferring to look on my face.

"I hear that cavern is larger than the church." Josh smiled at me and turned to look where I did, sharing my enthusiasm.

"It is! And it has the most remarkable view in all of Adams, perhaps in all of Robertson County. You can see forever, past Kate Batts's pond. John Jr. showed it to me." I paused and thought of John Jr. on the day he'd taken me into the cave. I had balked, disgusted by the slimy look of the smooth wet walls, the spiders magnified by the shadows thrown from his candle, but he had insisted I go on. He encouraged me step by step and I was never more grateful than when I emerged into the great cavern, hung with olive and purple stalactites, revealing the most lovely view. "Come springtime, perhaps I might ask Mother if you could help with the storing of the cheese and we might slip away. Then I could show you."

"I'd like that." Josh nodded, his cheeks pink with the cold.

Betsy Bell, do not have Josh Gardner.

I was attacked by the sudden arrival of the Being, and a terrible empty feeling struck the pit of my stomach.

You will not go to the cave with him.

Abruptly I sat down on a snow-covered boulder beside the path and Josh sat with me, undisturbed by the cold snow against his clothing, and equally undisturbed by the Being.

"I have thought a long time on our last encounter, Betsy. We must not listen. It does not speak the truth." He took my hand in his with great sensitivity and resolve, having clearly decided the best course of action was to ignore the Being.

Today! Today!

The Spirit's voice trailed away, dissolving like our frosty breath. I tried to recover my enthusiasm for the moment, but I was shaken, and remained silent, turning my feelings over in my mind. What if the Spirit spoke the truth? I felt afraid. Why could I not enjoy a walk through the cave with Josh? What would happen? Why did it speak so certainly against this happy plan for my future? I felt sorry for myself afflicted as I was, even in my most joyful moments, with strange forebodings of my future. I thought of Mother's advice to me to trust the unknown powers watching over us all. Josh squeezed my hand, kind attention in his face.

"Look at the majesty before us, Betsy! Is not God's world a lovely place?"

"It is, if God is with you," I answered, without thought or premeditation, and I believe I was nearly as surprised as Josh to hear myself profess such lack of faith. He turned and took my shoulders in his hands and looked into my eyes.

"Dear Betsy, never doubt that God is with you! Believe, there can be no greater God than He who walks with you." He drew my shoulders to his own and my cheek pressed against the cold wool of his gray jacket. He held me gently, silently, as if he knew I needed several moments to force away the tears rising in my throat. I think he understood I did not wish to cry. For several minutes we remained in our embrace, the sound of the snow-covered river a bubbling accompaniment to our quiet stillness. I felt again the rightness of our being together, but when I could breathe naturally, I drew away. Josh took his hands from my shoulders and for a breathless moment held my cold cheeks between his leather gloves. Lifting my chin just slightly he closed his eyes and kissed me again, this time so slowly and deliberately I could not doubt that it was so. His lips were warm and soft and he pressed them into mine with some certainty, and I pressed back, whereupon our two mouths gently opened and I tasted the sweetness of his soul. I allowed this ecstasy only for a moment, for though I knew his intentions were honorable with me, I remained troubled by the Spirit's words. I pulled back and looked quickly away, afraid to see disappointment in his eyes.

"How cold it has become." I noticed the gray air had darkened around us. Without further words, we stood and began our descent down the path. The wind picked up as we walked, and whistled as we reached the clearing.

"I wonder if we might soon see more snow?" I hugged my arms across my front, watching Josh untie the horses.

"Not yet," Josh said, frowning at the sky and then at our two restless animals tossing their heads, as if there was something in the air they could smell or see that we could not. "Here, Betsy, let me help you." Josh lifted me onto Moses and I recalled his hands about my waist in the fall when we were tormented with branches. At least the Spirit had not unleashed violence on us. I was attempting to comfort myself, as I felt unable to return to my prior state of pure enjoyment. The kiss we'd shared lingered with me as a precious gift I wished to take home and examine privately, but at that moment I had hidden it away. I watched Josh mount and settle himself, thinking the black snow-covered branches around us, so recently magical, seemed menacing and strange to me now.

We set out together walking on the path until the river turned again to stream, and there we steered our horses up the bank so we might ride beside the meadow. Abruptly Moses strained beneath me and reared up, as though startled by some hidden menace. I held fast, attempting to shorten his reins as we came down to regain control, but suddenly he seemed to be a steed I knew not. He jerked his head so my grasp was loosened and leaped up the embankment. The laden branches of the trees along the bank whipped at my hair and back as I struggled to stay astride him. I tore past Josh, who was meant to lead the way.

"Hang on, Betsy," he cried, as Moses raced to the crest of the hill. I heard the hooves of his horse pounding as he kicked her to come up behind me. Overcome with fear, I felt frightened and doubted my abilities.

"What should I do?" I called when Josh reached my side.

"Go faster!" Josh shouted, laughing, slapping Moses so hard on his behind he vaulted forward and I was forced to throw my arms around his neck and simply hang on for dear life as he burst from the trees and soared across the snow-covered field. As Moses let loose his strength, the ride became smooth as flying in a dream. My fear disappeared, swept away by the tremendous rush of cold air. Josh raced only a short distance behind me and we flew all the way to the southern boundary before Moses slowed for a break and Josh reined in his horse so we might stand together.

"Did you enjoy that, Betsy?" Josh's laughter burst from behind the frosty smoke of his heavy-breathing horse and I could tell he knew I had.

"Yes, thank you!" I laughed with him. The tension and fear I'd felt as Moses shot up the bank had dispersed like the flakes of snow kicked up and pummeled by the horses' hooves.

"It is like flying," Josh observed.

"Like riding on the wind!"

"I wanted you not to be frightened, dear Betsy." Josh was cautious in confronting my emotions, but kept a shy smile and his eyes on mine.

"I was frightened!" I readily admitted the truth, "much more than I care to say." I wanted to tell him how often I felt frightened. I wanted to tell him nothing could have been more right than his mastery of my moment of fear. I wanted to say how grateful I was that he had seen a strength in me I had not known I possessed.

"Sometimes when I am frightened, Betsy, I try simply to *feel* my heart racing, my wild eyes, my quick movements and tension in my limbs. This concentration allows me then to surge forth, as I bade you do, just now, and in the progress there I find release." Josh looked endearingly bashful as he spoke his wisdom and I knew I could trust him with my thoughts.

"Nothing could have been more perfect, Josh." Holding his smiling eyes to mine, I wanted nothing more than to stay in that white field for eternity, enveloped in our horses' breath, warmed by our inner excitement.

"I wish it were not so, but I must get home," Josh informed me reluctantly, looking away. "I promised my father."

"If you must, so be it," I replied, with more acceptance than I felt. I hoped my expression would convey my sincere dismay that we must part.

"God go with you, Betsy," Josh said and I smiled at his reminder as I turned Moses to home. Looking back, over my shoulder, I saw he was watching, not leaving, and I was glad. He waved and I kicked Moses hard, into another flying gallop, wanting again that exalted feeling of speed, feeling distinctly unafraid. I rode as fast as I could, churning the snow, all the way back to the stables. I tore into the barnyard, and scared Zeke, who came startled to open the stable door, scowling his greeting to me.

"Where's the fire, Miss 'Lizabeth?" He grasped Moses by the nose and helped me down.

"It is Heaven in the meadows, Zeke, sheer Heaven." I left him to feed Moses, thinking Josh was Heaven sent to me, a light amidst the dark things in my life.

The boys and Mother were gathered at the dining table for the midday meal. The boys had red cheeks and shiny hair, slick from their wool caps. They were amusing Mother with tales of their morning frolics and a general air of merriment occupied our house. Mother had mixed and baked more fruit-cakes than I cared to count and they were cooling on every sill, desk and table. Their luscious aroma filled our noses, and made the boys dip their bread deeper in Chloe's winter potato and onion soup.

"If only John Jr. were here, he'd take us for a sleigh ride, Mother." Joel raised his eyes from his bowl, but I saw him glance quickly at Drew and Richard, as though they shared a plan. I sensed a movement amongst my brothers to prevail on Mother in Father's absence for permission to hitch up the sleigh for an afternoon ride. They had thought of it, just as I had. "The whole winter will be ruined without John Jr.," Joel pouted, and I could see he had rehearsed. "Wait!" he sat up brightly as though a brilliant idea had just occurred to him and we all waited, expectant. "Drewry is old enough to drive the sleigh, and Betsy too!" He clapped his hands together with unrestrained excitement. I had to smile and I saw Mother do the same. I hoped she had been taken in.

"Please, please, Mother, might we take him for a ride?" I begged with more enthusiasm than I had shown for many weeks.

"'Tis good to see you so robust and happy, dear Betsy," Mother said, smiling and radiating contentment as strong as the sweet smell of her cakes. She looked at all our pleading faces. "All right then, you may take the sleigh. Enjoy your-selves, but be careful, and have Zeke help you bring it from the barn."

We stood in unison, noisily scattering our chairs, rushing

to crowd around the fire and gather our steaming boots and gloves. "Warm well your feet before you go," Mother cautioned. "I'll take back my permission if you don't!" she threatened, but we knew that was unlikely. It was just words, called after us like blessings, for she was already picturing her house still and silent, her fruitcakes cooling in peace. Drewry and I helped Joel and Richard with their things, then raced back outdoors. We ran down the hill toward the stables and again I was overcome by a feeling of wild abandon at the thought that Father was not present and could not object to our outing. I felt free and full of energy.

Our family sleigh was a true delight, considered a rare luxury by most in the county, who were not so fortunate to have one. Dean had taken months to carve the rails from rich mahogany, and it glided like magic across the snow.

"We'll have to fetch it from the tobacco barn," Zeke said. He was not enthusiastic, but when we reached it, he helped Drewry lift and carry the sleigh outside while I got the skins from the cedar chest. Father's owl was sleeping on its perch and I avoided looking at it. I concentrated on lifting the big bearskin and the two woolly sheepskins Mother had sewn together with her strongest spun thread. They would cover our laps and protect our shoulders from the cold. In the yard, Zeke had hitched Dipsy and another old mare to the harness and the boys were protesting.

"Zeke, please! Must we have Dipsy? We will go ever so slow!"

Zeke shook his head, and would not do it another way.

"I seen Miss 'Lizabeth here go ever so slow once already today."

"Never mind," I said quickly, not wishing to discuss with

my brothers how I'd spent my morning. "Climb up quickly, and we'll be off."

They scrambled up on the back bench and I cuddled them inside the bearskin, enjoying the glow of enchantment on their faces as they stroked the soft fur across their cheeks. They giggled, ready to go.

"Be mindful," Zeke gave his warning to Drewry this time. "I done told you, the first snow excites the beasts as it does us." Drewry laughed at the thought of Zeke excited over anything and, adjusting the sheepskins over my lap and his, he took up the reins.

The snow on the Adams–Cedar Hill high road before our house was as yet undisturbed, except by the track of an animal here and there. The trees lining the sides shook their limbs ever so gently as we passed, sending cascades falling to the ground. Richard and Joel squealed every time this happened and Drewry and I laughed at them. I felt very mature, like a lady, taking my sleigh down the road, and I pretended silently Richard and Joel were my children and I had a husband like Josh beside me instead of my brother. I imagined we were traveling to a Christmas service, or a grand event, to be followed by a music recital and socializing, like Thenny said people in Nashville did at Christmastime. I allowed myself to dream the day would come when all my life would be the happiness and light of my fantasies.

We were not far from the house when something appeared on the road ahead. At first I thought it was nothing more than a rabbit, then, instantly, I knew it was a witch rabbit, as certain as I could see the black spot on its left hind foot standing out against the white snow. I gripped Drewry by the arm.

"Slow up, and do not be afraid, but do you see?" I spoke

quietly into his ear for I did not wish to alarm the younger boys.

"A rabbit!" Joel shrieked with enthusiasm before Drewry could respond and the witch creature leaped forward, straight toward us, as if shot from the sound of his voice. The horses neighed and skittered backward, sending the sleigh bouncing sideways on the lane, and then the sly creature dashed between the rising horses' hooves, and we all near tumbled out.

"Whoa!" In unison Drewry and I tried to calm the old mares and hold the sides of the rocking sleigh to steady it. Joel and Richard fell off the benches to the floor, but they were so well bundled in the bearskin they remained unhurt.

"Stay there, 'tis a safer place if we must dodge rabbits in the snow," I told them. Looking down the road for the creature, I saw nothing apart from the tracks of the sleigh, and a big circle in the snow where we had turned halfway round. Drewry and I climbed out, and straightened the sleigh back behind the horses. We had just accomplished this and taken up our positions on the bench with the reins, when the rabbit appeared again, ahead, but darting to the right, into the woods. Despite our attempts to rein them back, the two mares pushed forward and gathered speed as they turned to follow the rabbit through the small wooded area above our planting fields. God was with us for certain, as the mares flew wildly through the poplars, the sleigh bumping crazily behind. We narrowly missed crash after possible crash.

"Close your eyes and hold on!" Drewry shouted.

I followed his instructions and did cease to watch, until we burst onto the white expanse of meadow, the horses full of speed uncommon for their age. Richard and Joel screamed with equal parts fear and delight as we tore up the flat, and I prayed desperately, please Lord, let us live. The rabbit bounced ahead, leading the horses to make a great circle of the field, and the tracks of the sleigh deepened with each turn, causing the wood to glide ever faster as the surface grew firm beneath the rails. The boys grew quiet and I realized we were on a frightful course.

"If you would drive us so, take us to Old Kate's farm!" I cried a challenge to the creature, hoping it would cease its endless circles. Drewry, without speaking a word of warning, pulled his gun from beneath the seat and jumped from the moving sleigh, tossing the reins to me in what I thought was a very dangerous manner. On the ground he stuffed his powder deep, struck the flint, and fired a lead ball so direct, the creature was struck down in just one shot. Joel and Richard burst into cheers and shouts of admiration and I was abruptly able to rein the horses to a stop.

The boys threw off their skins, and clambered into the snow to inspect the dead rabbit and congratulate Drewry. I too climbed out, but I had no desire to look at the rabbit's form. I could not even look at my brother who had shot it and my legs quivered, so weakened was I by the rise and fall of fear left in the pit of my stomach from battling the witch creature. I tried desperately to recall what Josh had said I must do to fight my fear as I stroked Dipsy's nose and loosened the bridles, allowing both horses to bend their heads to the ground and scoop up snow with their heavy pink tongues. From the corner of my eye I caught a movement, and looking up, I saw the witch rabbit, fast and well as before, heading back up to the road. I said nothing to the boys or Drew. I knew the creature was off to do some other mischief and, selfish as I was, I prayed the Being would torment some other persons for a while and not return to me. I thought it foolish to believe the Spirit in another form could die by Drewry's rifle, for a witch rabbit like any witch creature must experience no such thing as death. I thought there must only be regeneration and mischief for all eternity for such entities.

I wanted to go home. The skies were darkening and the smell of more snow coming was present in the air. The cold seemed to grow deeper with each passing moment and I wrapped my arms about myself, snug inside my greatcoat but knowing I would not be warm much longer. Drewry and the boys were arguing regarding what to do with his kill.

"If we bring it home Mother might make us rabbit fur hats," Joel said, his preference obvious.

"*Witch rabbit* fur hats," Richard added.

"Recall the jawbone and its relation to the Spirit. We will leave it here, where it lies," Drewry insisted, and the young boys were made to understand they would not have their way.

"If *you* wore a witch rabbit hat, sister . . ." Joel said thoughtfully, as I wrapped him back up in the bearskin in the sleigh, "if you wore a witch rabbit hat, perhaps the Witch would stay away."

I could not answer, for it occurred to me our prayers to God for deliverance had produced no noticeable relief, and neither had Dean's witchball or Old Kate's amulets. I had tested Josh's strategy and failed, and I could not tell Joel I thought we were beyond the help a witch rabbit hat might bring.

We let the horses walk to the very end of the meadow where the stand of poplars broke, by the road. The gentle motion of the gliding sleigh lulled us into silence, and I thought Richard and Joel would certainly fall asleep before we reached home. I felt an intense tiredness myself, particularly in my arms, and I leaned against my brother, glad he was guiding the reins, for I had seen a lot of riding for one day. We turned out of the meadow into the trees on the path toward the road and I became suddenly aware of a change in Drewry.

"Sister," he passed the reins to me, "I am so tired . . ."

He closed his eyes and I had hardly time enough to speak, "But Drewry," before he laid his head onto my lap, overcome, with a deep sleep. Over my shoulder I saw Richard and Joel also sleeping soundly and I realized it fell on me to guide the horses home.

I kept them on the path to the road, toward the hill and house. We jerked along, despite my attempts at hastening the mares by slapping their backs with the reins. They were fatigued and stubborn too. I began to feel nervous, as the tall trees shut away more and more of the dim gray light. I tried to imagine how much stronger I'd feel if it were Josh's curls lying on my skirt and I recalled his words to me, "There can be no greater God than He who walks with you." Unholy as I was, it was the way his lips parted when he said my name that I drew strength from, not the thought of God's protection.

We reached the foot of the hill and a tiredness unlike any I had previously experienced came over me and I grew somnolent, watching the horses' flanks rise and fall, hypnotic in their rhythm, climbing the incline yard by yard. In the next moment, it was as if I were waking from a deep sleep. The sleigh jolted sharply and my neck jerked up. Ahead in the road I saw Father on his horse, stopped at the crest of the hill. I rubbed my eyes to be certain and snow dropped from my gloves onto my cheeks. Yes, it was Father, but something was wrong, his clothing was at odd angles and his legs hung limp, as though he had no stirrups, and his spine slouched unnatural in his saddle.

"Look, there's Father!" I cried, shaking Drewry hard with my left hand, but he would not wake. The horses seemed to find their momentum at that moment and trotted up the hill toward him as though toward their stalls in the barn. Abruptly I wanted to go more slowly, for something about Father's appearance filled me with great trepidation. I saw a large black stain spreading out beneath his horse across the snow as we grew near, and I realized it was blood, dripping from his cloak and boots, and Father's face existed no more. Inside his woolen hood his skeleton glared, white as the snow surrounding us but dripping strange icicles of skin and muscle like the hanging slabs of meat in the cold storehouse. His teeth stood out terrible and crooked, with many missing.

"God help me!" I screamed and I must have fainted, for when I woke next I was in the barnyard and Zeke was standing over me.

"Miss 'Lizabeth, Lordy, you'll catch your death," Zeke said, his voice full of grim concern. "Lordy, Lordy, you'll catch your death," he repeated, worried, as I came slowly to myself, frozen in my position slumped over Drewry, still asleep on my lap. My face was turned to the right and I saw the sky dark gray, behind the stable. A light snow was falling and I realized it must have been falling for some time, as my arm before my eyes was covered with a thin dusting. I raised my head, and turned stiffly to check on my brothers, asleep on the floor, wrapped tightly in the bearskin.

"Get the young'uns to the fire and get Drewry awake. The sleigh must get to the barn before the snow. Landsakes, where was you?" Zeke's voice was full of urgency and I turned back to him realizing the horses must have driven us into the yard while we lay unconscious.

Father.

"He done come home," Zeke answered. I must have said the words aloud, though I did not think I had. "Spoke not a word, but he did not look well. Wake your brother, Miss 'Lizabeth." I shook Drewry with both hands and some frustration, and he stirred, sitting slowly upright.

"Sister . . ."

I wanted immediately to tell him, and Zeke too, what I had seen, to hear what they would make of it, but something prevented me from speaking. I found myself behaving as if we had just come from the lovely outing we had held in our hearts at the outset of the ride.

"We're home," I said, shaking Richard and Joel until they rubbed their eyes and climbed down from the sleigh. "Help to fold these skins." I made them stop, insisting they must not run immediately off. Why was Father back at home? The judgment in Cedar Hill was expected to require several days. I felt weak at the thought of greeting Mother at the door, for I wished not to expose her to the pain of the vision I had seen. If I remained silent, Joel and Richard would tell the tale of our adventure as an infinitely more lighthearted experience, as it had been for them. They ran ahead while I waited for Zeke to light a lantern for me to take to the barn.

"Hurry, Miss 'Lizabeth." He and Drewry took the horses to the stable and I went alone. As I walked, the skins were a giant pillow to my front and the lantern bounced so badly I was afraid I would accidentally extinguish it, but I could do no better at carrying it, as my load was bulky. I was filled with worry over Father's health and I regretted not having spoken my vision to Drewry and Zeke, for it occurred to me the Spirit knew and told all. I startled myself, having forgotten for a moment this was so, and I began to worry, would it tell of my kisses with Josh Gardner? Which would be more painfully revealed? My father's skeleton, or my first real kiss? I reached the barn door and opened the cedar chests, folding in the soft fur and skins.

Father's owl awoke and hooted bleakly when I closed the lid. Without the bundle of fur in my arms I shivered with the cold, and ran quickly from that frightening place. As I hurried up the hill, I hugged my arms across my chest and felt a curiously sickening excitement. I knew the Spirit would undoubtedly tell its version of the day when and how it pleased, and though much of what it spoke was ungodly lies, I thought at times the Witch had enlightened me with information, and I wished to know what had taken place on the crest of the hill. Why had I been visited with that vision of my father's skeleton? What evil work was effected on me there? For the mark of evil in this instance seemed to me as black as the bloodstain I had witnessed in the snow.

Mother met me at the door, her finger pressed upright against her mouth in the sign for silence. "Your father has returned, and he is resting. I wish him not to be disturbed, for he fares poorly."

I undid my wet boots before the woodstove in the kitchen and I noticed all the fruitcakes had been stacked in two towers in a corner. They wobbled dangerously and gave my brothers reason to tiptoe about in exaggerated quiet when they came in to huddle beside the fire. I went up and changed my clothes for dry ones and when I returned, Mother wrapped her own woolen shawl around me, warm from her breast. She insisted I eat my soup before the woodstove.

"You are cold to the touch." She felt my forehead with the back of her hand, but did not inquire at all into whether we'd enjoyed our afternoon outing. I saw she was clearly preoccupied with Father's illness and paced nervously in and out of her pantry, apparently uncertain which herbs she wished to dose him with. "Come, boys. It is the hour for you two to re-tire," she sighed and held her hands out for Richard and Joel. "I will tuck you warm in your beds." She went upstairs with the boys and I had the feeling she needed a task to focus her restless energy. I was glad she had not focused on me, for I was afraid she might notice my own preoccupation. Drewry and I remained in the kitchen, finishing our supper silently together.

Outside the wind whistled, blowing gusts of snow against the house. I listened for the Spirit's voice and watched white eddies swirling against the window glass, putting me to mind of ghostly figures crowding near. The mood inside had altered drastically since noon, for we were now somber and dis-traught, in contrast with our earlier exuberant merriment. Drewry and I did not speak, but our silence was alive with our unspoken concerns. I wished to talk about the witch rabbit, and of what I had witnessed while he slept, for suddenly I did not wish the Spirit to inform him before I had spoken my piece, but though I formulated the beginnings of sentences which might express my thoughts, I spoke none aloud. The Spirit arrived as I placed my plate in the washtub, but it spoke not to me, or about me, but to Father in his bedroom where he lay in his bed.

Jack Bell, die you will!

Drew and I ran to Father's room, followed by Mother, who hurried down the stairs at the sound of the Being.

Have you any last words?

This frightening query was followed by peals of laughter from the Spirit and I saw Father, looking not at all himself, at-tempting speech that would not come. He choked and gagged and waved his arms stiffly, as though in the grip of a seizure.

"Oh Jack!" Mother's hands fluttered helplessly around his

own. "Betsy, get me the good book!" I fetched the Bible from the parlor, and I saw my own hands shaking while my heart raced fast with the Being's laughter. Mother began to read from the Psalms, the prayer of the afflicted when he is overwhelmed.

"Hear my Prayer, O Lord, and let my cry come unto thee. Hide not thy face from me on the day when I be in trouble." She spoke evenly, without faltering, and I saw reading gave her strength. My knees and legs began to shake and I prostrated myself on the bare wood floor of Father's bedroom, sudden tears overwhelming me. I could do nothing to stop my crying, but mine was not the dominant voice in the room, for the Spirit loudly recited a perverted nursery rhyme.

> *Old Jack Bell went up a hill,*
> *To fetch a lady's garter.*
> *On his way down, he broke his crown*
> *And Betsy Bell came tumbling after.*

"Leave him be!" I disregarded its insolent song and pleaded with the Being. Never had I seen Father so clearly ill. The image of his skeleton dripping blood returned to me and I much regretted my earlier desire to hear anything at all from the Spirit.

"Incline thine ear unto me: In the day when I call, answer me speedily." Mother continued to pray, her face raised to the roof as she spoke, but her only answer was unearthly evil laughter. I carried on sobbing as though my heart would break open. "Elizabeth, cease your tears and remove yourself to bed, immediately." Mother was annoyed with me and moved closer to Father to try and still his flailing hands again.

"Drewry, go with your sister and comfort her. I will stay with your father here."

Sit as long as you like, Lucy. I am here to take him.

"Shall I fetch the doctor or the Reverend?" Drewry was concerned and appeared ready to bolt from the house. Mother stroked Father's cheek and frowned at the mention of the doctor.

No doctor.

"I think we ought to wait and see how he progresses. The snow is falling thickly, and he does not have a fever." Mother spoke slowly, with great consideration. "You may help most by departing this sad scene." There was a slight bitterness in her tone I found most upsetting, but I realized she was dismayed by Father's illness and our lack of faith. I thought guiltily back to the wild abandon I had experienced when Father was away in Cedar Hill and I found myself reluctant to leave, but Mother insisted.

"Go! The fury of your tears, Miss Betsy, will not raise your father's spirits." I saw he was stiff and pale in his bed, his eyes closed, an expression at once vacant and resigned on his features. He had ceased attempting speech, but the grim set of his mouth and the tension of his forehead gave over the pain he suffered, and I wondered, truly, was the Spirit attempting murder? The Being had engaged me in a covenant of secrecy, for I had witnessed Father's skeleton and innards dropping away and the dreadful unshared image would not cease beneath my lids.

"Let us say the Lord's Prayer together," I suggested, standing to recite the prayer, but the Spirit began to whistle an uplifting tune, in contrast to the emotions of the room, imparting I should hurry and finish with my business there, so it might do the same. As though our business with Father could ever be one and the same.

"Deliver us from evil," Drewry joined me in prayer, and reaching out he squeezed my hand and I was so overcome with sadness I had great difficulty continuing.

"Forgive us our sins," we said together, making our faces brave and sturdy in case Father opened his eyes, but he did not.

"Come away, sister, 'tis for the best," Drewry said, pulling me toward the door. The Spirit launched into a raucous and vile song containing words I know Father was pained to hear spoken in his home, coarse curses beyond what I had ever imagined. Mother turned her face to the floor in sorrow and despair, for the Spirit's song was so loud there was no opportunity to plead with it to cease.

Drewry and I retreated upstairs into our rooms and soon I lay shivering under my quilts, listening to the horrible songs downstairs and the wailing cry of the storm wind outside. Sleep was impossible. I tried thinking of Josh, and his lips pressed to mine. I closed my eyes wanting terribly to relive the feeling of warmth and happiness his kiss had provided, but the feeling I sought remained beyond my reach. Instead, the sour smell of whiskey on Father's breath filled my nose as if he stood over me and I knew it was a trick of the Being, attempting to poison the few good thoughts in my mind. Its malevolent laughter rose through the floorboards and behind my eyes the figure of Father's skeleton hid waiting. I lay paralyzed in fear and though I know not how it happened, I did drift into a dreamless sleep.

unspeakable

In the morning when I awoke I discovered Father had risen, seeming fit and whole and very much restored to his regular health.

"Thanks be to God for this meal we are blessed to receive." He bowed his head and said our grace at breakfast while I stared at him from the half-shut corners of my eyes, unable to believe he could be so sound and wholesome after the night before. "Work needs doing at the hog pen," he said, cutting the tasty wild turkey Drewry had killed, spreading Mother's butter liberally across his cornbread.

"Shall we see to it?" Drewry asked. Since John Jr.'s departure, Drewry as the eldest son had taken on new responsibilities.

"May I come with you?" I inquired, spooning butter onto my own cornbread, hoping he would hear in my plea my most sincere desire to be with him, and not my fear that his living hours were limited.

"Yes, darling daughter," he said, looking directly at me, as though he were surprised I had requested to accompany him.

He laid his napkin down and stood. "I wish to do it while the weather holds, so both of you, make haste."

We hurried through our breakfast and through dressing in our winter things, meeting Father in the hall where he slapped his leather gloves together, clearly anxious to set out. "Dean reports my fences are in need of some repair and I intend to divide the stock hogs from the porkers, for Easter fattening." He spoke his intentions to Mother, who stood beside the door and kissed us each quite tenderly, tightening our knit scarves securely around our necks as she'd done each winter since Drewry and I were old enough to venture from the house alone.

"Be helpful to your father, Betsy," she whispered in my ear before shutting the door tight against the cold.

We walked at Father's brisk pace, not speaking. The snow had frozen lightly in the night and made a satisfying crunch beneath our boots. We walked around the house and down the hill to the stables. Father led the way and so it happened Drewry and I were nearly struck when his left boot came flying off his foot and shot back up the hill. He stopped and looked behind, but did not speak, and I knew not how it had happened.

"I'll fetch it, Father!" Drewry called out and sensibly retrieved the boot, which had fallen near to him. Father leaned against him and they worked together, replacing it. We had not gone two steps more when it happened again, this time to the other boot, on his right foot.

Call your angels down, Jack Bell, for you are like the hog to slaughter.

"Fiend!" Father drew a sharp breath but attempted to ignore the Spirit's taunt. "Drewry, fetch my boot and lace it tight this time." He was clearly much annoyed, and I could see it was not easy for Drew to get the boot on him; the fit was close. I watched my brother pull the laces taut and tie more than one knot, but as soon as we set out, directly the laces became strings to the wind and, this time, both his boots flew off.

"I will go in my stocking feet through this snow, evil demon! You will not alter my course," Father said. He continued walking in his stockings and Drewry and I followed behind, witnessing the boots rise up from where they lay in the snow and fly, as if thrown by a strong man with accurate aim, striking our father two horrible blows to the back of his head. He fell heavily to the ground and we rushed to him.

"Put them on my feet again, children." He lay flat on his back, stretched against the hill with his eyes closed, as though he were sleeping in his bed. Drewry and I did what we were told, he did the right boot, and I the left. Gently, I brushed away the snow encrusted to the sole of Father's wool stocking and slipped the boot beneath his narrow foot, pulling it up around his heel. It was more difficult than I anticipated, and I had to use so much strength I felt myself grow warm inside my coat. I sat back, removing my gloves so I could better grip the laces, and I saw Father's eyes remained closed. I could not tell if he was living or dead he lay so still. I glanced at Drewry to see what he was thinking, but he was furiously lacing. I felt the bristle in the air of the Spirit close to me, and I followed Father's example and did not speak, hoping it might be just the cold. When his boots were well and completely secured, Father opened his eyes.

"I shall need your assistance," he grunted, rising to his elbows.

"Shall we return to the house, Father?" I inquired, but he shook his head and frowned.

"No, we shall attend to the business at hand." Slowly we

helped him to his feet and he leaned on our shoulders while we brushed the snow from his coat and trousers. He bore up strongly considering he was obviously much worried and disturbed, and we managed to reach the hog pen without further incident. Dean was waiting for us there and he detailed to Father the problem he'd experienced with a section of double-gated fence.

"Leave it be for now, so long as it will hold the hogs till spring."

"It will do that, masta, but not much more." Despite the concern in Dean's voice, I could see Father had clearly lost his desire to inspect the problem. This was most unlike him and Dean appeared surprised when Father wished to busy himself directly with the second task of separating the hogs. "Yes, suh, we got some good 'uns this year." He began to point them out but Father was distracted and Dean's brow furrowed with concern. "Are you feeling all right, masta Bell?"

"No, Dean, truly, I am not."

"Leave the hogs for me to sort then, suh. I will make certain the best is fattened up for you, for Easter."

"For sure you will, man, but perhaps I shall not taste it." Father paused and looked over his shoulder realizing Drewry and I had heard his despairing comment. He said nothing to us, but turned back to Dean. "Let us undertake it together, for I am here now and prepared to make the choices."

Drewry and I stood silently watching with an attitude of uncertainty regarding what might happen next, as Father and Dean walked into the pen. I felt the cold tension in my stomach and in my mind I heard the voice of the Being, *Torment the life from old Jack Bell*. I wished to know if Drewry shared my misgivings, but how could I share my fears without enlarging his? "Shall we say a prayer for Father?" I asked him.

"Betsy, I believe our prayers no longer have much meaning," Drewry answered. He bent his head and breathed a funnel of frost into his two gloved hands, clasped before him. He was clearly upset and perhaps troubled with the same prescient thoughts as I.

"Please, Drewry, we must keep trying," I insisted and he allowed me to turn him around, so we did not face the barn, lest Dean or Father wonder what we were doing, and he joined me in a short but hearty petition for Father's deliverance from evil.

"Dear God, with respect to all your ways too mysterious for ourselves to understand, allow our father to return to robust health. Cast asunder his demons and light his way!" Drewry, not overly hopeful, walked away from me into the hog pen and, not knowing what else to do, I followed, discovering the hogs had already been properly segregated as Father desired.

"Let us return to the house, children," Father called to us and we began to walk back in a silence most tense. We had just reached the edge of the orchard when again Father's boots flew off his feet and through the air, commencing to kick and strike him. We heard a loud crack, similar to a branch breaking suddenly from the weight of too much snow, or a gunshot near to our ears, and we saw Father suffer another blow to the head, which struck him to the ground. He lay in the snow on his back, but now his face twitched and jerked as though the demon had its hands on it again. His contortions were so violent that he appeared quite unlike himself and I was terrified by the spectacle before me, afraid he was converting into the demon itself.

Jack Bell, you did not find my tooth, but you dug an excellent grave!

Drewry rushed to Father's side, grasping his boots from the snow. He tugged first one, then the other, onto Father's stockinged feet with foolish determination. The boots flew off as fast as he replaced them and soon Drewry sat back, his purpose defeated. The laughter of the Spirit filled the icy air around us and it began to sing a piercing song of torment, an evil little rhyme.

> *Jack Bell*
> *Not well*
> *Time will tell*
> *You'll lie in Hell.*

Father's contortions ceased as abruptly as they had begun and the Spirit's song trailed away, dissolving into laughter, triumphant and rejoicing. I rushed to sit beside him, seized with the same impulse as Drewry. It was absurd but somehow I felt if we could just secure Father's boots to his feet we could protect him. As we labored to that end, I looked at Father's face and saw tears coursing over his still shivering cheeks. Clearly he was suffering the most profound despair. Covering his face with his hands he began to cry in earnest. What were we to do? Until that moment I had never seen Father cry and the visage troubled me deeply. His shoulders shook with quiet sobs and Drewry and I simply waited, his witnesses, too frightened and distraught to notice how stiff and cold our fingers grew, or how, when the snow gusted, it froze instantly to the folds of our coats.

"Children, my dear children . . ." There was more compassion and fatherly affection in his words than I had ever heard before. "Not long will you have a father to wait on so patiently. I cannot survive much longer the persecutions of this terrible affliction. My end is near."

"Say it is not so, Father!" I cried.

"Have courage!" Drew implored him.

"And faith in God Almighty's triumph over evil!" I reminded him of the right true path.

"So you say, my children, but I am dying here." He turned his eyes upward and began the most fervent and passionate prayer. "Dear Lord, thine eyes are on the ways of men and you have seen all goings-on amongst us. Pray, in your divine wisdom, allow this terrible demon to plague me no more." If the earth could have opened up and swallowed us, I felt it would have been a great deliverance, such was the tremor of fear that shook my soul. I raised my face to Heaven and silently begged the tragedy of Father's death would not be enacted before he might move from his position in the snow. "If this demon is some Devil spirit and an enemy to you, as it is to me, Lord, pray that I might greet it with courage. Instruct me in the ways and means how I might best expunge its evil influence from my life and from the lives of my good family. Forsake me not, but impart to me thy love and faith in the blessed Savior that I might leave this world in peace."

I waited until I heard his gruff "Amen," to take my eyes from the gray and darkening sky. The wind was rising and the clouds appeared heavy with snow. So intense were Father's prayers, I felt God most surely *was* listening and would intervene to stop the torture, were it possible.

"Let us return home." Father spoke evenly, and this time Drew and I were able to tie his boots and help him to his feet. I felt witness to a miracle, as clearly the Lord had granted him the solace he requested. Drew and I each had Father's arms about our shoulders and our progress was quite slow. As we walked back up the hill toward the house, a squirrel rustled through the orchard floor, searching beneath the snow for some acorn buried there, and I started, tripping over my own skirt, and naturally, I clung to Father.

"Oh Betsy!" In his fragile state, I nearly knocked him down. I, who was supposed to be supporting him, clung to the man in fear. I tried my best to control the wild anxiety in my breast, but I knew not the way. Each step our three pairs of black leather lace-ups trod was taken with determination, for we knew not if the Spirit might attack again. There was a faint bristle in the air, and though I hoped it was just the chilling wind, I knew it was most likely the Being, silently watching our struggle.

When we reached the door, Mother stood waiting. She had come out on the porch wrapped only in her woolen shawl. She had watched us laboring up the hill and I could see in her face the knowledge of what had transpired. Perhaps the Spirit had played it out for her. I did not ask.

"Here, Jack, let me help you," she said, hurrying to get Father into bed. His face had tightened through his jaw and he looked most uncomfortable.

"Lucy, a fungus grows inside my mouth and there are twigs inside my throat." Father revealed his sufferings to her and his eyes appeared covered with a film of glass. He did not focus on my face as I passed his arm along to Mother.

"Don't try to speak, shhhh, now." She and Drewry led him through the parlor to his bedroom where she had warmed his sheets with pans of coals.

I leaned against our thick door, closing my eyes. Time seemed to slow down. I heard the low murmur of Mother and Drewry talking in the bedroom and the hiss of the logs burning in the fire. The good smell of Chloe's fresh-baked cornbread drifted from the kitchen, and it did not seem right that all should be amiss. I felt oddly light-headed as though I was not entirely in my body. Heavy footsteps hurried toward me and Drewry returned.

"I'm to bring the doctor," he told me, his voice high with worry.

"Godspeed to you, dear brother," I said, recovering myself enough to wish him well. I opened the door to allow him out. The black branches of the two bare pear trees swung viciously with a rising wind. I wanted to call after him, "Stay home!" For what could the doctor do for a man being murdered by an evil spirit? But Drewry had the wind on his face as he ran for the stable and I knew my words would be lost.

I went to Father's room and sat in the corner chair, seeing Mother occupied the chair by their bed. Through the window I saw the early dark of the winter storm fast descending, though it was only midday. At his bedside under the window stood the table he had fashioned himself from hickory and cedar wood, made to match the stand of the bed he and Mother had shared since marriage, where he now lay, propped on white linen pillows, his head back and his eyes closed. His jaw was tight, his whiskers limp on his neck. He looked nearly lifeless, as I had seen him earlier in the snow, except for the hurried rise and fall of his chest. Mother lit the oil lamp, and the room began to glow with amber light. The house was gravely silent, save for Father's irregular breathing. Mother and I shared the same thoughts as we sat vigil. Have mercy, Lord. Have mercy on his soul.

At the sound of horses' hooves thumping through the snow, Mother rose to greet Dr. Hopson. I remained in my chair, where I'd passed three mostly silent hours, watching my father decline. Abruptly, I threw my fists into my eyes and gave a silent scream. I knew not what I wished to cry out, but there was something in me, something vile, a foul emotion, an evil wrong. I cried not at all. I gazed at Father.

The doctor entered the room with his coat dripping snow, Mother and Drewry close behind.

"He fares quite poorly. Observe his eyes and pallor," Mother said, clearly relieved to see Dr. Hopson. He set his bag on the side table.

"Have you another lamp? 'Tis dim in here."

"Betsy, fetch it from the parlor," Mother directed me as she stood over Father and held the lamp high to assist Dr. Hopson's examination. I found the other lamp in the parlor, and returned to watch the doctor lay his hands from Father's ear to jaw, feeling his throat with his thumbs.

"Has he suffered a blow to the head?"

"He has!" I cried. "The Spirit threw Father's own boot and struck him such a mighty blow he fell down on the ground. It happened twice, this morning." Dr. Hopson palpitated Father's scalp with his hands, exhibiting only in the set of his shoulders how ridiculous he found the truth.

"I feel no lump or wound. John Bell, John, can you hear me?" Dr. Hopson leaned over my father, who blinked his eyes and groaned, as though he were not unconscious.

"Jack!" Mother joined the doctor, attempting to cajole him from his stupor. "It's Lucy, Jack. And Dr. Hopson. Speak, if you can hear us." I moved to stand at the foot of the bed to better see, but no words issued from his lips.

"Father! Tell what happened, Father!" I squeezed the wooden bedpost and witnessed his eyes open. He blinked and in the shining lamplight I could see his pupils, bright and clearly focused.

"Ah," Dr. Hopson exclaimed. "What ails you, John?"

Father raised his right arm, returned to the land of the living, but unable to speak. His wrist quivered in the air as if it were a great effort for him to keep it aloft. His fingers twitched violently in my direction and then up to the ceiling before his arm collapsed back to the bed.

"He means you should bring the slate from upstairs, Betsy." Mother turned to me, requesting I should fetch it. I do not know how she knew what he meant, for no movement of his hands had revealed that to me.

"Go, Betsy!" Mother's impatience brought tears to my eyes. I turned and fled without a lamp. The parlor glowed with the warm red light from the hearth, but the hall and stairs were black. The day had come to an early end. It did not matter, for I felt as if I was moving through an even greater blackness, from which I would never emerge. At the landing I saw a light gleaming in the boys' room, and I made haste to it. Richard and Joel were on Joel's bed and Chloe sat between them, holding them both to her breast. Father would not have approved, but I thought it best that she was there to comfort them.

"Where is your slate?" I demanded. Richard purposefully left the bed and crossed the room into the darkest corner where his slate was set by his schoolbooks. He brought it straight to me.

"Is Father dying?" he asked, handing it over.

"No," I answered and left the room running, heedless of the dark.

Downstairs, Dr. Hopson had his quill pen and paper out and he was writing a note. He had lined several glass bottles labeled in his tall smooth cursive across the bedside table.

"At nighttime, give him a dose of this, and also whenever he complains of pain. This will soothe his throat. This tincture will improve his blood and restore him to strength. You may dose him three times a day until he has regained his color and voice, when twice a day will be sufficient."

"What is his affliction, doctor? Do you recognize the disease?" Mother appeared most concerned, but Dr. Hopson remained occupied recording his instructions and did not immediately answer. Father appeared to have fallen into a deep sleep, and his chest rose evenly, his breathing regular and calm.

"There are as many diseases in the world as there are people to fall ill with them," Dr. Hopson sighed. "Though I cannot say for certain what ails your John, I do not believe it is of a serious nature. He has no fever and his breath flows easily. I have looked into his throat, his ears and eyes, and found nothing amiss. He has no lumps or wounds. His pallor is disturbing, but perhaps he has attempted overly strenuous activity of late?" The doctor raised questioning eyebrows.

"He took a trip to Cedar Hill and back and complained of suffering the same ailment of the throat which I now believe prevents him from speaking. Yet this morning, he rose early in his customary habit and felt well enough to journey in the snow to the hog pen to separate the stock." Mother seemed uncertain in her description of Father's activities.

"Most likely he has a minor irritation of the throat which will be healed by medicine and rest in bed. From Drewry's face on my doorstep I should have thought much worse. Pray, do not be overly concerned by his condition, the causes of illness often remain a mystery, Lucy." Dr. Hopson turned his gaze to me, and in his eyes I saw his thoughts. Despite the testimony of the many friends, neighbors and strangers who had come through our home, he maintained his belief the Spirit's antics were created from my imagination. I could see if I were his daughter, he would have me appropriately punished.

"We are ever so grateful for your prompt response, Dr. Hopson. It is so unlike Jack to have an illness requiring rest in bed, we are naturally beside ourselves! Please, take a fruitcake home to Abigail and bid her enjoy it for Christmas." Mother lifted the lamp from the table to escort the doctor out.

"You do bake the finest fruitcake, Lucy Bell." Dr. Hopson smiled and closed the straps about his bag.

I knew what was wrong with Father was not at all what the doctor said, and further, I doubted he would be helped in any way by tinctures. I bolted to the doorway and fell down purposely on my knees, blocking his way out.

"Please, you must do something more to save my father!" I raised my hands up clasped in the posture of prayer to Dr. Hopson, and a sour expression of distaste fell across his features. Mother's eyes filled with tears but they did not overflow. Gently she sank beside me and the amber light of the oil lamp swung across the walls with her movement.

"Betsy darling," she spoke into my ear, "the good doctor has done his best. The Lord will care for Father in his every moment of need. Trust in God, for He is the only Savior for us all. Look, your father sleeps peacefully." She paused for me to look at him, his face a ghastly gray on the white pillow. "All will be well with him come morning." She pulled at my arm most urgently, digging her nails into my muscle, encouraging me to rise and move aside. I did so with great reluctance and the sobs I had previously kept quiet issued forth. It was an awkward moment, as Mother was torn between her manners and her sincere concern for me. The doctor heaved a sigh so loud I heard it through my tears. Opening his bag, he withdrew another bottle.

"Give her this," he said to Mother. "She is clearly overwrought." I grasped the bottle from the doctor's hands and threw it violently onto the bare floorboards, but it did not break.

"I'll have none of it!" I cried, thinking the Spirit was not present in any way, apart from its stranglehold on Father, so I must be responsible myself for this bad behavior. I ran through the darkened parlor and up the black stairs into my room, dark and colder still. No light came through my window for dark snow clouds filled the sky. I fell down on my bed and cried until the sobs choked at my throat. I cried until it seemed the Spirit had its hands inside me too, distorting my face, and then I stopped. I dried my eyes with the sleeve of my dress, and sat up, fairly ripping the laces through my boots. In a temper I pulled them off and climbed under my cold quilts. I did not undress, and I expected all would not be well, come morning.

Mother did not come up to speak to me, as I supposed she would. I guessed my behavior deemed me unworthy of receiving whatever calming tincture the doctor had intended for me. I heard her voice downstairs, talking with him, and then I heard the big door close and the sound of his horse thumping through the snow. I thought he must be a brave man to leave our home on a dark winter evening with no companion save a traveling lantern and a fruitcake packed in his saddlebag. But perhaps it was not bravery, but desperation forcing him to go, for despite his attitude of disbelief, it was possible he did not wish to spend any additional minutes in our cursed home. Who would? I fell to sleep and dreamed I was standing at the foot of Father's bed, trying to speak, but I was prevented from doing so by a fat and slimy frog stuck in my mouth. It was attached by one webbed foot to a place deep in my throat and pull as I might, I could not shake it loose.

I woke to the dull winter light of early morning. I heard Father's boots on the stairs, a sound familiar to my ears from countless mornings of his routine, and my first thought was, something is not right, and when I recalled the day before, my next thought was, how can he be fit to rise and light the morning fires? I lay deep beneath my quilts where it was warm, wary of rising into the frozen air. Down the hall, I heard him waking Drewry, Joel and Richard, and in answer to their inquiries, I heard him say he felt well rested and much recovered. Drew was quick to dress and I heard his boots join Father's on the landing.

"The troughs will be frozen, but perhaps only on the top." Father apprised Drewry with tasks for the day and I noticed he did not sound entirely like himself. There was a weakness in his tone, and his voice seemed altered. "Tell Dean to break the ice and cart new water up so all the stock may drink. And have him check the feed bins in the upper barn, for they are in need of replenishing." Their boots descended the stairs and I could no longer hear them clearly.

If he could rise, then so could I. The creases and wrinkles in yesterday's dress put me of a mind to change, and I picked from my wardrobe a gray wool dress that reminded me instantly of Josh Gardner's winter coat. Mother was setting out bowls of grits and molasses at the table where everyone was gathered, and she did not immediately look my way. I observed her chin was set in a line of sadness and the skin around her eyes looked pink, as if she had been crying. I sat at my place and the front door burst open, swirling in eddies of snow, the air bristling with the presence of the Being.

All work and no play makes Jack a dull boy!

Father twisted unnaturally in his chair, as though a strong hand gripped his shoulders. The spoons stood at their places and flew to his hands, and his fingers grasped them tight and jerked up and down above the table, clattering so awful a rhythm we were forced to cover our ears.

"Stop!" Drewry shouted. Father's hands were forced to move ever faster and harder, until the spoons pounded indentations in Mother's breakfast cloth, leaving marks on the table underneath. The racket and clatter was accompanied by the hoarse laughter of the Spirit, obviously delighted by Father's pain.

"Please," cried Mother, "he is not well, might you spare him this humiliation?" The Spirit ignored Mother for a few more moments of clattering silver, then one by one the spoons fell from Father's hands onto the floor. He did not speak, and his eyes turned glassy as we sat watching. A silence fell over us all. Joel moved from his chair to sit on my lap, and Mother stood to close the door.

"Please!" She begged for mercy from the Being and her face displayed how worn and sad she was, how, like Father, she felt the end might truly be near.

Luce, for you I would do most anything, but this is as it must be. Take old Jack to bed and leave him there, for he will not walk again.

I gasped, and Father slumped forward on the table, his head narrowly missing the bowl set before him.

"Drewry, help me, we must dose him with the doctor's tinctures!" Mother cried. With effort they managed to raise Father's arms about their shoulders and hoist him up, though he was limp and appeared unconscious of their ministrations. Because neither Drew nor Mother was as tall as he, his boots dragged the floor from his knees, as they headed to his bedroom. Joel burst into sobs at the sight of him being carted away and Richard came to throw his arms around my waist.

"All will be well," I lied, knowing it absolutely would not be. "Eat your grits." I spoke to give them the comfort of routine, and once I'd kissed their hair, they settled into their chairs and did spoon the food silently into their mouths. Mother and Drewry did not return, and soon the boys had finished.

"Run, throw snowballs at the squirrels." Chloe gave them direction, and I was grateful, for I was about to cry myself and I knew I would not be able to carry on pretending for their benefit. "Help to clear this table, Miss Betsy, so I can get to the washing." Mindlessly, I did what Chloe asked, carrying the empty bowls to the sideboard in the kitchen. Mother entered in a hurry to set the kettle to boiling on the woodstove. She did not speak and I was afraid to ask after Father. She went into the herb pantry and I followed, watching her lift great glass jars full of dried leaves and powders from the uppermost shelves of her cupboard. Abruptly she gave a start, for pulling down a jar, she beheld it empty and she grew very much concerned.

"Betsy, you must ride to Kate's, and ask if she can spare some valerian root. There was plenty here, yet now 'tis gone! No doubt the Spirit has whisked it away, for I need it for your father." Mother was clearly frustrated and upset.

"Must I?" I did not want to go, for I would be forced to take the path where I had encountered Father's skeleton and a visit to Old Kate's house was never to my liking, but Mother was desperate.

"You must." I could tell my reluctance irritated her and I did not wish to make things worse. I fetched my hat, my gloves, my coat, my boots and scarf, and when I returned to the kitchen, Mother gave me a fruitcake packed in a satchel for Kate.

"Betsy, yesterday is gone from us now, and all I wish to say in speaking of it is, do not shame yourself with weakness. Your Father needs his family to be mighty against affliction. All will come right when this illness passes." She helped me tuck my scarf into the collar of my coat, but she did not look into my eyes and, despite her reassuring words, I knew she was more worried than she had ever been. "Make haste to bring me back the root, and answer Kate whatever she asks regarding Father's illness." Mother implied Old Kate might have some knowledge that could help Father in his suffering, and I only hoped I could keep any measures she might prescribe straight inside the jumble of my mind.

I rode quickly there and back and when I returned Mother was tending to Father while Drewry, Richard and Joel sat solemnly at the table.

"How does Old Kate today, sister?"

"She had the root our mother requested."

"Will it make him well?" Joel held his chin in his hands, inquiring hopefully.

"Will it get rid of the Witch?" Richard asked, revealing he knew the source of Father's ailments.

"Who can say?" I sighed and we heard Mother's steps across the parlor and the hall.

"Have you the valerian, Betsy?"

"I do, and Mrs. Batts thanks you ever so kindly for the cake."

"Did she give you counsel on his illness?" Mother was anxious to hear Kate's recommendations, but I did not wish to repeat her remarks. Old Kate had crooked her index finger in my face and said, "Everyone has a time to meet their maker, Betsy Bell, and it sounds as if your poor father has started down that path. Make no mistake, the fiend that harrows you will do as it will do." I recalled the ugly brown color her finger was stained and I sighed, deciding to repeat her less offensive words.

"All Mrs. Batts said was, if she could cure troubles such as Father's, she'd be a rich woman indeed."

"A greedy woman is what she is now!" Drewry snapped, angered by this slander.

"Drewry!" Mother looked sharp at him, taking the root from my outstretched hand. "You are not Kate's judge. God will take care of that, and all else. Pray, make yourself useful. Engage the young ones in lessons of some sort." Mother appeared exceedingly preoccupied, as though she could not recall what to do with her own children.

"But Father has our slate," Joel protested. He was not overly fond of home lessons at any time.

"So he does. Go outside and play then." She looked over her shoulder and paused, listening a moment before continuing. "Or perhaps you'd rather brew valerian and slippery elm into a tea with Chloe and me in the kitchen?" She made it sound dull on purpose so the boys decided to leave.

"Do you want to come, Betsy?" Joel tugged at my hand, wanting me.

"No, I have just come in, go with Drewry." I felt tired and irritable and decided I would sit with Father while Mother concocted the herb.

Father lay in his bed exactly as he had the day before, tucked beneath the gray wool blanket. I saw Mother had dressed him in his heaviest cotton nightshirt, the one with the winter collar. His head was propped against the pillows in what looked to me a most uncomfortable and unnatural position, for his neck seemed tilted forward in a way that made the stern set of his jaw most menacing. I was startled to see how ill he looked. His face was gray and his eyes and mouth had sunk deep into his bones. His whiskers were uncombed and the skin beneath them seemed to have shriveled, so they stuck out in wild directions. He was not asleep however and he saw me enter. He did not speak, but his dark eyes flashed and he gestured weakly with his fingers splayed across the blanket that I should sit beside him on the bed. I took his hand.

"Oh, Father!" I cried out in despair, seeing his condition. He raised his head off the pillow slightly, and I saw the skin of his neck under his whiskers quivered with the effort. His lips moved, attempting to shape words, but no sound issued forth. He squeezed my hand and I understood he had something of importance he wished to tell me. I waited, but observed his face growing paler with each passing moment and I feared soon the very lifeblood would leave his cheeks.

"Pray, Father, do not trouble yourself to speak. Reserve your strength." I did not wish to cry and dishearten him, but I was afraid I might not be able to control myself. He gave a choking sound and fell back against his pillow, and the Spirit arrived, singing.

> *Howdy my brethren, Howdy yo'do*
> *Since I been in de lan'*
> *I do mi'ty well, an' I thank de Lord too*
> *Since I bin in de lan'*
>
> *Oh yes, Oh yes, since I bin in de lan'*
> *Oh yes, Oh yes, since I bin in de lan'*
> *I do mi'ty well, an I thank de Lord too*
> *Since I bin in de land.*

I recognized the song as common amongst the slaves. They sang it all over the lands, especially at harvest, but why the Spirit chose it followed no logic I could understand, except I guessed it wished to torment Father with the knowledge he would not set foot on his lands again. He would never walk through a field of lush tobacco ready for sticking, with a full heart of thanks for the Lord. Father ignored the voice and as it died away I felt the Spirit had gone. He lifted his hand, attempting with some urgency to express himself again. He tried to use his fingers to push his lips to form the words he could not speak, but he lacked control and so appeared to be attacking his own face.

"Please, Father, please! Rest quiet!" I could not make sense of his struggle.

Frantic with annoyance, he thrust his arm in spasm toward the parlor and I suddenly understood he wanted his silver flask and book of accounts. I left to get it, relieved to escape, if only for a moment, Father's extreme suffering. I ran across the parlor and grasped the walnut knob of his desk and pulled it, seeing Father's things carefully arranged inside. I thought what a sacred place his desk was, as I reached for the leather book, his quill pen and the bottle of ink. Without thought I lifted the silver flask and unscrewed the top, smelling the sour brew inside. The silky feel of the metal in the palm of my hand was comforting but I was worried, would he never drink from it again?

He was breathing regularly and his hands lay relaxed on the quilts when I returned. He managed to jerk his head forward in what I took to be a nod, acknowledging I had done right to fetch the book and flask. He tilted his head back and opened his mouth, and knowing what he wanted, I poured the whiskey in. I looked over my shoulder anxiously while I did it, for I did not know what Mother would make of this, but I could hear her still busy in the kitchen. Father jerked his neck forward and closed his mouth, but the whiskey ran from the sides of it, as if he could not swallow.

"Here, I will wipe it away." I used the sleeve of my dress and set the silver flask inside the pocket of my smock. He jerked his head again, this time toward the book of accounts, indicating he desired to write in it. I opened up the book where it was marked with a red silk ribbon on the last page where he had made an entry. Along the parchment he had drawn many lines, and columns of numbers stretched across the page. All the running of the farm was documented there, from the number of slaves and livestock and their cost, to the hogsheads of tobacco harvested and the price they brought at market. There were also annotations regarding the weather and what-not in the margins. I did not try to read it. Father twisted his neck the other direction and I understood he desired I should turn the page. I did so, but thought he must be mistaken to want a clean new sheet, without lines or marks of any kind. Summoning all his strength, Father held the quill and I hurried to open the ink jar, realizing he meant to write something down. I tried to prevent drops of ink from falling onto his quilts, but he seemed wholly unconcerned, focused as he was on wielding the pen. His letters slid across the page, much larger than normal and not easily discernible. When he finished he dropped the quill into the open book and pushed it away, toward me, so I could read what he'd recorded.

Forgive me.

I was about to tell him, yes, of course, I forgive you, only the Spirit spoke before me in a windy hiss.

Unspeakable.

A large stone, near the size of the river rocks that lined the front path, smashed down to the floor by the doorway. I jumped from the bed and stood with the book clasped to my chest, the bottle of ink balanced in my hand. The Spirit screamed into the silence.

Unspeakable, Jack Bell! Unspeakable.

"Go away, you wretched Being!" My anger surpassed my fear and Mother hurried into the room to hear it answer.

There will be no more of breathing in this house!

Despite the many instances of terror I had survived, the full hate and malice of the evil creature had never been so frightful to me. It was as if the Devil himself had spoken. Mother and I sucked in our breath, horrified, and Father too gasped, and then seemed unable to recover. He choked and coughed and the bones of his brow stood out as if his brain was swelling with the pain. Bits of white mucuslike material rolled off his tongue, thick and hanging from his tense jaw. Mother rushed to him, and holding his head back and his mouth open, she dropped Dr. Hopson's tinctures down his throat. In a moment he seemed to breathe again.

"Drink this, Jack," she said as she held the cup of valerian tea she had brought to his lips, and Father managed a sip.

It will be no use. I will kill him.

The Spirit spoke softly and calmly and Father closed his eyes. We watched in silence as he appeared to fall asleep. Mother sat beside him on the bed and lay her hand across his forehead, smoothing back his hair. He breathed an easy breath and so did I to see him peaceful. I felt inclined to leave Mother to comfort him, for I needed to return Father's book to his desk. Backing out discreetly, so as not to disturb, I forgot about the rock in the entrance, and stumbled, spilling ink directly down the center of the open book in my hand. I had neglected to shut it, but did so quickly in an attempt to prevent the ink from spilling to the floor. Mother glanced at me, but did not appear aware of the importance of the book, or my error. Her only concern was that I not wake Father. I felt suddenly light-headed and dizzy, as if I might faint, and I wondered, did the Spirit mean to strike my head into that rock?

I turned and walked with great speed to Father's desk, where I opened the leaf and set everything down in a jumbled pile. I took the flask out of my pocket and hurried to the kitchen to get a rag to wipe the edges of the ink bottle clean, for my fingers and the lowest feathers of Father's quill were already stained to black, and I wished not to spread the mess further. I opened Father's book at the desk to inspect what damage I had caused, and I discovered the red ribbon had been shut halfway in. It wagged at me, half red, half black, like the Devil's tongue. The words Father had written were completely obliterated and a black stain spread across the page where they had been, reminding me of the black stain on the snow under Father's skeleton. I ripped the page from the book, crumpled it into a ball, and threw it without thought into the fire at the hearth,

Betsy Bell. Unspeakable.

The spirit whispered softly in my ear, making the hissing sound I associated with its departure. My eyes were fixed to the satin ribbon. Ought I to leave it stained but whole, a horrible reminder of the havoc wreaked by evil, or should I cut it out completely and hope its absence was no reminder of the same? Before I could decide, the front door opened and I heard the boys in the hall. "There is another storm brewing in the north," Drewry said, stamping his boots, "and it looks to be worse than the last." I shut the book and the leaf of the desk, and thought I would return to it later when my head had cleared.

I went to my room and sat in the rocker Father and John Jr. had made for me. I wished my brother was present to spend the day in silent meditation and prayer for Father's recovery. I worried Father might die and never see John Jr. on this earth again. And what of Jesse and Martha and Frank Miles, who was like Father's own brother? I refused to believe it was possible. I looked out my window and saw the flakes of snow fell thick as swirls of eiderdown at a bed making, and the bare black branches of the fruit trees in the orchard were bent near to breaking with the force of the wind. The whistle of it bore down on my glass pane so it rattled in its wooden frame, and sharp gusts of cold blew inside, striking at the skin of my hands and face like tiny pinpricks. I wondered if the tiny stabbings I felt now were wind, or the Spirit. I felt sad I had become so accustomed to torture I could no longer recognize the difference between it and nature, but in the next minute, I thought it hardly mattered. Drewry appeared in my doorway.

"Someone ought to call the doctor, or the Reverend." He was restless and worried.

"Not in this storm." I shook my head and he followed my gaze out the window, where the view was rapidly diminishing to a few mere feet of moving flakes, and beyond that, all was white. "Will Heaven be so darkly white?" I asked Drewry, for the heavy flakes reminded me of angel wings, floating on clouds smooth as the white wall of snow gathering.

"Surely Father will recover, Betsy."

"God's will will be done," was the only reply I could think of, and I recalled Kate saying, *"It will do as it will do."*

"I'm going to find Dean. Father will wish to know the status of the farm. The boys are at their games. Do not allow them out," Drewry cautioned me, as if I was unfamiliar with the responsibility of their care.

"Do you believe I've lost my mind?" I let my anxiety fly at him.

"Do not be offended. I know not what your thoughts contain. I know only my own are dark with great foreboding and confusion. Verily, I wish no further misfortune on this house."

"Go visit Dean, brother." I could not seem to keep the mean sarcasm from my voice. "Ask him if his wife has a hairball for us to hang near Father's bed, or an amulet off Old Kate to keep away the witches!" Drewry simply stared at me in silent disappointment and left my doorway without speaking further. I could not seem to control my words or actions, for I had thrown Dr. Hopson's medicine to the floor, and crumpled the page from Father's book into the fire without a thought, and I had spoken thoughts I did not know I possessed to my brother. I rocked in anger, drawing my woven shawl ever closer about my shoulders. I wished to shield myself from the stabbing cold, but it seemed an impossible desire. I felt tremendously sleepy all of a sudden, and I tilted my head back and must have fallen instantly to sleep, for in the next minute Richard and Joel were pulling at my dress saying it was time for supper.

Mother and Drewry were at the table, silent, listening to the wind wailing outside the thick log walls of our home. Was it the Spirit singing dirges, or was it just nature, crying her strength? Mother had every lamp lit, so the rooms glowed warm and bright, and the fires were stoked high in the kitchen and the parlor. Chloe served us cornbread and sweet potato pancakes with blackberry jam, a comforting supper dish, but she tarried not long at the table, for Dean was stopping in the kitchen for his supper and she wished to join him there.

Mother said grace in Father's absence and immediately after the Amen, Joel asked the question on all our minds.

"How fares Father?"

"He is resting comfortably now and I believe the worst must be behind him." Mother smiled, but I could not believe she told the truth. I was surprised by her mood and her information, as Father had not looked to be recovering at all when last I saw him. Still, Mother continued to try and reassure us. "The good doctor's medicines seem remarkably effective, for all afternoon your Father has made steady improvement. The color is returning to his cheeks and most likely he will be on his feet again so we might enjoy our Christmas." I saw Joel and Richard exchange a glance and smile, attacking their potato pancakes with significantly more vigor.

"Perhaps after supper we might begin to plan our holiday, as it is scarcely a week away," Joel suggested, and around the table I saw a gentle easement in the tension of my family's faces. I allowed into my heart the small hope that Mother spoke the truth and my own evil feelings of foreboding were based on too many bad experiences. It was uncanny how my heart and mind worked together to create this future I very much wanted, though I knew it was entirely unlikely it would come to pass. I believed, at that moment, as the rest of the family believed, that Father's condition was much improved and I imagined in the morning he would rise as he had done every day for all my life, fully restored to himself. The shriek of wind against the glass panes and the flaring of the fire as it gusted down the chimney turned our table conversation away from his illness to the most pressing matters of concern regarding the farm.

"The pump at the well is frozen solid," Drewry reported, "and Dean fears the water at the garden pump may not outlast the storm."

"Was he able to dig the path to the necessary house?" Mother sliced her pancake delicately with the edge of her fork.

"He was, but related the snow falls so thick and so fast, before he was to the end of the path, the beginning was buried as deep as when he started. At the necessary house itself, the water is iced over and he mentioned tomorrow may be spent boiling kettles and churning the pit below."

"Yuk!" Joel wrinkled his nose with disgust.

"Our chamber pots will suffice," Mother said, clearly not wishing to dwell on the subject over our meal. " 'Tis too cold and blowing to use the necessary house, frozen or not."

"Zeke says the Negroes at the cabins haven't enough pairs of solid shoes to work in this much snow without losing their feet and being no 'count come spring planting." Drewry held his fork unconsciously aloft, awaiting Mother's reaction. She pulled a face, and I looked down, for I remembered how she had been most upset in the summer about the possibility of this very thing.

"What does Dean advise?" Mother asked Drewry, pausing in her meal, wiping her hands with the cloth on her lap.

"Dean says Zeke's brethren are worse off than the rest, and as he and his folk are necessary to any task, Dean is most concerned. All the Negroes do agree, this winter is unreasonably harsh."

"Drewry, I want you to go to the kitchen and tell Dean no one is to leave their cabins until this storm has passed. No one, except the hardiest of men to perform only the most essential chores, and even those men should not venture out if they haven't wrapped their sorry boots with hide of some sort. Tell him to stock their cabins well with wood, and tell him also, when the storm is over your father will have the cobbler out for Christmas boots and whiskey fresh from the doubler for everyone."

"I shall tell him now," Drewry said as he pushed his chair back from the table, pleased to be the bearer of this message.

When we finished eating we moved the lamps into the parlor, and each of us peeked into the doorway of Father's room, reassured to see him resting comfortably in bed.

"Let us list the joys of Christmas," Richard suggested, and Mother obliged him readily, citing sugared ham's head, brandied fruitcakes and sleigh rides to the neighboring farms. I listened, but stood aside to poke at the fire with Father's tool, and part of me was much distracted by waiting for the demon to descend. Because of my fear I did not wholly enjoy myself as the others appeared to. Or perhaps they all felt as I did, and simply hid it better, for I saw Mother, when she thought no one else was looking, casting watchful eyes to Father's sleeping form, and I noticed her descriptions of the lovely cakes with cream and put-up cherries from the summer intensified just as the wind outside howled stronger, and soon I knew she was putting forth her best effort to keep her family calm, despite what ills might befall us in the night.

"I love you, Mother!" I blurted out spontaneously, moving to sit beside her.

" 'Tis nice to hear you say so, Betsy. Now settle down, and I will read a favorite verse of Father's."

"I love you, too!" Joel did not wish to be left out when

there was affection to be had. He climbed up on her lap and she shifted her knees to accommodate him.

"Whatsoever thy soul desirest I will even do it for thee," Mother rocked Joel on her lap, while the room glowed with the light of the roaring fire and the lamps. Her smooth voice cast a serene spell over us all and despite my fear I became caught up with the story of the covenant of truth David and Jonathan had made until, abruptly, my peace was shattered by a shower of rocks in the hallway and the Spirit arrived, singing coarsely.

Row me up some brandy O

"Have mercy on us this evening," pleaded Mother, placing the Bible down so she could bring Richard onto her lap as well as Joel. I stood and poked the fire viciously, shouting at the Being.

"Why won't you leave us be?"

Drewry crossed the room to stand beside me, placing a restraining hand on my arm. I saw in his anxious features he was frightened the Spirit might cast me down, but it did not. It ignored us all, bringing into the room many ugly voices, until it was as if we sat at a barn dance with none but the roughest folk, engaged in chanting vile and hideous songs. We could not speak, for the noise in the room prevented any one of us from being heard, and when it became obvious the Spirit did not intend to cease this visitation, Mother led us upstairs to our rooms and tucked us into bed, while curses and musical vituperations carried on, ringing up through the floorboards.

"That which can't be cured, must be endured," she shouted. "I will sit with your father, and ignore this frightful revelry. You must try to sleep." I left my own bed as soon as she had gone and climbed into Joel's, encouraging him with my knees in his to snuggle up against me. He fell asleep quite shortly, nestled in my arms, and I found his warm and regular breathing so comforting that I did not mind how my position put a crick into my neck. I lay unhappy and distressed, more frightened than ever before, knowing the Spirit was about its final purpose, buried in the noise. I worried it meant to kill not only our dear Father but the rest of us as well, and I felt certain I would be the next to die. A howling like a marked hog rose from the noise and I wished suddenly the suffering would end at any cost. If death was to be the end of it, I did wish for it, for Father, for myself. This unlikely thought stewed a potion of darkness in my mind. I tried to pray to God, but found sufficient words absent. I thought of John Jr., and wondered, was he awake in this moment? Did he have any idea what was happening in our home?

Downstairs the curses and laughter of a brothel raged, and time again seemed very slow as I listened to the Spirit's destructive power. Every scratch of wind on the glass, every thump of snow shifting on the roof, gave me cause to fear the Being's hand would soon be on my head, or wrapped around my throat and I would not breathe again. I thought I did not want my last moments on earth to occur while I was sleeping, so though I did not know if I would live or die, I knew I would not sleep! Yet, as the hours of darkness carried on, I wondered, why had I been so cursed that God should will for me to live through this?

At dawn, the perverse merrymaking and the storm simultaneously ceased and all was quiet in the house. I heard the door open downstairs and then the sound of thumping on the porch. My brothers whimpered in their beds, as if they shared the same night terrors in their sleep. The light of day came through their dormer window and piles of blown snow were stuck against the glass, so the light was dim, but glowing, like white liquid in the air. I thought of angel wings again, and the ethereal quiet soothed me. The light had come and I was still alive. Maybe it was possible God did have a special purpose for me as Mother believed, and maybe I would live to see more propitious days in my future. I certainly was relieved to have made it through the night. Still, I did not wish to get up and out of bed as I was suddenly most sleepy, for it was cozy in the silent stillness with Joel's warm body stretched against my stomach. I was just about to close my eyes when Drewry sat up quickly in his bed opposite.

"Perhaps 'tis over now," he whispered and I wondered if he had ever really been to sleep himself. His wool trousers and linen shirt were impossibly wrinkled from the night, and I thought back to the days before the Spirit when Mother would have insisted on taking a box iron to his clothes before she would allow him to sit at the table. "It cursed all the night and never did repeat itself!" Drewry shook his head in wonder, and did not pause to observe the quality of the light, but hurried downstairs to supervise the lighting of the fires and to survey the nighttime damage from the storm and the Spirit. I heard Chloe rattling bread pans in the kitchen and Joel twisted and sat up, pulling all the quilts along.

"Betsy, is the Witch away?" Joel was wide awake immediately, and he woke Richard.

"Let's go and see." Richard rubbed his eyes and looked about his bedclothes for the stocking that had slipped off his foot in the night. I could not remain alone, so I also rose. I expected a scene of destruction in our parlor, but it was as it always was, everything in place. All the stones had been removed from the hall, for the thumping I had heard had been Mother tossing rocks off our front porch.

"Are you ill, dear Mother?" She shut the great front door and I saw that, like the rest of us, she had not changed her dress, and her face was as pale and wrinkled as Drew's shirt. She embraced me and I felt the chill of the outdoors on her and the hallway smelled of snow.

"No, child. I am just weary from no sleep." She ran her hand along my fuzzy braid and down my back. "But your father is improved!" She turned me round and pushed me gently toward the table, for our breakfast. "I watched him through the night, and though we were much reviled, your father did not wake. He slept peacefully until just before the dawn, when he awoke, as has always been his custom. You may visit at his bedside shortly, but remember his illness has left him weak and you must not tire him further. What news of the storm, Drewry?"

"None as yet. Dean is absent from our kitchen. I will go out after breakfast and inspect the lands myself."

"Oh Dean will be along, 'tis certain. Thanks be to you, Lord, we have survived the endless night." Mother added this sparse amendment to her grace and I assumed her weariness extended to her vocabulary.

"The snow falls no more," Drew informed her.

"A gift from God." Mother sipped a cup of dark tea very slowly as if she had made it too hot.

"May we build snowmen after breakfast, Mother?" Joel and Richard astounded me with their resilience.

"You may, but you must come in through the kitchen, as I believe Chloe and I might today begin some Christmas cooking and I can't spare her to mop up the snow you will bring back with you." Mother smiled, and for a moment I felt the day was beginning as many that had come before it had begun, with a routine of living that made us all comfortable.

But looking down, I saw the wrinkles in my sleeve and realized the fear of the night was still on all of us, marking our clothes less deeply than our minds and I knew our lighthearted conversation was all just pretense. I hurried to finish first and visit with Father to witness for myself his recovery.

"I have done. Might I go and visit?" I rose with my plate in my hand.

"Yes, Betsy, but be quiet and come away if he is sleeping." Mother continued to sip her tea very slowly.

Drew had built the fire to blazing at the hearth and it was warm in the parlor. As I passed Father's desk I felt ashamed for having ripped a page from his book of accounts, and I reminded myself I must organize things there after I saw him. I decided I would confess straight away, and be done with my guilt, but when I crossed the threshold of his room I sensed immediately something was very wrong. Father lay with his arm hanging off the side of his bed and his face was turned to the ceiling at a very odd angle. His eyes were wide open and staring, and his chest heaved upward as though he could not get a breath.

"Mother!" I screamed and Drewry and the boys came running with her.

"What has happened?" cried Mother, taking Father's hand into her own. She felt his wrist and found it pulsing quickly. "Jack, Jack, can you hear me? It's Lucy! What ails you?"

'Twas me, I did it. He is poisoned and will die.

The boys pressed against me, frightened, and I held them so tightly to my side my hand must have felt like the box iron on their wrinkled backs. Mother turned to Father's bedside table and there I saw a strange smoke-colored vial of blackish liquid, one third full and with its cork out, standing beside the tinctures prescribed by Dr. Hopson.

"What's this?" Mother raised the vial up to her nose and turned to us. "Who has brought this here? What is this foul-smelling liquid?"

'Tis poison, Luce. I told you plain, I done fixed him now!

The Spirit shrieked with glee, and Mother burst into tears as did Joel and Richard.

While you ate I dosed him down.

"I will fetch the doctor," Drewry said, touching Mother's arm. "Shall I?"

"Yes, you must!" Mother readily agreed.

"But Drew, the storm . . ." I knew the road was thick with snow and there might be more to come. Swathing out a path would be a trial for any horse, never mind the deadly wind and chill. I did not wish to lose my father and my brother in one day.

" 'Tis over now and for Father's sake, I must depart." He kissed Mother on the cheek and she did not detain him.

"Use caution as you go," she spoke softly through her tears. Taking Father's hand she sat beside him on the bed, adjusting his contorted body as the Spirit launched into a ribald song.

Row me up some brandy O

She ignored it and beckoned Richard, Joel and me to form a circle by the bedside holding hands. She led us in prayer above the Spirit's song.

"Yea, though I walk through the valley of the shadow of death I will fear no evil; for thou art with me." The Spirit alternated lines of its own verse with our prayer in the most confusing way.

Row me up some brandy O
For on a journey I will go!

"Thy rod and thy staff they comfort me."

Row me up some sailor's drink
For any sailor's ship can sink!

"Surely goodness and mercy shall follow me all the days of my life and I will dwell in the house of the Lord forever. Amen."

Row me up some brandy O
For on a journey I will go!

We remained in our small circle praying over Father, barely aware of the passing time. The air in the room bristled with the Spirit's ill feeling, and it continued to sing strident verses. I closed my eyes and felt a darkness unlike any other, terrible, cold and deeply empty, and when I opened my eyes it was there in the high corners of the room, a black and ominous fog, descending to the bed. Father's eyes remained open, but unseeing, and when Mother spoke to him he gave no sign he was aware of our presence. Mother held his hand and we prayed each breath would be followed by another.

I knew he did not have long and I realized only all the moments I'd spent with him in my life mattered now. They were all we would ever share, the sum of our time together. I hoped he knew I forgave him everything. His breathing seemed to happen more and more slowly and I saw tears were falling silently from Mother's cheeks onto the blanket. She looked as if her heart might break, and I thought of Josh saying, "there can be no greater God than He who walks with you" and I felt comforted. I wanted desperately to see him again and to spend all the rest of the moments of my life in his company, so when it came my time to go I would not be saddened with longing for my true love. Father's breath caught short, and abruptly from his throat there issued a sudden gurgling cry, unlike any sound he had uttered previously. His limbs shuddered like a rabbit shot in the field, and his chest rose and fell no more. His eyes remained open, staring unfocused at the ceiling. Mother gently closed his lids with a trembling finger and I saw one single tear roll down his cheek. Mother placed her ear onto his heart and sobbed without restraint.

"Your father has passed on."

I told you I done fixed him!

The Spirit could not contain its excitement and its most pleasant laughter filled the room. Mother responded not at all, but kept her head on Father's chest, crying bitterly. Richard, Joel and I held on to one another, not knowing what to do. We cried, but softly, beneath the Spirit's giggles, disbelieving Father had breathed his last.

I did it! He's dead! I will go and tell!

The Spirit's joy at its accomplishment brought rage into my soul. I wished to throw my body down and strike the floorboards until my fists and head were bleeding, so I might fall into fortuitous unconsciousness, and so be released from the pain of grief. I thought I could not bear it, yet someplace near my stomach lay the heavy stone holding me in my place, rendering me immovable. If the Spirit had not placed it there, I could not have remained still and silent in that chamber, witness to my father's death.

The Spirit left us to broadcast Jack Bell was dead to all our community. Though we were unaware of it, the Being had told Frank Miles the trapper nearly three weeks previous, while he was bagging coons. After his visit to our house in the spring Frank had returned to his mountain to find all his traps sprung and open and all his furs and hides gone to Indian hands, exactly as the Being had predicted. When the Spirit had spoken the news of Father's death to him, Frank had dropped his hides straight away and worn his horse near into the ground, traveling through the snow and storms to knock at our door, only minutes after Father breathed his last.

"Lucy! Tell me it is not true, tell me, Jack, my friend, is still amongst us?" He stood on our porch shaking snow off the bearskin he'd worn as a cloak on his ride.

"No! Dear Frank, he has passed away this very hour!" Mother fell into his arms in tears and behind Frank I saw the Reverend huffing his way through the deep snow up our steps.

"Dear Lucy, I came at once, is Jack seriously not well?"

"He has passed on, Reverend! Please, bless his soul!" Mother led the Reverend and Frank into the bedroom where she stood beside Father's lifeless body and tears rolled off her cheeks, falling in dark drops onto his quilt.

"He is eternally at peace, dear Lucy." The Reverend put one hand on Mother's shoulder, and the other on Father's forehead. I sat in the corner chair and Richard and Joel sat on the cold floor at my feet. No one spoke for a moment and the only sound was Mother's persistent sobbing, rising and falling along the valleys of her despair as Father's breath had done, before he'd breathed his last. We heard the sound of horses riding fast, then boots on the porch steps, and Drewry threw open our front door, arriving with Dr. Hopson.

"How fares John Bell?" Dr. Hopson shook the snow from his hat on our parlor floor as he crossed to the bedroom.

"He fares no more." Frank was the only person able to respond.

"Father! No!" Drewry raced to Father's bed and stared in disbelief at his still corpse.

"By what means has he passed?" The doctor gazed at his dead patient, adjusting his gold-rimmed spectacles. Mother remained overcome with tears and appeared not to have registered his question, as no answer came from her, though she did move aside, clutching Drewry, to make room for the doctor to examine Father's body.

"What's this? This is no medicine of mine." Dr. Hopson held aloft the smoky vial and Mother's sobs increased.

" 'Tis poison left by the Spirit," I answered, since she did not.

"Poison?" The doctor held it to his nose, then bent above my Father and smelled about his mouth. He put the bottle down and in a shocking gesture put his finger into Father's throat. When he withdrew it, we could see a touch of blackish liquid on its tip. "This substance must be tested," he announced.

"I'll catch a cat," Frank said and left the house at once.

"Boys, come away." Mother seemed to recover herself slightly and moved to take Richard and Joel by the hand, to lead them upstairs. The Reverend and Drewry gathered around the doctor's finger held aloft for them to see, but I hung back.

"He smells of this quite plainly, but I do not recognize the substance. And the bottle is unlike any I have previously viewed. Do you recognize it, Reverend?"

"I do not." The Reverend's gaze returned to Father and he shook his head with sadness.

"The Spirit brought it." Again I tried to communicate the details of the morning.

"How say you, Elizabeth?" Dr. Hopson turned and lowered his spectacles over his nose at me, frowning with distracted annoyance.

"Father was recovering until this morning, when I went to visit him and found he was severely worsened."

"In what state did you find him?" Dr. Hopson wanted every detail.

"His breathing appeared difficult and though his eyes were open, he was unable to see. He gave no sign he knew of my presence in the room. His arm hung from the bed as if disconnected from his body. It was horrible to see." The doctor squinted hard at me and I could tell he did not trust my accurate recounting of the facts. Drewry spoke up, supporting my rendition.

"When Mother and I entered, we heard the evil fiend which haunts us here report it had dosed him with the poison contents of this bottle."

"Where now is that fiend?" The doctor looked to the Reverend to confirm his skepticism but the Reverend Johnston had too many times been witness to our torment and a victim of the Being himself.

"That fiend may soon appear, good doctor. Call it not unto this house," the Reverend cautioned. "It came to me at dawn this morning to say it had poisoned Jack Bell and he would soon breathe his last and here I find it has come to pass." Reverend Johnston shook his head with heartfelt sadness.

"All of you are demented. This bottle and what it does contain must come from someplace!" The doctor was infuriated but all present ignored him, overcome as we were with grief and the reality of our situation. We were at the mercy of a demon from Hell and we knew not when, or in what way, we would suffer next.

Frank returned, carrying a burlap bag with a cat trapped inside. It thrashed and wiggled in a comical manner as he dropped it on the floor.

"Give me the bottle," Frank commanded and the doctor did so, while Drew and I moved closer. Frank sat on the chair and placed the bag between his knees, rolling back the burlap until the head of the cat appeared. I recognized the friendly golden barn cat I had stopped to pet on the day Richard was saved from the whirlpool of quicksand in summer. She was no longer a kitten, but she had yet to have her own. She hissed and spat at those assembled in fear.

"Wait," I cried, not wanting him to test the stuff on her, but Frank ignored me. Withdrawing a piece of straw from the pocket of his vest, he dipped it deep into the bottle, coating it with the blackish liquid. He ran it through the cat's mouth, wiping it across her tongue. In an instant, she jumped from the bag, whirled twice around, then fell sideways to the floor, and lay there, kicking out her legs. She gave a high-pitched yowl as if she suffered greatly, then a violent shudder passed through her and she was quickly dead. We stood silenced by this demonstration of the poison.

"Give it to me!" I lunged at Frank and grabbed the bottle from his hand. I ran into the parlor and threw the vial with all my strength into the fire where the glass smashed against the andiron. The men followed and witnessed the liquid contents exploding in a blue blaze that shot up the chimney in an instant.

"What have you done, Elizabeth Bell? We shall never know what was contained within it!" I could see the doctor was enraged, thinking I was an insolent and foolish girl.

Whoa, doctor, pray the day shall come when you might mix a tincture to stand with the likes of mine!

"Respect the dear departed, you wretched creature." Frank came to my side and placed his hand around my shoulder with such paternal tenderness I began to cry.

"Where is Mrs. Bell?" Dr. Hopson asked. He was shaking with fear or anger, I knew not. A few unmelted bits of snow fell from his cape to the floor as my own tears fell off my cheeks onto Frank's soft deerskin coat. Richard's slate had been set against the side table in the parlor and suddenly it rose into the air and we witnessed the Invisible writing a message in chalk, in a hand similar to Father's own tight cursive.

Jack Bell, December 20, 1820.

"How is this possible?" Dr. Hopson slid his glasses over his nose, as if he could find a place where what was happening before him could not be seen.

"You demon of the night! Show your face for this murderous deed. Come into my arms that I might match my strength to yours," Frank shouted. The Spirit appeared intrigued by Frank's invitation of a challenge and abruptly it allowed the slate to clatter to the floor and pushed me from Frank's side with such force I fell into Father's desk. Frank wrestled the Being and the doctor and the Reverend and Drewry backed against the walls and furniture as Frank thrashed about the room. Drewry had cast his coat on the parlor chair when entering with the doctor, and I saw him move with the same volition and speed he had used to shoot the witch rabbit in the field. He threw the coat on what wrestled Frank and with one motion and a cry, they hurled the bundle solidly into the fire. The coat smoldered into flames, but the Spirit had not been contained within it and struck them each blows to the face that left vivid red marks and they cried out in pain. A foul stench and odor worse than eggs rotting in the chicken coop overpowered the room.

"What a nasty business!" The doctor covered his mouth with his hand.

'Tis the smell of Jack, three days hence.

I ran to our front door and cast it open wide. I flew down the porch steps and caught my skirt on branches fallen from the pear tree, standing like black knives in the deep snow of our path. I ran, past the frozen well and the horse tie, until I reached the road, where I could run no more. There I fell into the snow as though into a faint, face down, and I cried and cried. I felt the thumping of my heart and listened to the heaving of my breath, and I knew for certain in my soul the day was approaching when they would thump and heave for me no more.

the rattling thistles

"Betsy, you must not be forlorn. Your father has eternal rest."
Mother took me in her arms the moment I passed back
through the door, but her voice caught in her throat and I
could feel her breast trembling as she held me close. She
stroked my braid in silence and did not give in to tears.
"You're too cold. Change that dress for another, and wrap this
about you." She draped her shawl over my shoulders and
turned me toward the stairs. "Come before the fire when you
are dressed. I will brew some tea."

The smell of Father three days hence was gone from the
house and the Spirit too seemed absent. Dr. Hopson stood
shaking his head in our parlor and he did not look pleased.

"The inclement weather, so late in the day, necessitates my
staying on."

"Were the weather fine as summer, I would stay here this
evening to sit vigil with the body of so outstanding a soul as
John Bell." The Reverend's tone was firm to the doctor, but
turned soft when he spoke to Mother. "Jack will be deeply
missed."

"We are glad to have your company, Reverend, and we are much in need of your spiritual guidance," Mother said, acknowledging his concern.

When I had changed my clothes, I returned downstairs and Mother brought me a steaming china cup of light-colored sweet tea. I settled into my skirts on the rug, beside Joel and Richard, who were listening to Frank Miles tell stories with indomitable enthusiasm of Father in his younger years.

"John Bell could shoot more rabbits in a day than we could bag." Frank shook his head, in admiration of the feat. "And he was strong! I saw him at Thorn's barn-raising hold a wall completely on his own." He leaned toward my brothers with his elbows on his knees, pure adulation for the dear departed in his weathered face. Joel's beautiful eyes were red from crying and he was very pale, yet he did smile at Frank's recollections. The Reverend cleared his throat and opened his Bible carefully, so none of his parchment notes fell out. He read to us in a voice much subdued.

"The righteous perisheth, and merciful men are taken away, none considering that the righteous are taken away from the evil to come. He shall enter into peace."

A silence fell over the room and I felt acutely conscious of Father's corpse. As if the Spirit ran a finger up my spine, I became aware of the shell of him, lying still in his bed, growing grayer and stiffer and larger with each passing minute. I feared the next act of the Being. Would it parade Father's corpse about the house? Or shatter the glass of the windows with stones? Or breathe on the fire so it shot tendrils of flame out from the hearth into our breasts, stilling all our hearts? I knew not what to expect, but I waited for something, and listened, and in the silence, my mind repeated, *the evil to come*. This was what I waited for. Did the Reverend's thoughts tend like mine, toward dwelling on the nature of that evil? When next it came, what form would it take? Would my corpse soon lie beneath my sheets? I felt if Father had entered into peace, while I must remain waiting for more evil, clearly he had the better situation.

Forgive me. Forgive me. Forgive me.

I wished desperately I had answered him, all is forgiven, Father, but the opportunity had not arisen and soon he would be in the grave. To forgive him now meant nothing. I looked to Mother, sitting straight and tall in her chair, her bun balanced at the nape of her neck, her hands calmly folded in her lap. She was composed, but many fine new lines had grown overnight, around her eyes and mouth, and a tired sadness hung about her form.

"I believe I shall retire in John Jr.'s room this evening," she said. I watched her stand and the Reverend, Frank and the doctor politely rose. "Betsy, help me with the pallets."

"Go, Lucy, trouble yourself not at all with our arrangements." Frank took her arm and embraced her and she consented, stiffly.

"Thank you, Frank, I do not believe I shall sleep, but I shall pray and think on my memories of Jack."

"There will be many," he reassured her, but Mother pulled away, herding us up the stairs with her skirts.

The next morning dawned gray and cold again and I woke to the sound of Dean's shovel striking the cobblestones as he tried to clear the path for our community to pay their last respects. I dressed and went downstairs to find my brothers all awake and sitting at the dining table with the Reverend, Frank and my Mother, engaged in breakfast conversation.

"Dr. Hopson has departed, and with only bread and tea for

his breakfast." Mother shook her head, but I saw there was not much else on the table, except a jar of blackberry jam. I moved it closer to my place as I sat down.

"I assume Dr. Hopson was in a hurry to be rid of us," I sighed, opening the jar, and Mother frowned at my rudeness, but did not speak.

"He will return for the burial service scheduled two days hence," the Reverend reminded me, most politely.

"Yes, the burial . . ." I saw Mother was dressed in her warmest boiled wool and I realized she planned to go with the men and my brothers to pick the site of Father's grave. Dean appeared in the doorway, and Mother acknowledged him with a smile.

"Ah, Dean, what of the grave?"

"The ground is froze solid, Miz Lucy. Zeke say he done buried a man in a snowstorm once before, and it may be some help to build a fire and keep it burning through the day and night. Even so, he say the digging of the grave will be a trial of strength for many men on account of the weather." Dean spoke politely to a place somewhere beyond Mother's right shoulder.

"It will be as it will be." Mother's voice broke and she paused and I realized the words she usually spoke for comfort were difficult for her to utter. She took a deep breath and folded her hands calmly on her lap before she sighed and continued. "The storm has subsided for the moment. Pray, send a man to fetch Mr. J. Bratton the cobbler. Tell him if he comes at once we will be eternally indebted and he will be well compensated for his troubles. Tell him all our Negroes need new shoes."

"Yes, ma'am." Dean was clearly pleased and the Reverend did not raise his brow at Mother's generosity.

"Speak freely, Dean," Mother said, correctly sensing there was something else he wished to say. "Speak to me as you would to my dear departed husband."

"Masta Bell done been my master ever since I was a chile, Miz Lucy, and if it please you, I wish to be a help to the man who do his coffin." Dean's eyes filled and he had trouble finishing his speech, but Mother smiled, listening to his curiously formal request, for most certainly he was the obvious choice as the person most capable of crafting Father's coffin. Father had engaged Dean to help him fashion every piece of furniture about our house, and he had said there was no carpenter better than Dean in the district.

"I had hoped *you would be* the carpenter, dear Dean." I saw Mother break with convention and try to meet his eye.

"Oh yes, Miz Lucy, I will make it fine." Dean looked down with emotion but Mother raised her eyebrows at him, hoping he was thinking along the lines of her own mind. Earlier in the fall Father had taken Dean to Springfield where they had purchased some lovely and expensive planks of walnut wood. Father had intended to make a dining table for Jesse and Martha but then they had moved, and the wood had not been used.

"Use the walnut wood, Dean, and know Frank Miles has volunteered to supervise the digging of the grave, so you need not concern yourself with that."

"That wood is the finest, ma'am, and Zeke, he say he knows the ins and outs of digging." Dean nodded his head in vigorous agreement with Mother, but still kept his eyes to the floor. "Miz Lucy, with the help of the good Lord, this casket will be worthy of the man." I wondered if he sheltered tears within his lids.

I watched everyone leave from the front window in the parlor. Frank and Drew walked on one side of Mother, and the Reverend took her other side, his hand on her elbow, crooked like the bare black branches of the trees they trudged beneath. They traveled slowly down the path Dean had shoveled, and Richard and Joel followed behind, straying frequently into the snow. I watched them kicking it, sending tufts up in the air that surely soaked their boots. I wondered where they were headed. Mother had suggested the plateau on the north end of the property up above the stream, where Father had let the thistles grow after Drewry stole the jawbone from the Indian graves. It seemed an odd choice to me, but there was a lovely view of the Red River and the tobacco fields from there, and I trusted Mother to know what Father would have wanted.

"I am going now, Miss Betsy, to fetch my girls for the preparations." Chloe stood in the hall, and I could feel her shrinking back from the bedroom off the parlor where Father's corpse lay. "Little Bright wants me to tell you, she sure is sorry at your father's passing."

"Thank her kindly," I said, thinking the last time I saw Little Bright she was in line to have her head shaved of lice, while her mother was busy oiling my hair. I thought of the time Father had made her eat tobacco worms, and I found it hard to believe she was truly sorry at his passing. We were silent for a moment and from the cabins I heard the wailing of the slaves. Their deep voices howled in mourning for Father's soul, or perhaps they cried with joy that they might soon have shoes. It was difficult to tell, as the melody of their grief did not have words I could understand; it rose and fell, rhythmic and distant.

"Check the fire keeps lively, Miss Betsy, and I will soon return." Chloe hurried back through the house, leaving from the kitchen. I realized I was alone and I grew cold, as if a large hand of ice lay across my back. Frightened, I thought it was my father's hand and I expected he had risen from his bed to tap me on the shoulder. I could not turn around to see if it were so, and I endured my fear, repeating to myself, Father's body lying in his bed was nothing but the shell of him. His body was like the barn, emptied of its harvest crops. I stared at the white expanse of our lawn, and thought of Ignatius Batts sitting all the days at his front window, the same unseeing expression on the features of his face. I wondered if he saw as I did, nothing but shapes and colors without meaning. The cold air carried the uncomfortable sensation of waiting, waiting for some unpredictable evil, and the hand of ice on my back did not move.

On the road I saw a horse and rider of familiar stature taking the turn onto our path. He rode quickly and though he wore a cloak with a hood around his head I recognized Josh Gardner dismounting at our horse tie. My heart quickened as he looked up to the house and I wondered if he could see me at the window, for he hastened in the tying of his horse. I wished to rise and open the door, but the cold air in the parlor was so intense I felt frozen in my spot. I wanted to tell him of Father's last breath and how I knew in my soul the importance of deep love. I wanted to feel Josh's warm arms circling me and holding me safe, but though he had more distance to cover than I, it took me until he was knocking to move my frightened body to open our door. I saw instantly so much kindness and concern in his gray eyes, I did not know how to say what had happened, and I was grateful he spoke first.

"Say it is not so, the evil Being has dealt a fatal blow unto your father?"

" 'Tis true! He lies cold as stone in his bed, poisoned by the menace." Sudden tears filled my eyes and Josh pulled me to him in embrace without a thought of who might see. Only I knew we were alone. The one other person in the house who might have cared lay dead.

Betsy Bell, do not have Josh Gardner.

The Spirit filled the hallway with its warning, and a sudden wind whisked eddies of snow inside the door.

"Be gone, you evil demon! Your horrors are accomplished here!" Josh held my face in his two hands, still gloved and cold. He covered my ears so I might not hear the fiend's command.

Betsy Bell, do not have Josh Gardner.

It repeated itself without a change in tone.

"Please, go!" I pushed Josh back away, onto the porch, for I did not want to die, and I knew the Being was capable of many tortures.

"But, Betsy." Josh grasped my arm and firmly held it. "I must pay my respects," he insisted. "Are you alone with that foul creature?" He stepped back inside.

"Go, Josh! If ever you had a care in your heart for me, please, go, now!" It was most painful to make that loathsome request, for I knew he would not stay if I so entreated him. I wanted more than anything to be transported to some other house where I might live another life and associate with him, yet I did not want to fight the Spirit.

Betsy Bell, do not have Josh Gardner.

"Quiet, you horror, leave her be!" Josh shouted as I managed to turn him around and, using the heavy cedar door to my advantage, I pushed him out. He did not physically fight my requests, and I was glad, for my resolve to be rid of him was weak indeed. A sudden wind blew under the door and up my skirt, pushing snow into a tidy line before my feet. I heard a crack, like a gunshot, and I ran to the window in time to see Josh jump nimbly away from a branch falling with great velocity off the pear tree. It smashed into the snow, and Josh was not struck. He stood on the lawn, shouting, but his words were unintelligible to me against the wind. He faced the house, apparently determined not to leave. The pear trees swayed above him, dropping sheets of snow onto the ground, freeing the mighty armlike branches. I feared they would come alive with the Spirit's mischief and harm him with their black and pointed ends.

"Go, Josh!" I shouted through the window, then turned away, unable to watch him remain. I fled up to my room and from the stairs shouted loud into the house, empty of all except Father's corpse and the ugly Spirit, "I am still alive!" I yelled, "I am alive!" I threw myself down on my bed on my back and closed my eyes. If I lay still long enough would it kill me? Would my heart be frozen into silence, and would I lie in my position forevermore, never rising from the bed, but descending in a box into the ground? Dear Lord, I will fear no evil . . . I made an attempt at prayer, but found I could not encompass the thought of the Lord in my fear. I felt the cold stone in my belly and I knew suddenly what it was, a grave marker. The Spirit had placed the stone inside me, so to mark where I already was dead.

On the day of the funeral, the house swirled with activity as the snow had swirled on the day Father died. It filled the distances and made it impossible to see three feet beyond what lay directly before our busy hands. Mother chose my dress for me, a woven wool dyed with hickory nuts to the dark brown of autumn bark. Martha had left it behind.

" 'Tis nice with your hair," Mother told me, though I

doubted it mattered. Richard and Joel had suits fashioned from the same cloth and they wore them without protest, a testament to their deep sadness. Drewry wore dark gray, as did Mother, Frank and most of the rest of the community, as black elder and juniper berries were plentiful in those parts and often used to dye the winter wools. We were a somber crowd, but our preparations were much the same as those for a party.

"Help Chloe move the table up against the wall." Mother busied herself giving instructions. I spread our whitest linen, ironed by Chloe until it shone, and she put the fruitcakes out, leaving spaces for the biscuits and sweet breads we knew the neighbors would bring. I went to the kitchen pleased to see Chloe had fetched five sugared hog's heads from the storehouse and arranged them on a platter. I craved the taste of the brown-sugared meat along my tongue, but I thought of Father and how he too had felt a special liking for the sugared hog's head. It pained me to know we would never share another.

"They're bringing in the coffin . . ." I heard Drewry shout from the hall and I hurried back to see Dean and Zeke carrying in the dark and shining box. Dean had toiled through three days and nights to complete Father's coffin, and it was indeed a master's work. He and Zeke placed it on two tables Mother had set together, perpendicular to the hearth, and I saw the shine was from liberal amounts of wood oil Dean had rubbed into the finish. He had carved a pattern of intertwined tobacco leaves along the side.

"It seems a shame to hide so fine a piece beneath the ground." Mother held her white cotton handkerchief up to her eyes, staring at the lovely empty coffin in our parlor.

" 'Twas masta Bell's own idea." Dean took a step forward, touching the wooden vine. "We were talking one day after Miz Lawson died and he told me, 'A tobacco vine ought to circle my box for what more vigorous emblem could a man wish for?'" Mother began to cry and Dean and Zeke appeared likely to join her. I could easily hear Father making that remark.

"'Tis time the body should be placed inside." Frank hung his massive head.

"Children, leave us to it." Mother sighed, waving Joel, Richard and me into the kitchen where Chloe patted our backs and slipped bits of brown sugar melting off the edges of the hog's heads into our mouths.

"On the count of three . . ." I heard Frank Miles from the bedroom, instructing, "Heave!" I imagined Father's corpse was heavy as the stone above the phantom treasure. How would they maneuver him from the bed into the box? I licked the sweet and sticky sugar off my lips and tried not to picture the scene.

"Jack! Jack!" Mother cried his name in pain and we heard Frank's strong hammer driving nails into the walnut. A bad odor I recognized as the smell of Jack three days hence replaced the lovely hog's head in my nose. "I cannot bear it!" I heard a clatter in the parlor and Mother burst into the kitchen, her handkerchief over her mouth.

"Oh Miz Lucy! Make no memory of him in death!" Chloe hugged Joel close to her. Mother did not reply, but pressed her back against the door between the kitchen and the dining room, and her expression clearly wished to keep the day ahead away. The back door burst open and the cold came in, along with Old Kate and Mary Batts.

"I heard them nailing, so we came around the back. Dreadfully sorry to hear of your misfortune. I done brought a nut-meat pie, with our regrets." Old Kate thrust the pie toward Chloe, who took it with one hand, prying Joel's arms off her waist with her other hand. "Ooh, the stench of death is foul in here!" Old Kate wrinkled up her nose, withdrawing her amulet from her coat and dress. Mother sighed and wiped her cheeks. Standing straighter, she recovered herself. I heard a knocking behind the pounding of the hammer and I realized the community was arriving to pay their last respects to John Bell, landowning upright tobacco farmer, my father.

"We so appreciate your kind concern." Mother thanked Kate and drew Joel from Chloe, allowing her to open the door to place Kate's pie on the dining table.

"Lucy, I also made you this . . ." Old Kate reached inside her coat, removing a scrap of velvet stuffed with herbs she dared to call an amulet. "You can have it, free of charge, and I suggest you wear it, as it has herbs to keep the evil off."

"Thank you, Kate," Mother replied and as she reached out to take the gift Kate caught her hand, speaking close to her ear, but I heard her whisper.

"You have tolerated enough, now, Lucy. Grieve not for the dear departed, for he shall suffer this earth no more." I could not stand to listen to her penny wisdom and I retreated to a solitary ladder-backed chair placed in the corner of the parlor behind the coffin. I saw Thenny arrive with her family but I purposely did not look to her and I believe she could well sense I did not wish to speak, as she followed her mother into our dining room.

When next I looked at the arrivals, I was pleased to see Josh Gardner, accompanied by his father. Mr. Gardner and my father had not been friends, so I knew he was present only at Josh's insistence. I was momentarily heartened, but then I remembered the Spirit's warning, and I became afraid to speak with him. Josh looked about the room for me and, seeing my position, frowned. I saw him try to catch my eye but I pretended I had not by looking down at my two hands folded on my lap.

The parlor filled quickly, and the Reverend and Frank Miles moved to stand before the casket, so I was mostly hidden from view. I sat listening to the somber murmur of voices, feeling, as I had on the afternoon when I was alone staring out into the snow, the sounds in my ears and the shapes before me had no meaning.

"Betsy, Betsy . . ." I looked up and there stood Josh. Having paid his respects to the Reverend and Frank to get to me, he stood at the head of the gleaming casket, and I had the sense he had been a long time waiting for my attention. "I want to tell you how I long to relieve your grief. I did not wish to leave your house the day before yesterday, but I did wish to respect your wishes, though they were contrary to my own." Josh bent and lifted my hand from my lap to his lips. I allowed it, but Father's coffin at my elbow made the gesture grimly formal.

"Thank you, Josh," I replied without a smile, for my despair was large. I saw behind him our parlor was full and overflowing into the yard, reminding me of the Spirit's early days. How the crowds had come. I tried to focus on the individual members of our community wrapped in their warmest cloaks in our parlor, but I could only see a crowd of familiar faces. Who was simply curious regarding supernatural acts of murder and who was there to pay their last respects to a man who had wielded power in his dealings amongst them? Only a few had really known my father.

"Betsy, your father has gone to where we all shall go, though I mean not to further sadden you with that thought." Josh sighed with some frustration, but carried on. "Truthfully, it is hard to know what to say to you, but I did find a most modern poem that expresses some approximation of my thoughts, and in later moments perhaps it may provide you small comfort." From inside his vest pocket Josh withdrew a piece of smooth folded paper, which he deposited onto my lap. "Perhaps I may call on you again soon?" He squeezed my hand with affection. I shook my head no, most absolutely, as I was too frightened by what the Spirit might do to us. There was a shuffle amongst the crowd and Josh was forced to move aside. Frank and Drewry set a wooden bench before the casket and many people shifted, their backs to me. I opened the paper on my lap, easily able to focus on Josh's perfect script.

"Mutability"
by
Percy Bysshe Shelley

We are as clouds that veil the midnight moon;
   How restlessly they speed, and gleam, and quiver,
Streaking the darkness radiantly!—yet soon
   Night closes round, and they are lost for ever:

Or like forgotten lyres, whose dissonant strings
   Give various response to each varying blast,
To whose frail frame no second motion brings
   One mood or modulation like the last.

We rest.—A dream has power to poison sleep;
   We rise.—One wandering thought pollutes the day;
We feel, conceive or reason, laugh or weep;
   Embrace fond woe, or cast our cares away:

It is the same!—For, be it joy or sorrow,
   The path of its departure still is free:
Man's yesterday may ne'er be like his morrow;
   Nought may endure but Mutability.

Where had he discovered such blasphemous poetry, and what was his meaning in sharing it with me? I was intrigued, and set to read it over when the Reverend climbed up the bench in front of me and began to speak to the assembled in his loud church voice.

"None of us liveth to himself, and no man dieth to himself. For whether we live, we live unto the Lord, and whether we die, we die unto the Lord; whether we live, therefore, or die, we be the Lord's." A rush of cold air blew up the hill and in our door, chilling all persons present until we were as frozen as stones in the stream, buried under ice and snow.

Oh here's success to brandy, drink it down, drink it down,
Oh here's success to brandy, drink it down, drink it down,.

The Spirit filled the room with a hundred voices on the chorus, so outside the sound resonated as if our home were a rumbling brothel. Inside, the people in the parlor bowed their heads and shivered in silent prayer. At least, I hoped they prayed, and did not bow their heads to hide their laughter, as the Spirit made a mockery of Father's life.

Oh here's success to whiskey, drink it down, drink it down,
Oh here's success to whiskey, drink it down, drink it down,
For it always makes you frisky,
Drink it down! Drink it down! Drink it down!

The picture of Father draining his silver flask at his desk occupied my mind, and if not for the heavy stone in the pit of my stomach that held me in my place, I believe I would have fallen on the floor under the casket in tears. The Reverend shouted the Lord's Prayer and Frank cursed the Spirit, but no voice could compete with the voice of the Being in song.

"We shall end this torment!" Frank pushed through the crowd and out the door, and I could see in the set of his deer-skinned shoulders he was full of anger. I stood and climbed the bench beside the Reverend, so I might see out the window Frank's plan of action. He tore through the crowds running down the hill to the horse tie where Zeke waited with the sleigh that would carry Father's coffin to his grave.

> *Be like me, and good for a spree,*
> *From now till the day is dawning,*

"'Tis time!" Satisfied the horses were ready for the journey through the snow, Frank turned and ran back up the path toward the house, shouting, "We must go now, to the grave!"

> *Good for any game at night, my boys,*
> *Good for any game at night,*

Drewry, the Reverend, Mr. Thorn and Calvin Justice simultaneously understood Frank's intent and the Reverend stepped heavily down to the floor to help the men lift the coffin.

"Yea, though I walk through the valley of the shadow of death, I will fear no evil, for the Lord is with me." He led the room in prayer and struggled to balance his corner of the coffin as they turned to the door, but the Spirit would not allow the Reverend to be heard and increased the number of voices singing its wicked tune.

> *My father he was a great drinker,*
> *He never was sober a day,*

And when he'd roll in, in the morning,
Oh these are the words he would say.
I'll never get drunk anymore,
I'll never get drunk anymore.
The pledge I will take, the whiskey I'll shake,
Oh I'll never get drunk anymore.

"Let us get on with it!" Frank shouted, and holding the head of the coffin he guided the men and Drewry forward. The crowd parted, moving somberly, in contrast with the ribald Spirit. I followed the Reverend and Calvin Justice, who carried the foot of the casket, and I was careful not to look at who I passed. In the hall, Mother handed me my coat, my gloves and hat, and she wrapped her warmest lamb's wool shawl around my right arm and her left, so we were both encompassed. We descended the porch steps together, with Joel and Richard following us closely, bumping against our backs.

And when I lay down in me coffin,
These are the words that I say.
I'll never get drunk anymore.
I'll never get drunk anymore.

I looked up and saw the lawn of snow was filled with strangers, all silent and willing to wet their boots that they might tell their grandchildren *they were there* on the gray winter day when John Bell was buried and the Being who killed him sang the songs of a brothel.

Oh row me up some brandy O
For on a journey I will go!

We walked slowly on the path Dean had shoveled under the pear trees and down to the horse tie, where the casket was loaded into our sleigh. Dean had removed all the benches except the driver's, but still the coffin had to be tied with ropes on both ends to prevent it from slipping out. I could easily imagine the catastrophe of the casket flying through the air, the wood box breaking into splinters, Father's stiff corpse rolling into the snow. Frank climbed quickly on the bench and whipped the reins against the horses' backs.

"To the grave!" He whipped them wickedly and the sleigh took off at a great speed, toward the barn, and all the crowd gasped and staggered back, afraid they would be hurt.

"He wishes our ordeal to be over," Mother whispered into my ear, explaining Frank's urgency, patting my arm under the shawl. The Reverend and Calvin Justice and Drewry walked alongside Mother and me, through ruts and gullies of snow. The path was too narrow to hold all present, and it was difficult going, what with stepping in the imprints of the horses' hooves and buggy wheels. I watched my black boots stepping, crunching through the snow, and I was happy to have a point of focus, for it was all I could do to keep from running back to the house and gorging myself on sugared hog's head, not attending my father's burial.

> I was not in my bed until late,
> 'Twas only an innocent spree,
> My wife for my coming did wait,
> While sleeping I thought she would be.

At the barn, the horses neighed and whinnied, as if the Spirit ran snakes through their stalls. The chickens set up squawking, the cows mooed in fear and protest, and the hogs began to scream and wail, as if they all were marked and called their angels down. It was the most horrendous expression of animal sounds I had ever heard.

> *I found her in temper and tears.*
> *Oh! she cried, it's a sin and a shame,*
> *And she scratched both my eyes and ears.*
> *But I told her I soon will explain.*

A loud screeching filled the air, and I thought it was the Spirit, but then Drewry cried, "Look!" pointing to the sky. Above us, Father's owl flapped, dangling its tether, loudly celebrating its freedom. I wondered how it had been liberated, but watching it soar to the forest along the river I thought at least one being would profit from Father's untimely demise.

> *And when I lay down in me coffin,*
> *These are the words that I say.*
> *I'll never get drunk anymore.*
> *I'll never get drunk anymore.*

I looked over my shoulder, surprised to see the long line of mourners trudging through the snow as we made our way on the path across our meadow toward the poplar trees and the road. What a testament to Father's renown. I turned back to walking, fairly certain there was no one in that procession, judging by the bowed heads and somber attitudes, who did not wish the whole thing over, just as I did. I put my attention on the toes of my wet boots, for I was frightened as we reached the poplars and began ascending the hill. I did not wish to cross the place where I had seen his skeleton.

"Follow the tracks of the sleigh!" Mother called ahead to

Calvin Justice, who was in the lead with Drewry on his right. The Reverend had fallen back somewhere in the line. I wondered if he had the stamina for such a long walk.

"I know the way, Mother," Drewry called back to her, reminding us that he knew the plateau well, as it marked the site of his most constant regret, the day he had stolen the jawbone. The cold burned the skin of my cheeks and I squinted, looking ahead, where we must turn off the road, to pass through the forest of elm and maple that led to the northern plateau. Large black winter birds gathered in the bare branches of the woods, and I felt they watched our parade, dispassionate as the white snow of the forest floor. We walked and walked, in the path made by Frank and the sleigh, and finally did reach the clearing on the northern plateau. I was surprised at the size of it, for three hundred strong men could join hands and make a circle there. Frank had driven the sleigh right up beside the northern edge where the large hill of red earth stood like a wound in the land.

"Oh Betsy!" Mother stumbled when she saw the earth dug out of Father's grave. She leaned heavily against me.

"'Tis almost accomplished, Mother, do not be afraid," I whispered in her ear, and pulled her closer inside the shawl as we walked the final steps. The Spirit stopped singing as we crossed the clearing. In the sudden quiet, a wind rattled the bordering field of thistles, and I recognized the sound as what was visited on us long ago, before the Spirit spoke. I remembered hearing conversations buried in the rustling and their hissing made me feel I would soon faint and fall into the gaping pit I drew ever closer to. We stood and looked into the hole of red earth and waited for the Reverend to make his way through the crowd behind us, trying to ignore the rattling thistles setting all our nerves on edge.

"God does remind us we are as nothing to the force of His Will and nature." The Reverend's cheeks were bright red and he breathed heavily from exertion, but I could tell he wished to begin the service immediately, for he strode past Mother, Frank and me to the top of the grave where the stone would be set.

Greetings, Old Sugar Mouth!

The Being laughed as the Reverend adjusted his coat, and standing with his back to the river, he removed his Bible from the special pocket Mrs. Johnston had stitched for him. Before he could begin his eulogy, a mocking cry rose from the winter birds.

Goodbye, Jack Bell
You're off to Hell!

The Spirit screamed with great vehemence.

"Lord God, forsake us not!" I heard Calvin Justice cry an earnest prayer from somewhere behind me and then every noise the Being had ever visited on us descended. Stones dropped and bird wings flapped, hideous gulps and choking swallows filled our ears, and Mother sank to her knees, in the snow, crying, unwound from the shawl that had kept us together.

"Finish this dreadful business! Bury the man!" Dr. Hopson pushed toward us, shouting in anger. He kneeled beside my Mother while Frank, Calvin Justice and Drewry hastened to unload the casket and lower it on ropes into the grave.

Goodbye, Jack Bell, I fixed you!

The Spirit laughed, but nobody else attempted to speak. I felt I could not stand it one moment more, then they pulled the ropes out of the pit, and the Reverend threw in the first handful of earth.

"Return unto the ground; for out of it wast thou taken: For dust thou art, and unto dust shalt thou return." He shouted over the loud laughter of the Being, and Frank took up the spade and began to shovel, fiercely. Dr. Hopson had his arm around Mother, attempting to raise her to her feet. I looked away, and over my shoulder I saw Thenny had positioned herself beside Josh in the half-circle behind us. She was speaking in his ear, and I watched until I saw him turn and begin to answer her. I looked away from them both and saw shovels of red dirt and snow splattering across the gleaming dark wood of Father's coffin. Let Thenny and Josh say what they liked, about Father, about my torment, about the evil inhabiting my life and how my battles with it should be waged. What did either of them know about my suffering?

Old Jack, the soil falls over your head!

"I cannot bear it." Mother stumbled back when she stood, then clung to me, so I nearly fell myself. The Spirit laughed and continued singing.

"It would be best to depart." The Reverend abandoned his position, realizing the Spirit was not going to allow him to speak. Calvin Justice took Mother's other arm and encouraged her to leave, though the dirt in the grave was not yet the height of the coffin. The earth was frozen in clumps, and it made a hollow sound striking the wood. Mother looked to Joel and Richard, who stood with tears streaming down their faces by the sleigh.

"Betsy, bring the boys." She turned to walk between the Reverend and Calvin Justice and I followed, taking my brothers' gloved hands in my own. I avoided all eyes by staring at the snow, and the gray and hickory coats I passed reminded me of so much dried tobacco and ash, rather than my friends. I listened not to the murmur of gossip hissing through the procession, but to the rattling thistles under the Spirit's rejoicing.

mother's illness

The new year of 1821 arrived without a single dropped stone and without a song from the Being. We had not heard from it since Father's funeral. I hoped our most welcome respite would be permanent, yet I felt the evil Spirit's absence and the absence of my father constantly. I also deeply felt the absence of Josh Gardner, for he had obeyed my request at the funeral and had not come calling.

"I believe the Witch's curses unto Father were its goodbye unto us," Drewry suggested one evening when he saw me looking anxiously to the window at the sound of a gusty wind. He recognized how I feared the Spirit's return in every noise.

"I do hope that is the truth," I answered, but I was uncertain.

"'Tis a waste of good energy to speculate regarding what will be, children," Mother said. "The Lord directs our days. Concern yourselves solely with right actions, and trust God for all the rest." If Mother felt as insecure as I did she hid it well, and on her advice I tried not to ruminate excessively on all that had happened to us.

We had hosted the town at Father's funeral but since then, the path to our front door was allowed to fill with snow when it fell, and we were left alone to grieve. I went about the tasks of my former life under Mother's instruction, continually amazed to find my hands and legs worked just as they had always done, unaltered by the dead weight of tragedy settled in my soul. I missed Father greatly and often woke in the morning thinking I heard the sound of his boots on the stairs, but as the weeks passed I began to feel a small sense of relief, for it occurred to me perhaps the Spirit's purpose had been accomplished and we would hear from it no more.

One afternoon, our quiet grief was interrupted by the arrival of a man employed to carry the mail from North Carolina. He brought a letter for us from John Jr. and Mother read it aloud in the parlor.

My Dearest Mother, Sister and Brothers,

I have received the news of Father's passing. The evil demon spoke it to me on the day of the foul event and though I was afraid, I did not believe it, until your letter, dated December twenty-first of our year gone past. I wish to return home at once, yet I must acquire new horses for myself and Isiah, for ours were uncurried and hobbled on the road, and when we reached this destination I found the sides of my animal streaked with dried sweat lather and mud, and this where his ribs were not showing through. I have the funds to replace them, but I have not done so as yet, for I believe it was Father's desire I bring the affairs of this estate to a close, and many issues here regarding livestock & land & improvements to the land, and many additional items not worthy of the ink required to list them remain unresolved, and until they are satisfactorily brought to a close, I will remain in this place.

I pray constantly for Father at peace in Heaven, and for you, beloved family. May we be delivered from all evil.

Yours always,

John Jr. Bell

Mother folded up the paper and tucked it in her apron, and I could see she was disappointed the news was not of his imminent return. Her general frustration increased, when less than one week later we had word from Jesse and Martha.

Dear Mother, Sister and my brothers,

I hope this missive finds you in good health. I received your message regarding Father's passing, and I am ashamed to say I had already heard the news from that evil demon that plagues your house, for it visited us announcing its triumph over my father. We prayed it was not so, but alas! How cruel! We would pack our buggy and brave the winter storms to return and comfort you, but for the one happy detail of this letter—Martha is carrying our first child, and already more than half her time is gone, and the midwife cautions against travel.

Mother stopped reading and laid the letter down on her lap.

"Martha? With child?" Joel was amazed to hear he would soon be an uncle.

"Our first grandchild . . . My first . . . What does your brother mean about the midwife? It would be no trouble to midwife to Martha." Mother was annoyed and frowning, and I could see she was upset they did not plan to return.

"Read on," I encouraged her.

I say this next, hoping you will accept it in love, and will not be offended—Now that Father has passed on, might you consider leaving Adams? We have a homestead much larger than we can fill, and the land is arable as paradise. All crops grow with little effort, as the Being did predict. Apart from the visit we received at Father's passing, we do not hear from the Spirit that tormented us in Robertson County. Has John Jr. completed his journey? How is Betsy? And Drewry? Richard? And Joel? We should welcome you into our home, at any moment of your choosing, and we pray for you, always.

    Your loving son,

    Jesse Bell

Mother folded his letter and held it in her hands on her skirt.

"What say you, Mother? Shall we prepare to depart?" I could see Drewry was ready to leave at any moment, and he itched with hope that Mother would wish it so.

"I think not, Drewry." Mother sighed. "This is our home, and our livelihood, we cannot up and leave. What would your father say to that?" She looked irritated, acknowledging our circumstances were not to her liking, but were entirely beyond her control.

"I will be out with Dean then," Drewry said, clearly disappointed. "The pump at the well is frozen again and needs fixing." Mother nodded as Drewry left, for she had set him up with the majority of Father's tasks. If I needed Drew for any reason, I looked first to where the hands were working, as he was certain to be there, the sole white face amongst the slaves. Richard and Joel followed him, as they did most every morning, for they were never bored with sledding down our hill.

The snow had not melted, and on one or two occasions, more had fallen, though we had experienced no further heavy storms.

"Betsy, get the loom," Mother announced, tucking the note away, determined to think on what disturbed her later. "I shall try again to teach you the finer points of weaving." I was not happy with her choice of how to spend our time and after several hours of constant effort on her part and mine, she admitted my weave had to be torn out and done again, it was so uneven.

"I find this thrusting and shoving motion impossible to master!" I made an excuse for my sorry work.

"Elizabeth, even your spinning, which is not your strength, is better than this weave." Mother held my efforts up to the light, and the cloth appeared to be a fishnet. "Enough. Retrieve your sewing, child, for 'tis wise to work to your strengths." I was happy to abandon the clumsy loom for the needle and thread, for my thimble fit just right on my thumb, and through the dim winter afternoons of our mourning, I found I could sew for hours without a tangle.

Toward the end of January, Mother and I sat together sewing in the parlor. The light was at my back and my needle moved smoothly over and through the white cotton shirting of the new tunic I was stitching for Drewry. I was having a moment of thoughtless contentment, absorbed in the repetitive motion, when Mother gave a groan and I looked up, surprised to see she'd dropped the cloth she worked onto the floor.

"Uh, Betsy, I feel unwell. I believe I must lie down." I studied her face. Her cheeks were flushed and red and small tendrils of her dark hair appeared damp at her forehead. What was the matter? Mother was never ill. I laid my sewing down and stood to help her.

"Mother? What is it? What ails you?" She shut her eyes and leaned farther back against her chair. She did not rise, or immediately reply.

"Dear Betsy, just help me to my bed." I took her arm and we slowly walked across the parlor. I could not go into her bedroom without thinking on Father's passing, and I imagined it must trouble Mother also, to sleep each night in the bed where he had died. I wondered if it was in her mind to have Dean build a new one. She had said nothing of it. She sat down heavily and I removed her boots, while she struggled to untie her sewing apron.

"My bedclothes, Betsy. I would have them . . ." Though it was the middle of the day, I helped her dress in nightclothes. "'Tis cold . . ." she said, shivering. I pulled the quilts up high around her neck for the room was chilly, even with the fire next door in the parlor.

"What may I fetch for you, Mother?"

"Water," she answered in a hoarse whisper that was frightening, and I hurried to the kitchen. Dean and Drewry had managed to unfreeze the pump at the well, and Chloe had drawn a pitcher, so the water was fresh and cold.

"Mother is feeling poorly," I told Chloe and saw my hands shook slightly as I poured. I returned quickly, but when I reached her, she was sleeping, with her head at an odd angle, reminding me of the last head I had seen lying askance on that pillow. I set the water on the bedside table, and put my hand against her forehead, pushing back her hair. I found her flesh burned hot as embers from the fire under my fingertips.

"Please, no," I whispered, wishing I might take away what ailed her.

"Why is Mother in bed?" Richard and Joel asked when they tumbled in from playing out-of-doors.

"She is feeling poorly. Please, be quiet! Play checkers or some other game upstairs." I ushered them from the room and returned to sit beside Mother all the rest of the day. She continued in a fever, waking only briefly to ask for water, and twice she fell back asleep before I could hold the glass to her lips. I grew ever more concerned and sat in prayer and fear, for it was in my mind the Spirit had not finished with us. Did it mean to murder my family, one by one, before my eyes? I made an effort to cease all thoughts of my own pain and concentrate on Mother's suffering. I prayed the Lord would care for her, body and soul. The room grew slowly dark and I did not move, but simply listened to Mother's raspy breathing, hoping any moment she would awake, recovered. Near suppertime, I heard Drewry come in, and Richard and Joel ran immediately down the stairs to greet him.

"Mother is not well!" I heard Joel's fear clearly in his declaration and I felt guilty having left the two of them alone all day with little explanation. I hurried to the hallway to tell Drewry myself what had happened, and I was there before he'd hung his shot bag on its peg.

"It came on her very sudden, brother. She dropped her sewing and said she wished to go to bed." I held my hands clasped to my breast with anxiety and Drewry clearly saw my worry.

"Do not distress yourself, dear sister. Most likely she has some minor ailment, requiring simple rest." He unshouldered his gun and turned away to hang his coat and I stood most surprised, for I had expected him to say he'd saddle his horse, though it was already dark, and ride the cursed ride to Dr. Hopson's home.

"Drewry, I believe we must call Dr. Hopson," I said, gripping his arm, most urgently.

"Betsy, has the Witch been here?" Drewry spoke softly to me, raising his eyebrows high, mindful of Richard and Joel beside us. I was silent, thinking how the Spirit had been on my mind, but not present.

"No, no . . . 'tis not the work of the Being. She has a fever."

"What does Mother say of fever? A day to run its course, and feverfew for two." He smiled, reciting Mother's familiar rhyme regarding when to use the herb feverfew for treatment. "If she is not improved in the morning, I will ride for the doctor." He cast his glance to Richard and Joel, who listened as though they were nothing but ears. Joel's eyes were watery, and I realized Drewry would make a good father when his time came, as his voice and reason successfully reassured me and my little brothers.

"Let us eat our supper."

Chloe had boiled turnips and made squirrel gravy to pour over the biscuits, and we took our places at the table. I was grateful Drewry led the conversation, telling an anecdote he'd heard from Dean.

"There was a slave, working for a farmer we don't know, outside Robertson County. Someplace far away. Dean said he heard the tale from Aggie, who heard it from her cousin, who knew the wife of the slave." His opening was intricate enough to force Joel and Richard and me to concentrate, and I suppose that was his intention. "The slave, they called him John. He stole a hog from his master, because his master had so many, he thought the shoats could not be counted, and he thought the master would not notice were there just one less. So, he caught a hog and killed it and put it in a bag and was hauling it down to where the other slaves were waiting to get the fixings for a feast when his master rode up after him, asking, 'What you got there, John?' " Drewry made his voice momentarily gruff, a bit like Father's had been when sussing a transgression. "The slave, he answered, 'A possum, sir,' for he was brave and hungry, but the master, he paid close attention to all his stock, and he had seen John make every effort to better his lot. 'Let me see it,' the master demanded." I laughed at Drewry's imitation, for he turned his mouth way down at the corners stretching his jaw in a comical way. "John had to open the bag, but when he did, he jumped back, feigning disbelief, shouting, 'Whoa! master! It is a shoat now, but it sure was a possum a while ago when I put 'im in the sack!' "

Joel and Richard and I laughed at this silly story and after supper when Drewry and I went to check on Mother, I heard the boys playing a game of slave and master, with Joel pretending to act surprised there was no possum in his sack. I heard them laughing, while Drewry and I stood in Mother's room, observing and assessing her condition.

"She is burning," Drewry said and frowned, placing his hand across her forehead. "What did she say of fevers? The strongest folk burn hottest?" I recalled her saying so, when Joel was ill, and yet, I was uncertain again. I shook my head, close to tears with worry. Mother was the one who knew what to do with illness. She knew what tea to make, what herbs to rub against the skin. I realized I had taken her knowledge for granted, and faced with her illness I did not know how to react. I wished I had paid better attention throughout my life, so I might know the cure, but which herb was used to treat what disease was as foreign to me as how to make the shuttle fly through the loom. I felt I was a most unworthy child.

"I know not what she said of fever," I stammered and Drewry frowned, but seemed to understand.

"I told you, sister, if she is not better by morning, I will ride to fetch the doctor." He turned the lamp down low, but left it burning on the bedside table, in case she woke in the night.

We rose early the next morning to find Mother much worse than the day before. She was now pale with the fever and would not properly awake. While Drewry and I stood over her, deciding on a course of action, she called out in her sleep.

"Jack, Jack . . ."

"She is dreaming," Drewry offered as an explanation, but she thrashed her head on the pillow and I thought it most distressing she believed Father was in the room with us.

"I think you must call for Dr. Hopson." I squeezed Drewry's hand and he did not argue, but left immediately, and was gone by the time the boys came down for breakfast.

"Whatever you do, be quiet today," I told them, forgetting I wished to be nice. "Mother needs her sleep." The tension of harboring illness in our home again descended and I watched the boys spoon Chloe's creamed buckwheat quickly into their mouths, as if they could eat their fear.

"Shall we have a sled race, Joel?" Richard understood it was better if they were out-of-doors, and after they had finished their food I helped them put on their winter things. I wrapped their scarves tightly around their necks in the hall, but I felt I was a poor substitute for Mother.

"Will she be made well today, sister?" Joel's knit hat slid down over his brow, and he pushed it back with a mittened fist.

"The doctor is on his way." I did not comfort him as I should have, but I could not. I kissed his bare cheek and sent him off to play, and returned to Mother's bedside, hoping she would wake and instruct me in the means to treat her illness.

"Jack . . ." His name came forth in a whisper as I crossed the threshold, and her eyelids fluttered, as if she woke.

"No, Mother, it is Betsy, here beside you. What must I do?" She did not answer but a groan and the next moment she had turned her head and lay asleep again.

The hours passed slowly, while I listened closely to her breathing. Several times she mumbled Father's name, but did not wake, and it was near the dinner hour when I heard hoof-beats on the road and I left her to meet Dr. Hopson and Drewry at the door.

Dr. Hopson entered with his head down, so I saw first the shiny black of his top hat, before his wary eyes met mine in greeting.

"How does your mother fare, Miss Elizabeth?" He looked anxiously toward the parlor, slowly withdrawing his arms from his greatcoat. He removed his scarf and handed it to me.

"She is hot as the fire and will not properly awake."

"Has your demon visited?" I felt he watched me too closely as I hung his things, as if I knew not how to do it.

"No," I answered simply, then added, "sir," with respect, for despite my resentment, he was the doctor and Mother was ill and in need of his services. I saw his shoulders shiver and he hunched forward, as if he walked into a strong wind re-quiring fortitude as he passed over the thresholds of the par-lor and the bedroom. I followed, feeling no sympathy for his trepidation. He placed his leather bag on the chair and pro-ceeded to examine Mother in silence. He felt her head and frowned, then withdrew an instrument from his bag.

"Undo the laces of her nightdress," he commanded, and I did as I was told, surprised to feel Mother's chest was hot as the woodstove with a fire within. The doctor stretched his instrument from his ear to her breast, intently listening.

"She has the pleurisy," he announced, "but the exudation of liquid in the chest cavity has not yet occurred."

"What do you mean?" I had heard of pleurisy. Becky Porter's Aunt Mabel had died of it.

"She may get worse, before she improves. If she improves." The doctor lowered his glasses, and wrinkled his nose with displeasure.

"What must we do?" I was horrified to hear his prognosis.

"Have your girl prepare sugared slippery elm and mint tea, and broth, and spoon it to her mouth. Dose her every mealtime with a dropperful of this." From his bag he pulled a tincture labeled *butterfly root* in his tall script.

"Is this the cure?" I turned the glass bottle over in my hand, trying not to think how it reminded me of the Spirit's poison.

"What cure there is. It will depend on the strength of the inflammation and the strength of her lungs."

"What will depend?" I knew I must sound as stupid as the bedpost, but I could not accept his words.

"Her improvement will depend." He closed his bag and looked away from me, taking up Mother's hand at the wrist. He pulled a silver watch on a chain from his vest pocket, and stood counting the beats of her racing pulse, and then he sighed. "Her improvement will depend on the strength of the inflammation in relation to the strength of her lungs." He put the watch away, and I thought I saw pity and some regret in the gesture, so I grew most concerned.

"Mother has more strength than most!" I meant to reassure myself, as clearly he did not intend to.

"Here, she must be propped up on her pillows." With

more kindness in his tone than he had previously allotted me, Dr. Hopson showed me how to arrange Mother so she lay half sitting up. "The exudation will be less in this position." He stepped back and sighed, as she thrashed her head violently, left and right, when we moved her.

"Jack . . ." she groaned.

"Good Lord, she calls for him!" Dr. Hopson turned away and busied himself closing his bag, and I thought I saw his hands tremble slightly, tightening the buckle. "I will return to-morrow," he cast an unreadable eye on Mother, "to examine her progress." I followed him out of the room and into the hall, where he turned to me, expecting his coat and hat. I froze, thinking he must not leave. What was I to do for Mother?

"Dose her every mealtime, with the tincture. And don't forget the broth." He frowned, seeming aware of my confusion. He spoke over loud, as if he meant Chloe in the kitchen to hear his repeated instructions, and I realized he thought I was incompetent. I recovered myself enough to hand him his coat, still cold from his ride to our house.

"Thank you for coming." I did not feel polite, I was so worried, but Mother occupied my mind, insisting as she would have that I behave responsibly.

"I am a physician, Miss Elizabeth! I took an oath to treat those who are diseased." Dr. Hopson turned his back on me, and hurried out the door.

I went to the kitchen to tell Chloe what to do, but when I got there I saw the kettle was boiling and the jars of slippery elm and mint were already on the sideboard. Chloe stood by the soup pot, plucking the last feathers from a plump chicken that had only recently lost its head.

"You heard the prescription for her care?"

"I did, and we must get the medicine inside her, for I done seen the pleurisy before, and it is a nasty ill."

At supper, Chloe served the chicken meat with boiled hominy, and the broth was kept back to spoon to Mother. The meat was most delicious, but I was terribly distracted, for looking around the table, I had the uneasy feeling it was growing larger as its number of attendants shrank. The places once occupied by Jesse, John Jr., Mother and Father sat empty, and I was afraid every one of us would soon be absent.

"We must make Mother well!" I hit my fist down on the table, and Drewry, Joel and Richard jumped, engrossed in the silent tension of illness.

"Sister, let us take turns, and dose her through the night." Drewry's concern had greatly deepened after hearing the doctor's diagnosis.

"Mother will be well again." Richard refused to think there could be any other possible outcome to her illness.

"We must pray it will be so." I smoothed my napkin on my skirt, looking down so he could not see my eyes.

"Why not ask the Spirit if it can heal her?" Joel suggested.

"No!" In unison Drewry and I both reprimanded him. "Call not that ungodly entity," I warned.

"It did like Mother best," Joel said, shrugging his shoulders at our vehemence. He returned to chewing his meat. I knew he was thinking of the time the Spirit had saved Richard from the whirlpool of quicksand and all the rest of us from the falling tree, but all I could think of was the bottle of poison on Father's bedside table, and the voice of the Being proclaiming, *Jack Bell, off to Hell* and *Betsy Bell, do not have Josh Gardner.*

Drewry took the boys upstairs after supper, so I might have the first turn by Mother's side. The fire hissed and

sparked in the parlor and Mother's breath came irregularly. I
placed the lamp on the table, and tried my best to coax spoon-
fuls of butterfly root and broth down her throat, but some of
it spilled down her chin and I had to wipe it away with my
sleeve. I thought of when I had poured whiskey into Father's
throat. I had not known it would be his last drink. Mother's
skin still burned like fire, and her lips were the red of a tomato
in summer, ripe to bursting. I thought of the times she had
taken care of me as I lay ill and I refused to think on what our
lives would be like without her ever-present caring and concern.

"Jack . . . Jack!" She twisted her neck, resisting my attempts to feed her medicine. She breathed out heavily, as if
she fell more deeply asleep, and I sighed, frustrated, for she
had not woken for near three days.

"Mother, it's me, Betsy, can you hear me?" I decided I
would read to her from the good book, an inspiring passage,
though I knew not if she could hear.

"I will lift up mine eyes unto the hills, from whence
cometh my help. My help cometh from the Lord, who made
Heaven and Earth. The Lord is thy keeper: The Lord is thy
shade on thy right hand." There was a sound like the flutter
of bird wings under a shrub and without cold winds or noise
to announce its return, the Spirit spoke in a comforting voice.

Poor Luce, poor Luce, I am so sorry you are sick.

"Please, torment us not!" I cried. "Have mercy on Mother,
for ever she was good to you." The Spirit did not reply and
gave no other sign of being present, and though my fingers
holding the Bible began to shake, I continued reading.

"The sun shall not smite thee by day, nor the moon by
night. The Lord shall preserve thee from all evil: He shall preserve thy soul."

Be quiet, Betsy. Let her sleep!

The Spirit admonished me in the most condescending tone, but I prevented myself from responding with anger.

"What is her fate? Can you help her?" I knew it was wrong of me to ask an evil demon favors, yet I feared with Mother in such serious condition the Spirit and its power over life and death was, as Joel had suggested, perhaps our best hope. It did not speak to me again but directed its ministrations solely to Mother.

Luce, poor Luce, I am so sorry you are sick.

"Ohhh," Mother groaned as though she suffered greatly, "I am too ill to speak with you." I was amazed to hear her voice.

That's all right.

The Being's tone surpassed Mother's own in soothing tenderness.

I will be back in the morning. Rest, Luce. I promise you will feel better.

I had no reason to trust the Spirit, but its promise entered my heart and gave me hope. I felt comforted, for in all my efforts through the day, Mother had not spoken a word, yet the Being had elicited a response. Drewry arrived to relieve me and I told him all that had occurred. He listened, then put the back of his hand to her forehead.

"I believe her fever has broken."

"Thanks be to God!" He looked into my eyes and I understood we were both aware we had the Spirit to thank, though neither of us said so.

Mother rested well through the night and in the morning she awoke showing awareness of her situation.

"Betsy, help me to my pot." She needed my arm to assist her and hold her as she squatted. I could tell she was embarrassed to have me there, but also grateful. "I fear I am most truly unwell." She moved slowly back to bed, leaning heavily on me, for the journey to the corner of her room exhausted her.

"Dr. Hopson came while you were sleeping yesterday. He says you have the pleurisy, but if you rest and swallow down his tinctures, you will soon recover."

"What tincture did he leave?"

"'Tis butterfly root."

"Did he leave no milkweed?"

I'll fetch it.

The Spirit spoke like an eager child, and all of a sudden, a glass jar labeled *milkweed*, in Mother's round cursive, appeared on my lap. I clutched it instinctively as it arrived so it did not fall from my knees and break open on the floor. How had it materialized? I knew not! I held up the jar and inside was the milkweed herb, already ground into a fine white powder.

"What am I to do?"

Mix it in a boiling kettle, two parts water to two parts weed.

"Yes . . ." Mother nodded, weak and fragile, sinking back in her pillows.

How do you fare today, Luce? Are you much recovered?

"Yes, thank you, but I am not yet myself completely." Mother was honest with the Being and seemed to bear it no malice.

What can I do for you? I wish to be of service.

"You are kind."

I do not like to see you ill or disconsolate, dear Luce. I will make you well.

"God gives us health and strength."

Speak not. You must rest and I will sing to you.

I sat with the milkweed on my lap, unable to move from my spot, mesmerized by the sweet music of the Spirit's song.

This day God gives me strength of High Heaven
Sun and moon shining
Flame in my hearth
Flashing of lightning
Wind in its swiftness
Deeps of the ocean
Firmness of earth

This day God gives me strength as my guardian
Might to uphold me
Wisdom as guide
Your eyes are watchful
Your ears are listening
Your lips are speaking
Friend at my side

The song was so profoundly moving, I felt I might shed tears from the pure beauty of it, or perhaps it was just my relief over Mother's turn for the better that made me weepy.

"Thank you," Mother mumbled, polite even in illness. She gave the slightest smile and I saw she too had tears gathering in the wrinkles at the corners of her fevered eyes. She closed them, as though she would return to sleep, and in my ear the Spirit whispered.

Betsy, make the milkweed!

I had forgotten I was meant to do it, I was so absorbed. I almost asked, why did you not provide it ready-made? Yet I thought twice before questioning the Being. I went to do the task and in the kitchen questioned Chloe instead.

"I must make a milkweed tincture for Mother and the Being has returned to sing her lullabies, promising she will improve. Just now, did you feel the Spirit in the kitchen? The jar it brought came from the pantry, here." I looked up on the shelf and saw the place where the jar usually stood between *marjoram* and *mint* was empty, and I turned to Chloe, who had her back to me, busy at stoking the woodstove so I might set the kettle on to boil.

"Miss Betsy, I do say, I feel that 'haint all the time, all the time, and everywhere." She looked around the kitchen and rolled her eyes to the corners of the ceiling, as if she feared it listened even as we spoke.

"If it heals Mother quickly . . ." I did not know what to say, or what to think. If it saved our mother's life, must it be redeemed in my affections? I made the tincture of milkweed as instructed and returned to wait silently at her bedside to dose her with it. Before long, her eyes fluttered open and her head shifted forward off her pillows. Immediately the Spirit spoke.

So, Luce, how do you feel now? Are you much recovered?

"Oh yes, thank you," she replied in a hoarse whisper, but she did not look at all well to me. Her lips were swollen with white blisters and her skin was pale and dry where before it had been flushed. She was recovering, but clearly she was still unwell.

The doctor is on his way, Luce, and he will be most impressed.

"Betsy dear, help me." Mother tried to raise herself with an elbow and found she could not lift her own weight. I pulled her up to sitting and she whispered she would need the chamber pot again.

I will be silent while he visits for I make him quite uncomfortable.

The Spirit spoke like a gossiping woman, though its intentions appeared kind.

I will be of service to you, dear Luce, in every way.

I wondered if it could be trusted, as I helped Mother to the corner and back.

I will fetch whatever the doctor prescribes for you.

True to its prediction, Dr. Hopson soon arrived. I heard the hoofbeats in the yard and a greeting shouted out to the boys who played on their sleds up and down the hill. I rose from Mother's side and went to meet him at the door.

"How fares your mother?" he inquired, removing his greatcoat and top hat, inspecting me as before, from his lowered glasses. He looked as if he doubted I had properly cared for her.

"The inflammation is not so strong as her constitution, Dr. Hopson. You will find her much improved." I turned away, hiding a small smile as I hung his coat, and he quickly went to Mother's bedside.

"Hello, Lucy Bell, how do you fare?"

"I am weak, but feeling better than before." She looked up at him with wide eyes and he placed a hand on her forehead.

"The fever has broken, indeed, a good sign." He took his instrument out and listened to her lungs, nodding, postulating, "I expect the tincture is the cure." He looked on the table to see how much we had used and noticed the bottle of milkweed.

"What is this? Milkweed? Who made this?" He turned to me, inquiring.

"The Spirit told me to," I answered truthfully, knowing he would not like it.

"So you have had a visit from your demon friend, Miss

Elizabeth?" He shoved his spectacles down his nose with impatient annoyance.

"It was not a demon this time, doctor. It sang a gentle song and spoke the recipe for the milkweed tincture at Mother's request."

"At your request?" The doctor raised his eyebrows at my mother, who nodded an affirmative reply, but spoke no explanation.

"How odd, your demon is an evil murderer one day, and a ministering angel on the next." Dr. Hopson shook his head, unwilling to investigate the matter further. I knew he was implying something, but I could not say exactly what. I wished the Spirit would speak, for I felt it was my defense against the doctor's doubts. But the Spirit was not at my beck and call. There was silence, except for Mother's quickened breathing, until the doctor sighed.

" 'Tis a good sign the fever has lifted, but the illness is still a danger. You must drink a broth to improve your strength, and prevent a worsening in your chest."

"I have no desire for food." Mother spoke softly, but Dr. Hopson heard her.

"You must eat, desire or no. Your body is weak with affliction. If you do not wish to leave your children orphans, rise not from this bed for the next month." I was surprised by the severity of Dr. Hopson's warning, surprised and displeased he could imagine such a horrible outcome to her illness.

The next day I stood by her bedside attempting to discover what I might fetch from the kitchen, or the storehouse even, that she would like.

"I have no appetite," Mother lamented and I was greatly

frustrated, as I felt Dr. Hopson's orders must be strictly adhered to, despite the Spirit's assurance she would improve.

"There must be something, Mother. Chloe's sage cheese? Clotted cream?"

"Betsy, there is nothing I desire. Save, perhaps, a sweet summer cherry." She looked down at the quilt, dismayed she could think of nothing I could possibly bring to her.

Ah, Luce, a cherry is a pure delight.

The Spirit spoke from the ceiling and I looked up surprised to see a rain of cherries falling as stones had fallen down our stairs. They appeared from nowhere, a darker, more purple-red than any off our trees in the orchard.

Taste them!

Mother and I exchanged a glance, was it safe? Were they poison, and a trick? The skin of the cherries gleamed like Dean's arms at work in the fields of summer.

Dear Luce, they will heal and help you. I cannot bear to see you ill! Eat them!

Mother obediently plucked a cherry from the pile and dangled it briefly over her lips before biting into the sweet meat of it.

" 'Tis like a beam of sunlight in my wintry soul." She licked her lips with her dry tongue. "Thank you."

What else would you like, dear Luce? Speak its name and I shall fetch it for you.

The Spirit pressed her for more information as to her cravings.

"The fruits of summer are my favorites," Mother ventured, hesitant as a child, receiving undeserved gifts.

'Tis summer now in many tropical environs.

Again, from the ceiling fell a rain of fruit: sweet plums, peaches, large purple grapes, green figs and hazelnuts, in such abundance I was forced to gather them off the floor into my skirt.

"How lovely!" Mother graciously accepted the offerings. "But I am much too weak for cracking nuts."

Hold out your hands.

I stopped collecting when I heard the sound of nuts splitting apart. Mother stretched out her palm and the meat of the hazelnuts dropped straight into it, while the shells dropped over the floor, clattering at my feet.

Fetch a basket, Betsy.

The Spirit ordered me around like a slave and I nearly shouted, I do not belong to you! Only the look of gratitude on Mother's face and the ripe peaches at her fingertips silenced my urge to anger. I told myself I must thank the Being for the luscious gifts it brought to my dear mother, for rather figs and hazelnuts rain down on us than we become orphans.

the gifts of the spirit

Mother's convalescence was long, but by no means dismal, as the gifts of the Spirit overflowed in every wooden bowl and woven vine basket in our home. The fuzz of fresh peaches stood up like the new whiskers on Drewry's chin, screaming they had just been plucked off the tree, and the strawberries brought by the Being were red as fresh blood, the leaves still sticky with small prickers. Mother was confined to home, and Dr. Hopson came once a week to check her progress.

"Your recovery is remarkable," he proclaimed, after listening to her chest with his instrument.

"The Lord protects and heals us," she answered, smiling. She did not look me in the eye when Dr. Hopson was present, for we both knew her recovery was entirely the good work of the Spirit. It did not speak or perform any miracles of apportation while the doctor was in our home, but he saw the gifts it brought strewn everywhere. Only once did he mention them.

"I know not your secret in obtaining such delicious fruits of summer." He adjusted his spectacles to focus on the gray winter fog outside the window in Mother's bedroom, and I thought he would expound a theory of his own, but he merely sighed. "Yet, John Bell's cold storehouse is legendary in these parts, and however you have managed it these fruits are certainly a heavenly cure." He left with purple plums and grapes carefully packed in his saddlebag, but I wondered if he dared to eat them at his home.

By the end of February, Mother was able to walk about in her bedclothes, unaided, and she could sit at the table for supper. She could not yet dress and sustain a day of her usual activities, but she asked Drewry to let it be known she was ready to entertain callers.

"I desire some news of our community. How is Reverend Johnston? And the Thorns? And what of Calvin Justice, where has he been hiding?"

They are afraid, dear Luce. They grasp not the other worlds.

"Never mind about all that." Mother was pragmatic in her approach. "I should just like to hear of this world, going on about us." The Spirit laughed, charming as a tin music box.

You are such a sensitive soul, Luce, I must tell you, you are right in all your actions. This other world you will forever wander, and your moments of now are most precious.

I thought about that statement while I poured boiling well water into cups of milkweed sweetened with just a little sugar, the way Mother liked it. I stirred and stirred to make the herb dissolve, but try as I might, I could no longer conceive of another world of forever. I missed Father and my faith seemed to be fading, along with my happy memories of Josh, into the darkness of Father's murder and so many long days of illness as my lot. All happened against my prayers, where was God in my long suffering?

Mrs. Johnston and Mrs. Thorn responded immediately to Drewry's invitation, arriving the following morning. Old Kate saw them on the road to our place and she trailed along without an invitation, but Mother was pleased to entertain them all at her bedside.

"Lucy, we were much disturbed to hear of your illness, so sudden after your tragedy. We have prayed daily for your swift recovery." Mrs. Thorn clasped her hands tightly to her knee, as soon as she settled into her chair, appearing to be most kind and concerned. I wished she had brought Thenny.

"At church, the Reverend has you constantly in his prayers," Mrs. Johnston said, but she was distracted by the large basket of fruit on the bedside table.

"You must sample it," Mother offered with a smile, following her gaze.

"Forgive me for staring, but where have you found such treats? Mr. Thorn will carry no fruit approximate to this for many months." Mrs. Thorn leaned forward for a better view. "Has Dr. Hopson brought it here, from that newly opened store in Springfield? We did hear they carry much that is exotic from downriver, but I had no idea!"

I brought them, ladies, and I will bring some more!

The Spirit announced its presence with a hail of black cherries that shocked Mrs. Johnston and Mrs. Thorn immensely. They twisted their necks wildly to see from whence the fruit did fall, but Old Kate thought quickly and held her skirt out to catch the fruit.

"My word, 'tis like the loaves and fishes here!" She laughed as her apron filled.

"The miraculous is ever possible." Mother looked radiant and in the best of health, as if the Spirit's demonstration of kindness caused her to rejoice.

"But, Lucy, if the demon brings them hither, is it not the fruit of the Devil?" Mrs. Johnston spoke softly, very much concerned.

"Do her pink cheeks look like Devil's work to you? Clearly what haunts this house is more complex." Kate popped a cherry in her mouth and Mrs. Thorn gasped.

"Is it true what they say of you, Kate Batts? Is the origin of this unusual visitation inside *your* iron pot?" Mrs. Thorn stepped outside the bounds of permissible speech with this query and I wished there could be an end to the accusations.

"Fear not, the fruit is good and healthful. I have subsisted on it for several weeks." Mother calmed her guests, seeking to prohibit further discussion of Old Kate's possible hand in our mischief, and the Spirit interrupted with a silly song.

> The world seemed topsy-turvy, and people of renown
> Were doing the most outrageous things,
> When the world turned upside down!

"What is its meaning?" Mrs. Thorn leaned forward and whispered her query to Mother, leaving Old Kate out of it.

"I know not the Being's meaning. I know only this fruit is the sweetest and most succulent ever tasted and I believe it has greatly contributed to healing my pleurisy."

"'Tis the least it could do, having murdered your husband," Kate said bluntly. A shocked silence followed her remark and the room grew tense and so quiet, I heard the last of the cherries rolling over the floorboards into the sloping corner. "Lucy, I mean not to offend," Old Kate began to apologize, but seeing the smug set of Mrs. Thorn's chin, she simply shifted the blame, "unlike some others present . . ."

Mother looked down at her hands, resting, filled with fruit

on her quilt, and the pain she must have felt was not evident on her face.

"Not so, Kate, cherries are my most favored summer delight and these do look delicious." I could tell Mrs. Johnston felt sorry for my mother, educated as she was in our long suffering, and she wished to save the discussion from Kate's vulgarity. Though Mrs. Thorn glanced uneasily her way, she took the bold step of tasting the fruit. "If you don't mind," she said as she plucked a cherry from Kate's lap.

"If ye then, being evil, know how to give good gifts unto your children." Mrs. Batts stood, apparently addressing the Spirit, quoting from the Scripture, requesting further gifts. She held her apron at both corners, hoping more fruit would fall.

A wicked doer giveth heed to false lips; and a liar giveth ear to a naughty tongue!

"You would be the one to know of that! Offend me not!" Kate gathered her apron in one hand and rested the other on her massive hip as she spoke to the empty ceiling. "The Lord knows my faith is true. A gift is as a precious stone in the eyes of him that has it. 'Tis written in the Proverbs." She turned to Mrs. Johnston, who was slowly chewing to the pit of her cherry, casting a serious, doubting glance at Kate.

"Verily, Kate quotes the Scripture accurately," Mother interrupted, sighing. "Please take the fruit home with you, we have more than enough." The ladies hastily rose, realizing Mother had suddenly tired of visiting.

"Be well, Lucy dear, we shall call again." Mrs. Johnston took Mother's hand in her own, patting it affectionately.

Chloe had prepared muslin bags full of fruits and nuts for the ladies and I helped her distribute them at the door. All the way down our path we heard them discussing excitedly the health benefits of fruit from the Spirit. I laughed and realized suddenly I had experienced a moment unafraid and without anxiety. It was pleasant to suck on cherries in the winter and to laugh, knowing Mother was well and protected by the Spirit. I wondered if it could be possible that we were finally to reap some benefits where pain had previously been sown.

Sunday morning, Mother requested I take a basket of fruit for the congregation to enjoy at church, and I set out in the buggy, driven by Zeke, along with Drewry, Richard and Joel. The snow had mostly melted but the ground was still hard and dead and the branches were completely bare. The thicket and the hedgerow were a mass of gray brambles, reminding me of the tangled basket of old wool Mother had asked me to wind. I was grateful to have left it behind. Though it was still very cold, a pale sunlight glinted in the sky, a gentle reminder spring was coming. The clopping of horses' hooves on the roads through the woods multiplied as we grew closer to the church and met our neighbors. Thenny's father's carriage crossed the bridge into the yard just before ours. Excited, I adjusted the basket of fruit in my lap. Chloe had wrapped it well in a summer muslin cloth so the cherries and grapes would not spill from the edges. The churchyard bustled with talk as we rode in and I heard neighbors greeting neighbors, checking their Sunday invitations to meals following the service. It felt like a long time since folk had gathered at our house. Zeke stopped the carriage and the boys climbed out ahead of me. I had to make certain the basket was secure on the floor before I climbed down myself. Straightening my coat I looked for Thenny in the yard, but did not see her.

"Come, sister," Drewry called to me from the church steps as the Reverend's treasured brass bell began to ring. I hurried to join my brother and we entered into the church in silence, walking quietly to our places in the pews. Reverend Johnston stood in front at his wooden pulpit, nodding greetings and waiting until the church had filled and the clanging bell had died away to begin his sermon. I was wearing a new red velvet bonnet Mother had stitched for me during her convalescence and the satin ribbons tied under my chin tickled my neck when I breathed. I knew it was wrong and sinful of me, but my greatest excitement in coming to church was the possibility Josh Gardner would be present, and I had seen him, sitting behind and to my left. I felt his gaze on the back of my head and I hoped he did plan to speak with me.

"Today we are in the house of the Lord together," the Reverend began. "May we be blessed with the Spirit of the Lord!"

"Amen."

"Let us rise and sing his praises. A charge to keep I have . . ."

"A charge to keep I have, a God to glorify."

The congregation sang together mightily and as I opened my throat and let the song pour forth I felt a surge of warmth and happiness within, for with Josh's eye on my profile I felt my faith in God's good nature returning inside me. I was exalted by the many true voices joining my own. It crossed my mind to stand and proclaim "the Spirit of the Lord is in me," as Old Kate liked to do, but I thought better of it. I knew there were still those amongst the congregation who felt I was to blame for all our troubles, and I wanted no aspersions cast and no excess attention. It ought to be enough in the house of the Lord for me to feel exalted and for Him to feel me feeling it, and I hoped He would.

I recalled my promise to Mother and as soon as the sermon ended, I made my way straight to the buggy, wondering if it would be too brazen to fetch my basket up to the Reverend to hand out at the door of the church. I pictured myself standing beside him, distributing the delicious fruit, but what would be the response? I was nervous and uncertain how to go about my task when Thenny tapped me on the shoulder and I turned to see her two gloved hands outstretched in the shape of a cup.

"Might I have some cherries from the Spirit, Miss Betsy?" she joked and giggled, pleased to see me. "My mother has told me everything!"

"Yes, you must!" I surprised her, undoing the muslin cloth so quickly cherries fell from the edges onto the floor of the buggy.

"My, Betsy, you have fetched them *here?*"

"Mother believes we should share our good fortune with our community."

Thenny helped me gather them up and followed my example in popping every other one into her mouth. We had not spoken since Father's funeral, but the resentment I had felt toward her gossiping about me on that day had completely dissipated, and I was very glad to see her and share her company. I wondered what she knew of Josh. Under my bonnet ribbons I cast my eyes about to see where he was and I saw him striding across the lawn, away from his father's buggy, toward us.

"Miss Betsy, what a pleasure to see you, beautiful as ever and long missed." Josh took my hand in his and I blushed. Thenny was impressed with his forward nature and stood with her mouth hanging open for a moment before quickly thinking to tease Josh.

"Wait till you see what she has in her basket!"

"Some sweet summer fruits from the tropics." I pulled my hand from Josh's and reached for a bunch of grapes from the basket to give to Thenny. She dangled it in jest coyly before Josh's mouth, daring him to take one in his lips. He took a step back, raising his eyebrows in mock fear.

"I hear say such fruits will rot your insides and turn your brains to worms, is it not true?"

We dissolved into laughter at his expression and yet our giggles did not last long, for Mrs. Thorn hurried over to us and her stern expression reminded me briefly of Father.

"How fares your mother, Betsy?" Mrs. Thorn brought silence to our party.

"Very much better, thank you. She asked I might give you more fruit to carry home, as we have such a surplus."

"Most certainly," Mrs. Thorn replied with a smile, but I saw her look nervously sideways under her bonnet at Mr. Thorn, to see if he was watching her stash away bunches of grapes and plums in her coat. He would have been hard-pressed not to notice something was happening at our buggy, for as if there was one mind within the congregation, more people now approached.

"How fares Mrs. Bell?" cried Kate, huffing from the back of the crowd. She probably wished to be certain I had noticed her and would save some fruit for her to take home to Ignatius, but her calling out had the effect of turning the crowd's attention toward her, thus enlarging the circle.

"She fares well, and requests those who wish to, come away today with a sampling of the sweet summer fruit provided by the Spirit at our home." Though I was nervous, I used the opportunity of an audience to broadcast my purpose.

"Taste it not!" cried a voice from the back and I recognized Dr. Hopson's wife, Abigail, out on the edge.

"I have tasted it and suffered no ill effects." The Reverend strode confidently down the hill from the church doorway, defending me. "The Lord works in ways mysterious to us. We know not how these fruits have come here, but clearly they are healthful and good in the dark winter, and the mark of the Devil is not on them." He strode right up to me, and picking a peach from the basket, he took a bite.

"Reverend!" Mrs. Hopson was clearly upset. "I have seen everything! When a man of the cloth preaches he has eaten the fruit of a demon and claims to suffer no ill effects! I will not come again to this church, for Satan must now be in your soul." It was a heavy charge to be levied at the Reverend, especially before so many, but he bore it well. He raised his voice for all to hear and quoted the Gospel of John.

"Beloved, believe not every Spirit, but try the Spirits whether they are of God: No man hath seen God at any time. If we love one another, God dwelleth in us, and his love is perfected in us. We have known and believed the love that God has for us. God is love; and he that dwelleth in love dwelleth in God and God in Him."

A spontaneous chorus of Amen! rose from the crowd, and the Reverend carried on.

"I say these offerings come in the purest Spirit of the Lord our God, a miracle provided to heal the soul of a woman so good and kind in our community that God has visited on her severe afflictions to show us what He means by the right true path, and by purpose and love. God has made Mrs. Lucy Bell a widow and an example for all of us, Mrs. Hopson, and I pray, rethink your decision to taste not the sweet summer fruit offered here."

"That's right, Reverend," someone called, and another shouted, "'Tis so! I heard those who taste the fruit have been improved." There was a nodding of heads and murmur of agreement about the yard and people pushed forward to get nearer to me, to take a sample of the Spirit's gifts.

Mrs. Hopson turned her back to the crowd and began walking to her carriage where the doctor was waiting for her.

"It was not God that made Lucy Bell a widow, Reverend," she called loudly back, over her shoulder, and I knew we would not be seeing her or the doctor at our church again. The Methodist service of Calvin Justice was closer to their home anyway. I would not miss them. Hands reached out for fruit and I loaded them up. Thenny helped me do it, but we were somber, especially compared to our earlier mood. Vernon Batts came up behind me and hissed in my ear.

"Does the Devil's fruit taste sweet to you, Miss Betsy?" I threw a plum at him, but he caught it fast and laughed, turning away. I hated his mean accusations, but hearing my mother described as horribly afflicted and a widow did more to dampen my good mood than Vernon's evil talk. I was relieved when the basket was emptied and with well wishes for my mother, the crowd thinned and departed.

"Thenny, come now!" Mrs. Thorn called my friend away and there remained only Josh Gardner and my brothers.

"Miss Betsy, might I trouble you for a ride to the crossing?" He touched my arm as I folded the muslin inside the empty basket and I felt my face grow hot.

"The crossing?" I repeated stupidly, not knowing how to answer.

"My father must ride to John Polk's house and I would prefer to make my own way home, which I can easily do through the woods from there."

"Of course, we will gladly take you." I felt somewhat flustered, as I did not wish to draw any further attention from the community with my actions and I was not certain what the

Spirit might say about me riding in the buggy with Josh at my side. At the same time I was loath to discourage him in any way, as I had truly missed him. I climbed up and he climbed up and sat beside me and we waited silently while Drewry and the boys climbed in. We were so close I could feel his sweet breath moving the air around my face. Drewry caught my eye under my bonnet edge and raised his brows in question, and Josh turned to speak to him.

"It won't trouble you to provide a lift for me to the crossing will it, Drewry?"

"No, 'tis no matter at all." He leaned out the door instructing Zeke and we set out, in silence. I was conscious of Josh's thigh and shoulder as we bumped down the rutted hill toward the bridge, and I tried to lean as much toward the side as possible, lest Josh think wrong of me rubbing up against him.

"A lovely sermon, wasn't it?" Josh attempted polite conversation, but I kept my eyes on my skirt and my gloves in my lap and not on the red velvet ribbon at the edge of my face, for I could feel Josh's eyes on my cheeks, and without my control, I felt them growing ever warmer, until I was certain they gleamed as red as the ribbon itself. Richard and Joel burst into a fit of unexplained giggles and I leaned forward and swatted at them, as you do at flies, with the muslin cloth from the basket.

"The Reverend is born to his calling," Drewry answered Josh as I did not, for I was unable to speak, silenced by silly fears. What did Josh think of me? Did he think I had told my little brothers of the kisses we'd shared? Did he think my love was openly declared for him inside my family? I felt wholly unlike myself.

"Soon it will be spring, for the smell of it is promised now in the chilly morn." Drewry did me a kind favor, chatting with Josh.

"I believe the best fishing will be on your land, under the cavern, where the mighty tree has fallen and made such a pleasant dam." Josh bumped his leg accidentally on purpose into mine and I saw Drewry frown. I could tell he was wondering how Josh was aware of the spot, but he did not ask.

"There, and in Kate Batts's pond, where the fish are always biting." They speculated further on where the best fishing spots were likely to be come spring, and I remained quiet and withdrawn. I wondered, could it be possible for Josh to be filled with the same longing I experienced every time I saw his gentle face? I did not believe right then that it was so.

Betsy Bell, do not have Josh Gardner.

The Spirit suddenly hissed in my mind, but it did not speak out loud. I felt the pinpricks of its touch up and down my hands and arms as we traversed the rutted road. I said nothing and I bore them without flinching, pleased they did take away the heat from my cheeks. We soon reached the crossing and Zeke reined the horses to a stop. Josh climbed from the buggy with a lighthearted jump, turning quickly, holding up his hand.

"Thank you kindly, Drewry, Miss Betsy, boys." He tipped his hat at Joel and Richard, making fun, and for the first time I looked into his eyes as he waved farewell to me. What I saw most clearly announced the love he felt. "Miss Betsy, tell your dear mother I will pray for her swift and full recovery. My mother has also been ill and incapacitated so I have been most needed at my home. This is my first outing in several weeks, and I am well pleased it resulted in our meeting." That was clearly as much as he could say in front of my brothers and Zeke about how he had managed to obey my wishes and not call on me. My heartbeat quickened and I knew he was the one soul who could best understand the heavy weight of my continued isolation, but I was too frightened to ask him to call when he could.

"Please wish your mother a swift recovery from our family as well!" I had to lean out the window and shout, for Zeke had whipped the horses and we were rolling off.

"Betsy and Joshua, swinging on a swing!" Richard and Joel started in with the schoolyard teasing song and I could tell they were begging for me to swat at them again, and I did so, with much more enthusiasm than when Josh was in the buggy.

That afternoon, the boys told Mother all about Josh hitching a ride and how nervous I became. She laughed until she coughed, then smiled and patted my hand.

"Perhaps our Betsy will soon have a beau . . ."

"Stop, Mother! Josh Gardner is kind indeed, but he begged a ride purely for convenience." I was not ready to announce my love for him and I changed the subject. "Nearly all the members of our congregation did sample the fruit, and they were happy as Old Kate to get it." I hoped Mother would not admonish me for insulting Mrs. Batts. "And the Reverend spoke of you in the yard as a soul singled out by God." I left out the part about why he had done that, and also everything about Mrs. Hopson, because Mother was still very fragile and I thought it best not to worry her with any little details that might make her sad. She coughed again and frowned, and I wondered if she guessed at what had prompted the Reverend's praises.

"Betsy, I would have you take a look into John Jr.'s chest. Last year before our troubles started up, I had it in my mind to stitch us both new dresses for the Easter celebrations. At the bottom, you will find two bolts of printed cotton, ten yards each. Fetch them hither."

I did as she asked and when I returned, I laid the bolts slightly unrolled on the parlor rug at Mother's request.

"Choose which you prefer." One was a very pretty white with tiny blue roses printed on it, and the other was a solid pale blue with a darker stripe. I had nothing made of printed cloth and I was fascinated by the pattern.

"Might I have the dainty flowered one?" I asked, choosing the fabric I knew would brighten my mood every time I saw it.

"You may," Mother nodded and reached for my hand. "I have something else for you." She opened the robe she wore over her flannel petticoat and pulled a piece of paper from inside the folds of her nightdress. She handed it to me and the texture of it was unlike any paper I had seen before in ream or book. A woman in the most beautiful modern dress was printed on it.

"The Spirit brought it," Mother explained. "When I woke from the nap I took while you were at church it was in my fingers and the Being says it is from the French Almanac of this very year. Shall we make you one just exactly like it?"

"Might we try?" I marveled at the sophisticated style. Mother gave her answer with a willing nod and I thought she was most likely very bored with lying about every day, and glad to have the activity of dressmaking. It seemed a good measure of her restored health that she wished to spend hours cutting and pinning. Chloe helped me move the chairs off the rug and Mother and I laid out the fabric with the paper picture in the center. We studied it carefully before cutting the cloth.

"The skirt will be the widest of any you have ever owned." She adjusted her knees on the pillow Chloe had brought from her bed.

"And there are so many pleats in the waistband to sew." I stared at the picture, attempting to see how it should be done.

"Yes, it will require many tiny stitches to make it up right." Mother finished cutting the front panel of the skirt. "I have found the challenge for your skills, Miss Betsy, or rather, the Spirit has." She sat back and coughed again.

"Shall I help you to your bed now, Mother?" I was worried she was attempting too much.

"No, I should like to cut it all today. When this dress is finished, your skirt will sway like a bell when you cross the room." She smiled at the thought.

"Mother, it means so much to me to see you so recovered." I felt exceptionally lighthearted. She had me stand with my arms above my head and just my petticoat on while she gathered yards and yards of the crisp cotton around my waist, to pin it up. We worked all day and burned the lamps awhile after supper to finish the pinning.

In the morning after breakfast, I began to sew. I had decided I would follow Mother's example and devote every day to the completion of my dress. I was sitting at the chair by the front parlor window stitching away, when the Spirit spoke.

The deed is done and not one of you did try to stop it.

The next moment brought a knock at our door.

"What was that about?" Mother was crocheting lace for my sleeves in the chair across from me. "I am expecting no callers." She stood, pulling her robe close around her, opening the door. There stood Calvin Justice with his hat in his hands. He refused Mother's invitation to step inside.

"I bear news of a dreadful tragedy, Lucy. Young Amanda Ellison has drowned in Old Kate's pond."

"Oh!" Mother's hand flew to her mouth and she let out a cry as if she'd been struck. "How did it happen?"

"The story of her last hours was related by her friend Gertrude, and all was revealed to have happened exactly as the Being foretold it, nearly one year previous. Do you recall the night? We talked of witch creatures."

"Of course I do recall it." Mother shook her head.

"The Reverend wished to warn the parents . . ."

"But Jack did not want to frighten the girls . . ." Mother and Calvin Justice stood silent a moment and their expressions told how they felt most painfully responsible. "God must have wanted her sweet voice in his choir of angels." Mother sighed, choosing to attribute the tragedy to God's will.

"The funeral service is tomorrow at three. I must go and inform the Thorns." Calvin Justice looked away down our path and I could tell his penance for himself was to carry the news through the district.

"Thank you so much for coming. We shall attend the service." Mother gently closed the door and I stood up, dropping my sewing to the floor.

"I should have told her, Mother. I thought of it when I saw her at the schoolhouse." I recalled with regret how my eyes had purposely avoided Amanda's. I had been too embarrassed and uncertain to tell her my thoughts, yet now she was dead and the prediction had never been foremost in my mind. "How awful, I should have done something!"

"Betsy, this did not occur because of anything you did or did not do. God must people his Heaven with some young souls." She patted my back and tried to comfort me but I felt she too was upset. We stood and cried awhile together but soon crying caused Mother to cough and I insisted she lie down. I returned to busying my needle for the rest of the day and most of the next. I sewed until my thimble had rubbed a blister and it was time to attend Amanda's funeral. It was Mother's first outing since her pleurisy, and though I felt she was still too weak, she insisted on going.

"Losing a child is the worst evil God suffers on the faithful," she whispered into my ear while we stood in the graveyard behind the church. I knew some in the congregation had heard about the Being's forewarning but out of kindness to the Ellisons' grief and to our family, no one spoke cruelly about us, though I wondered what they were thinking. Did they know we had decided not to tell the Spirit's prediction because we did not wish to scare the girls? Did they know we had not believed this tragedy would actually come to pass? Once again, because of our troubles, misery was unleashed in the world. Perhaps they thought Mr. Ellison ought to strike us with a red-hot poker from his forge, as the Spirit had everything to do with the witch creature heron and, thus, his daughter's drowning. I bowed my head in prayer, exceedingly contrite, curious to know if I had experienced my knowledge differently, could poor Amanda still be living? At the time there had been so many odd occurrences, the thought of a witch creature drowning her and what I could do to prevent it had been impossible to ponder.

When the Reverend pronounced Amanda laid to eternal rest, Mr. Ellison broke down in tears beside the grave.

"Thou art a selfish God!" he cried, beating the ground with his fists.

"Take Richard and Joel back to the buggy, Betsy," Mother hissed into my ear, so I did not witness how the faithful managed to comfort him. I wanted to know what words they spoke to help him with his loss, for I wished to say them to myself.

the unknown thrill

By March the ground had thawed and it was time to turn the earth over and ready the fields for spring planting. The subject on everyone's mind was how to grow a successful tobacco crop without Father. Dean and Mother knew all about the soil, the seedlings, and how best to grow the plants, and when John Jr. came home, as we hoped he would soon, he had knowledge of the harvest and the markets. Certain aspects of my life I had discovered to be easier since Father's passing. It made me uncomfortable and I would not have confessed the truth to anyone, not even Josh, but I did not miss him lying down with me. I had seen Little Bright one day and called out hello to her, pleased Father could no longer object. Yet I was worried the farm could not be profitable without him and I missed his reassuring presence at our table.

It felt odd, approaching our first season without Father's dominant skills. The dawn arrived ever earlier and so increased my anxiety, but Drewry simply rose with it. He left the house each morning with his gun and his woolen coat, hoping he might shoot a wild boar or turkey on his way to meet

Dean in the fields. He saw the ox team hitched to the iron plow and driven nearly all day for a week of the spring weather, so soon every field had been plowed up and over, leaving mountains of red earth behind for the slaves to shape into rows and plant with seedlings.

"Let's play plow blade towns again." Joel turned to Richard at the breakfast table, certain he had a willing partner for his game. Each day since the plowing had begun, the boys had come home with dreadful cakes of mud on their woolen stockings. Mother had Chloe wash them out at night and hang them by the fire all evening so they could dry for the next day, and our house strongly smelled of rich red earth.

"When will John Jr. return?" I asked Mother, for I felt he knew the most about how Father conducted business.

"Yes, John Jr. . . ." Mother allowed herself to dreamily not answer my question or finish her sentence as she sipped her tea. I wondered if this was the effect of the milkweed and butterfly root. She seemed truly calmer and more relaxed than ever before in a way that concerned me greatly. How could she be so secure? I thought we might soon be on the brink of financial distress without Father. I could easily imagine the evils of poverty, all I had to do was picture Old Kate's farm, but Mother appeared confident on all aspects of Father's business.

"Don't you worry, Betsy." She shook her head and reached to pat my hand, and despite the fact I knew she was growing stronger every day, I noticed the blue veins rose high on the backs of her fingers, and I worried further. "There will be no trouble with the crops," she reassured me. "Dean has the knowledge and the know-how."

"And the shoes!" Drewry smiled across the table, for he

was well aware of the good feeling she had created amongst the hands, having provided them with boots.

"Perhaps today I will put on a smock and venture out for a look-see at the state of my garden."

"Do not go out too soon, Mother, for a chill remains in the air," I cautioned her. Since Amanda Ellison's funeral we had successfully kept Mother at home, but as the winter days gave over to spring, she grew most anxious to work outdoors.

"Elizabeth, I am now blessed and warmed by the fruits of summer, but if I wish to grow my own, I must soon direct the pruning, for the time to do it has nearly passed me by."

"Have Chloe stay with you and carry the clippers," I advised, for I knew she was still weak.

"Miss Betsy," Mother laughed, "thank you for your kind concern, but I believe I am wise to my own condition." Her laughter caused her to cough a little and she grew serious with me. "You have suffered enough, dear girl; the loss of your father topped with the anxiety of nursing your mother, and the absence of your oldest brothers. I know you are frightened by the knowledge of all that has come before now." She paused and I could tell she meant the Spirit and its unpredictable horrors. "But you must strive to keep your thoughts on tomorrow, for therein lies your opportunity to better the days, each as they pass."

"I do try, Mother." I felt as worried as before.

"Of course you do, Betsy." We sat in silence for a moment and then Mother smiled again, observing me. "The Easter holiday fast approaches, and 'tis your birthday before that, in just three weeks' time. Would you like to have a luncheon party?"

"I could invite Thenny and Becky Porter . . ."

"Chloe and I could bake a molasses and caramel cake for you." Mother was most girlish and I recalled her face during the summer at the dance when she'd coaxed Father to his feet. "What a good suggestion, I must say, even though it was my own. It is hard to believe you are near fourteen already."

"Near fourteen, but this past year seems to have contained more than a lifetime of experiences."

"Dear child, I know how you must think it is, but older and wiser as I am, I tell you true, God willing, you have much still to experience in your years ahead." Mother rose from the table and took her cup to the kitchen, and I retired to the parlor, for all I wished to do was sew the tiny stitches into the pleats of my dress. I spent the remainder of the day and a good many more sewing away, and I did make fair progress.

The night before my birthday, a storm blowing from the south sent great clouds rolling over our house and a downpour fell, lasting all the dark hours, so we slept to the rush of wind through the tree branches and the pattering of rain on the roof and windows. When I woke early, a bright sun teased my ceiling and, looking out my window, I saw steam rising in wisps off the ground, bringing to my mind the picture of angels ascending to Heaven in droves. I opened my window and smelled the rich red dirt and the bark of the trees loosening their sap for growing, and I recognized the delicious odor of the world returned to life.

I put on my oldest plain cloth dress, one I had nearly outgrown, choosing it because it did not matter how dirty it became. I grabbed my boots and ran downstairs and through the kitchen without stopping to check on Mother, to have breakfast, or say good morning to Chloe. I felt possessed with urgency of movement, compelled to be part of the beauty. I ran through the shrub of Mother's perennial herbs, successfully wintered over, through her fallow garden plot and out into the orchard, where the purple bark of the plum trees shone like the skin of the Spirit's cherries. Tiny pink blossoms and new green leaves steamed everywhere over my head, undaunted by pruning. I raced down the hill, behind the stable and past the dairy house and on, and by the time I reached the first planting field, I was completely out of breath.

My chest heaved and I was warm inside my coat. Hastily I shed my jacket and hung the winter garment on the post marking the boundary of the field. They had plowed it yesterday and puddles gleamed in the paths. I climbed up to sit on the fence and soak up the sun so I might steam to Heaven also, for there is nothing so tantalizing as a spring chill burned away by the Tennessee sun.

I wanted to remove my boots and go barefoot in the red mud, splashing in the new puddles as Richard and Joel would have done, had I bothered to fetch them along, so I balanced on the fence and untied my shoes without further thought. I felt the wood of the split log fence fairly icy under my bare toes, and I shivered. Hoisting my skirt up to my knees, I jumped.

The red mud was delightfully squishy, warm and cold at once, and so smooth it made me squirm. I stood in a clear puddle and saw the sparkling sun reflected as a million jewels of light behind my head. I wiggled my toes breaking the water apart into many fractured pieces, then I waited, still in the center, until the image formed again. At the bottom of the pool the mud oozed and I felt the small pulsations of worms crawling under my heels. I thought of Father in the field; *these worms make our soil the richest in the district.* A wind blew through the newly leafed trees and the steam off the ground rushed over me like a passing cloud.

Oh that I had some secret place where I might hide from sorrow;
Where I might see my Savior's face, and thus be saved from terror.
Oh had I wings like Noah's dove, I'd leave this world and Satan;
And fly away to realms above, where angels stand inviting.

The Being sang like a choir, from all sides of the field, with many harmonies, and when it had finished, all the birds in the trees nearby were inspired to try their own songs. I had a strong sense that something good and wonderful and important might happen, but I wasn't sure what it would be. At the very least I was a year older! I dug my toes deeper in the muck. A meadowlark in a tree nearby began to sing alone, heavily influenced by the Being. I jumped from my puddle to the next one in the row, then on, from puddle to puddle, until I had splashed to the end where I turned back, to splash down the next row. Even though it was my birthday, I thought Chloe might be annoyed about the mud accumulating on the edge of my petticoat but I couldn't stop until my skirt was wet and dripping and my feet tingled, almost numb. I decided I had best put my boots and coat back on and return for breakfast.

"What does possess you, Miss Betsy?" Mother was at the table in her nightdress when I arrived back home.

"It was so lovely, Mother! The mist appeared like angels on their way to Heaven."

"In good time and God willing we will all get there." Mother spread blackberry jam on Chloe's morning biscuits. "After I have dressed and you have had your breakfast we will wash your hair and body, for you are not wearing your beautiful dress with mud covering your feet."

We had just put the final stitches in the lace of my dress the day before. I hurried through my meal and helped bring water from the stream for Chloe to boil on the stove. Mother decided I should have my bath in the kitchen so Chloe stoked the woodstove high until the room was heated to summertime temperatures. Mother filled the tub and I dipped my hair in the water and remained bent over while Mother wove soap and lather through it with her capable hands. I loved the gentle touch of her hair washings when done for cleansing and not for killing lice. With my head upside down, I saw two yellow balls plop into the tub and the warm water splashed into my eyes.

Cut the lemons and pour the juice in her hair.

"Oh, thank you!" Mother appreciated the Spirit's gift, for though she used lemons in the summer to part the tangles and add the shine, in my birthday season they were a rarity.

"I will squeeze 'em down, Miz Lucy." Chloe finished straining the juice just as Mother finished pouring the rinse water over my head.

"Close your eyes," she warned me, and I felt the cold tickle and smelled the tart juice of the lemons running over my scalp. She rinsed it once more, then Mother had me dry my head, and sit in the chair. Her wooden comb slipped easily through my wet locks, the strands separating like threads in the loom.

"Open up the door, Chloe, for it looks to be a lovely day outside." With the door open I could see into Mother's garden where the sky was blue and bright with spring sunshine and all the trees of the orchard had opened their blossoms delighting in the onslaught of buzzing bees and pale new butterflies.

"It is near time for your friends to arrive. Go and dress, Miss Betsy, for Chloe and I must ready the table." I jumped with excitement from the chair, happy my special day was to be so beautiful.

Thenny and Becky arrived together, accompanied by their mothers, and I greeted them in the hall.

"Betsy, how it does become you!" When I heard Thenny compliment the job I had done on my dress, I knew she was sincerely impressed.

"Will you turn a circle, slowly?" Becky did not remove her coat before expressing her admiration. "In France there can be none finer!"

" 'Tis so, because our Betsy is here." Mother joined in the compliments.

"May I?" Becky ran her hand along the bodice seam admiring the tailored fit I had achieved. All my other dresses were the old style, the bodice done up in smocking or darted pleats, but this one had a smooth fit across my bosom, and the lace Mother had made was featured prominently at the edges.

"How ever did you make the pattern for it, Lucy?" Mrs. Thorn was an excellent seamstress and was interested in the new style. "So many tiny pleats."

"I shall show you the paper after our meal, Helen," said Mother, promising to give her the secret.

We moved into the dining room and my hem swayed like a bell over my petticoats, exactly as Mother had promised it would. I felt very proud to have made it myself. We sat at the dining table laid with a brocade cloth and Mother's special china. Chloe served cold sliced ham, wild turkey, hot corn biscuits, grits and beans, and the conversation divided into two, one amongst the mothers, of dress styles and fashions from the French Almanac, and one amongst us girls.

"Betsy, last week when lessons started up again Josh Gardner came to the schoolhouse each day his responsibilities allowed, his only hope that *you* would be present. He told me so. He is for certain sweet on you." Thenny went straight to the heart of every matter and Becky giggled, keeping her eyes riveted to my response. I felt my face grow hot.

"Thenny!" I admonished her presumptive nature but I could not keep from smiling.

"It's true, you love him." Becky squeezed my arm. "You are the perfect coupling of souls and temperament."

" 'Tis certain!" Thenny grinned as if she'd made the match herself. "Ask your mother if you might go walking with him on the Saturday before Easter."

" 'Tis the traditional day for the Lovers Promenade." Becky held her hand up to her mouth as she pronounced the word *Lovers* and giggled after.

"Pray, tell us what causes your amusement, girls?" Mother turned to us.

" 'Tis your daughter, Mrs. Bell. She wishes to ask if she might promenade with her beau, Josh Gardner, on the Saturday before Easter."

"Thenny Thorn!" Mrs. Thorn and I together called her name with indignation.

"I said no such thing!" I objected.

"That's all right, Betsy, I do give my permission." Mother smiled sweetly at me, and Thenny clapped her hands, excited, her purpose accomplished.

"I have a present for you." Thenny jumped up and left the table returning with a parcel wrapped in thin fine paper I recognized as off the oranges in her father's store. I was slightly annoyed with her for arranging my affairs, but I tried to be gracious, unwrapping the present carefully, discovering a length of blue satin ribbon.

" 'Tis the color of the flowers on my dress!" I was pleased with it.

"Mother and I thought you might use it for a bonnet." Thenny was unusually demure.

"How pretty, thank you." I kissed Thenny on the cheek for her kindness.

"We brought a little something too." Becky withdrew a beautiful paper fan from the pocket of her skirt.

"How lovely." I inhaled the finely carved sandalwood, opening it wide. "I adore it!" I stood and held it mysteriously below my eyes, strutting across the dining room to the hall and back, pretending I was a great lady with my swaying skirts and elegant fan.

"It suits you perfectly." Thenny and Becky laughed in unison as I paraded before them and the mothers smiled, indulging me.

I have something for you too.

I stopped my gay mockery and extended my hands to receive what I expected would be grapes or cherries from the Spirit, but instead into my open palms fell a beautiful silver comb to wear in my hair. Inlaid with mother-of-pearl, it was curved to exactly the right proportions.

"My goodness!" Mrs. Porter held her hand to her breast and grew pale as a muslin cloth.

"I told you." Mrs. Thorn had clearly discussed the gifts of the Spirit with Mrs. Porter before arriving, and she was more concerned with examining what I'd received than comforting her friend.

"Let me help you to try it." Mother deftly twisted my braid on top of my head and secured it in place with the comb. I turned to face my girlfriends and was pleased when Thenny and Becky both gasped at the effect.

"'Tis breathtaking. I shall fetch the looking glass, for you must see yourself." Mother hurried from the room.

"Wear it like that when you go with Josh," Thenny whispered in my ear.

"You look ever so sophisticated, doesn't she, Mother?" Becky nudged her pale mother, poking her shoulder until she nodded her agreement.

"Yes, yes, Miss Betsy, that you do."

"I wonder where the presents come from . . ." Mrs. Thorn spoke her query softly, and Mother returned, handing me her small mirror. I looked and saw the silver glinting in the light, and I was truly surprised, for I did look beautiful. The raising of my hair atop my head revealed my face to have a delicate jaw and fine neck, most often hidden. They told the truth, it was a becoming style. I thought instantly of Josh, and wondered what he would think. I wished to open up the door and have him standing there, to admire me in my finery.

"I am blessed indeed," I told my friends and we returned to the table to cut the cake and eat.

"I wish your father could be here with us this day." Mother squeezed my shoulder and I stared down at the lovely brown glaze of the caramel cake, thinking how it reminded me of the warm mud between my toes in the morning, and the swirls in the frosting suddenly looked like the worms in the earth Father was buried under. I thought of how good I'd felt with the warm sun on my back, knowing how lovely the day was going to be.

"For certain he is watching from his place in Heaven," I replied, unwilling to allow any melancholy thoughts to spoil my party.

When the girls had gone, I went up to my room. I took the comb from my hair and laid it on my chest beside the pretty fan and the length of satin ribbon. Looking out the window at the blossoming fruit trees in the orchard, I thought my final pleasure of the day would be to take a horseback ride along the creek. I hurried to change my fine dress for a plain cloth one and ran quickly back downstairs. Mother and Chloe were in the kitchen.

"I am going out, Mother, to inspect the lovely spring," I called.

"And I am going for a nap, Miss Betsy, as your celebration has tired me plenty."

I was happy she did not object. I took my wool coat from the wardrobe in the hall for I knew I would need it riding, as the wind would still be cold. I could not find my riding bonnet so I grabbed my velvet church one. The bonnet was too nice to ride in, but it was my birthday and I could not be bothered to look for another more practical one. My hair had come undone from its braid, slippery from the Spirit's lemons, and I did not wish to take the time to do it up again, so I just tucked it carelessly inside. I thought of the wintertime when I'd met Josh Gardner in the woods and I hoped he would be there now. I felt possessed by a nervous exuberance as if something truly exciting were soon to happen to me, and if I did not keep moving, the unknown thrill would not be realized. I allowed the front door to slam behind me, and I nearly tripped over my own feet running down the hill.

Riding away from the stables on Moses my exhilaration only increased. Pea green clover carpeted the path down to the stream and I expect Moses enjoyed the soft plush pile beneath his shoes. The smell of new grass, sassafras and spicy forsythia drifted on the breeze, while bunnies scattered away from us under the bushes. I kicked Moses hard with my heels and galloped down the path along the stream. The ties of my bonnet came undone and I caught the velvet ribbons just before losing it to the wind. I stuffed it in my coat, and my hair tumbled down my back. I loved the feeling of it flapping on my cheeks like yellow silk, tangling and smelling of fresh lemons. I thought of the wooden bowl Chloe had used to pour the lemon juice on my head, and I imagined all the love and happiness in the world had been strained into that golden liquid and poured over me. I felt blessed to be alive.

I turned the corner and rode under the gray elms, already in leaf. The sun filtered in, making fairy light, and there was something in the green and shifting patterns that brought to mind how magic things could happen. I looked to the clearing ahead and there was Josh, standing by the stream, allowing his horse a drink.

"Betsy!" He turned at my approach. "Our Lord is good to me. Once again, I wished for you, and here you are."

"Josh! I too have wished for you." As in the instance when I threw Father's paper in the fire and the poison down into the grate, I could not blame my wrong actions on the Spirit, for it was not in attendance. I dismounted Moses and threw the reins carelessly around the closest bush. I ran smiling and surefooted over the mossy rocks straight into Josh's open arms, laughing as he did. He held me as if it were the very thing he'd been waiting there to do.

"It was as if your voice spoke without words into my heart," I whispered into his coat, understanding my earlier excitement most clearly, for here was the thrill I had sensed.

"I have been waiting, Betsy." He stepped back and wrapped his fingers through my hair, drawing my face to his. He kissed my lips, and I opened my mouth to him. I did not think how sinful we were, for I felt certain we were doing exactly what we should be doing. "There are some who would say this is wrong-minded of us . . . ." Josh breathed into my ear, hesitating, but I encouraged him.

"How can that be, when we most truly love one another?" It seemed to me God inhabited our hands, helping us to find the right true places on each other that were meant to be touched, and the feeling was unlike anything I had ever experienced before. Josh did not speak again but with his eyes and hands and lips and tongue, and all his meanings were returned from in my soul, filled to overflowing with desire and a gratitude toward him so deep it could have filled the sky above us.

We lay together, our clothes and minds undone on the damp floor of the clearing, watching the sun finish the day. I thought of what Martha had told me of the joys of womanhood and I was surprised how she had not conveyed the half of it. The places where our skin was bare grew cold, but still we did not move. I curled inside his arms breathing deep the mingled smells of new grass and damp wool and the delicious aroma of his skin. I wished the light would never quit, and the day never be gone.

"I would not have done this, Betsy, only I do intend to marry you. I would never wish to do anything you did not want."

"But I did want it, Josh, the same as you."

"You are Heaven on earth, Betsy. I would have you for my wife." Josh tilted my chin upward with his hand and kissed me. I felt a great swelling inside and realized that until he mentioned marriage I had completely forgotten about the Spirit and its evil warnings. For those unconscious moments I had been happy. "Say you will be mine, Betsy," Josh pressed me. "I will love you forever."

"I am yours already, Josh, you can't have forgotten so soon." I tickled the bare skin of his belly with my fingertips, teasing him. What joy it was to touch him there, admiring his muscles, taut and lean. It was terribly exciting. I wanted nothing more than to lie with him on the damp forest floor for the rest of my life.

"Betsy, I have not forgotten." Josh took my hands in his, rolled up and straddled me. "I will never forget, but I must always have you." He bent and kissed me deeply and I wrapped my arms around his neck.

"There will be no other match for me, come what may." I felt I might begin to cry and I did not know if it was pleasure or pain, bringing tears into my eyes.

"What do you mean, 'come what may'? Why do you worry so? The Spirit that murdered your father is gone, its evil is accomplished, and 'tis certain we were meant to have each other. My father says there is land more fertile than our own across the mountains in Kentucky. We can go and homestead there."

"But the Spirit is not gone, Josh." I turned my cheek to the ground, aware how soft the moss was, how full of water, like my eyes. I thought to tell Josh it was my birthday but I was so saddened by holding the thought of the Spirit and Josh and my future at once, that I did not tell him. I also did not say I felt he had given me a gift of the greatest significance. He got off me and lay next to me again. Taking up my hand, he kissed it, silent. It pained me to think he did not really know the depth of my fear and experience. I sat halfway up, leaning on my elbow. "What if I say we must go *now* to Kentucky, or never go at all?"

"If you say now or never, I say yea, let us depart! I do love you truly, Betsy. But I believe our families would not understand such haste and unto your dear mother I would cause no greater sorrow than what she has already suffered." I was chastened by the thought of my mother and impressed with Josh's maturity, but I sighed, knowing it might very well be now or never, for my future beyond that moment loomed uncertain, and I was afraid once we parted I might never see him more.

"Betsy, kiss me, and picture in your mind the very many days of our future together." Josh spoke as if my inner thoughts were written on my face. "I love you and have loved you since the day I visited your home and you did drop the wool. You saw it roll a tie between us! I have suffered mostly silent through your torment, but I am certain the love I feel for you is stronger than the strongest evil, and here, united in this love, we are stronger together than any unworldly creature. God has blessed us, and given us such strength in love, nothing can harm us. You must have faith, Betsy, and trust me." Josh finished his confident speech pressing his lips into mine, and I parted my own, allowing his tongue in my mouth. I wanted to believe his words, and I encouraged myself to be swept up in the passion, but the sun had disappeared behind the trees and the breeze chilled my exposed skin, so I was forced to pull away.

"I must go, I must," I told him.

"Do you love me, Betsy?" He held on to my forearm as I attempted to rise.

"I do, more than you know, dear Josh. But it is complicated. I can't forget all that has happened . . ." Josh drew me back into his arms and with my ear pressed against his bare chest I heard his heart beat strong.

"It will be all right." Josh stroked my hair and I felt safe and content, but remembered suddenly the winter night Father had carried me up to my bed, and lay with me. He too had promised all would come out right and it most certainly had not. I shivered, and though Josh tried to squeeze me closer, I managed to pull away and hastily depart.

Riding home, I began to worry, for I knew Mother would be wondering what had happened to me. The light was truly at its end under the blooming elms. I had to kick Moses and trust he knew the way. When I reached the stable, Zeke was not about, but a lantern had been lit. I did not bother to lead Moses to his stall, I was in such a hurry, and he neighed at me on my way out, as if to say I was ungrateful and mean.

"Sorry," I called back to him, hoping Zeke would soon return. I hastened up the hill toward the house. My undone hair was full of twigs, clover and bits of moss, and though at first I tried to comb it with my fingers, I quickly gave up, and stuffed it in large handfuls up inside my bonnet. I was absorbed completely in what I might say by way of explanation to Mother, and I did not see the commotion in the yard until I was on top of it.

There at the hitching post stood two horses I did not recognize and beside them Zeke and Isiah, and up the path on the porch steps there stood John Jr. I ran past the well and under the pear trees.

"I rode my horse near to the ground to be here today," John Jr. called down to me and in the light of the lamp Mother held I saw his face told the story of his journey. His cheeks were so gaunt, they looked hollow above his dark brown beard, and he bore a new resemblance to Father. I stopped myself from running into his arms, and stood frozen at the bottom of the steps, staring, my hair protruding in wild strands from my velvet bonnet, hoping he would not notice my coat was damp from an afternoon on the ground.

"Good son, we have prayed for your safe journey home. And for you to arrive today on Betsy's birthday, what a gift!" Mother stroked his arm.

"A terrible shame you were not here when Father was laid to rest." Drewry appeared behind Mother and though his lament was certainly honest, there was a pinched quality to his voice.

"Oh, brother, we so desired your presence . . ." I ceased thinking how I might be perceived, for John Jr. standing before me was a sight I had often wished to view. I could not contain my pleasure and I bounded up the steps, hugging him with both arms around his waist.

"That evil Being did torment me with our father's fate." John Jr. squeezed his arm around my back, and I thought of Josh's arm so recently fingering the same place. A silence fell across the porch, for it had been some time since the Spirit had been called the "evil being" out loud, and we had all made great efforts not to discuss Father's murder.

I gave to your good mother all your news, John Jr.

"Speak not, you evil creature! Get back to Hell and stay there!" John Jr. raised his fist.

I would have told you more tidings had you a mind to listen.

"No upright man listens to the Devil's voice."

"Come in, my son, for we must sit and feed you supper. Tell us all your news, and your many adventures too." Mother ignored the Being, and grasping John Jr.'s arm she pulled him into the house, communicating with her eyes that many things had changed.

"Brother! Brother!" Richard and Joel careened down the stairs and attached themselves to John Jr.'s legs. I laughed, pleased my brother's arrival home had eclipsed all concern for where I might have been. I removed my bonnet and coat and hung them in the hall, surreptitiously shaking my skirt for spare leaves and twigs caught in the hem. I wanted to go upstairs and tidy my appearance, but I was afraid to draw any further attention to myself through absence.

"The good Lord blesses us today." Chloe's smile was tender and relieved as she laid the table, "I did wonder, chile, if you was ever coming home."

"I did wonder that myself, Chloe, and more than once as well," John Jr. responded, laughing, but I noticed the line of his jaw was serious and much aged.

Supper was the leftover meat and biscuits from my luncheon party, which did not excite my appetite, but John Jr. ate heartily, between stories of his travels.

"Was it only squirrels and skunk you had to eat, brother?" Joel was curious regarding all the details.

"We ate plenty of squirrels, but never a skunk, and in all the countryside we never did taste a ham so sweet as Chloe's." We watched him wipe his mouth with satisfaction, and all of us felt amazed and grateful to see him in his place at the table once again. He looked around at us, smiling, but then turned abruptly serious. "Tell me, what is the state of the farm? In the growing dark it was impossible to see."

"For certain we shall have a crop for you to bring to market, brother, for I have planted much of it myself." Drewry sat straight and tall, speaking quickly.

"Drewry knows everything having to do with the slaves and the planting, John Jr." I wished to support Drew, but he shot me such a withering glance I wished I had kept quiet.

"Everything?" John Jr. took a teasing tone, and used a knife to pare the ham off the bone on his plate. "How is Little Bright these days?" At first I thought John Jr. was sincerely asking Chloe, but then I realized she was in the kitchen, and he had not meant the question for her. Mother let her fork drop on her china plate.

"John Jr. Bell!"

I knew immediately what he meant, though I had not been thinking of it. I was horrified to realize Little Bright had been taken advantage of by Drewry, and if John Jr. knew so much about it, he might have taken similar liberties himself. But how could he speak of it at the table with Mother present?

"My most sincere apologies, Mother, though Drewry is of age for it. My long days away were spent in company much more coarse than this fine family." He stopped eating and clasped his hands together, pretending prayer. Mother sighed but the corners of her mouth turned in a half-smile, to say he was forgiven. I believe she was simply hypnotized into agreeability by seeing his face.

"Still Drewry is a young buck now." John Jr. could not quit and mocked him further. I expected Mother to slap him, but before she could speak Joel looked up from his plate, smiling.

"Of age for what, John Jr.?"

"Of age for what you be far away from!" He laughed deeply, but Mother interrupted his pleasure.

"John Jr., I know you have seen and suffered a great deal in your travels, but we have seen and suffered much at home as well. Do not be base and licentious at your father's table." Mother summoned harsh words to end the discussion, but I could tell she was not as upset as she pretended, and I knew it was true, Drewry had been with Little Bright. I looked at him, blushing a dark red under his early tan.

"I see the weather on your face, dear brother." John Jr. also noticed.

"Yea, for I have worked the fields a plenty in your absence." Drewry looked him in the eye, and John Jr. nodded, an understanding made.

"Tomorrow we shall take pleasure working them together."

"You will find it better than you left it, for our slaves are in excellent humor. Mother provided them with shoes at Father's passing."

"There was snow several feet deep . . ." Mother spoke softly, remembering, and we were silent a moment.

"I could not eat a mouthful more, my belly will pop my trouser buttons." John Jr. pushed his chair back, and I watched him stand and stretch his lean form.

"Let us move to the parlor, and read a passage." Mother got slowly to her feet and Joel and Richard quickly followed her.

"How could you?" I whispered to Drewry, left alone at the table with him. "And you could have told me." I was annoyed.

"It was not the way he makes it out, Betsy, and you have enough to think on with your own affairs. There is no need to trouble yourself with mine."

Chloe came from the kitchen to clear away the plates and I felt she was careful not to look at either Drewry or myself. I wondered with some anxiety what he meant by my affairs. Did he suspect what I had done with Josh? I did not wish to discuss it further and thankfully neither did he. We both stood quickly and adjourned to the parlor, leaving Chloe to clean up alone.

John Jr. was standing silently before Father's chair with his eyes cast downward.

"Take it for your own," Mother sighed, collapsing into her chair, opposite. "Your father would want you to, were he here with us tonight."

"I can never be happy in my life again when every day I feel the horror of my father's murder." John Jr. turned from the chair to the fire, and withdrawing a dull pewter flask none of us had ever seen before from his shirt pocket, he took a long drink. I thought truly, he was his father's son.

"You must be your best self in the face of adversity, John Jr.," Mother said, her eyes filling with tears as she looked up to him. "I know you are capable of great strength and tolerance, for the Spirit has praised those qualities in you in every report given over to me during the many months you have been absent from your home." She wiped at her eyes with the back of her hand and the rest of us were quiet. My back was itchy where my dress had been damp and was now stuck to my skin. I squirmed in my chair, unhappy John Jr.'s presence required all of us to relive Father's passing.

"He will never know any of the good things I may possibly do!" John Jr. turned to look at Mother and I saw that his eyes, already widened with the drink, contained a flash of youthful anger.

If your father could speak he would assure you, you do satisfy.

"If my father could speak he would still be alive, and not murdered by you, evil demon!"

You know nothing. I could imitate his voice exactly and compose his words so you might never know it wasn't him that spoke, but it is not my purpose to deceive you.

"You have no purpose, Spirit of the damned!"

You know nothing of my purpose.

"Pray do not argue further. This house has seen enough malevolence." Mother held her hand up to John Jr. imploring him to stop and cause no conflict. I hoped he would recognize how weak she had recently been, and respect her request. He frowned and was silent.

People who have gone on and left their bodies do not in this era talk to those left behind, John Jr. Bell. They will not in the future either. There is enough talking going on in the world today without the souls of thousands of years past having a say.

I laughed at this, for I could not help it. The idea of a million dead departed chatting away, filling the everyday air with their ancient concerns, struck me as humorous. Mother smiled also, appearing relieved I had broken the tension, but John Jr. was not amused. He lifted the heavy poker and jabbed at the logs in the fire Drewry had made, sending sparks up the chimney.

"Your true nature is evil, and I know it is so." John Jr. spoke softly toward the grate.

My true nature, you will never know, as you knew not your father's.

"My father's nature was beyond your comprehension," John Jr. objected.

The Spirit laughed, at once condescending and mean.

What I could tell you of Jack's true nature. Instead let us talk of how I returned your mother to the land of the living, and nursed her with gifts from the tropics.

The Spirit was most concerned its kindnesses were emphasized to my brother, and Mother sighed, obliging it briefly like a willful child she wished would learn a lesson in manners.

"'Tis true, John Jr., as the Being relates. For certain you

have heard of my illness and recovery? The Spirit told me my messages to you were delivered."

"Mother, have you *faith* in a murderous demon?" John Jr. was incredulous, his opinion of the Being solidly formed. I could see abhorrence spreading in a dark blush across his features, as though we betrayed Father's memory with our tolerance for it.

"My faith is in God, son, for He inhabits all things." Mother reached for his hand. "Even the many we do not understand." I watched them sit, silently holding hands for several moments until John Jr.'s countenance revealed he had grown calmer.

Chloe brought in the tea tray along with the remains of my caramel cake. She set it on the table, and nervously I jumped up to do the pouring, anxious to change the mood. For the first time, I felt Mother's eyes on my back, appraising the twigs stuck in my hair, and I wondered, what did she see? Was there a mark of dampness on the back of my dress? Would she think to wonder why? The teacup I held rattled in the saucer when I turned to deliver it, and I saw her frown.

"Betsy, bring my brush along with my tea. Your hair is outrageously tangled, and I would put it in a braid." I hoped her instructions to me were meant only to dissipate the tension further by bringing normal routines into the room, but I feared she suspected something amiss. I hurried to her dark bedroom and took the brush up off her chest of drawers, carefully avoiding looking to her bed for I was thinking of Father, and it was easy to conjure the image of his corpse lying there. I hastened back to Mother's side, kneeling before the fire, and she began to brush my hair.

"Tell us your most exciting story, brother," Joel pleaded.

He took his piece of cake from Chloe and sat on the rug at John Jr.'s feet.

"That would be the storm of lightning at Bailey's Crossing . . ." John Jr. smiled to see that despite all our trauma Joel was still a trusting child, relishing a good evening's entertainment.

"Did it get you, John Jr.?" Richard sat cross-legged beside him, encouraging him to tell the tale.

"We had been on the road for three long weeks of terrible weather. You recall the rains last spring? The heavy ones that went on and on after Clara Lawson hanged herself?" He looked quickly to Mother, as if he would apologize for the reference, but felt it was essential to conjure up weather we could picture. I felt Mother nod to him, absently brushing over my tangles. "The rain was like that, endless, and in the afternoon, the wind whipped up. The tracks in the road were a swamp beneath the horses' feet. We were striving to reach Bailey's Crossing, for we were greatly in need of supplies, but the animals stumbled and sank near to their knees each step in the muck and the road had not been properly cleared, so branches whipped and struck our sides, and it was very slow going." Abruptly the sound of loud rain splashing into mud filled our parlor. "Leave off!" John Jr. turned his head with great annoyance to the fire as if the Spirit would speak from there. "I can tell it well enough alone," he snapped, but the Being did not answer, though the sound of rain did stop, and he continued.

"Isiah and I were unaware the demon was present in the storm until it spoke. *'John Jr. Bell, stop this instant or your head will burst like a melon!'*" John Jr. did an excellent imitation of the Spirit's most commanding tone. "We heard a thunderous cracking sound and a bolt of lightning was hurled from the sky into a tree before us on the roadside. It crashed down across our path, and if we had gone one foot farther it would have meant our skulls crushed for certain!"

Now they know, I saved your life, and your lowly slave.

"'Tis certain you were there, creature of the damned, but 'tis as likely you did _cause_ the damage as relieve it." John Jr. took another drink from his flask.

"It nearly got you, brother, just like it nearly got me in the whirlpool of quicksand!" Richard clasped his hands in excitement. I tried not to flinch when Mother ripped through an impossible knot in my hair.

"It saved you, Richard! It didn't _get_ you," Joel objected. "Tell it again, John Jr.," he begged.

"I have many more stories I know will interest you," John Jr. laughed, "but I believe you have your own share."

"One day in winter Drewry shot a witch rabbit!" Joel was anxious to recount that story.

"And pretty Miss Sallie Barton from Virginia came to call," Drewry spoke up.

"Not tonight, dears," Mother interrupted, "for it is growing late. Perhaps you can continue telling tales in the comfort of your beds." Mother did not wish to observe John Jr. hearing Drew's description of Sallie Barton, I could tell, and I certainly did not wish to relive our sleigh ride. "I must finish Elizabeth's plait." Mother continued to pull the twigs and leaves from my slippery hair. She did not speak to me about it, but she did place her hand on my back, smoothing the wrinkles in the cloth. I hoped she did not know what I had done that day. I wondered if I knew myself. John Jr. stood.

"I will take the boys upstairs, Mother. So many nights I have longed for my bed, I am looking forward to this rest. Provided it will be undisturbed." He spoke to the walls and ceiling as if he hoped the Spirit was listening and would heed his desire.

"It will be peaceful, I am certain," Mother said. "It has been for some time. You know not the depth of my joy over your return." She tilted her cheek and John Jr. bent and kissed her. Taking the boys by the hand, he climbed the stairs, returning a different person to his same old room.

the life of all that lives

The following morning was a Saturday and I awoke to John Jr. shaking my shoulder.

"Will you come to the cavern, sister? Drewry is out on the lands and Mother has taken the boys to Thorn's store. I greatly desire to see Father's best view. Will you come?" I wondered if he had something private he wished to tell me. Something had changed between us, exactly as I had felt it would before his departure, but what it was I could not say. So much had happened, I knew not how to tell him of the many events he had missed while he was away, or even how to accurately express my feelings. I pulled my quilt up to my chin, blinking to focus on his face. He reminded me of Father in so many ways, it made me sad. And yet, in the gleam of his teeth, smiling his inquiry, I saw my brother's true nature. His soul lived for adventure, though unlike Drewry, he might meet it simply to practice restraint.

"I will," I answered, pushing back my cover. I would not pass on an opportunity to visit the cavern, as I had not been there since last I went with him.

We set out directly after eating breakfast. The sun was pleasantly warm and large white clouds rolled behind the treetops. I carried a saddlebag of our warmest woolens which could suffer mud, and our lunches, and John Jr. carried his rifle on his shoulder, as well as a coil of rope, in case of an emergency. The oil lantern he'd fetched from the barn swung carelessly in his right hand and twice he bumped my knee, until I fell to walking a step behind.

"'Tis nowhere more lovely than Father's land." John Jr. spoke over his shoulder, invigorated with the spring.

"In truth?" I was curious what the rest of the world was like, despite my suspicion it was much the same as where we walked.

"Betsy, there is land vastly different from this."

"In all aspects?"

"In all aspects. I saw mountains so tall they stood in the clouds, with faces of sheer rock one hundred times the size of Father's cavern." John Jr. adjusted the rope on his shoulder and I remembered he had always enjoyed climbing. He would not exaggerate. "The land past here is God's great majesty, but many settlements are evil and corrupt." His lips curled into a grim frown reminding me of his face when he teased Drewry over Little Bright, and I wondered what else he had seen in his travels.

"How say you?"

"I tell you, Betsy, there are parts of this great south where impecuniousness has caused whole communities and their outlying districts to go to wreck and ruin. The larger cities are filled with swindlers, wanting only to fleece you. Our father has provided for us well here, Betsy."

"That is understood by me." I had the feeling there was something more he wished to say.

"All men will not have your father's or your brother's good intentions toward you, sister." I could see he was concerned for me. "There are men in this country who would dishonor you as quick as they would blink an eyelid and with less thought as well. With your beauty, you must be aware."

"I am aware, John Jr., but you forget, I am unlikely to travel far from this secluded farm." My response reassured him and he left it at that. I wondered what he had observed on the evening of his arrival as I strode unconscious of his presence up the hill? I had committed a grave sin, I knew, but it was between me and the Lord and Josh Gardner. Besides, I felt my brother was hardly one to give advice.

We reached the sinkhole that marked the cold storehouse and we stopped there, before the mighty wooden door. Dean had carved it from a massive oak felled by himself and Father, such a feat of strength he had recalled it before doing battle with the black dog witch creature. Set into the knoll of the hillside and reinforced with stones, it was a formidable sight. The iron padlock and chain were kept well oiled and when John Jr. fitted in the key, the lock snapped undone. The handle Dean had carved was long enough for many pairs of men's hands, as in the winter it took more than one person to heave it open. John Jr. and I grasped the smooth wood together and pulled with all our strength, until the foot-wide door creaked, gave way, and the cold air smelling of smoked meats and cheese blasted our faces.

"We must dress out here." John Jr. took the satchel off my shoulder and we pulled out all the clothes, leaving only our lunch to carry in the bag. I put one of Mother's old wool gardening smocks over my plain cloth dress and John Jr. wore his oldest woolen coat. I watched him expertly light the lantern after striking the flint and steel to get his char cloth going, igniting the flame in his tinderbox.

"Are you prepared, dear sister?"

"As ever I will be."

He went first, descending the stone steps into the wide room of the larder.

"Look at the prosperity we enjoy, dear Betsy. Look on it!" He raised the lamp and I saw we had two sides of pork and two of beef strung near the wall where it was coldest, while wooden shelves built to stand alone held cheese wrapped in muslin and quantities of butter blocks. Sitting in pewter bowls of icy water was enough butter to cover all the cornbread eaten in Robertson County. There were fifty-pound sacks labeled *sugar, hominy, cornmeal* and *oats,* stacked crosswise on the highest shelves. I did not often come to the storehouse and our abundance *was* astounding.

There was a natural slope down to the back of the room and John Jr. went that way. The passage narrowed slightly and then more, until the walls became so tight we had to turn sideways and slide along. We did this silently for nearly half an hour, winding our way back through the rock of the massive cavern. It was damp in places and very tight in others and, as I moved along, I felt the chilling rock pressing my body hard, and I had to hold my breath to squeeze through. John Jr. had the lantern before him and the passage grew completely dark as he rounded a corner more quickly than I. Without the light I could not see my hand before my face.

"Go more slowly, brother," I called ahead.

"Hurry, it is not much farther," he called back. I was happy I had worn my oldest ragged bonnet, for even though John Jr. was in front and got the worst of it, the spiderwebs were thick and I did not like the feel of them on my cheeks and hands.

We emerged from the small passage into a large cave some thirty feet high with walls the color of ripe figs and giant dark stalactites hanging from the ceiling. I felt as I remembered feeling last time I had visited; as if I'd entered the most unusually sacred church. I knew abruptly John Jr. and I were not the first to see the pleasures of this place. I wondered why it had not struck me before.

"Brother, do you think the Injuns once lived here?"

"Injuns, or maybe animals."

He held the lantern up and we examined a stalactite.

"See how the minerals contained within our earth cause the cone to shimmer?" John Jr.'s interest in geology was deeper than I'd realized.

" 'Tis lovely," I agreed, marveling at the swirls of color, but as I stared at the icicle of rock, the flame of his lantern wavered and I thought I saw an ancient and unfamiliar face staring from inside the cone. I gasped and grabbed John Jr.'s arm.

"What, Betsy?" He turned to me, surprised, but I did not say what I had seen.

"Let us move on and have our lunch, dear brother, for I am nearly faint with hunger."

We carried on to the back of the room, then climbed upward through a short but wide passage that served as the hallway to the great mouth of the cavern. We entered there and I noticed first how smooth and flat the floor became, and, looking up, I saw framed by the gigantic arch of rock the gorgeous view of Father's acreage spreading far below.

"What's this?" John Jr. did not face the panorama as I did, but rather turned away and held the lantern high to better see the concave wall rising on our left. I looked where he pointed and saw a pile of something that resembled bones in the corner, under the shelf of rock.

"Never mind. Look at this!" I insisted he survey the land, and moving past him, I settled on my knees in the arc of sunlight bathing the floor right at the mouth of the cave. I looked down at the river and the fallen elm, the perfect fishing hole. I thought of the day I'd stood below with Josh, admiring the icicles hanging from the arched mouth above where I sat now. I wished heartily he was by my side.

"The floor is smooth as window glass, John Jr. Let us spread our luncheon here."

"Are you growing, Betsy?" John Jr. came quickly over, teasing me, unshouldering his gun and rope. He set the lantern down and sat cross-legged at my side.

"'Tis nowhere more lovely," he said, resting his hands on his knees, looking out. I saw he was completely satisfied with what lay before him, and yet, deep sadness etched contours in his face and made his spine too stiff. I recognized his mood, for I had seen it in myself and Drewry. His blessings were not enough to provide sufficient relief from his pain. I wished to make him understand how ready I was to leave behind our times of dread, and be able to enjoy the warm excitement a handful of black cherries or innocent kisses in the woods could bring.

"You know, dear brother, the Spirit saved our mother from her death." I started the discussion I realized we must have.

"I know only the Spirit murdered our father and has done damage to the souls of all his children and his wife. I will not hear you speak in its favor, little sister."

The pile of bones we had chosen not to approach set up rattling in the corner, and turning our heads, we saw them rise to do a noisy dance. The clinking of their joints against the stone made a nasty rhythm, reminding me of the spoons the Spirit beat in Father's hands his last day at our table. The clatter echoed large out of the mouth of the cavern.

Know you, John Jr., your mother is an exceptional human, protected from each existing wickedness by her goodness and gentleness toward every creature of whatever kind.

"Please stop, I beg you, hurt us not today!" I grew afraid, because the sound increased under the Spirit's words until it was truly deafening.

Lucy Bell appreciates the smallest tribute rendered her; extended by a madwoman, an evil demon or a most demanding man.

"Your only virtue, creature, apart from certain kindness to our mother, is you do not profess to be other than you are, and declare yourself an outcast from Hell and a murderer!" John Jr. shouted at the Being.

Yea, I am outcast, but I have many virtues unknown to you. You will not understand all I say, but you will know I speak the truth.

"You speak not the truth. You speak of murder and wrongdoings, of buried teeth and treasure and other stories proven false."

The things I have told others which were not true are not important. They were told to prove to you the foolish ways of men. Did I tell you true I had poisoned your father?

"Your falsity is all of you, not only what you say."

No, no, John Jr. Bell. I am true as the drop beneath you from this cave into the river. I am true as the hard ground below.

"Please stop," I begged the Spirit, fearing the next moment would see my brother hurled over the edge to certain death. The bones collapsed back into a pile and the sound of their clamoring died in echoes off the walls.

Though I have the gift of prophecy and understand all myster-

ies and all knowledge, and though I have all faith, have I not charity, I am nothing. I will leave you be, John Jr.

The Spirit held a firm but less menacing tone with my brother and I detected gentleness within it, as though it educated a well-loved child.

A demon is not the only Being who laughs at the foolish things men do over and again, and encourages them to carry on in folly, so as to laugh the more. The evil in men's hearts surpasses all the evil made in Hell, for it is one and the same.

"Why did you murder Father? In all your talk never do you say a reason why."

For the good of future generations.

"I see no reason there."

Someday you will have a daughter and you will know my reason.

"You need not speak to me of future good. I will not believe you and I do not want to hear it."

I could kill you too, John Jr., but I will not.

"Kill me, for I am doomed to misery alive, tormented by your presence!" John Jr. was as beside himself as ever I had witnessed.

I will not kill you for the good of future generations.

The Being continued its patronizing yet tolerant tone.

"Spirit, you speak nonsense and lies eternally! Kill me, or begone!"

Why wish for death?

A bone flew across the cave from the pile and rapped John Jr. lightly on the head not hard enough to hurt, but hard enough to anger him further.

You will be dead much longer than alive! There are many things I could tell you, many things I should like to say to someone with enough compassion and intelligence to understand.

"Tell me," I begged, interrupting, engaged by the Spirit's speech.

My tellings are beyond the grasp of the human mind. Your salvation will be faith in unknown power, therein lies Heaven on earth.

"Your lies are tiresome, demon."

When you understand me, John Jr., you will understand the truth. I live forever, and all living beings are part of me. One who does good is never overcome by evil. I can not tell you all my powers for they are endless, but know, I am the life of all that lives, the intelligence of the intelligent, and the strength of the powerful Beings. I am unending time and silence, I am music and all secrets. Everything comes from me. I am your most dear friend.

"You talk well when you like," John Jr. said, tossing the bone back across the cave. "But I shall never believe a word you say." He looked again at the beautiful vista of Father's land. "Betsy, unpack the luncheon," he commanded.

"I am not so famished now as I was before, dear brother." I was in fact most anxious to depart, for a horrible cold dampness had descended in the cavern, and I recognized it as the cold spot I had felt in the woods when I was only nine and unaware.

I am unspeakable and all truth that is spoken.

The Spirit rattled the pile of bones one last time, and left us alone.

Over the next few weeks I gradually became aware I had learned something very important from the Spirit's talk in the cave, and though I could hardly articulate it, the learning was growing inside of me. I walked through sweeping and dusting, washing and polishing so slowly Mother began to complain my tasks were being accomplished at the rate of the moon. I was thinking so hard about other things I could not concentrate on a cloth in my hand. I was thinking about unending time and silence, and about the intelligence of the intelligent and the strength of the powerful Beings, and also I thought a great deal about Josh. I was slow at my tasks, but quick to get away after the dinner hour, for Mother liked to lie down in the afternoons, and that meant I was free to meet Josh in the woods.

We both tried to be there as often as possible, sometimes indulging in the exquisite passions we had shared on my birthday, but most often playing like children together. We plucked new leaves off the trees that circled and hid us and we pretended they were boats racing down the streams. His managed to reach the finish line of the little rapids before mine most consistently and he took as his prize kisses up against the elms. The hours flew by, each day it grew late too soon, and though we met as often as possible, I did not feel it was enough, for those hours simply enjoying our time together were brilliant with laughter and silly fun.

On the Friday before the Lovers Promenade Josh and I walked all the way to the fishing pool under the cavern. We sat down together on a large boulder near where the stream poured down in a waterfall into the pool. I looked up at the gaping mouth of the cave and thought suddenly of the pile of bones in the corner. I realized I had learned as deep in my soul as the cave was recessed into the rock above, that the Spirit and all its actions were way more than I could comprehend. I was about to tell Josh what the Being had said to John Jr. to see what he would make of it when he spoke to me of a conversation he had had with his father.

"He has been asking me, Betsy, since your father's funeral if I feel a *particular* affection for you." Josh squeezed my hand in his, and smiled, but his eyes held a most determined aspect. "I know it has been your wish to keep our affections circumspect, but I was bound by my heart and my love of the good Lord to speak the truth in a matter of such importance, so I told him as I have often told you, I mean to have Miss Betsy Bell to be my wife."

"You told him that? Dear Josh!" I was surprised, for he knew I felt it best we live from one meeting to the next, as the Spirit made my life so unpredictable. When I thought of marrying Josh, I heard immediately the Being's warning in my mind. *Betsy Bell, do not have Josh Gardner.*

"My father has a property in the fertile land of Kentucky that already has a log cabin erected. He has promised it to me so you and I can begin a farm and family there. When shall I speak to your mother and brother, Betsy? I am anxious to put our love before the altar of the Lord our God and sanctify what we know to be true and right. How say you?" Josh was pleased and excited by his plan. He brought his fingers to my face and I took hold of them, pressing them to my lips to make the sign for silence, for the very mention of a future happy life with him clouded my enjoyment of the present moment. I knew it was not to be. "Betsy, why do you not see the blessing offered in this change?" He held my face as though in prayer.

"Josh, why do you not see the happiness of this present moment? Why must you be looking to plan our future instead of enjoying my company now?" I took his fingers from my cheeks allowing my irritation with the subject to be apparent, but then I placed his hands in my lap hoping to remind him of all we had shared and must be grateful for.

"Very well, Betsy, I will not dwell on the subject." Josh sighed and squeezed my thigh playfully before pulling his hands away, grasping my shoulders. "But it is one we must return to, for the future will come, planned or not, and my intentions are honorable with you, Betsy Bell, though I begin to wonder about yours, darling girl!" Josh teased me, but there was a frustration in his voice I had not previously heard, and to hear him call me "darling girl" reminded me of Father, and caused me pain. I went limp when he embraced me, for I felt again the heavy stone in the pit of my stomach. Was I more connected to a dead man and a boulder than I was to my warm lover's body? I looked up at the mouth of the dark cavern and I felt afraid.

Later that same day, we received a letter from Jesse announcing that Martha had successfully borne their first son without trauma or tragedy.

"They have named him John, but plan to call him Jack, as we did your father." After sharing the news, Mother folded the letter and retired to her bedroom to be alone, leaving me to wonder why such a happy issue caused her to grow sad. I realized there were those who might say the same of myself and Josh. Why did thoughts of a happy future with him seem overwhelming and impossible to me? I suddenly understood Mother's sadness was for all she had lost at Father's passing, all the news and years they would not share, and that was how I felt it was going to be for me as well. Only instead of years of memories I would be left with only months. I went early to bed and fought self-pity until I fell asleep.

The next day was the Saturday of the Lovers Promenade and we were blessed with a bright, strong sun that gave us all a taste of summer heat. I woke in the morning to find the curse of blood between my legs. Although not a lot was flowing, I felt slightly unwell and thought instead of walking I ought to lie all day in bed. The tight waist and all the buttons in my special dress seemed impossible. Even though I greatly desired Josh to see me in it, I was uncertain if I could manage to get it on. I went downstairs intending to ask Mother for help.

"Betsy." Mother was sitting at the dining table resting her chin on her hand, and before I could speak of my dress, she turned to me. "Your father's book of accounts is missing. I looked for it today to show John Jr. the tobacco records and discovered it has disappeared from its place in Father's desk. Drewry knows nothing of it. Do you?" She raised her eyes to mine. I thought of the red silk ribbon, the wagging demon tongue. If Father's book of accounts could speak, would it cry more than *forgive me*?

"No, I know nothing of it," I lied, realizing I had never returned to it, though I had meant to the day before Father had died. Where was it now? I felt suddenly ill.

I have taken it!

"For what purpose?" Mother let her hand drop to the table with consternation.

Your Jack, so fond of judge and jury, will be judged by what was written in the book.

I felt extremely uncomfortable. Did that mean his request for forgiveness would not be acknowledged? Why had I ripped away that page and burned it? My impulsive actions seemed to have larger repercussions than ever I intended. I forgave him everything. I hoped God knew I had. I hoped Father knew. I realized suddenly it was myself I had now to forgive. I thought of the Spirit's words to John Jr. in the cave. *Have I not charity, I am nothing.* I must have charity for myself.

"Well, if you might find some way to return it, all the running of the farm he documented there."

And much else as well, but you will not see it again.

"If that is so, then I will cease to worry over it." Mother sighed and turned to me. "What's the matter, Betsy? You look pale."

"'Tis my time to bleed again," I told her, happy to change the subject, "and I wish to wear my finest dress to the picnic."

"Oh, never mind, Joshua will not know. Your red petticoat will be completely hidden by the bell of your skirt." Mother sighed again. "I will help you prepare."

It took almost two hours for me to dress and pin up my hair in the sophisticated style with the Spirit's comb, but finally Mother had finished with me and I was released out-of-doors. I still felt queasy, but I was growing excited about the stroll by the riverbank before our community. I walked down our hill to the road to see if I could spot Josh's carriage, for he was due to arrive, but I saw nothing but bunnies, nibbling on the clover and buttercups, growing in ever larger patches on the ruts of our road. My womb cramped and twisted and I turned back, walking to the horse tie where I could sit and wait. I wondered if I should tell Josh it was my time to bleed, but I was not sure how to raise the subject. Zeke walked past me, a fishing pole in his hand, heading toward the river.

"Where might you be going, Zeke?"

"Miz Lucy done asked me to fetch her up some fish for Easter, so I be on my way."

"Mind the Spirit don't mess with your fishes!" I teased him, for we had recently heard a rumor the Spirit was being blamed by some for the disappearance of bait off their hooks when no catch was resulting.

"Your mama don't like no phantom fishes for her supper,

do she Miss 'Lizabeth?" Zeke winked at me and I noticed as he set off smiling he had a fat pocket of tobacco to help him enjoy the day. When I turned back around, there was Josh's carriage, coming down the road.

When we arrived at the churchyard Josh jumped down and pulled the footstool out for me to disembark, grasping my arm with such commanding certainty, I felt my stomach fill with excitement. "Let me help you, Betsy. Your hair and dress are more lovely than the day," he whispered in my ear and gently closed the door. We were about to pick our path when Thenny and Becky, walking with James, Alex, Mary Batts and Ephraim, approached us.

"Have you heard, Betsy, about the heron on Old Kate's pond and Mr. Ellison?" Thenny did not wait to greet me before speaking her news. I looked to Mary but she looked away, ever stoic.

"Tell it again, Thenny!" Becky giggled, and cast down her eyes.

"Mr. Ellison, as he said he would do at the funeral, has made it his single purpose to shoot that heron off the lake, and only today he has accomplished it."

"What is so remarkable in the killing of a bird?" Alex Gooch raised his arm and closed one eye, posturing he pulled the trigger of a gun. I wondered if he was pretending for my benefit, or did he really know so little?

"The bird was no ordinary bird, silly! It was the witch creature that drowned Amanda. Recall it now?"

"Thenny! We are to have a jolly day, cease to be morose," I chastised her.

"I am not morose. No, I am well pleased, for that witch creature is dead!" Thenny pouted slightly and was silent for a moment but could not prevent herself from going on. "Not only is it remarkable Mr. Ellison did kill it, but the heron *did not float* as naturally it should have done. Instead it disappeared where he felled it, and sank to the bottom of the lake."

"Oh Thenny!" Becky giggled and James joined her with a nervous laugh.

"Next you'll be thinking it was the witch heron eating the bait off the hooks this spring." I meant this as a joke, but from the silence that fell I understood it had been suggested as a real possibility before the group met up with us. A tense silence settled over us and Josh attempted to change the mood.

"Well, friends, shall we walk along the river? This is a promenade . . ." He held out his arm to me.

"Yes, let's," I readily agreed. Mary Batts passed by my ear, whispering.

"Mother says fear of that heron will keep the boys from swimming in our pond come summer."

"Is that a good thing?" I answered her cryptically and stepped aside. Looking round, I saw the riverbank was crowded with members of our community strolling and picnicking and farther downstream there lounged a large group of Negroes, fishing and eating corn cakes in the shade.

We let Thenny and Alex and Ephraim and Mary and James and Becky move in front of us, and I held back with Josh so we were last on the path. When we had passed the clusters of people near the bridge and finished the superficial convivial greetings exchanged there, I allowed Josh to hold my hand as we walked, enjoying the heat of his fingers and the warm sun on my head. The others were far ahead around a bend in the river so we could not see them and I believe they sensed we wished to walk alone.

"Come, Betsy," Josh pulled me off the main path onto a

smaller cow path leading down to the water. Violets dotted the carpet of purslane and chickweed on the riverbank, and I noticed a patch of red sassafras towering over wild iris in bloom, a sight most certainly a gift from God. Josh stopped me when we reached a thick stand of elms that hid us well.

"I think of nothing save you, Betsy Bell." He pulled me to him, firmly. "You and our own log cabin. You must allow me to speak to your mother and brother and we must set a date to be wed, as your previous troubles have passed and the time has come to move forward."

"The Spirit is still with me, Josh."

"I wish to marry you, Spirit or no, dear girl."

"If only it were so simple . . ."

"It is! Say you will marry me, Betsy, for you are my destiny and I am yours." He put his hands on my shoulders and drew my face to his and I relaxed, breathing deep his smell and the spicebush around us, scents of longing.

"Let us see," I managed to mumble, allowing him to push me up solidly against the smooth trunk of the elm, allowing his hands to roam around the bodice of my dress. I winced as he felt my breasts but hoped he would not know it was a tender time for me.

"What shall I see that is new to me?" Josh teased me, and quickly kissed my neck. "Marry me soon, Betsy. Marry me and every day we can share in the pleasures of each other and make together a new life." He squeezed my shoulders and forced my eyes to his, insisting I respond.

"Would that I could give my answer yes. Would that it could be so." I tried to squirm away and look down at the river, but he shook me just slightly, as though he feared I was not entirely in my body.

"It can be so, you foolish girl! You are only afraid. Remember in the winter when you were frightened riding up the bank? Remember how you flew across the meadow when I slapped your horse? You trounced that fear and then we laughed together! Was that not happiness? We must marry, Betsy, let us tell everyone today!"

"No! If you force me to an answer, Josh, I must declare it no! Not now! Ask not for me to do it!" I gripped his forearms with my nails and felt tears rise in my throat. I shocked Josh with my despair.

"Betsy! Don't cry, you will always be loved by me and sure I will protect you, so you need not be afraid." He held me close, calmly communicating the strength of his love for me, but the tenseness of his elbows revealed his desire to resolve the matter was firm. "This very afternoon I will go to your mother and John Jr. with my request, and then you must say yes."

Betsy Bell, do not have Josh Gardner.

The Spirit hissed through the breeze in the new leaves. The hard tree was against my back and Josh's body pressed my front and, despite its pleasures, the image came to me of an animal in a trap. I wondered, did the fox feel this way when it recognized its next movement would be its last? Why must Josh force the issue? Why could we not carry on forever as we were?

It cannot be.

The Spirit spoke exactly to my darkest fears and I felt the heavy stone within my belly, as I always did when Josh proposed his plans for our future.

Betsy Bell, do not have Josh Gardner.

"You would listen to a fiend from Hell, the tormentor of your soul, and not to this plea to stand beside me before God's altar, united in purpose?" Josh demanded.

"Josh, it is not my doing."

Betsy Bell, do not have Josh Gardner.

"It will be your undoing, darling girl." Josh moved his hands from my shoulders up my neck to hold my face. His fingers pressed against the comb at the back of my head and I felt the silver prongs dig into my scalp. "I implore you, ignore the mean foreboding of this demon." The love in his face was certain and I did wish to have it, but I was too afraid.

"Josh, be thoughtful of the matter. How can I marry you? Our future would be so afflicted as to resemble my father's last days. Many times this Being has told the truth and I fear horrible affliction might come from our union. I cannot marry you, for I cannot cause you torment. I love you, before the eyes of the Lord, you know I love you, as I have opened every part of myself to you." I ceased speaking, for a dark expression I did not like was settling on Josh's features. He did not understand me.

"You have indeed. You cannot mean to refuse me now." He slid his thumbs under my chin and tilted my face up as though he would kiss me, but did not.

"Dear Josh, it is because I love you, I *must say no,* we cannot marry." I managed to speak the words despite the voice inside me crying, yes, say yes, say yes.

"Betsy Bell, if this is your true answer to my proposal I will go from here and never more will see you. I know not what else there may be for me in life . . . I fear there may be nothing, for you have been my dearest hope, the adoration of my soul. Say you will reconsider." Josh allowed his fingers gently to caress my neck and I swallowed.

"I could not forgive myself if I were to cause a painful future to be yours," I answered him, turning my eyes to the ground.

"Betsy, you know not the future nor its course." Josh slipped his hands around my shoulders.

"I know the Spirit knows, and you have heard how it commands me." I wished he could see it as I did.

"That creature of the damned knows nothing of my love for you."

"Josh, you do not understand!" I shook my head with frustration and he let go of me, dropping his hands to his sides.

"I understand." He nodded his head and I could see he was angry with me. "I understand you are finished with our love."

"No . . ."

"Betsy, if you do not intend to marry me, I will leave you now and never see you more."

"How can you? Do you not love me as you said?"

"I do. I love you and wish to sanctify our covenant together, but what *you* wish, I cannot do, for I feel it is unkind of you not to accept my worthy proposal." He raised the back of his left hand and touched my cheek and lips, with confidence and longing. I knew not how to answer him for he had turned abruptly sensitive and calm. I had the momentary sense he knew something I did not, and I ought to trust him, but I could not be certain. I wondered fiercely what it was he knew.

"What shall I tell the others?" I asked, stalling for time while I tried to think of how our disagreement could be resolved.

"You must tell them you are free of me if you will not allow our marriage." He turned to walk away and I noticed the light gray wool he wore was exactly the color of the elms that had sheltered us. My eyes filled with the red light of the waving sassafras and tears and I moved to run after him.

"Wait!" I called, but a thick white fog descended on the bank, and I could see nothing but ribbons of mist. I looked for Josh, but he had disappeared into the cloud. I tried to find the path we had taken, but I could not. Trees appeared where I thought there were none, blocking my progress. I cried out loud, what have I done?

Betsy Bell, do not have Josh Gardner.

I caught my beautiful dress on a stinging nettle as I moved between the elms and I knew it would be ruined, but I did not care. I stopped tripping through the fog and sank to my knees, giving my forehead to the ground. I listened to the river and tears rolled from my eyes onto the purslane and violets. I could not have Josh Gardner for my love, and all our tender moments shared were over. I thought of Father and his dying face and I cried harder for my losses; my father and my own true love.

I am leaving now.

The Spirit whispered in my ear and I knew all was over, for its voice was papery and soft, rustling like the pages of Father's book of accounts, closing in my ear. I sat up and saw the fog had lifted and the woods and river were bathed in sunlight. I was not far off the path.

"There is too much unexplained!" I yelled, but my words were lost to the rushing water. I stood and ran up the path hoping I might see Josh, but he had gone. The comb in my hair had loosened and I pulled it out with great regret and hurled it down the bank into the water. I stood watching it sink, sad I would never see it again.

In the evening at supper we were all gathered in our places around the dining table. The fire burned at the hearth in the parlor and Chloe served early peas and skillet cornbread in gravy, a simple meal, as the next day was Easter and a hog was to be slaughtered for the occasion. I had heard the one they'd marked, wailing, as I walked up our path, but I cared not at all for the fate of the pig. I was sullen, tremendously downcast over what had transpired with Josh. I was thinking I should join the hog and wail myself until my angels came to get me, as surely, there must be a better world. But if it was inhabited by numerous unearthly Beings resembling the Spirit, then it was no place I wished to go.

Mother said grace, and John Jr. said Amen, and we commenced eating. I had not swallowed my first mouthful, when there came the sound of a bed frame being smashed to bits in the parlor. My first thought was the Spirit had finally decided to destroy Father's last resting place. We all rose and went to see what the matter was, but we found no evidence of any breakage.

"Well, shall we resume our meal?" Mother turned to leave, but took not a step, as a heavy stone of iron rolled from our chimney and bounced from the grate onto the parlor carpet where it burst into a ball of blue sparks and the Spirit spoke.

I am leaving now. I will worry you and your people no more.

"Goodbye!" Mother called, as though she wished it well, but I felt suddenly overcome, as though I might faint. I knew the Spirit was leaving because its purpose was accomplished. It had tormented the life from Father and prevented me from having Josh Gardner. I spoke up, allowing my upset to be apparent.

"Why? Why was I so tortured?"

Do you not see my reason in my actions, Betsy Bell?

"All I see is how you caused my suffering." The injustice of it was intolerable to me and I thought of Father speaking in church, his back rigid with anger.

Your worst torment was slaps and pinpricks, not so sharp as your own fears. All your suffering was not caused by me.

"It was! Did you not murder my father and cause me to renounce my love, never speaking to the reason why?"

I am all things. I am evil and evil seeks no reason. You would be wise to live content with that mystery without your irritable search for meaning. Your feeble mind cannot contain knowledge of all that lives. You cannot comprehend my reasons, or the lack of them.

I had the feeling the Spirit was not telling me the truth.

"I comprehend you better than you know. Your pleasure has been my suffering, and now you will depart, assured my life will be one of pain and loneliness." I felt the wild abandon I'd experienced on the morning of the sleigh ride, when I'd known Father was gone and I could behave as I liked.

"Betsy . . ." Mother shook her head and frowned at me, discouraging me from continuing. I pictured Josh's gray honest eyes and the love he held for me and I realized suddenly what he had known that afternoon that I had not; if I was blessed enough to share a single purpose with him it was my responsibility to embrace it, come what may. I recalled the day when we were attacked at the bridge with sticks and I had returned home to find my corn husk dolls blown away by the wind. Forces of nature I could not dictate, but what of my own future? I knew, though it felt buried under the heavy stone in my belly, I knew the right true path for me was to live in love and not in fear, or longing. What had I done? Why had I refused Josh Gardner? A fury such as I had never experienced before filled my body and I shouted, "Go, Spirit! Be gone and know I will do as I like, regardless of you, reason or no!"

Betsy Bell, what thoughts rage inside your head? You understand nothing.

"I understand I have had enough of your malevolence and you shall not leave any more than you already have behind. I shall have the love that I deserve." I felt certain it was as Josh had said, our love was stronger than any otherworldly creature.

You will do as you will. I did not come here to torment you only.

I thought of Father and the dying slant of his head, his breath stuttering away. I thought of Clara Lawson hanging from a rope inside her barn and of Amanda Ellison floating face down in Kate Batts's pond. I thought of the doors closed forever to Old Kate's wares and of my brother struggling through storms for no good reason. I thought of Sallie Barton and John Jr. and how they never would meet or marry.

You are only one amongst the many suffering souls in this world and there are many other worlds as well, where many suffer.

"But I have finished with your torture," I said, wanting more than anything for this to be the truth.

I too will soon be done with you, Betsy Bell.

The Spirit hissed into my ear and struck me hard across the face as it used to do before it murdered Father. I cried out in pain and brought my hand to the place where I had been struck.

I am the strength of the powerful Beings.

The Spirit raised its voice to the level of thunder.

"Betsy, allow the Spirit to take leave of us. Do not shout after it. It has said it will worry us no more." Mother was upset and took up my arm protectively, but it was too late. I saw a white light flash across the room like the lightning bolt that had split our giant elm in two. An unbearable heat burned in my belly as though the Spirit had replaced the cold stone with red-hot coals.

"No!" Mother drew her hand quickly back as my dress burst into flames. I was frightened, but I felt nothing. Behind me John Jr. called for Chloe to bring a pail of water.

"She is burning, you must stop this! Stop it!" Mother flailed her arms against the flames but the fire simply grew stronger and brighter in the wind she created.

"I will live!" I screamed, determined to withstand the Spirit's abuses of my flesh. I raised my arms above my head, surprised I felt no pain, though the flames consumed me. I was still able to speak, but tendrils of fire shot from my mouth with my words so I chose them carefully. "I will have Josh Gardner for my husband and my life. It is not God's wish that I should suffer further."

Do you believe you know the mind of God?

"I know He charged me with a special purpose, one I struggled to apprehend and did ignore until this very day."

John Jr. took the pail of water from Chloe and stepped through the fire of me, pouring it over my head. It evaporated instantly, having no effect on the flames.

Speak not of what you know not, Betsy Bell.

"I may speak best of what I know most deeply. Hatred stirs up strife, but love covers all sins. I love Josh Gardner, as the fig tree putteth forth green figs. It is my nature."

Nature is what you know not.

"I know what love is and how it does deliver and delight." A massive flame shot from my womb and licked the parlor curtains, scorching them to black.

"Please, stop! You must not do this!" Mother sobbed and I saw Joel and Richard shrinking up against the wall. Though I continued to feel nothing I could see they were afraid for me.

"Cursed I have been," I continued to argue with the Being, "but now I am blessed to know love, and you shall not take it from me. One who does good is never overcome by evil, you said so yourself, in the cave." The burning fire in my body subsided instantly. The flames ceased to flare from my arms and I was left with a warmth so rare and beautiful it felt as though God had breathed into my soul. My dress was black and scorched but there was not a mark left behind on my skin.

"Thank God! Thank you, Lord, thank you for sparing my child." Mother prostrated herself on the floor by my feet. I wondered what she thought of my declaration of love for Josh, and I wondered why she thanked the Lord and not the Being.

Are you prepared for the responsibility of your affections?

The Spirit changed its tone with me and spoke reasonably.

Any fool can say I choose this love, but you know not what will befall you on the course.

"For certain I will never know if I do not take my opportunity." All at once I felt possessed of an urgent need to saddle up Moses and ride through the night to Josh's home. What if he was packing for Kentucky?

Betsy Bell, do not have Josh Gardner.

The Spirit returned to its menacing hiss and this caused me to let my temper loose. I knew it was dangerous to do so, but like the days when I crumpled Father's page from his book of accounts and threw the poison in the fire and ran to Josh to let him love me, I no longer could control myself. I screamed at the Spirit.

"If you must stay and torment my days with Josh, so be it. I would rather be tormented and together with my love than separated by your evil and left to a lifetime of longing for what I already have. Do what you will, but know *I will have Josh*

Gardner." I shouted so loud the back of my throat felt ripped open by the words and suddenly I was growing and expanding until my head hit the ceiling and my elbows became notched in the corners of the room.

"Oh Betsy!" I saw Mother clasp her hands together in prayer down on the floor, now very far away. I felt the Being inhabit my soul on the screech of my rejection of it, slinking into my body so I had the urge to vomit and emit the great darkness welling inside. What was the dark? Subterranean, cold and frightening like the walls of the cavern, like the fear of the early nights of the visitation when I waited alone for the maddeningly cruel abuse. It was the fear in the room with Father before his death, the unspeakable cloud of black, a darkness smelling like dank earth. I could not properly breathe, for it seemed my lungs had remained tiny when the rest of me expanded. The Spirit whispered in my ear.

When I placed my hands on your shoulders in the woods when you were only nine, I saw your fate, Betsy Bell.

I felt as though my swollen limbs might burst and rain blood down. I wanted to be released, but I could not speak. All at once time stopped, all breathing ceased, and into this stillness the Spirit spoke only to my soul.

You saw me in the light in the forest.

I thought of that first time, the light flashing as if someone walked with a lantern in the woods.

You felt the chill of me.

I felt it at that moment, for the dark was cold, and icy like the earth on Father's coffin.

You heard my voice inside the wind.

I recalled the rattling thistles and the conversation buried in them.

Do you ask the wind, why do you blow across my cheek?

A velvet hand brushed against my face.

Accept the gift I have been to you.

I did not understand what the Spirit meant. I thought of the silver comb dropping into my hands on my birthday, but I knew it was something more than that.

I came here to protect and guide you, Betsy Bell, though it may be difficult for you to understand my ways and means.

I thought of Father in the fields explaining why Little Bright must eat the worms, had he not said it may be difficult for you to understand?

When I said I once was happy, but I had been disturbed, did you not know I spoke to you?

I had known, and it was true, once I had been happy, but I had been disturbed. Abruptly I felt I was lying in my bed with Father. He grunted "darling daughter" in my ear just like he used to and I could smell the sour whiskey on his breath. My stomach rose thickly and I feared I would for certain hail vomit onto the parlor carpet.

All that is over now.

How ever did you protect me? I did not speak the words aloud, I was incapable, the world was frozen silent, but the Spirit answered my thoughts.

I took possession of your nights, then I did poison him! There was much you suffered I could not affect. I did what fate allowed. You should be grateful, instead you throw away my gifts, like your comb into the river. You do not listen.

Only God can protect me, if He exists.

I did not want to accept the Spirit's claim, for it seemed to say the murder of my father was a benefit to me. Repulsive as it was, I felt this could be true and part of an infinite plan my mind was too small to comprehend. I did not want to think on it.

God inhabits all things, you and me for certain. You are a special girl, willful as you are. The wisdom of the ages is available to you. Look in your heart, Betsy, for God is there, as real as I am.

Very far away, buried in the breathless silence, I heard the wailing of the hog outdoors and I understood how it was they knew when they were marked and it was time to call their angels down. There was much unspoken knowledge but it was possible to hear it. The hogs knew of their future as God spoke it to their hearts and they did listen. This was the Being's gift to me, this knowledge of all things, spoken and not, unending time and silence, the life of all that lives. I understood it for a moment, but only for a moment.

Betsy Bell, do not have Josh Gardner.

I felt as though the Spirit removed me from my body and threw me out across a great stretch of rolling green fields of time, hurtling me toward a log cabin in a clearing. I felt as I had when I rode up the hill and saw the vision of Father's skeleton. I knew there was something mean and ugly behind the door, and frightened it was my future self, I did not want to look. The Being laughed and the door swung open and I did see myself, older and holding a broom, sweeping the floor, crying. A huge sadness unlike any I had ever known before made my sweeping heavy-handed and the dust off the bare planks itched my nose. I did not know what was wrong, but I seemed frightfully alone in the woods. The Spirit was not present, yet somehow I knew that was part of my sorrow. The future me wished to talk with the Being and could not. A huge regret ached inside me. Abruptly I felt I was falling backward through a night sky, spinning, with only the light of the stars. I grew very cold and it seemed far too long since I had taken a breath.

This is why you must heed my counsel. Do you wish to lose your love?

What you have shown me is harsh and cruel in my future and my past.

I felt as though any moment I must relinquish consciousness and cease to be. I did not want the future the Spirit had shown me, and yet I struggled to remain living.

This is the last time we will speak, Betsy Bell. Do not have Josh Gardner, for with him you will learn the meaning of despair.

Why should I believe you? You have tormented me most grievously. You said you came to bring me buried treasure. You said you were of Kate Batts's making. I know you to be most like the witch rabbit on our sleigh ride, evil, and capable of regeneration and mischief for all of eternity.

All that is true, but so is what I tell you now.

Your protection was a curse to me.

Why do you persist in your wrong thinking? I am your most dear friend, yet I have a mind to smash you like the bed frame, Betsy Bell, for you are an ungracious participant in your own education.

I thought of Mother pulling tight my braid, insisting I keep my faith in God contained within my head. How was it possible? I was distracted by the many events of my suffering. Yet, how foolish and wasted were my days, abused and fearful. If only I could have the chance to claim the love I knew was meant for me. Only the image of Josh's full lips made it possible for me to hold out against the Spirit's crushing grip on my breath.

Were you not certain in the knowledge I WOULD speak? My words appeared as possibilities in your heart before they were uttered in your ears.

There was the swoosh of a bird wing and I had the feeling

I was waking from a dream. I was still the size of the room but I could breathe and I could see Mother's lips moving in prayer at my feet, so time had resumed. My lungs filled easily without gasping.

"You cannot frighten me with a vision of future tears. I have already known the limits of despair and it is my resolve to find peace in sharing love." My head was dizzy and my speech broke unevenly into the silence.

The dark is more vast than you know and it is within you.

"I know the darkness, I know it, for you have brought it to me with your rattling thistles and foul poison and bad memories." It was difficult to choke the words out, but I was determined. "You say you are the life of all that lives but I am all that lives as much as you! I am *more* of it than you, for I have what you do not, which is a body and a single mind. Do what you like with the dead and the unborn and the thousands of souls having their say in the other worlds. Know everything you will, but understand you cannot know the pleasure of two lips pressed together or rays of sun against your cheek. I am alive and you are not!"

You are a beautiful girl. Be of it, but not it.

I thought the Spirit meant I must fulfill my potential and I hoped it would agree with me in how I should do it. I thought of Dean striking the witch dog down and Kate Batts filling with Spirit without encouragement from the congregation. I thought of Chloe mixing lye and ash to make a perfect soap and of Mother sorting the beans for seed and drying. I pictured Mother engaged in any simple task, sewing, or cutting the lavender blooms in the garden, or wrapping our scarves around our necks to protect us.

A sad sigh filled the room and I could feel as well as hear it. The black nausea within me began to dissipate as though the sigh opened the door in my breast and released it all. The cold darkness fled my body and I could see it as a cloud of black leaving the room. I watched it hover at the window, then thin itself and slip through a crack in the parlor sill. That it could all add up to just so much darkness in one soul. I was overjoyed to see it released and gone from me. Whoever placed it there, my father, God or the Being, it no longer mattered, for I would no longer be afraid. The depths of God would not be for me like the long drop from the cavern to the fishing hole. Instead they would be part of each moment lived. I planned to fill my soul with the lightness I had felt on my birthday. A lightness that smelled like lemons and let me know I was blessed by God.

You threw away my gifts, Betsy Bell. As the worms give richness to the soil, so evil and suffering give depth to the soul, for without them there is no good, no joy. It may seem heavy knowledge for you to hear, but it is your responsibility to use it wisely.

A sublime warmth overcame me and I thought of the days after John Jr. and I had met the Being in the cave. I recalled the hours of dusting and sewing when I had thought deeply about the intelligence of the intelligent and unending time and silence. I had understood more about it than I had realized. I could accept as truth what the Being said, and I recalled feeling its intention to protect me before it spoke for the first time. I had not understood it then and I had abruptly forgotten I ever felt it. I understood it now.

"My past will be ever present and my history will inform my future actions," I reassured the Spirit.

Nature will take its course with you, Betsy Bell.

It was difficult to comprehend, the knowledge of all things, but I had the feeling of it, like the velvet hand against my cheek and the sweet meat of the Spirit's cherries in my mouth. I felt my limbs and head shrinking back to my regular size and my whole body tingled as if the Being had run pins and needles through my veins. I gave my forehead to the parlor carpet as earlier I had laid it on the purslane and violets and months previous I had laid it in the snow, crying after Father breathed his last, certain in the knowledge the day approached when my own heart would thump and heave no more. The snow, the flowers, the parlor carpet, the plank floor of my room, my forehead had laid against them all. I felt the light inside me spreading from my fingers to my toes, melting all the sadness I had suffered. The stone in my belly was gone and I knew it would not return. I thought back to when I was nine and felt the Spirit in the woods and wondered how God's good earth could have such cold and frightening places and I understood for certain, God's good earth contained it all.